CRIMSON IS
THE EASTERN SHORE

DON TRACY

BARONET PUBLISHING COMPANY, New York

Baronet Publishing Company, New York, N.Y. 10022

International Standard Book Number: 0-89437-030-8

Printed in the United States

First Baronet printing, August 1978

For Harold Matson

Foreword

THIS BOOK MAKES no attempt to be an authoritative history of the War of 1812 on the Eastern Shore of Maryland; that has been done by historians better qualified than the writer.

If there ever was an Anthony Worth, a Gracellen, a Jett Worth, a Task Tillman or a Charles Rawlent or a Vivian Dangerfield, their existence or the existence of anyone resembling them is not known to the author. No maps of the period show a Fairoverlea or Larkspur Hill on the Miles River, no Squire Wills ever lived at the Indian Queen Inn at Easton Town, no Peartree Creek is traced on any chart of old Talbot County. These people, these places, the parts the writer has them play in history, are all fictitious.

Certain other characters, such as Admiral Cockburn, Captain Nicholson, Lieutenant Dodson, General Benson and other officers, both British and American, named herein—with one exception—were real persons and did most of the things these pages have them do. The exception is the character of Sir Peter Porter, who is entirely a product of imagination.

The War of 1812 in Maryland was fought as the book relates. The towns were burned, the battles took place on the dates set forth, but the reader should be able to easily spy out just where fact lapses into fiction, as in the episode of the Dragon Footguards at Fairoverlea. There were no Dragon Footguards or if there were they have been treated with unlikely silence by history.

This foreword is not intended as an apology; it is, instead, fair warning that the writer has taken generous liberties with history in his effort to offer a book intended more to entertain than to provide a field for serious study.

Part One

Part One

1

"PULL! LIVELY ALL!"

Jett Worth leaned forward in the bow of the longboat, peering into the mist that was just lightening under the rays of the rising sun.

"Pull hearty and we're home!"

It was a devil of a thing to make a landing like this, with the schooner towed aft like a heifer led to a cowpen. But the wind had deserted just before dawn and *Heron* had to be safely hidden at her mooring in Peartree Creek before curious eyes were up and about. A lady in *Heron's* trade had to to careful where she was caught out, of a dawn; those damned revenue cutters were apt to pop up where they were least expected.

Jett pushed his low-crowned beaver hat further back on his head and wiped the fog moisture from his brows. His eyes searched the vaporish dimness for the landmarks that showed him the channel of the creek. There was the old hickory stump that he and Task—and Gracellen, too, when she was a child and just learning to splutter and splash—had used as a diving place. To port was the big elm that held in its crown, hidden now by the fog, the eagle's nest that had been there since the Indians owned the country that was, in this year of 1810, Talbot County, on the Eastern Shore of Maryland.

3

"Steady, all! Avast!"

The oars backwatered as the mist curtain, shredded by a sudden morning breeze, parted to show the dock that stood out from the shore. The men on the thwarts rested, breathing hard; towing a schooner as deep in the water as was *Heron* was no child's play, ever, and with the tide against them it had been a struggle.

Behind the longboat, the bowsprit of the schooner slid out of the mist and swung toward the dock with the prod of the creek's current. Jett Worth watched, his eyes alight with satisfaction, as *Heron* came as neatly into place as a well-trained mare into her harness and the lines went out to the men who waited on the pier. He cupped his hand about his mouth as he yelled up at the deck that loomed over the longboat.

"Take over, Mister Greer! I'm going ashore!"

A bearded face thrust itself over the taffrail and nodded; a blunt hand gestured an informal salute.

"Aye, sir," boomed a heavy voice, "and tell *The King* we made our sails earn their wages this voyage."

"Depend on that!" Jett called back. "Give all hands leave as soon as my uncle's men take over. A couple of extra tots, too, Mister Greer, for the work they've done."

"Aye aye, sir."

Jett Worth reached for the side of the pier and lifted himself to the planking with a lithe spring. He settled his hat on his head, brushed at his trousers and straightened to face the three men who confronted him.

It was an ill-assorted trio. One man was tall, gaunt, hawk-nosed, with a face that never seemed to have smiled. Although the day promised to be hot, he wore a greatcoat, dampened now by the morning mist, and clamped on his narrow head was a cap of sorts that was better fitted for winter wear than for July. The second man was short, dumpy, round-faced and pop-eyed, possessed of a perpetual giggle. The third was a huge brute who wore a striped knit shirt, a seaman's tasseled cap and a pair of canvas breeches held up by a wide leather belt from which protruded the ugly hilt of a dirk.

4

"Cap'n Jett, sir," the big man said, with a knuckle at his fore-head. "Welcome home to Fairoverlea."

"Thank you, Will Roan," the schooner's captain replied, "and you, too, Tom Womble—I see you've got no thinner since I've been away—and you, Marsden." He turned back to the towering Roan, smiling up at the bigger man.

Jett Worth was a stripling in comparison with the hulking Roan but his bearing made up for his lack of bulk. Where Roan's features were blunted, scarred and coarse, this man's face was finely chiseled, extraordinarily handsome. But no one not reck-lessly in his cups would ever dare fling the taunt of pretty-lad at Jett; his eyes, the set of his shoulders, the air of command that fitted him as well as his doeskin breeches, ruffled stock and shin-ing boots, all gave due warning against that mistake.

"Well, Roan," he said now. "I'll wager you thought they'd grabbed us for sure this time, didn't you?"

Roan shook his head, his answering grin yellow-toothed.

"Not you, Cap'n Jett," he rumbled. "Though you cut it pretty fine, if I c'n say so. Another hour and the Miles would have been fair crawlin' with vessels. Y'r uncle's messenger, Filkey, sighted y'r signals at three bells and came a-gallopin'. The King, of course, ordered us down here to light y'r landin' but"—with an upward glance at the fog-cleared sky—"y'don't seem to need any torches or lanthorns, do ye, sir?"

Jett laughed as he shook his head.

"Better a parasol," he said. "Greer lost the wind in the river, though it was my fault, really. I went below to get into something respectable for the landing and he brought her in too close to catch what little breeze there was left. He doesn't know the river as I do, not havin' been brought up on it, but he'll learn. Aye, he'll learn."

He looked about him, sniffing the freshening morning breeze, his bronzed face reflecting his delight.

"Fairoverlea again," he said. "Heaven will have to put on her best bonnet to come up to this." His smile broadened. "Though

5

you and I will hardly have the chance to compare the two places, eh, Womble?"

The fat man giggled throatily.

"I doubt my wings are still saved for me, Cap'n."

"And mine have moulted long ago," Jett nodded. His voice changed, dropping its lightness, as he turned back to Roan. "My uncle—he's well?"

"Hale and hearty as ever, sir," Roan replied. "He bids you to Great House as soon as y'r duties are finished here. He'll be glad to see you back safe and sound. I think he's been worryin' these past few days, you bein' overdue."

"I'll bet he's fretted like a schoolgirl," Jett laughed. "It'd take a lot more than an overdue vessel of his to make him lose a wink of sleep, God bless him."

He turned to watch the men warping the schooner into the dock. The job was tidily done, with no confusion, no bawled orders, none of the hubbub that usually attended the docking of a vessel of her size, home after months at sea. Jett nodded and turned back to the wide-shouldered giant beside him.

"I'd best get up to the house then," he said. "I'm starved for a meal out of Fairoverlea's kitchens. I forget when I had decent food last but it must have been years ago."

He started to leave the wharf and was stopped as Tom Womble stepped forward, a pudgy forefinger at his eyebrow.

"Y'r pardon, Cap'n," he said, "but did ye remember the trifle I asked ye to attend to f'r me?"

"Aye, Womble," Jett nodded. His smile disappeared and a scowl replaced it. "But first, I'd better find out if my uncle approves of you havin' these things at Fairoverlea. You said it was just a bit of fun to make the wenches laugh when you gave me the name of that Portuygee, but, my God, those pictures would make a Marseilles whore blush! I'll show 'em to my uncle and if he says you can keep 'em—"

"Oh, 'fore Gawd!" Womble bleated, "Ye'd not do that, sir! Why, The King would flay me within an inch of m'life, sir!

6

Throw 'em overboard—let the crabs have 'em! I was mistaken— I don't want 'em, sir! I didn't mean to—"

"Oh, belay, Womble," Jett laughed. "Mister Greer has the things for you. But keep 'em well hid save when you use 'em for your—er—your curious pastimes."

"I will, sir!" Womble promised, fervently. "Indeed I will, sir!" Touching his forehead again, the round little man waddled toward the gangway that had been lowered from the deck of the docked schooner.

"A folio of unusual prints," Jett explained briefly to Roan. "Doubtless needful in poor Womble's case. We'll not mention 'em to my uncle."

At the shore end of the dock clustered a gang of some fifty Negroes, all lean-bodied, heavy-shouldered blacks who were naked except for brief drawers. A pace or two apart from the gang stood a huge black man, Roan's equal and more in size, who carried a blacksnake whip looped loosely in one hand.

"Titus still handles the lash, eh?" Jett asked the dour Marsden. "I'd ha' thought they'd ha' killed him by now."

"They've tried," Marsden croaked. "Twice since ye sailed, sir. But, as you say, Titus still handles the lash. And"—with a mirthless twist of his bloodless lips—"I still handle Titus."

Jett Worth and Roan passed the silent file of slaves, the towering Titus, and mounted the rise along the path that led from the dock to a cart road.

"If my uncle brought this road right down to the pier," Jett grumbled as the two men turned into the lane, "he could unload a vessel with half as many hands as he needs now, having them hand-carry everything to the warehouses. I've spoken to him about it a hundred times but he won't listen."

"Nay, sir," Roan answered. "He's set in his way about that. Says he's used the blacks this way ever since he started and there's been no trouble to speak of, so why change and risk bringin' down a hornet's nest about us all?"

"Hornet's nest!" Jett scoffed. "Who'd dare make trouble for my uncle? Don't they call him *The King* in these parts, Roan?"

"Well, maybe, 'tis best to be careful," Roan said cautiously. "Times change, y'know. Then, there's always that damned Tillman—he'd welcome a chance to make trouble."

The two men passed through a cluster of outbuildings, the dairy, the laundry house, the smokehouse, the stables, the other sheds and lean-to's that grouped themselves behind the Great House of Fairoverlea. Jett cast only a fleeting glance at the manor house itself before he preceded Roan through the narrow, virtually hidden, side door set in a niche between the kitchens and the main part of the house. Time enough to renew acquaintance with Fairoverlea, he told himself, when his business with his uncle was finished; the place deserved more than the few minutes' greeting he could afford it now, with Anthony Worth waiting.

The door opened onto a passageway which turned abruptly toward the front of the mansion and led to another door beyond which lay the office of Anthony Worth whom many people in that part of Maryland's Eastern Shore called *The King* in admiration, in fear, in envy, in gratitude, in hatred.

Jett rapped, his tattoo echoing in the hallway. Beyond the door there was a stir, the creak of a chair, and a voice boomed out.

"Come in!"

2

ANTHONY WORTH rose from behind the broad desk as his nephew entered the beautifully appointed office. His big hand went out to meet the grip of this youngster who had brought in the *Heron*. The two men looked at each other over the firm clasp, neither needing words.

Anthony Worth was past his sixty-third year by more than five months, that July day of 1810. He looked twenty years younger and his friends and enemies—particularly his enemies—could swear that his mind was as agile as it had been when he had first come out of nowhere to the Eastern Shore, a half-grown boy of fifteen, and set to work at building his fortune.

He was six feet three inches tall, without a suspicion of the shoulder droop or belly swell that marked most men ten years his junior. He weighed better than sixteen stone and not an ounce of it was fat. The teeth that shone now in his welcoming smile to his nephew were his own, the reddish-brown, grey-streaked hair that he still wore in the clubbed fashion that was becoming more and more rarely seen in this Nineteenth Century was no wig. His grey eyes needed no spectacles, his ears could pick up a whisper at an uncomfortable distance, in all his life his only use for doctors had been to patch his wounds and set his broken bones, of which there had been no dearth in earlier years.

9

He had buried three wives and was in his third year of marriage to his fourth, Vivian, a woman young enough to be his daughter, certainly, and not impossibly his grand-daughter in a day of early marriages. He had sired eight children and, ironically, had not one living son.

He was what he had determined to be from the first, the richest, most powerful man within three days' hard riding or tight-hauled sailing. If, in the gathering of his fortune and the building of his power he had trodden on laws and lives, why, surely, those must have been foolish laws or persons to have dared try to stand between Anthony Worth and his goals.

There had been many an outraged cry raised against *The King* and all of them had been stilled, openly or covertly, by means of gold or guile, threat or crushing blow, as they arose. There was a susurrus of whispering about Anthony Worth as there had been from his first day on the Eastern Shore and this he laughed at or ignored, as he always had. Or appeared to, at any rate. If a persistent whisperer fell upon hard times, suddenly and mysteriously, there was always the possibility that it was the just hand of the Almighty, who must hate all slanderers.

Now the silence that had stretched between the two men, uncle and nephew, was broken by Anthony's bluff growl.

"So ye're finally of a mind to bring *Heron* in, eh?" he asked. "Ye'll ruin us all some day, waitin' till blazin' high noon to swish your butt up the Miles River so the ladies can see how fine you look in y'r new Frenchified clothes."

Jett Worth shook his head, grinning.

" 'Twasn't my clothes, Uncle," he protested. "I would have been here hours ago but I knew an old man must have his sleep."

Anthony's brows drew down in mock ferocity.

"Old man, eh?" he rumbled. "I can still outrun, outdrink and outfight ye, ancient as I am."

Jett's smile widened.

"Outrun, outdrink and outfight?" he asked. "The sailormen have a different boast, there bein' no room for running aboard ship."

"That, too!" boomed Anthony Worth. He flung a hand toward the chair set against the wall opposite his desk. "Sit down, lad. There's a lot to tell me. Ye're overdue by a week, at least. Was there trouble?"

"A little," Jett nodded. "We were two days past the Capes when —" He broke off and his face twisted in a wrenching spasm. Anthony's florid features went almost white as he leaned over his desk.

"What's wrong, Jett?" he demanded. "Ye're ill? Ye've been hurt?"

"Nay, Uncle," Jett quavered, his face still agonized. "But a whiff from the kitchens, just came through that window there and my belly griped me so badly, not havin' been fed since—"

"Fool!" Anthony snarled in disgusted relief. He reached for a bell pull beside him and hauled on it. At once, a door in the west wall of the office opened and a liveried black popped in.

"Some breakfast for Captain Jett, Joseph," Anthony ordered. "Bring it in here. Coffee or rum, Jett?"

"Coffee and brandy," said the *Heron's* skipper. "Coffee for the meal and I'll need the brandy to sustain me durin' the answering of your million questions, I know."

Anthony shot a glance at bulky Will Roan, standing just inside the hallway door, and hesitated visibly before he spoke.

"Ye'll have a glass with us, Will, and then best get back to the schooner and oversee the others. I'll call you when I'm through with my nephew."

"Aye, sir," Roan answererd. His tone was spiked with his pleasure at having been invited to share a glass with *The King* and Cap'n Jett. That was something he knew Marsden would never experience; it was a sure sign that he, not the beaked skeleton, was the top man of the trio of Anthony Worth's lieutenants.

The brandy came and the three men raised their glasses in a toasting gesture. Then, when Roan had left, the breakfast was brought in and set beside Jett's chair. He sniffed, exhaled in bliss and plunged into a meal of fried ham, eggs, cold fowl and beef,

11

hotbreads and biscuits, while his uncle, elbows on the desktop and chin on his knuckles, began his questioning.

"Ye spoke of trouble. What was it and how bad?"

Jett shrugged, chewed and swallowed.

"Not too bad, but bothersome," he said, when he could speak. "Just past the Capes a damn revenue cutter, the *Gull* as I made her out, tried to chase us. We ran away from her but only because the man handling the cutter must have been drunk or a fool or maybe both. If I'd had the cutter—"

"*Gull?*" Anthony asked. "And she gave you chase?"

"If you could call it that. She made all the motions, certainly, but as I said we ran away from her while the nincompoop did everything wrong."

"So?" Worth asked. "Well, ye'll not be hurt by cutters makin' motions, will ye?"

Jett eyed his uncle over a chicken drumstick he held, then snorted a laugh.

"So ye've friends there, too?" he asked. "Before I sail again you'd better give me a list of your friends so I'll not be cracking on sail when there's no need."

"And that list you'll never get," Anthony replied, shaking his rusty head. "That kind of friends can sell their loyalty to somebody else as fast as they sold it to me. Or"—and his smile chilled —"one of 'em might find himself all inspired by patriotism one day and seize you for the nation's good—and his share of the prize money. What other trouble?"

"The British!" Jett rapped out venomously. Then, as his uncle's face darkened, he went on rapidly. "Oh, I know we trade with 'em, we risk our necks to trade with 'em and the Frenchies, but, by God, some day—"

"Some day ye'll let that boy's temper of yours lead you to a yardarm!" Anthony broke in. His fist pounded the desk. "I like the British little better than you do, Jett. But so long as they buy our cargoes at our prices I'll put up with their sneers and the rest. Go on; what happened to stick in your craw this time?"

Jett finished a slab of ham and reached for the eggs.

"Frigate *Severn*, forty guns," he said, his voice still edgy. "We were nineteen days out when she spoke us, ordered us to heave to for an inspection. Inspection! Press gang, that's what!"

He speared an egg and watched the yolk spread.

"We had the letters you furnished me, of course," he went on. "So I came about and hove to without a qualm. Aboard came a sprig of a lieutenant and a squad of marines. Ah, that lieutenant! If I'd known—"

"Stop punishing that egg," Anthony commanded, "and either eat it or get on with the story!"

"I showed him the letters. They must have proved to him who we were and where bound. He strutted and posed and spoke to me like a cabin boy till my fingers itched to—ah, I'll get on! Finally, when he found nothing in the letters to give him leave to seize us, he told me down his nose that he must search my vessel for deserters from"—his voice mimicked the nasal drawl of a haughty Englishman—"'His Majesty's ships of wah.'"

He finished the egg while Anthony Worth waited impatiently. Jett wiped his mouth on a napkin, and pushed back his plate and reached for the coffee jug and mug. The big man at the desk drummed his fingers on the polished wood as his nephew drained the mug and wiped his mouth again.

"At your leisure, young sir," Anthony jerked out as Jett's hand went out for the jug again.

"Your pardon, Uncle, but salt beef and ship's biscuits—"

"*Will you get on?*"

"Aye, sir. Well, this young sprout feels he needs must return to his frigate with something to show, so he points out the mulatto, Jim Storey, as a wanted deserter from the fleet at Bermuda."

"Storey!" Anthony ejaculated. "By God, they made a strange pick! I told you to sign Storey on only because he was in a bit of trouble and needed to be out of the way for awhile. 'Twas the first time he'd ever been outside the Chesapeake, whilst most of the others—but go on."

"Truth, sir, I was almost tempted to give 'em Storey to be rid of him," Jett grinned. "A worse hand never sailed with me and I was afraid Greer or somebody else would heave him over the side anyway before many more days. But that lieutenant burned me so I said be damned to His Majesty's fleet at Bermuda, that was my man and if he took him off I'd raise a stink at the Admiralty when I got to his precious England."

"And that stopped him?"

"Aye," Jett nodded, "but only after argument and him taking advantage of every occasion to tell me what he thinks of Americans, trying to provoke me into something he could use his marines for. And you condemn my temper, sir! If it had been you—"

"They could have had Storey," Anthony smiled. "A worthless hand gone, a mulatto who's forever runnin' to me with his troubles because he thinks for some reason he's my responsibility —I note your smirk, Jett—a liability crossed off my account books, I say, and no pother or fuss."

"He'd have gone back to Severn all a-blow with himself," Jett muttered.

"My boy, he went back to the frigate just that way, in any case. You don't know British naval officers if you think your tantrum did aught to change his opinion of himself. But never mind —ye discharged at Liverpool?"

"Aye, sir," Jett said. "Then took aboard what Nappy needed from the British he's warrin' 'gainst and ran the blockade into the little port you'd arranged for."

"Under what flag?" Anthony Worth asked, hunching his wide shoulders.

"Strooth, sir, I've forgot what flag we flew that day. There were so many of 'em it might have been the Chiney pennant, if they have one."

"And your voyage home?"

"Head winds or no winds but no trouble beyond that. We ran away from a sail below the Leewards that might have been British or might have been a freebooter." He grinned briefly. "One of Roan's old comrades, maybe."

" 'Twas never proved," Anthony Worth said primly. "You mustn't believe gossip about a loyal hand like Roan, my lad."

"Oh, sir," Jett said with mock humility, "I don't believe a word of the story. No, my good Roan is as pure as driven snow, as is the merry Marsden and the saintly Womble."

He reached for the brandy decanter and splashed liquor into a thin-stemmed, fluted glass. Anthony shook his head as his nephew glanced inquiringly at him and the *Heron's* skipper replaced the stopper, sipped at the drink appreciatively.

"They say in England," he told his uncle, "that Bonaparte will be beat this year. They say his cause is in the death throes now."

The King humphed.

"And the Frenchies," Jett went on, "say Boney will cross the Channel when he's ready. The Dutch say be damned to them both and the Portuygees say they hope the war lasts forever." He drained his glass. "Which sentiment," he added, "we both approve. But what's the situation here?"

Anthony Worth shrugged and spread his broad, spatulate hands.

"More politics ye'd not understand if I told ye and be bored by if ye understood," he said. "Jefferson's out, y'know, and that stiff-neck James Madison, is in. The Embargo Act was repealed because New England forced it but no trade, still, with England or France, as you well know. Henry Clay's War Hawks are hot for a fight with England. The Federalists want none of it. The— but you're not listening!"

"Your pardon," Jett Worth said, "but I was remembering a remark the lambkin Roan made. Something about there being trouble with Tillman. That means that Task bears a grudge against us?"

If a shadow crossed Anthony's face, it was a fleeting one. His eyes were calm, benign, as he said: "Task is a friend of yours, I know, Jett, but he's a stubborn one." He sighed. "I'm afraid he does hold a grudge against me, though not against you, I'm sure."

Jett laughed and stretched out a hand for the decanter.

"Why, then," he said, "we'll get my beauteous cousin, Gracellen, to set him to rights. You've but to ask her to smile at Task and she'll have him believing all we Worths are pure gold, friends to man."

Anthony's eyes shifted to beyond Jett. Their grey depths warmed.

"Why not ask her yourself, then?" he said, quietly. "Your beauteous cousin, Gracellen, has just slipped in the door behind you, Jett."

3

JETT WORTH pushed back his chair and sprang to his feet, turning toward the door.

"My dearest cousin!" he cried. "More beautiful than ever, if that's possible."

His deep bow was not entirely mocking nor was the kiss he planted on her upturned cheek entirely cousinly, even though the day was not long past when he had teased her, lorded it over her and sent her into blazing fury from the lofty eminence of his six years' advantage in age.

"Phew," the girl sniffed. "You smell like a rum barrel, Jett, and it's not yet nine o'clock of the morning."

"Drunk only with your loveliness, pet," Jett protested. "Who could blame me if I staggered at sight of such a vision?"

"You're not improved, I see," Gracellen said, her lip curling. "I hoped that being chased all over the ocean by warships would send you home with some sense. I should have known better. Morning, Father."

She passed Jett to go to her father and bend over him, touching him lightly on the forehead with her lips. Anthony caught at her hand and held her there for a moment; it was all too seldom that this girl whom he adored above all others was this close to him, now that she had stopped being a child who had made his knee her sanctuary, her gangplank to the world of fancy, the court where all her wishes had been voiced—and granted.

Jett, looking across the room, thought again how much Gracellen was the daughter of the father. The girl, at seventeen, was as tall as she ever would be and for that Jett was thankful; he had feared for a time that she was going to match Anthony in height. Now her body had stopped striving for that impossible stature and was devoting itself, Jett's appreciative eyes told him, to perfecting itself in other ways.

Yes, Gracellen was tall, taller than most women of the day, but the rounded softness enhanced by the green morning dress she wore shaped a picture that made smaller women seem scrawny, runty, incomplete.

She had the reddish bronze hair that Anthony Worth had had in his youth and she had her father's grey eyes. Her mouth was Anthony's, not as broad as his, perhaps, but with the same firmness and—as Jett knew well—the same set to its corners when she was angry. Her nose, Jett thought idly, must have come from her mother or some long-gone Worth; it was sharp and high-bridged where Anthony's was blunt and broad at the nostrils. Gracellen's chin was all her father's, with the same stubborn line, the same jutting implacability when its owner was set upon a course.

Jett had been told that Johanna Igleway, Anthony's third wife, Gracellen's mother, had been a beautiful woman, even as beautiful in her way as Vivian. He had seen a miniature of Johanna but the artist had been a hack and the tiny enamel had been little more than a tinted blur. Beautiful or not, he decided, Johanna's looks had not been needed to make Gracellen the reigning belle of Talbot County; Anthony had taken care of that.

"Stop staring, Jett," Gracellen said, coolly. "Or is there some egg on *my* chin, as there is on yours?"

Jett's hand swooped for the napkin and then paused above the serviette as Gracellen's laugh tinkled and Anthony's rumbled. Jett grinned and bowed again.

"I keep forgetting," he said, "that you're still not in pigtails

I can pull, Gracellen-aleen. My, my, seventeen and still a spinster!" He turned to his uncle. "Even you must be hard put to raise a big enough dowry to make a man risk his neck marrying her, eh?"

"Bah!" Anthony snorted. "There are times when I wish she had a squint or a wart on her nose. Come noontime, you'll see the cavalry troop begin cantering up the lane from the highway and they'll keep up that parade till all hours unless she sends them all packing which, thank God, she does sometimes so her old father can get at his work or his sleep."

"Then all the *pretty* girls are married, eh?" Jett asked, blandly. "The poor young men, to have to ride out here to keep in practice with their wooing till the pigtailed crop ripens."

"Damn you!" Gracellen flared. "You and your rickety-rackety tongue! I'll have you know—"

She stopped as Jett's smile spread. Her down-drawn mouth quirked, trembled, and then she laughed.

"Oh, Jett," she said, "it's good to have you back—you know it is! Things have been so dreary-dull around here that I've been half mad. All these men with their solemn words and solemn manners, saying things they've read in some silly book. And when I tease them to see if they're human, they turn pale and beg my pardon, as if they'd stepped on my foot."

"Task Tillman, too?" Jett asked, innocently.

Color tinged Gracellen's face as she raised her chin.

"Task Tillman," she said in a stilted voice, "isn't welcome here, Jett. And—and I'm glad. Yes, I'm glad!"

"I see," Jett said gravely. "Well, the fellow always was a hound, of course, and I'm happy to see you've found it out. He's—"

"He's *not* a hound!" Gracellen cried. "He's—" She broke off what she was about to say and looked down at the floor. Anthony Worth cleared his throat and spoke quietly.

"Well, whatever he is," he rumbled, "he's a damned suspicious young man; ye'll agree to that, Gracellen."

She raised her eyes and nodded, her mouth firming.

19

"He's that," she said, "and I—I don't understand, Father. I mean—how could he think you'd do such a thing?"

"Such a thing as what?" Jett asked curiously. His cousin turned to him with a swirl of skirts, her eyes hot now.

"He thinks Father burned his tobacco barns, that's what! How could he think such a thing, the man who said . . . who said he . . . had a regard for me?"

"Task's barns were burned?" Jett asked slowly. "He thinks—"

"Yes, all his barns burned in a thunder storm and all his tobacco with them," Gracellen went on. "And when Father went to him and offered—"

"We'll not speak of that," Anthony interrupted.

"I will speak of it!" the girl snapped back. "Do y'know what he said, Jett? When Father went to offer him help he said he'd take no help from a man who'd put a torch to a man's barns with one hand and offer an—an enslaving loan with the other. Ohhh!"

Jett's eyes sought his uncle's and Anthony hunched his shoulders in a wry shrug.

"Father should have put his whip to the man!" Gracellen cried. "*I* tried to the next time I met him, out riding."

"*Tried* to?" Jett asked.

"He—he caught my wrist," Gracellen faltered. Her face flamed more pinkly as she avoided Jett's gaze. "He—he prevented me from lashing him."

Jett Worth looked at his cousin, his dark eyes thoughtful. That furious blush, he decided, plainly said that Task Tillman had done more than catch Gracellen's wrist and turn the whiplash.

"I see," he said, one corner of his mouth rising. "He caught your wrist—that's all?"

Gracellen glared at him, then tilted her nose.

"You're as big an oaf as he is!" she rapped out. "Worse!" She swept out of the office, slamming the door behind her. A swirl of spicy musk eddied about the room.

" 'How strongly sounds the lady's nay,' " Jett quoted, " 'when in her heart she shapes it yea.' She's been in love with Task Tillman since she can remember, Uncle. It's a damned shame that—"

"Let's get on with our work, Jett!" Anthony Worth broke in roughly. "You brought the lading bills or are they on the *Heron*?"

"Greer has them," Jett answered, "and he's checking them with Roan and Marsden. It was a good voyage, sir, though I say it m'self. The gold is in my strongbox aboard, safe enough."

"Aye," Anthony nodded. "It would be safe scattered on the dock at this place. It had better be. Let's go down to the schooner. I need the walk."

"Certainly," Jett agreed absently, and then: "How long ago was it that Tillman's barns burned?"

His uncle waved an impatient hand.

"Six months or so," he said. "What does it matter? I have my own troubles to consider and they mount higher every day, it seems."

"And Task blamed you?"

"The lad was overwrought." Anthony rose and started toward the door to the passageway. "I hadn't the heart to challenge as I probably should have when he insulted me. First, he's your friend and then, too, he'd worked hard and one night's fire wiped him out. Who wouldn't be half mad?"

Jett rubbed a ruminative thumb across his lower lip, slouched back in his chair, as Anthony paused at the doorway.

"Well?" the big man asked, his voice gravelly. "Shall we get on with our work or would you ask me more questions? What bothers you now?"

"Nothing, nothing," Jett said, shaking his head. "But—but, sir, the Tillmans certainly have the worst luck, don't they? First, Larkspur Hill is burned down in a fire that sweeps everything, big house, outbuildings, barns. And now Task—"

"I have nothing to do with keeping lightning from striking," Anthony said harshly, "and it was lightning that did the damage both times."

"Aye," Jett murmured. "Lightning."

Anthony Worth dropped his hand from the brass door knob and walked back into the office and up to his nephew's side.

His blunt fingers closed over the shoulder of the younger, slighter man and his voice was grave when he spoke.

"Jett," he said, "Providence never saw fit to give me a son who lived. My first, little Anthony, died of the pox that killed his mother, Mary, forty years or so ago. Honoria bore me Matthew who lived only long enough to be christened. Johanna gave me a third son, Charles, but he was another sickly child who died after a few days.

"Aye, Providence has dealt harshly with me in the matter of sons, perhaps for sins that I'll never admit nor deny—no, not even on my deathbed—but Providence, if it deals with these things, relented enough to give me you, my poor dead brother's son. I've tried to raise you as I would my own boy; I've tried to give you everything my son would have."

"Uncle," Jett said in a low voice, "I don't think the words have been writ down to tell you how grateful I am to you for what you've done."

"Then listen well, Jett. As well as you've done till now, you'll do better—much better. Your course is charted, lad. Accept my orders 'cause they're meant to serve your best interests. *And leave all else to me!*"

He paused and his hand tightened on Jett's shoulder, his eyes locked with his nephew's.

"As you love me," he went on, "apply yourself to the plans I make for you. Guard yourself 'gainst prying into things about Larkspur Hill and the Tillmans that rouse your curiosity. There are certain strange things about that place and those people. Of course, there's only the youngest, Task, left now but the stories about his father, Randolph Tillman, and his brother, William— all these are things that don't concern you. They'll never touch you, I promise. But if you be foolish, thoughtless, disobedient enough to peek and pry where you shouldn't, then you'll be hurt, nor can I help you though you perish!"

It was Jett who finally dropped his eyes before his uncle's steady stare.

"I'll remember," he said, huskily.

Anthony's hand dropped from his nephew's shoulder and his voice rose to a level of cheery bluffness.

"The morning's wasting," he said, "and here we stay, gabbling like a couple of geese. Let's get to work, lad."

High overhead, a turkey buzzard glided in wide circles, looking down on Fairoverlea. It could not know, or if it ever had known it could not remember, that there had been times in the past when Anthony Worth had had work to be done and the buzzards had eaten well.

THE SAME buzzard or one just as shaggy-feathered, as obscene, volplaned over Larkspur Hill a few minutes after Jett and Anthony Worth had finished their tense talk in the office of Fairoverlea. The winged scavenger picked out a movement and veered over to investigate, then slanted away; it was a living man astride a living black stallion and the buzzard was not interested in things alive.

The horseman was moving slowly up the dusty lane that led from the fields to the house set in a grove of chestnuts. This was no great, sprawling mansion as was Fairoverlea; this was a modest frame house of a dozen or so rooms, built for shelter and not for show. The place where the Great House of Larkspur Hill had once reared its magnificence was marked now only by the open graves of the cellars, growing deep in pokeweed.

Task Tillman passed the ruins with the ache that always struck him, even after all the years that had rolled by. It was an ache born of rage, first, and then a dull, devouring hatred for the man he knew, *he knew*, was to blame for the fire and every other disaster that had ever struck a Tillman—Anthony Worth.

That hate sustained him, kept him working against odds that always seemed and often were hopeless, but they made Task Tillman older than his years. Now, as he swung down off the stallion in the yard behind the house, there was a moment's droop to his wide shoulders before he straightened them with an obvious effort, threw back his head.

"Jobie!" he called. "You, Jobie!"

There was a stir within the barn and an ancient Negro emerged, blinking, brandishing a scrap of harness in his own defense.

"Jus' settin' out of the sun, fixin' up thisyere strop," the black said. "Been workin' on it 'most all mornin' and I still can't git it right. Old eyes ain't what they was, Marse Task."

The white man started a bitter opinion of hands who slept in the shade in the middle of a working day, then bit off his words as he summoned a tired smile. Old Jobie was long past his working days but he had served Larkspur Hill well when he was a young buck. Let him sleep his days away now; by the way things looked it didn't make much difference if any of them slept or worked at trying to keep Larkspur Hill going. Since the fire had taken his tobacco, the bankers in Baltimore were baying at his heels.

"Give Lucifer a rubdown," he told Jobie, "and saddle him up again with the other gear. I've got to go to Easton Town this afternoon."

"Yazzuh," the old man nodded and then: "I heerd some news this mawnin', Marse Task."

"News? Who brings you news when you're so busy with your harness fixing? And I didn't see anybody ride up here this morning."

The white-haired Negro shook his head and chuckled.

"I gits the news jus' the same," he laughed, and Task knew that was true. How they did it, no white man would ever know, but the blacks had their own means of spreading the news from place to place. Let something happen in Easton or even Queen's Town in the morning and before nightfall every black in Talbot County would know what had happened and why.

"All right," Task said, impatiently, "let's have it, Jobie, and don't drag it out into a half hour's telling. I've got things to do before I start out for town."

25

Jobie dropped his voice to a conspiratorial hush.

"Marse Jett Worth brought in the schooner at dawn t'day," he almost whispered. "He back again."

Task stiffened slightly. Jett was back again, eh, with a schooner packed to the gunwales with stuff that would make Anthony Worth richer after making fools of the revenue cutters? When Jett had been a boy he had always said he was going to be the best ship's captain afloat and he was making a fair bid for that name now, at twenty-three. If his uncle gave him only a fair portion of the money he made for Anthony Worth, Jett must have plenty now.

While he—but he wouldn't begrudge Jett his success. He had never allowed his hate for Anthony Worth to spread to Jett and he wouldn't start now. They had been friends through everything and God knew Task Tillman needed every friend he could find, even if one of them was the nephew of Anthony Worth.

"You be goin' see him?" Old Jobie asked. "You think mebbe he drap ovuh here whilst he's home? Be like old times with Marse Jett and Miss Gracellen—"

"I don't think he'll come over here," Task interrupted bluntly, "and I know Miss Gracellen won't."

"Too bad, too bad," Old Jobie mourned, shaking his white poll. "They was good times when the three of you young'uns was playin' around here and Marse Randolph, *he* was here, too, and—and—"

"You'd better get started on Lucifer," Task cut in and turned on his heel. He stalked toward the house, leaving Jobie muttering about the good times, the old times.

Damn the old man, Task told himself fiercely; why did he have to bring back the old memories on this day of all days? If things didn't go right at Easton that afternoon there'd be no more Tillmans of Larkspur Hill and Anthony Worth could sit at Fairoverlea and warm his black heart with his final victory.

"Tillie," he told the black woman in the kitchen as he entered, "I'll want a tub in my room and some water for shaving. Let me know when it's hot."

"You want *hot* water, day like t'day?" Tillie asked, dubiously.

"With the dirt that's on me, I might have to use lye," Task flung over his shoulder. "I'll be at the desk when the water's ready."

"All the time washin' in hot water," Tillie was grumbling as he left the kitchen. "Wash the skin right offen you some day, you see. You *nevuh* had no sense, chile."

"Chile." Tillie was another one who dwelt in the old days, the good days, and never would admit that times changed or even that a child could grow to be an oversized hulk of twenty-three with a bankrupt estate on his hands. He walked down a narrow hall to the front of the house, entered the room that served as an office-parlor and went to the desk set against the far wall. He pulled down the front of the old piece, one of the few good things saved from the fire, and stared at the books.

The books; the implacable, damning ledgers. There they lay in a stack that went back thirty years when there really were good days at Larkspur Hill.

"The saga of the Tillman Family," he muttered sourly as he sat down. "From Randolph to William to Task to *Finis*."

He started to take the ledger that held the past year's bad news from the top of the stack and an unaccountable urge made him slide out the bottom ledger, instead, a ledger inscribed in the impeccable hand of his father, Randolph Tillman. Perhaps it was Old Jobie's reminiscing, perhaps it was the news that Jett Worth was back, perhaps it was because he had been thinking of Gracellen that morning—whatever the reason, he opened the old ledger and began reading, as carefully as though this was all new to him.

Seventeen Ninety-Five. He, Task, had been eight years old then and no little boy anywhere was living a better life. True, he had no mother—she had died when he was born—but Randolph Tillman had never let him feel the lack. Task still remembered his father as a great gentleman who was never too busy, never too preoccupied, to give his son time and patience and thoughtful understanding.

Seventeen Ninety-Seven and there was the last entry made in

Randolph Tillman's flowing script. He had begun to rebuild Larkspur Hill and he could have brought it back to all its grandeur if he had not been found dead that terrible foggy morning, lying in the lane with his big grey standing patiently beside him, looking down wonderingly at Randolph Tillman's crushed skull.

A deplorable accident, everybody agreed. Perhaps a glass too many in Easton Town before he had started out that night to ride back to Larkspur Hill. An accident? But nobody had ever seen Randolph Tillman so drunk he couldn't sit his horse and the grey had never had a fractious bone in his body.

Murder, Task Tillman knew now, just as he knew the fire that had swept Larkspur Hill the year before had been set by hands that hated Randolph Tillman.

But the ten-year-old boy knew nothing then beyond the grief of losing his father and if William had ever suspected the truth he had drowned his dangerous suspicions in the liquor that had brought shabby days to Larkspur Hill and brought William's own death when he was but twenty-two and Task was fourteen.

It was hard to remember his older brother, William, and perhaps it was best not to try to remember him because the memories could never be kind. Better to remember the days spent with Gracellen and Jett Worth when the three of them were growing up. In Jett, Task found the companionship his father's death had robbed him of. In Gracellen he found a love that burgeoned amazingly one winter afternoon at Fairoverlea and still endured.

Yes, it still endured in spite of the discovery of his father's diary that described what had happened on an afternoon of Seventeen Eighty-Eight and explained many things to Task Tillman.

The old desk at which he sat now had kept its secret well; Task might never have found the hidden compartment if he had not lost his temper one hot, humid day when he had been sweating over figures that would not come right and a drawer he had tried to open had stuck obstinately. He had tried coaxing out the drawer, moving it from side to side in its slides and finally, in a rage, he had yanked at it with all the strength in his hard shoulders. The whole front panel of the drawer had ripped loose

28

and that had meant removing part of the side panelling so that Jobie, who was good at such work, could make the repairs Task's blundering had necessitated. And there, behind the damaged drawer, was found his father's diary for Seventeen Eighty-Eight.

Why Randolph Tillman had put the slender volume there, no one would ever know. There had been a thousand times that Task had cursed the fact that he had found it. But there it was and under the date of September ninth, Seventeen Eighty-Eight, Randolph Tillman had written:

On this day, a disturbing scene with Anthony Worth at the vestry meeting. It of course concerned the poor girl he is keeping at Fairoverlea, Mistress Johanna Igleway. The girl came to Fairoverlea as nurse to Worth's wife who died almost a year ago.

It came to my attention some time ago that Worth had mistreated the lass to the point where she is now with child and facing scorn and shame unless he marries her forthwith. Mistress Igleway comes from a good family fallen on hard times and surely is no creature to be used in such a shameful manner.

Several days ago I addressed a note to Worth, warning him that unless he pledged his word to take immediate steps to right this wrong I would demand that he be ousted from the vestry. To this letter I got no reply nor did I, indeed, expect one from such a man as Worth.

Therefore, when the vestry meeting convened I made my demands that Anthony Worth be expelled as a despoiler of a young girl in his charge. He replied to the effect that what took place at Fairoverlea was his business and not subject to my meddling. I fear I lost my temper complete as did he and I did something I had vowed I would not do—I made a remark about his origin and his antecedents, something which was sadly beneath me.

Never have I seen such mingled hatred and fear on the face of a human being. It was as though the man were stricken with a seizure for an instant and then he seemed to recover. I was amazed, as I am certain the other vestrymen were, by the change in his manner. He instantly apologized to me and the rest of the vestry and swore he would marry the unfortunate girl on the morrow. With that he rode off, still a man shaken as I had never thought to see Anthony Worth.

I fear I have made a bitter enemy this day and I regret it. I will make an effort to repair the harm my temper wrought as I want no ill feeling between Larkspur Hill and Fairoverlea. I hope I am not a coward but I would feel a certain uneasiness at knowing Anthony Worth hated me.

Johanna Igleway, the diary showed, was married to Anthony Worth the day after the vestry meeting. Her child was delivered a month later and was Ruth, Gracellen's oldest sister, now Mistress John Blake of Chestertown with seven children of her own.

And Randolph Tillman's efforts to patch things up with Anthony Worth appeared to have succeeded; there was frequent mention of the two men hunting together, dining in company and otherwise acting as two good neighbors who had both forgotten a regrettable incident.

Nine years had passed between the time Anthony Worth had looked at Randolph Tillman with hate and fear and the foggy morning Randolph Tillman had been found dead; eight years had passed between the vestry meeting and the fire that had destroyed Larkspur Hill. But as surely as though Anthony Worth had proclaimed the fact in the public square at Easton Town, Task Tillman knew that Worth had been biding his time, smiling at Randolph Tillman, eating at his table, while he plotted his destruction.

Anthony Worth's eyes had betrayed him for just the fraction of a second Task had needed to know what he had done. That flicker, that one drop of the big man's guard had come when Task had mentioned—oh, quite casually and with a smile

30

—that he had happened across his father's diary and the way the book had been discovered.

"Oh, I want to read it," Gracellen had said excitedly. "It must be full of old mysteries if your father put it in a secret compartment."

Task had even forced a laugh somehow.

"No mysteries at all," he had said. "Indeed, my father kept a very dull diary, I'm afraid. It was his idea of importance to list every least thing that happened at a meeting of the vestry back in 1788."

The shot had told. For that half-breath, Anthony Worth's eyes had blazed before they had gone back to their look of quiet amusement.

"And those meetings, I tell you, Gracellen," he had told his daughter, "were very dull affairs, indeed. Many's the one I've sat through, struggling to keep awake. Seventeen Eighty-eight —why, I served on the vestry with your father in that year, Task."

"Yes sir," Task had nodded and he had managed to keep his voice almost indifferent. "He mentions you on several pages, sir."

"You must bring the diary with you some time when you call," Anthony Worth had smiled. "I'd like to refresh my memory on just what weighty matters we did discuss." He had turned to Gracellen, "Seventeen Eighty-eight," he had added, "was the year I married your mother, dear."

He had looked back at Task, his face composed, his smile warm. It was impossible that this man could be a murderer. . . .

It was true. Anthony Worth's eyes had told Task that it was true; now his smile, his complete ease of manner might be daring Task to prove it.

"You water hot, Marse Task," Tillie called from the doorway.

Task rose slowly from the desk chair. Those old ledgers and the memory of the diary had set him to wool-gathering when he should have been totting up his accounts so that he would have a businesslike report to give Squire Wills. Not that he needed

31

ledgers to tell him the situation. Since his tobacco barns had burned, fired by the same kind of "lightning bolt" that had struck Larkspur Hill fourteen years before, there had been nothing but a black picture to show.

Anthony Worth's victory was almost complete. He had burned Larkspur Hill, then killed the Master of Larkspur Hill when it was evident that Randolph Tillman could come back, was coming back. God alone knew how much of his hand was in the tragedy of William. Now, by judicious use of the torch again at a time when Task Tillman was finally on his way, it looked as though everything that was required had been done.

Squire Wills was Task's last hope and Squire Wills had little reason to feel kindly to Task.

5

BATHED AND shaved and wearing his best riding clothes (patched and darned in places but of good quality originally), Task let the black stallion, Lucifer, jog along the sandy lane at the pace of a hack. His appointment with the Squire was for two o'clock, according to the old man's brief, stilted, note and there was time enough and more to reach Easton Town by then. And he needed to think, get his apologies, excuses and explanations readied.

"Though all I'll be able to say in the end is forgive me and help me because you were my father's dearest friend," he told himself bitterly.

It would not be enough. It had been too long since Squire Wills and Randolph Tillman had sat over their tankards and pipes, arguing politics or philosophy or any other subject that could be broached. And during the years since then he had not treated the Squire as he had deserved to be treated; he had virtually ignored the old man and Squire Wills would not be apt to forgive him easily for his ingratitude.

When William had finally swigged the drink that killed him, it had been Squire Wills who had made the trip to Larkspur Hill to try to bring some order out of the chaos William's tippling had brought. It had been the Squire who had advised

Task on what could be sold (which was little enough) and what should be kept; which slaves should be sent to the auction, which debts were the more pressing and which could be staved off for a time, which crops should be planted, how the meagre handful of cash William had left should be used. It had been Squire Wills who had held off the herd of creditors with the plea that Task be given a chance to show his abilities; it had been the Squire who had saved Larkspur Hill.

And in return, Task had let his labors tie him to his fields or, if there had been an empty hour or so at hand he had gone to Fairoverlea and Gracellen, not to Easton to see the old man. Even since the tobacco barns had burned and he had called Anthony Worth a villain to his face, bringing Gracellen's riding crop lashing at him, he had not gone to Easton, partly because of his shame at having neglected the Squire, partly because for a time his despair had been so black that he had wanted to see no man who might offer him hope.

Now he was going, hat in hand, to beg for one more chance. He was going on a fool's errand. Squire Wills would laugh at him, and rightly so.

Well, let Larkspur Hill go, then. Let whoever bought in the place carry on the struggle against Anthony Worth. But there would be no struggle. *The King* would seize the property the minute it was thrown on the green. That had been Worth's aim, his purpose, for all the years that stretched between this day back to the afternoon when Randolph Tillman had denounced him for what he was, lecher, seducer, violator of all things decent, breaker of laws and men's hopes and spirits.

The King, damn him, surrounded himself with rich men whose wealth depended on Anthony Worth, with cowards who were willing to sacrifice their own ambitions and plans in exchange for the uncertain security that Worth allowed but never guaranteed those who did his bidding; with blackguards, freebooters, cutthroats like Roan and Marsden and Womble who found safety from the law in Worth's service; with reckless young men who found excitement—and gold—on his vessels that flouted every maritime law laid down by the Government at Washington; with smugglers who used the Peartree Creek landing; with slave-runners and slave-snatchers. All these, from landed gentleman to skulking outlaw, bowed to Anthony Worth, did his will, prospered if they pleased him and suffered if they did not.

And this—this monster was the father of the woman he loved, the only woman he ever had loved, the only woman he ever would love.

"Gracellen," he groaned aloud. "Why in God's name were you born to *him*?"

The black pricked up its ears and sidestepped mincingly, shying at nothing, tired of the workhorse gait it had set for itself out of pure devilment. Task reined in the stallion sharply.

"You wanted a walk," he told his mount. "Walk you will."

Lucifer blew through his nostrils, shook his head, fought the bit and then subsided, snorting again in disgust. There was no joy, these days, in being saddled. The man on his back was a lump when once, and not so long ago, he had been a delight to carry.

Gracellen, Gracellen, the stallion's rider cried inwardly, why did this have to happen to us? You were not even born, I was a baby, when your father and mine came to grips. It was your own mother my father sought to save from shame and yet because he spoke for Johanna Igleway's good name we've been brought to these black days.

And if my father hadn't spoken, would you be here to try to stripe me with your little whip? Anthony Worth more probably would have thrown Johanna out of Fairoverlea like a slave wench who had pleasured him for a spell, had my father kept silent as the others did. And then you never would have been born.

So if this is right, then that must be wrong, and how can that be wrong if this is right?

With a curse that broke in his throat like a sob, he struck at the stallion with his crop and raked Lucifer's flanks with his spurs. The black reared in indignation, then sprang forward joyfully. Task hunched over the horse's neck, his eyes bleak and unseeing, keeping his saddle by instinct as Lucifer broke into a headlong gallop.

Down the road raced the stallion, a long plume of dust drifting up behind him. Across wooden bridges they thundered, around bends in the road that would have brought swift disaster if they had chanced to meet a lumbering oxcart, on and on they flew, the stallion half mad with jubilation over this, his first decent run in too long, the stallion's rider bowed by a burden that would not be outdistanced by any horse, no matter how fleet.

Their wild passing brought housewives running to the windows, made slaves in the fields straighten and stare in wonderment. A man driving a farm wagon yelled something as they swept past. A flock of chickens scattered in a flurry of feathers and a shriek of cackling. A dog that ran out from a farmyard missed being run down by a scanty inch and fled, ki-yi-ing.

("Is it a courier?" they asked each other as the dust of the passing horseman drifted to earth again. "Has the war come at last?")

The outskirts of a town came flying toward them and Task Tillman was brought back out of his blank, blind despair by the strangled squawk of a man in a wide straw hat who leaped from the road to the safety of a ditch with a flapping of coat-tails.

"Runaway! Runaway!" he howled from the weeds where he had landed. "Take cover, all!"

Task reined in and looked about him dazedly. By chance, Lucifer had brought him to Easton when it could just as well have been Queen's Town or even Georgetown, for all the control he had had over the reins.

He drew Lucifer down to a walk, turned him and went back to the man who was climbing from the ditch, goggling at him.

"Your pardon, sir," he said. "The animal got out of hand for a minute. Are you hurt?"

The man in the wide straw hat that somehow had stayed on his head worked his prominent adam's apple convulsively.

"Ain't hurt," he said, "but I lost five years of my life between

36

the road and the ditch." He peered up at Task, narrowing his eyes. "Say, ain't you Mister Tillman, out Miles River way?"

Task nodded and the man in the straw hat smiled.

"Thought I recognized you," he said, proud of his accomplishment. "Ain't seen you in town lately. Not since—well—I heard about your barns burnin'. Sorry to hear about it—everybody was. Damned shame, the bad luck you folks have had! First the fire at the big house, then your daddy havin' that awful accident, then your brother goin' off so young and now the barns. I'll say to you, truly, there never has been a family in Talbot County higher thought of than the Tillmans. I mind the time your daddy—"

"Yes," Task cut in as the older man drew a deep breath. "Thank you. I've got to be getting along if you're sure you're not hurt. I'm late for an appointment."

"You trot along," the man grinned. "Ain't nothin' wrong with me a few drams at the Indian Queen won't cure. Sorry about your barns burnin' down. Like I said before, everybody in town felt real bad when they heard about that."

"Thank you," Task said again and urged Lucifer into a canter toward the town.

Damned old gabber, ready to start talking the first chance he got and he'd keep on going till sundown if you'd let him.

But that, he reproached himself in the next breath, was a mighty poor way to think of a man who had been friendly after having had to jump for his life from in front of a damned fool who raced his horse with his eyes closed! And the man had sounded sincerely sorry about the bad luck of the Tillmans.

"You're sour to the core," he told himself aloud. "You've been sitting out at Larkspur Hill feeling sorry for yourself so long you've forgotten how to be human. The world's not to blame for what's happened; all your troubles are the fault of one man. Keep remembering that and you might do better. You might even remember how to laugh again."

The change in Task Tillman may have been slight but it was still true that some of the tight lines were gone from his face and

37

the scowl that had been habitual for so long was lifted as he rode on. He even managed the semblance of a smile as he responded to the hails of the first groups of men he passed on the street corners near the Square.

The town, he noted, was bustling. There were more people on the streets, there was a new air of urgency that he had not seen before. Everywhere were small knots of men, oblivious to the heat of the sun that poured down, deep in earnest conversation, all, Task guessed, talking about the war. There were men in uniform to be seen here and there, members of the militia companies that seemed to be springing up like mushrooms all over the Eastern Shore. These private companies chose their own uniforms and the accent was decidedly on color; there were men in bright green tunics and in glaring blue, others in white and silver reminiscent of the French troops of the Revolution. There was even one young man who paced along the street resplendent in a scarlet jacket identical with that of a British Hussar.

"That sprout," Task smiled inwardly, "is going to have a mighty busy time if we do go to war with the Redcoats. He'll be ducking bullets from both sides."

It was one of these uniformed men, a tall figure in a claret tunic, white breeches, brass-embellished shako and sword, who called sharply from the brick sidewalk as Task neared the Indian Queen Inn on Washington Street.

"Hey, Tillman! I want to see you!"

Task reined in and looked back, fighting the return of his scowl. He had hoped to get past Charles Rawlent without having to speak to him or, at least, without more than a sparse nod. He had never had any love for Charles Rawlent and the man in the claret tunic, he knew, had always had less for him; they had eyed each other with mutual contempt since they were boys.

"Hail, the great soldier," Task muttered beneath his breath as he watched Rawlent's approach with murky eyes. "The nation's safe now, by God, with that nancy-ann ready to defend us."

Rawlent came up to the side of the black stallion, one white-gloved hand on the hilt of his sword, the other thumb hooked over the wide leather belt at his waist. His perfectly booted feet were spread as he looked up at Task, squinting into the sun.

He made a handsome figure and he knew it. His mirror and the years had taught him that he was the handsomest man in Talbot County, certainly, and probably in all Maryland. His features were almost impossibly classic, his body was perfectly proportioned, impressive now in his well-tailored uniform. If his schoolmates, when he was a boy, and his classmates at Saint John's College had named him an egotistical fop, their derision had not bothered Charles Rawlent; he had waved it all away as born of jealousy.

He had been a *beau ideal* since his early teen years, the most sought-after young man on the Eastern Shore as a dance or dinner partner, though few men included him in any stag gatherings. Fair-haired, beautifully mannered, drawling in an affected tone which was supposed to be the London style, Rawlent had played the genteel young gentleman all his adult years, until just recently. Now, Task sneered, he had donned the armor of Mars, well-cut by the best Baltimore tailors.

Task's amber eyes surveyed the tunic, the sword, the shako for a moment as Rawlent looked up at him.

"Pretty," he said briefly. "The uniform, I mean."

Rawlent's face stiffened and a curl came to his mouth.

"I'm glad you approve, Tillman," he returned. "I'd thought that anything connected with fighting a war was quite odorous to you."

Tillman's eyes narrowed though he kept his chill smile. The rein with which he stopped Lucifer's curvetting was hard-hauled.

"Just what," he asked quietly, "are you talking about, Rawlent?"

The other young man waved a white-gloved hand airily.

"When you refused to report for the drill," he drawled, "we all thought the idea of being a militiaman was beneath you, naturally."

"Drill?" asked Task, with dangerous calm. "What drill and whose orders told me to report, President Madison's?"

"Ah, you know what drill all right, Tillman," Rawlent sneered. "I sent a man to your place a month ago or more and ordered you to report for drill with the Dragon Footguards here in Easton Town twice a week, on Tuesdays and Thursdays."

Task turned leisurely in the saddle and hooked a leg over the pommel to peer down at Rawlent as an indulgent parent might rest himself to listen to a child's prattle.

"Was that your doing?" he asked. "I was away from Larkspur Hill when your—er—*order* came but Tillie told me that somebody in fancy clothes had been there to ask me to go somewhere. From what I could make out, I'd missed an invitation to a masquerade ball."

Task's voice was not loud but it was strong enough to carry to a group of men standing several paces away. The snicker that rose from the group was loud enough, too, to tint Charles Rawlent's ears with scarlet. The hand at his sword hilt clenched in a spasmodic grip.

"If you mean that as a joke," he grated, "it's a damned poor one. There are some men in these parts who don't call it a masquerade ball to get themselves ready for a war."

"War?" Task asked. "You're forever talking about a war. What war?"

"The war that's bound to come," Rawlent barked. "The war with England. Or have you been so busy working with your niggers, hoeing corn, that you haven't heard about that?"

Task Tillman's sun-coppered face went grey beneath its tan and his hands bunched into splay-knuckled fists. The group that had snickered was silent, tense, expectant, now. Then, as Task relaxed, a sigh (relief, disappointment?) breathed out from the onlookers.

"I'll pass that remark, Rawlent," Task said evenly, "because I *have* been working in the fields with my hands. You see, I owe some money and even if it means handling a hoe to help get a crop, I'm bound to get one and pay up what I owe." His eyes glimmered. "As *most* gentlemen would be bound, or don't you agree?"

There was a buzz from the group of eavesdroppers; Rawlent's reputation for paying his debts was not the best on the Eastern

Shore. The man in the shako twisted his mouth in a crooked line as the shot went home but he recovered quickly.

"Perhaps, then," he murmured smoothly, "the Dragons might be better off, after all, to struggle along without your valiant services, Mister Tillman."

"A heavy blow," Task murmured in like tone. "But tell me, Rawlent, where do you get your special warnings of this war of yours?"

"I need only to know what every patriotic man in America knows! Henry Clay has sounded the warning often enough."

"Ah, Clay," Task nodded. "A model of calm deliberation. And when will Clay declare this war? And by what authority? I thought the Congress—"

"Congress be damned!" Rawlent shouted.

"Tut, tut," Task smiled. "Dangerously close to treason, that. But seeing we're old friends I'll forget you said it."

"No friend of yours, Tillman!" Rawlent cried as the laughter of the spectators sounded. "No friend to any scoundrel who'd set fire to the tobacco barns he'd emptied in the night and then cry misfortune to the people who loaned him money!"

Rawlent's voice resounded over the street and the adjoining Square. His blunt charge stopped every tongue within hearing distance as faces swung toward the man on the horse and the man in uniform. There was no sound except the drone of the cicadas for a second and then Task's voice came, low and level and coldly furious.

"Now, by God," he said, "you've done it!"

He slid from his saddle and was on Rawlent before the uniformed man could draw the dress sword that hung at his side. Task's fist swung in a blurred arc and the crack of its meeting with Rawlent's jaw was a pistol shot. The claret-jacketed man went over backward with a crash that raised a cloud of dust from the street; his shako sailed a dozen paces away where it came to rest, rocking idly on its visor, its white brush dirtied, its brass emblem smeared with manure.

Task looked down at Rawlent, trembling, his snarl inhuman.

"Get up!" he spat. "Get up and use your sword on me, if you can!"

Rawlent rolled over, pushed himself half up, and then saw Task's eyes. The officer sank back to the dust, his eyes wide, his mouth gaping loosely.

"Get up!" Tillman roared. "Get up or show these people what kind of a coward they have to keep the British away when Henry Clay starts his war!"

Charles Rawlent's mind must have still been numbed by the blow when he made his reply in a squeaked bleat.

"If there was no law 'gainst dueling," he managed, "ye'd pay for this with a bullet in your guts, Task Tillman!"

There was a roar of laughter from the men who had watched the brief scuffle. True, there was a law against dueling but, so far as anyone could remember, it had never stopped Eastern Shoremen of quality from resorting to The Code when the occasion seemed to demand it.

Task Tillman drew back a step and put his hands on his hips. His voice dripped contempt when he spoke to the man on the ground.

"A duel—with you?" he asked. "Why, I'd be ridden out of the county on a rail for mistreatin' a girl! By God, maybe you *are* a girl! Let's see what those fancy pantaloons hide!"

He started for the cringing Rawlent and stopped at the touch of a hand on his arm. He swung around, ready to accommodate a friend of Rawlent's, and looked into the kindly, troubled face of Squire Wills.

"Nay, Task," the old man said quietly. "Please, lad, let's leave it at this. Enough harm's done now, I fear, and let's not make it worse. Come along, Task, to the inn."

"But this lying dog—"

"I know," Wills interrupted, "but what's to be gained by shaming him further? Get your horse and let's to the inn."

Nodding, Task walked to Lucifer's head and slipped the reins over to take them in his hand. Slowly, and with the elderly

Squire walking beside him, he turned his back on Charles Rawlent and the burst of babble that mounted to a roar.

The two men and the horse had nearly reached the inn's courtyard when a high-pitched, womanish scream came hurtling after them. Charles Rawlent had found his voice again.

"You'll pay for this, Tillman!" screamed the leader of the Dragon Footguards. "Traitors, blackguards, scum—by God, we'll deal with such as you when the proper time comes!"

6

"AND SO, sir, you see my position," Task Tillman said, evenly, an hour later. "I admit I have no right to expect you to help me again after the way I've treated you, but—well, sir, I've been all through that."

The two men were in the small, slope-ceilinged room of the Indian Queen Inn which comprised the living quarters of old Squire Wills. The Squire lived here by preference; financially, he was able to have one of the finest places in Talbot County if he so desired. But he was a childless widower with a distinct disinterest in manor house living, so he chose to stay at the inn, close to the court where he still used his keen mind and silvery tongue occasionally to confound his legal opponents.

He was one of the few men in those parts who still wore the knee breeches, the tricorne hat, the powdered periwig of the Eighteenth Century. His rectangular spectacles might have been those the great Benjamin Franklin had worn. His speech was liberally sprinkled with phrases as antiquated as the massive silver buckles he wore on his square-toed shoes. Yet no one, not even the children, ever laughed at Squire Wills; those legal sharpshooters from Baltimore and Philadelphia who had been foolish enough to treat the old gentleman as a senile eccentric had learned swiftly and to their sorrow just why the Squire was so respected along the length and breadth of the Eastern Shore.

Now he pulled at the long-stemmed clay pipe he held and slumped lower in the wing chair by the narrow window that looked out over the Square. Had it not been for the occasional puff of bluish smoke that came from between his lips, Task would have thought the Squire was dozing as the story was told, the plea made. The old man's eyes were closed behind the spectacles, his free hand lay limp in his lap, his feet were loosely crossed at the ankles.

The silence stretched while Task ransacked his mind desperately for some word he might have overlooked, some argument that might convince the old man that he was worthy of another chance. A wasp buzzed through the window, circled the room, flew out again, and still Squire Wills made no move to give his answer.

Well, Task told himself, it had only been a drowning man's straw, at best. If he had failed in this, at least he had tried. He could go back to Larkspur Hill and face the bleak certainties with at least the cold comfort of knowing he had done everything he could, even going so far as to ask help from a man who had every reason to despise him as an ingrate.

Squire Wills' quiet voice made Task start as it came from the depths of the wing chair.

"Task," the old gentleman said, quietly, "through all this you've said Anthony Worth is to blame for everything. But aside from that diary of Randolph's, a diary that's twenty-two years old, you have no evidence, not a shred, that he or his servants—if that be the name for them—burned your barns."

"Evidence?" Task asked. "What evidence is ever found against Worth? Men have tried to get evidence against him for years. Most of them couldn't pin down a thing. The few who have, and you must know there have been some, sir, have had their mouths shut, by one way or another."

"Aye," Wills sighed. "That's been the whisper in this county for fifty years, I trow. Many men have come to me, seeking my feeble assistance in the courts against Anthony Worth, yet when I ask for evidence on which to rivet my case there have been only bits of hearsay, fragments of gossip, worthless scraps of conjecture."

He sighed again and puffed at the churchwarden pipe.

"I ofttimes think," he went on, "that Anthony Worth has been made the whipping boy for this county. He has been charged with more base villainies than any one human, even Anthony Worth, could plot, much less carry out."

Another tiny cloud of tobacco smoke escaped from between the old man's lips.

"So, Task, let me give you this warning, if you meant it when you said you valued my advice. 'Twould be wise to keep your rash charges to yourself. You speak of murder and house-burning and they are dangerous charges to bring against a man without proof. Aye, 'tis best to tread softly, softly, in matters where Anthony Worth is concerned."

Despair swamped Task Tillman and in its wake came anger. This man, he thought, had been his father's best friend and had been a friend to him and yet now he showed that he, too, was afraid of Anthony Worth. Or worse, was paid by Worth to make certain that people who came to him with their complaints against the Master of Fairoverlea were discouraged at the start.

He rose from the ladderback chair and reached for his hat on the highboy.

"I've taken up too much of your time, Squire Wills," he said, keeping his voice steady. "I thank you for listening to me and, regardless of the loan, I hope to see you more often than I have in the past."

The Squire's hand flapped as the bewigged old man spoke.

"Oh, sit down, Task, sit down," he commanded, wearily. "'Od's fish, why must you youngsters leap to unworthy conclusions like a frog at a gnat? Sit down and rid yourself of the notion that because I cautioned you I fear Anthony Worth—or am in his pay."

"Sir, I—"

"Oh, yes, you thought that—'twas printed on your face in big letters." The oldster straightend in the wing chair and laid aside

46

the pipe. "I take no offense, Task. I once was as young and as hasty as you at seizing the wrong thought, if you can believe it. And I loved your father too much—aye, and you, too—to see you suffer by a thoughtless doubt of an old man's integrity. Sit ye down, I say, and try that decanter by your side. Peach brandy that's made for me by a friend near Saint Michael's. Have a sup and give me a glass and we'll talk over what we must do."

The brandy was velvety, delicious fire and its glow dissolved the stone of hopelessness that had weighted Task's belly at his thought that Squire Wills was aligned with the enemy. For the first time since he had entered this room, indeed, for the first time anywhere in weeks, Task Tillman relaxed, lowered his taut guard.

"Now," said the Squire, smiling, "that improves the day, eh? First, let's at this vexing money puzzle. What's the sum total of your needs?"

"I can survive the pressing—"

Wills' raised hand cut him short.

"We'll not speak of surviving the immediate crisis," the old man objected, firmly. "A body can survive on a crust but it can hardly thrive on that diet. Nay, lad, I asked the sum total needed to get you in the clear again."

Tillman swallowed hard before he answered.

"Eleven thousand dollars, sir," he said.

Squire Wills did not seem staggered by the amount. He pursed his lips and brought the forefingers of his hands together under the point of his chin, his eyes half-closed behind the spectacles, but his attitude was one of deliberation, not doubt. Task waited, anxiously but with none of the dread that had filled him earlier. After a brief silence, Squire Wills nodded.

"Aye," he said, "we'll have no difficulty in finding that somewhere about. I was considering where best we could lay hands on the money with the least possible delay. This is Tuesday—would Friday be agreeable?"

"Sir," Task said in a choked voice, "I can't tell you how much I—"

"Best not try then, lad."

47

"And you'll not lose by this, I swear it! I said before that if Worth—" The Squire's grey brows lowered. "I mean, sir, that if misfortune tries to sneak up on me again, I'll be ready for him—it. If it means setting guards with guns about my place, I'll do that, too."

"I have another plan, mayhap, and one less warlike," the Squire offered. "Make your peace with Anthony Worth."

Task stared in astonishment at the old man in the wing chair.

"I—you mean—surely you know I couldn't!" he gasped.

"You can," Wills said, his voice almost solemn, "and with all my heart I hope you do."

"But—but—"

"Now listen to an old man, Task. Hear me out, though I drone on like the dotard I fool myself I'm not—nay, listen."

He leaned forward in the chair and his voice took on a depth that echoed his sincerity.

"Listen to me as I listened to you while you called Anthony Worth a murderer and the man who burned Larkspur Hill and your tobacco barns. Lad, you know Randolph Tillman was my dearest friend. You know—or I hope you know—that if I thought Anthony Worth killed Randolph, I'd call him out tomorrow, old as I am, and I'd kill him, somehow. If I truly thought Worth burned Larkspur Hill and your barns, if I thought the man was so evil that he'd spend the years biding his time, plotting Randolph's death and ruin to Randolph's son, I'd smash him like a poisonous viper.

"I do not like Anthony Worth. I know that he has flouted the law at every hand; he has become an arrogant power in this county. I would not have him at my table, I would not give him of my peach brandy, I despise all he stands for—ruthlessness, sharp practices, ostentation in all things. But because I cannot like a man, I cannot brand him a murderer. Don't you see, Task, you have no proof! Can't you realize that you've built this whole dark case against Anthony Worth on nothing but a deep and damning suspicion?"

"The diary—" Task muttered.

"There is the diary. It says that in Seventeen Eighty-eight, Anthony Worth and your father had differences in a vestry meeting over Worth's right to maintain in his household a young woman who had been his dead wife's nursing maid. I know about that meeting; I was there. I saw the whole thing, heard every word that was spoken."

"I didn't know you were at that meeting, sir," Task said.

"Aye," Squire Wills nodded, "and the thing distressed me because I thought my friend, Randolph, was wrong in the whole affair."

"But the girl was seduced by Worth!" Task exclaimed. The Squire shrugged.

"Seduced?" he murmured. "'Twill offend ye, no doubt, lad, but in the case of Anthony Worth it was ordinarily the other way 'round. Never to speak ill of Johanna Igleway who lived to be a gracious lady, but there was none who could see her eyes when Worth was near who could but know he needs must fend her off with a club if he would keep her pure for long."

He stretched out a hand in a placating gesture.

"Ah, Task," he said, "forgive an old man's evil thoughts, if that they be. I forgot Johanna was Gracellen's mother."

"Gracellen means nothing to me," Task lied, stiffly.

"No?" the old Squire asked. "Then I was wrong, I see. But to get on; the falling-out twixt your father and Anthony Worth, I say, concerned Worth's household, not Randolph's."

"But Johanna was with child. My father—"

"Aye, your father spoke out in vestry meeting when it could have all been done so much more different, so much more kindly. Randolph Tillman usually was the kindest, most thoughtful man on earth but the Devil got into him that day. He flayed Anthony Worth with vituperation that made my blood run cold. He must have regretted it when he came to his senses."

"His diary did say he was sorry," Task muttered grudgingly.

"Ah, you see? He admits it was a mistake—what man can say he never made one, even Randolph Tillman? But hear this: Anthony Worth had every reason to be furious enough to call

49

your father out, but did he? No, he apologized to the vestry and to Randolph, they shook hands on it and he wed Johanna the following day, as I remember it. And Task, your father and Anthony Worth were friends after that. Randolph was a better friend to Worth than I could ever bring myself to be."

"But—but couldn't Worth have been—"

"Planning your father's death for the next nine years?" Squire Wills asked. He sat back in his chair and shook his head slowly. "Task, I ask you can any man believe that? Can you blame me when I say you're wrong? You've always been wrong about this thing, you've burdened yourself with a hate that is as senseless as it is unworthy of you."

He leaned forward again.

"D'ye see what you've done, lad? You've seized on this black suspicion of yours and you've pinned the blame for every bad thing that's happened to you on Anthony Worth. Your father was killed in a fall from a horse—strange that a horseman such as he should die that way but stranger things have happened—and Anthony Worth killed him, bashed in his head and made it seem that he had struck his skull on a rock in his fall.

"Before that, Larkspur Hill burned in a terrible fire. Ah, you say, 'twas not lightning did it, 'twas Anthony Worth!

"Now your tobacco barns go up in smoke. Again, no lightning was to blame for that, 'twas Anthony Worth! Good God, boy, rid yourself of this delusion of yours before you go mad!"

His tone gentled as he left the wing chair and crossed the room to rest a hand on Task Tillman's shoulder.

"You've had more than your share of misfortune, Task," he said, "and mayhap you'd be something more than human if you did not find your thoughts twisted by your troubles. But if ye'll have me, I'll be your friend and together we can prove that misfortune can be beat by hard work and a brave spirit."

His hand pounded Task's shoulder gently.

"So make your peace with Anthony Worth," he said. "Cast out your devils, Task! Your father would want you to give me your promise to do this, lad."

Task Tillman kept his eyes fixed on the worn planking of the inn bedroom's floor. It took a long struggle for him to answer Squire Wills and his voice was low when he spoke.

"I hope to God you're right in this," he said, "but—I promise."

7

AT THE moment Squire Wills was asking Task's promise in an upper room of the Indian Queen Inn, Jett Worth was entering the inn's taproom.

Booted and spurred, Jett cut as handsome a figure in riding garb as he had earlier in the clothes he had donned for his landing at Fairoverlea. The gallop from the estate on Peartree Creek to Easton Town had been an exhilarating change from the months of bracing against the pitch and heave of a schooner's deck and Jett's eyes were shining with pure joy of life as he strode into the heavy-beamed, smoky room.

The place was jammed. The sun outside had driven a good many of the sidewalk orators out of its rays and it appeared that most of them had sought relief from the heat in the glasses and mugs of the taproom. The place might have been darker than the street but it could not have been much cooler, what with the press of bodies, the clouds of tobacco smoke and the heat of conversation.

Jett started edging toward the bar but the first man he tried to squeeze past seized on him with a loud cry of welcome.

"Jett, lad! Home again after—how long has it been?"

"Sixteen months, two weeks, two days," Jett smiled. "A devilish long voyage to Hispaniola, I say."

"Hispaniola, hah!" snorted the man who had hailed him. "How was it in London on this trip?"

"London, Mister Peters?" Jett asked wonderingly. "Why, surely you know that all trade's forbidden twixt us and England or France."

Peters, a stringy man in a mustard-colored coat and blue breeches, threw back his head and howled with laughter. His roar brought other heads swinging and there was a general surge toward Jett, standing a step inside the doorway.

"Jett Worth, it's good to see you . . . What's the news from Europe, Jett? . . . Is Boney goin' t'lick the British? . . . When do we pay the Lobsterbacks their due for the *Chesapeake*, Jett—soon?"

Still harping on the *Chesapeake*, Jett told himself, his mind's lip curling, as he responded to the greetings showered on him, shook hands with those able to reach him. Would they never forget the whole sad affair?

More than three years had passed since that day in June, 1807, when Captain Barron had taken the American frigate *Chesapeake* out through the Virginia Capes with some vague, misshapen plan of clashing with the British *Leopard* and yet the Eastern Shore of Maryland spoke of the disgraceful affair as though it had happened yesterday. He, Jett, would think these people, in fact all Americans, would be happy to forget it as soon as possible but still the tavern loungers, the ladies at their teacups—aye, even the great minds in the Congress at Washington—spilled endless words about the "battle," if it could be called that.

Jett had another term for the fight between the *Chesapeake* and the *Leopard*. He called it a damned noodle-headed farce. For look you: *Chesapeake*, according to the untwisted story, went out looking for the fight with only forty guns against *Leopard's* fifty-two. *Chesapeake* had a green crew under a green captain; *Leopard* had been fighting the French, the Dutch, the Spanish fleets for years and was more at home under fire than she was at anchor. And then, after the first exchanges and with only three of his crew down, Barron had ordered his colors struck! And it was this strange encounter that roused the patriotic fervor in the people's breast!

"Hell's eternal fire," Jett had said when he had first heard of the affair, "I could give a better account of myself with *Heron* and a fowling piece loaded with buckshot!"

Now, as the throng about him thickened, Jett laughingly held up a hand.

"I've just ridden a far piece over dusty roads, gentlemen," he said. "What little news I can give you will have to wait till I wash down some of the sand in my gullet."

They made way for him then and pressed about him as the barkeep slid a foaming tankard of ale across the board to him. Jett drank deeply, then drank again. He banged the empty tankard down on the counter and called for another as he turned to face his eager inquisitors.

"I'm afraid I must disappoint you, gentlemen," he said, "if it's news of Europe you're hot for. I told you I took my vessel to Hispaniola and Hispaniola it will be till Hell freezes over. I've clearance papers from Port au Prince if you're still unconvinced."

Another laugh. No man in the taproom would dare say it but few in the place doubted that The King could furnish his captains with clearance papers from any port in the world and have them appear more official than the real thing.

"But I had a drink with a Britisher in one port," Jett went on, disregarding the laughter, "and he told me some things you may not have heard. England's certain there'll be no war with us. She thinks Madison's afraid that if we declare war New England will secede."

"And well they might, the Yankee bastards," growled a burly man in a plum-colored coat. "When the Embargo Act kept us from tradin' with the foreign countries, either in our vessels or theirs, the squalls from Boston could be heard down here."

"They had a right to squawl!" protested another. "Timid Tom Jefferson, cutting the nation's throat by forbidding all commerce lest England become angry at our selling to her enemies. If he

54

had had his way, our ships would rot at anchor while he trembled under the bedcovers!"

"And Madison's no braver," cried somebody from the back of the crowd. "Shilly-shallying the time away instead of showing England once and for all that we're ready to give her again what we gave her once, a drubbing!"

"And are we?" Jett Worth asked before he buried his face in the tankard.

"Are we? Why, of course we are!" came the answering babel. "Don't say you doubt it, Jett!"

The young, dark-faced man in riding clothes lowered his tankard, swallowing his draught of ale.

"Aye," he said calmly, "I do doubt it." Then, as a rumble arose from the men surrounding him, he held up a slender hand. "Don't mistake me, gentlemen," he said. "I'm for my country, heart and soul and with whatever services I may offer as a sailing man. But you said we were ready to give England a drubbing *now*. I say it would be God's miracle if we were not beaten in a month's time if we fought now, as we're situated."

"Strange words, Jett Worth," somebody said in an ominous voice.

"Are they?" Jett asked imperturbably. "This war, if there be one, will be mostly a sea war, at the start at least. And do you know our Navy's strength right now? And England's?" There was a confused murmuring which Jett's clear voice cut through. "We have seven frigates, gentlemen—*just seven*! We have some leaky cutters, a few barges, a sloop or two I'd not risk my life on to sail from here to Norfolk. England has more than *one thousand* ships of war, from the seventy-four's down to eighteen-gun brig-sloops."

"And all of 'em kept busy with Bonaparte's war," a voice called.

Jett nodded, sipping at his ale.

"Kept busy, aye," he acknowledged, "but only 'cause the British Admiralty wants to keep 'em busy. I've seen their blockade—I mean, I've heard of their blockade of France, and England is using three vessels where one would do, only to keep 'em busy."

55

"But why?" asked Peters. "British stupidity?"

"No, Friend Peters," Jett said. "The British Admiralty is not half so stupid as it's credited with being. The Admiralty fights a constant battle with the Parliament for money. The Admiralty is always hungry for more; the Parliament is always looking for a way to give less. This war with Bonaparte has given the Admiralty a chance to dip deep into the purse. Boney's threat to invade has frightened the most niggardly pinch-purse in Parliament. Now that England has the greatest fleet the world has ever known, the Admiralty intends to keep it up to full strength. And how Parliament would howl if ships of war were sailed back to England because they weren't needed in the French blockade!

"So, three ships where one would do is the rule. But it wouldn't be the rule if we declared war. I say we'd bring such a fleet down on us, warships England can well spare from the Channel, the Mediterranean and the commerce lanes, that we'd be overwhelmed!"

"That's on the sea," the man in the plum-colored coat said. "They had the fleet in Seventy-six, too, but they found it did them little good in the end."

Jett sipped reflectively at his tankard while approving cries arose about him. He waited until the clamor had quieted, then spoke again.

"About war on land," he admitted, "I know nothing so I'll not speak for myself. But a man who's close to me and who's generally right says this: In Seventy-six we were fighting for independence; England was fighting what she thought was a puny rebellion till near the end. The troops she used against us were not her best, her generals were not her finest. Nay, nay—hear me out! This man says and I say, too, we could have whipped England's best to win our independence but we had no need to. Fortune smiled on us.

"Now, should we go to war with England over what she thinks is her right to rule the seas, we'd find a different temper in our old enemies. England lives off the sea. To threaten her there is to point a sword at her throat. She'd fight with the best she had and

56

she has troops seasoned in a half dozen wars. We'd fight with—what?"

"Our army! Our militia!"

"Our army?" Jett asked. "Three years ago, Governor Wright told the Adjutant General of Maryland to detach nearly four thousand men from the militia to the National Army. How many militiamen went? How many are still in the Army?"

"Their term of service ran out," somebody explained, "and we did give the National Army near two thousand men."

"So," Jett nodded, "and have others taken their places? What's the state of the Army? Does anybody know? The President ordered eleven regiments formed two years ago but were they formed? What arms have we and are they any good or relics of Seventy-six? Is our Army like our Navy and why should it be different?"

"The militia, then!" Peters said. "Our militia would rise overnight in every town and village."

"Oh, aye, the militia," Jett said. "I passed a company as I rode in. Charley Rawlent was leading them in drill. They made a pretty sight. I never saw a neater drill."

He tossed a coin on the bar and adjusted the stock at his throat.

"Please remember, gentlemen," he said, "I am for war with England. I hate the bastards more, I think, than any man in this place. But I say that as we stand, *as we stand now*, 'twould be a reckless thing to pick a fight with England. Let her wear herself out fighting Boney while we grow strong, then strike! Five years from now, if we start building a fleet and an army today, we could destroy her wherever she chose to fight."

He nodded, then stalked to the door, the handsome, jaunty, self-confident heir to the throne of *The King*, Anthony Worth.

8

OUTSIDE the taproom, he collided with Task Tillman.

Task had just left Squire Wills and was on his way to the stable, deep in conflicting thoughts that tore at him from every side. He had promised the Squire he would make his peace with Anthony Worth; he had heard Squire Wills make every one of his convictions of Worth's villainy seem empty suspicions; he had felt the first gnawing of self-doubt. True, he had found the money he had despaired of finding, the money to save Larkspur Hill, but even this seemed of secondary importance now to the promise he had made to the old Squire.

Small wonder, then, that Task, busy with his mind's puzzle, failed to see Jett until he crashed into him. Both men stepped back with apologies and both men's faces brightened as they recognized each other.

"Task, by God!" Jett said and his hand shot out in greeting. "Talk about running into somebody!"

"Jett!" Task seized the other's hand and wrung it. "I heard you were back!"

"At dawn today. And how are things, Task? How's—"

He stopped, clamping down on whatever he had been about to say, cursing himself for asking Task how things were doing when he knew full well by what Gracellen and his uncle had told him that things were doing very badly indeed with Task Tillman.

Task saw Jett's embarrassment and moved to ease it.

"A little bad luck," he said swiftly, "but—well, nothing fatal."

"I—I'm sorry, Task," Jett stammered. "I heard of this second fire, of course, and I—well, damn all, it was a stupid thing to say."

"You were always a nitwit," Task laughed. "Remember the time you blatted out about how much Mistress Everett's new baby looked like their white overseer? I thought Old Everett would murder you for sure that day."

"Not half as bad as the time you. . . ."

They plunged into their reminiscences, these two who had been friends for so long, as boys swimming, fishing, sailing and hunting together; as pupils under the birch of old Doctor Mulliken (long gone, now, may his soul have plenty of cherubim cheeks to put blushes on) and later as classmates at Saint John's College in Annapolis.

The old days, the good days that Jobie was always prating about, Task reflected. Could it be, if what Squire Wills held was true, that some semblance of those days could be brought back? Could the flavor of the times before the discovery of that 1788 diary ever be recaptured?

". . . and so she said: 'You're standin' on it, sir,'" Jett finished. Task laughed, although he had missed the joke.

"How was this voyage, Jett?" he asked. His friend shrugged.

"Wind and water and mains'l and men," he replied, "as always." He jerked his head toward the taproom door. "A drink?"

Task gestured toward the courtyard stable.

"I've got to get back to the place," he explained. "I've got a lot to do before dark. Another time, Jett, and thanks."

"I'll ride with you to the fork, then," the slighter man said. "I thought I might spend the night in Easton but it's too damned hot and there's nothing but war talk here. I'll go back along with you." He hesitated. "That is, if you'll have me."

"And why wouldn't I, for God's sake?"

59

"Well—well, to be honest, I found out at home that you and my uncle—yes, and Cousin Gracellen, too—are all at logger-heads these days. I was afraid this—er—misunderstanding might have soured you on me. I hope not, Task, but"—his chin lifted and his dark eyes lost their smile—"I'd better tell you now that if there's some kind of feud brewing, I'm a Worth and proud to be one."

His words were plain enough in their meaning: *Never forget I'm loyal to Anthony Worth. If the lines are drawn, count me against you, Task Tillman.*

Task walked on a few paces, searching for the right words. He found what he hoped were them when he reached the courtyard.

"Listen, Jett," he said in a low voice. "I've held some black thoughts against your uncle ever since—for quite a time. They didn't concern you or Gracellen, believe me. I don't think that anything can happen that will ever make me leave off our friend-ship, Jett."

"Nor make me change my friendship for you, Task," Jett put in. "But this thing you hold against my uncle, can you tell me what it is? I don't mean to pry (*If you peek and pry*) but—well, I thought perhaps I might help clear up whatever's amiss."

Task shook his head grimly.

"I can't tell you what it is—or was," he said.

"Was? Why then, you mean the thing's over?"

"I've just given Squire Wills my word," Task said heavily, "to make my peace with Anthony Worth."

"For that I'm glad," Jett said warmly. "I know my uncle will be glad, too. You'll find him ready to meet you more than halfway, Task; I'll swear it!"

"We'll see," Task said briefly.

They went on toward the stable, Task Tillman and Jett Worth. Seldom had two such opposites in looks and manner ever been attracted to each other in friendship. Jett was quick, graceful, handsome, thoughtless, charming, laughing. Task, and especially since the discovery of his father's diary, was more sober, slower in speech and movement, given to little laughter.

Jett was dark, slim, small-boned. Task Tillman's hair was light, bleached almost white now by the hours spent in the fields. His frame was wide-shouldered and narrow-hipped; he had big hands, big feet. Stripped for a swim, his body would have made a sculptor's fingers itch for a chisel.

When he shaved, his glass showed Task Tillman a square, solid face, not as sharply etched as Jett's but never to be called heavy-featured. The sun-bleached brows over his amber eyes gave him a deceptively mild appearance. He could not be called handsome if Jett were used as a model, and certainly not if Charles Rawlent were; neither could he be said to be lacking in good looks. Many a girl in Talbot County had sighed over Task Tillman who had enjoyed Jett Worth's company, his manners, his wit, and never considered him more seriously for all his charm. As many caps had been set for Task as had been for Jett when the two were growing up, but there never had been any girl for Task but Gracellen Worth and this the fond mammas and young ladies of the county had finally been forced to accept.

They waited, these oddly-matched friends, while hostlers led out Lucifer and Worth's chestnut mare. The two men swung into the saddle, Jett with a lithe agility that made it seem he lived on horseback instead of on a ship's deck, Task easily enough but without Worth's flair. They headed out of Easton Town toward the road that led to the Miles River.

Leaving town, both men saluted and were saluted by other horsemen coming into Easton, the drivers of carts and wagons, the foot travellers, all bound for the street corner debates that would convene again as soon as the sun had eased a bit.

"The place is bustling, for certain," Jett remarked as they passed a group of five horsemen cantering toward Easton. "You'd think there was a muster by the way they're streamin' in."

"It's the war fever," Task said. "Everybody, even oldsters and brats, play at soldier these days."

"And you? Has Charley Rawlent enlisted you in that dandy troop of his I saw on my way to town?"

"Hah!" Task snorted. "By the way I last left Master Rawlent,

61

the only thing he'd enlist me for would be as a target at shooting practice. Did you hear what happened between us today?"

"Not a word," Jett said, "but then, that was my own fault. I took the speaker's stand at the taproom and blabbered so that nobody could get in a word. What happened?"

Briefly, Tillman told his friend of the scene on the street, of Rawlent's arrogance and of the snarled slur that had brought his fist cracking against Rawlent's jaw. Jett doubled in his saddle at the story of the gorgeously-clad fop sprawling in the street, squealing about the dueling law, and then sobered.

"I'd have given plenty to have seen it," he said, "but I wish it hadn't happened, Task."

"That pimple," Task grunted. "There never was a night I'd lose a wink of sleep over anything he might do."

"Do himself, no," Jett agreed, "but the man has a nasty tongue and from what I hear he's bound on making himself some sort of a hero nowadays. He bankrupted himself outfitting that militia company out of his own pocket, my uncle told me, and in some way he has the ear of Governor Bowie at Annapolis; this also from my uncle."

"You think Governor Bowie will sail over here to chastise me for making his young friend wet his pants?" Task asked, his mouth quirked. "Or will Rawlent's hand-dressed soldiers ambush me on some back lane?"

"No, Task, be serious. We know Charley Rawlent and what he's worth, so does the county, and ordinarily I'd cry hooray for you for what you did. But with this war fever, any man in a uniform can do no wrong. People who laughed at him today when he went arse-over-head will cry shame tomorrow because Charley wore a uniform and you wore none. They'll say you struck a gallant defender of his country and, by God, they'll be saying you love the British and hate the Americans before they're through twisting it around. You'll see."

Task scowled and hunched his shoulders.

"Well, let them, then," he grumbled. "If a man must swallow an insult from that nit to be a patriot, I'd rather be a renegade.

This whole place is turned upside-down, it seems, when a man who doesn't know one end of a gun from another can order other, better, men to drill under his command."

Jett laughed and leaned over to whack his friend on the shoulder.

"Cheer up," he said, "and drop that scowl. You've got company in your position. I'll bet the taproom back at the inn is buzzing with talk about how Jett Worth is a traitor because he thinks we'd be fools to declare war on the English right now."

The two men jogged along the road, their horses' hooves raising a dust cloud that wavered after them. Task was silent for the space of half a mile before he turned to the man beside him.

"You travel to all parts of the world, Jett," he said, "while I'm stuck fast at Larkspur Hill. D'you think there'll be a war?"

"I don't know," Jett said, slowly. "I know this: I know England's not hot for one. I heard talk in Liverpool—oh, it's no true secret I was in England on this last voyage—that most of the people in high places there don't like the high-handed way the British Navy deals with our vessels and so makes trouble. I tell you, Task, and you can win a wager on this, that if there is a war, we'll have to declare it."

"And win it!" Task Tillman said fervently.

Jett cast his friend a sidelong glance, then looked straight ahead, unsmiling.

"Oh, aye," he said, "we'll win it, doubtless. For isn't it true that one American is worth a dozen Englishmen when it comes to a fight?"

If there was irony in his voice, Task missed it as he nodded solemnly. He, like most of the men his age, too young to have tasted the bitter truth of war in the Revolution, sincerely believed that an American with a musket in his hand was the greatest soldier the world had ever known, that an American sloop was a match for England's most formidable ship of the line. Randolph Tillman had fought with Smallwood's Maryland Brigade under Washington and had survived the horrors of Valley Forge; he could have upset his son's staunch naivete had he chosen. Task's

63

father, though, had seen enough misery to clamp his lips closed when the war was mentioned. Task had grown up envisioning the Revolution as one sweeping American victory after another, with the Redcoats throwing down their arms and running or begging mercy on their knees at the first American volley.

The years did nothing to correct this fantasy. Such Revolutionary War history as he could get did not come from textbooks but from the flapping mouths of garrulous old soldiers whose merciful memories had blanked out all recollection of the reverses, the blunders, the ineptitude, the stark cowardice suffered by Washington's army. As Task grew up, these oldsters added splashes of gaudier, braver colors to his boyhood picture of his country's invincibility in arms.

Nor was Task unusual in holding to his trustful misconception; the confidence prevailed everywhere in the infant nation and those who counselled caution were denounced as cowards or traitors. In Congress, such a brilliant, learned man as Henry Clay thundered his prediction that America's tiny Navy could sweep England's fleets from all the seas, once given the signal to start fighting.

Madison hedged, balked, played for time while the War Hawks screamed for action. New England held to a peace at any price policy, not because New England understood the country's weakness but because a war would cripple her shipping, cut the flow of gold pouring into New England ports to a trickle or shut it off altogether. Just as Pennsylvania, Maryland, Virginia and the Carolinas had cursed Massachusetts for "starting the Revolution," so New England now cursed the rest of the nation for trying to start another war.

Meanwhile, in this year of 1810, companies of militia in bright uniforms marched and counter-marched, wheeled and marked time, while wives and sweethearts watched and fluttered their kerchiefs and tapped their toes to the thump of the drums. And Madison's Regular Army grew shabbier and shabbier, a discontented crowd officered by frustrated young men from tiny West

64

Point with its ten graduates a year, or by senile holdovers from the War of Independence; Madison's seven-frigate Navy stayed in port while its thoughtful officers prayed the day would never come when they would be sent out to meet England's might.

9

Tᴀꜱᴋ, bound up in his visions of American victories, was silent during the rest of the ride to the fork in the road where the way to Fairoverlea branched off from the highway that passed Larkspur Hill. Jett, busy with his own, more somber, thoughts, made no attempt to revive the talk until he reined in at the place where the two men's paths parted.

"We always were great ones to spend time together without saying a word to each other," Jett smiled, "but there are a thousand things we've got to talk over when we get a chance." He rose in his stirrups, easing the muscles that had been put to unaccustomed use.

"Let's make it soon," Task nodded. "We'll empty a jug together, arguing about whether little Rosie, the tavern keeper's daughter in Annapolis, liked you better, or me."

" 'Twas me, of course. But when can we get together? There's no telling when my uncle will have me sailing again and from what I hear you're busy in your fields from dawn till dark." He slapped a thigh. "Why not today, Task? Why not keep on with me to Fairoverlea right now?"

"Me go to Fairoverlea?" Task asked. "Oh, no!"

"And why not? Oh, I know you and my uncle are at odds but you said back in Easton that you were bound to settle this thing. What better chance than now to do it?"

"But—but I couldn't," Task protested. "You don't know the details, man! Your uncle—Gracellen—no, Jett, I couldn't."

"Again, why not?"

"The—the time's not right," Task said lamely.

"You numbskull," Jett grinned. "The time was never better if you really mean to end this senseless quarrel. I'll act as the go-between, you see. I'm just back from a long voyage and I can't do anything wrong in the eyes of my uncle and Gracellen—at least for the next few days. They know what friends we've been. What could be more natural than I ask you home with me to dine? I tell you, this occasion's made for it."

"There's too much to be done at Larkspur Hill," Task muttered.

"Rot! There's nothing to be done there that your men can't take care of and you know it!"

"I'm not dressed," Task offered, weakly.

"Good God, this is no state dinner, man! I'm not going to change and my uncle probably will come straight to the table from the warehouses. Aunt Vivian will be dressed to the nines, as usual, but if Gracellen hasn't been riding this afternoon she's been sailing and she'll have on whatever she's been wearing. Hell, Task, you'll probably outshine us all except Vivian, just as you are."

"I can't," Task said desperately. Jett's smile faded as he curbed his fretful chestnut.

"What kind of man are you, Task?" he asked quietly. "I know you've loved Gracellen ever since she was in pigtails and she loves you as much, I'll be bound. Yet you balk and shy like a nervy colt where I'd suppose you'd leap at the chance to see her again, straighten things out between the two of you."

"I do want to see her, Jett, but there's your uncle and—"

"And you said you wanted to bury this bad feeling between you," Jett cut in. "Did you mean it when you said that or have I been listening to a lot of talk that didn't mean a thing?"

Task's eyes met Jett's and the tow-headed man summoned a smile as he shrugged.

"Of course you're right," he said, "but it's an almighty hard thing for me to do. I'm as scared as a shot-at cat."

"Come on, then," Jett laughed. "It'll be like having a tooth yanked, soon over. With me there as master of ceremonies I promise you it'll be all but painless. Come on, I'll race you to the oak by the drive."

He put spurs to his mare and was off before Task could dredge up any more arguments, galloping down the road toward Fairoverlea. Task kept Lucifer in check for a moment, his brow wrinkled, and then he shook out the reins, sighing. He dreaded what lay ahead but he knew that Jett was right; with Anthony Worth's crown prince beside him the situation might be uncomfortable but it would not be intolerable, as it would be without Jett there. And there was Gracellen at Fairoverlea. He would be able to see her, be close to her, hear her voice, inhale her fragrance.

The thought coursed through him, sweeping away his last resistance. His spurs touched Lucifer's flanks and he bent over the black's neck.

"Make tracks, bag o' bones," he said. "The lady's waiting."

Jett's mare lost her long lead halfway to the big oak that marked the driveway to Fairoverlea and Task was waiting when Jett rode up, laughing.

"That's two drinks I owe you when we get to the house," he said. "That nag of yours is a thunderbolt. I'd hate to try to run from you in any chase that meant my neck. And oh, my poor behind! No matter how high I lifted it, this damned mare insisted on coming up to whack it. Another quarter of a mile and I'd have to eat standing up tonight."

The two men cantered up the drive shaded by towering pines. There was a sharp turn in the lane and there, beyond the aisle of trees, stood Fairoverlea, majestic in the afternoon sun.

Both men had known Fairoverlea all their lives, both had seen it countless times in all seasons and at all times of day. Yet neither Jett Worth, whose home it was, nor Task Tillman, who once had sworn he never would visit it again, could come out of the pines to see the Great House without being struck anew by its beauty.

Anthony Worth had built the first section of Fairoverlea in 1766, four years after he had appeared on the Eastern Shore as a boy of fifteen, indication of the fury with which the boy had attacked his future. The first building proved to be an odd-looking affair, a two-and-a-half storey structure, two rooms and a hallway wide. It was a long, plain, narrow house that resembled a luxurious warehouse with windows more than anything else.

"I have my plans," young Worth had told those who questioned him, chided him, laughed at him. "I know what I'm doing."

It required seven more years and his first daughter, Anne, was four years old before his plan for Fairoverlea began to take shape. At one end of the first building, Anthony put up a square structure, a full three storeys high, with slender columns reaching from the porch to the roof. Then it was seen that the first building had been built as a huge wing for a main building that had to be of tremendous proportions to suit the original structure. Most men would have built the main building first, adding wings as the money became available. Not Anthony Worth; he put up the great wing first, to stand as an inescapable challenge to him, a demand that he provide the body of the house. As the wing was a challenge, so was the one-winged structure; in 1775 the second wing completed the picture.

Now that he had his Great House, Anthony Worth set about making it the finest on the Eastern Shore. His country was at war and the furnishings he must have from England were unavailable; it was impossible that fine furniture and silver, china and glassware, draperies, linens, carpets, even wallpaper, could be brought from England to the colonies England was trying to throttle, but, magically, such pieces began to appear in Fairoverlea. At war's end and while most Americans were celebrating their new Constitution, Worth was quietly celebrating the arrival of the last item needed to complete Fairoverlea's interior.

How was this done? There were a score of versions, all different, but Anthony never offered an explanation. He needed these things; he got these things; by what means, to Anthony, was of no concern to anyone but Anthony Worth.

Fairoverlea stood on a rise facing the Miles River over a broad sweep of lawn dotted here and there by weeping willows and maples. At the shore in front of the house was a narrow dock, used as a mooring place for the shallops and skiffs Anthony and his family sailed for pleasure and travel, up and down the river.

The main dock, the place where the *Heron* had come in that morning, was in Peartree Creek, nearly a mile behind the Great House, and, as the saying went in Talbot County, Peartree Creek had no sand or mud bottom but one of pure gold for Anthony Worth. It was a twisting inlet, its entrance from the Miles hardly discernible, its banks a tangle of honeysuckle and briars, pines and alders. A clever man who knew its channel could sail a schooner or buckeye up its length; a skipper strange to the creek's vagaries would be aground before he had proceeded the length of his own vessel.

Inland from the tortuous riverward narrows, Peartree Creek widened into a basin, broad and deep, that served as The King's harbor and this was territory forbidden to anyone without Anthony's bidding. There were no signs marking this as posted land; there was no need of signs. Everyone in those parts knew that to enter on Fairoverlea land by the pine-shaded drive was to receive a warm welcome at any hour; to intrude on Anthony Worth's domain by any other route was to court unpleasantness, if not disaster.

Few had tried to satisfy their curiosity about what went on around Peartree Creek. Worth's brief word that he would not take kindly to prowlers in that section of Fairoverlea sufficed to warn off most snoopers. The reckless adventurers who had tried to creep through the woods to peep at what they might see discovered that they had barely left the road before they were met by the dour Marsden, the hulking Roan or Tom Womble, whose chortle somehow did not seem to go with his eyes. On each of these rare occasions, the trespasser had been given a curt order to get out.

One young Easton buck, emboldened by whiskey, had refused point-blank, telling Will Roan that he'd go where he pleased and be damned to him. Later, in court, Roan had sworn that the young man's two broken arms had been suffered in a fall as he was trying to lead the youth—"far gone in his cups, Y'r Honor" —up to the Great House and safety.

"There's swamp holes that got no bottom where this gentleman was, Y'r Honor," Roan had explained, "and if he'd made a mis-step I doubt he'd ever be seen again. There's cases of people strayin' in there and never comin' out, y'know. I but tried to help the young gentleman, sir, and he grew violent, flung himself about and finally fell, heavy as a sack o' meal, against this big rock, injurin' himself terrible. I then carried him to Mister Worth and a doctor was called."

It was a regrettable accident and Anthony Worth was grieved, both by the young man's injuries and by the wild story, product of whiskey, no doubt, that the man told the court. All in all, it was a sad thing to have happened but it served to discourage trespassing on Fairoverlea.

As Jett and he neared the Great House on the drive that swept up to an oval in front of the porch, Task saw a tall, straight figure rise from a chair, shade her eyes for a moment and then turn abruptly and enter the house. Even at that distance there was no mistaking Gracellen and Task's heart leaped before it thudded back to its rocky resting place. He had expected no more, but the sight of Gracellen sweeping into the house, chin up and nose held high, made him wish he had not listened to Jett's arguments.

"The fair Gracellen-aleen," commented Jett, wryly, "has fled to her dressing table to primp."

"Look, Jett," Task said, huskily, "maybe another day would be better for this visit. I mean—"

"Ah, my God!" Jett cried. "We'll not go through all that again! Courage, man! What kind of soldier are you going to make in this war that's coming if you get weak in the knees at a long distance sight of a seventeen-year-old girl?"

71

"Well, but—"

"Whenever you need a best man at your wedding, don't call on me. The one who takes the duty will have to hold you up 'cause you'll be fainted dead away, I swear."

He swung his chestnut around to the side drive that led to the stables and Task followed on Lucifer. The sound of the horses' hooves brought an identical pair of young Negroes running, their white teeth shining, their bare feet spurning the crushed oyster shell of the roadway.

"Ha, the Heavenly Twins!" Jett shouted. "Avon and Devon. Ever see such worthless rascals put up in pairs before, Task? If one can't find a way to trouble, the other can, and my uncle can't give the wrong 'un over to Titus for a tanning 'cause he's never sure which one's to blame."

The boys, barely more than pickaninnies, sounded their clattering laugh as they nimbly caught the reins tossed to them by the two riders. This talk of Titus, they both knew as well as Task, was joking; they were house hands and Titus with his whip could never touch a house servant. Of course, they realized, that if they ever did anything *real* bad, they could be banished by a nod of The King's head to the barracks where lived the field, dock and warehouse hands and then Titus would be more than a joking threat; Titus would be a nightmare come true.

Dismounted, the two men crossed the rear courtyard and went up a short flight of steps to a door set in the west wing of Fairoverlea. They entered a hall that was pleasantly cool and dusky after the glare of the July sun outside.

"First to the gun room and we'll have those drinks I owe you," Jett said easily. "And from your backing and filling I'd say you need a whole flock of them, Task. Let's fill you with Dutchman's courage before you brave the terrors ahead of you."

"A drink," said Task fervently, "would go very well right now."

The slighter man's boots echoed in the hallway as he paced the short distance to a doorway opening onto the gun room. It was a panelled den, lined with racks that held shotguns of all types, sizes and gauges, from scarred and work-worn veterans with enormous barrels, used in raking flocks of geese and swan, to women's dainty fowling pieces with stocks inlaid with ivory. On a table in one corner of the gun room sat an array of decanters and glasses and it was toward this that Jett Worth made his unerring way.

"Whiskey or brandy, Task?" he asked over his shoulder. " 'Twill be whiskey, to jolt you out of your numb fright."

The amber liquor gurgled into tumblers and Jett turned, handing a glass to his friend.

"Get this inside you," he ordered, "and when that's down you'll have another. Before we leave here we'll have you swaggering like a bully and ready to give Gracellen back as good as she sends. Ye'll broadside her, man, and make her strike her colors without a struggle, with enough of these to sail on."

The whiskey was good, smooth but potent. Task felt the liquor's warmth course through him and, imagined or not, there was a surge of much-needed confidence. He did not protest as Jett took his glass and refilled it; he tossed off the second potion as quickly as the first.

"Water? But no, ye'll not want to spoil the drink. Besides, if my uncle ever found out you'd watered his whiskey it would make it that much harder for me to bring the two of you together. Another?"

Task shook his head, inhaling deeply. That second drink had gone down a little too hard on the heels of the first. Jett toyed with his glass, sipping, and then looked up at his friend.

"Tell me to mind my own business if you want to, Task," he said, grinning, "but what happened when Gracellen came at you with her riding whip? I haven't heard the details."

"Oh, Lord," Task groaned. "You would remind me of that, just when I'd braced myself with whiskey to meet her. I—I guess I lost my head, Jett. She was furious, of course, over—over something I'd said to your uncle and she came at me without warning. I barely had time to catch her whiphand wrist as she swung and —well, I truly didn't mean to pull her toward me, but I did. And—and—"

73

"And there she was, right in your arms," Jett finished, "and you did the only possible thing a man could do." Task nodded wordlessly. Jett sent his laughter whooping through the room. "By God, I wish I could have seen that!" he gasped. "My fire-eating cousin goes out to whip a man and winds up being kissed! No wonder she lights up like a beacon at the thought of it! What a wonderful thing to happen to her!"

"And what was that, Jett?" asked an amused voice from the doorway. "I'm in a mood to hear about wonderful things."

Both men turned and both men bowed, deeply and instinctively. Framed by the doorway stood Vivian, fourth wife of Anthony Worth.

10

IT WAS said by the greybeards of Talbot County who had known him since he had first appeared upon the Eastern Shore scene that each of Anthony Worth's wives was younger and more beautiful than her predecessor.

Mary, the first wife of Anthony, had by all accounts been a plain woman who was considerably older than nineteen-year-old Anthony, a widow whose dead husband had left her slaves, a tidy amount of gold, and property that was now part of Fairoverlea. Three years after Mary died in 1778, Anthony had married Honoria, who had been his own age and, by the same accounts that had described Mary, a comely woman. Johanna, first nurse to Honoria, then mistress to Anthony and finally his wife, had been at least ten years his junior when he had married her the day after that fateful vestry meeting. And after Johanna's death in 1795, Anthony Worth had waited twelve years before he had sailed to England in one of his own ships and had met and married Vivian Dangerfield in London.

Even those who had known and loved Johanna could not help but admit that Vivian, Englishwoman though she might be, was the most beautiful of all the women Anthony Worth had married.

"And as strange," they were likely to add, "as she is beautiful."

Strange or not, Task told himself as he straightened from his bow, for sheer unalloyed beauty there was not a woman he had ever seen who could come close to Vivian, not even Gracellen. He gazed at her in frank admiration as she came into the gun room.

She wore a shade of deep green which fully complemented her olive complexion and which had been cunningly cut to draw men's eyes to the form it enveloped. It was no blatant dress but on the other hand it certainly was no burdensome cloak. Task's breath, so recently engaged in a struggle with the second whiskey, caught in his throat again as he fought to keep from staring at the low-cut neckline that seemed only idly concerned with its duty of covering Vivian's splendid breasts. He dropped his eyes, but the rippling swing of the woman's hips beneath the green silk proved no less disturbing than the expanse of powder-dusted flesh above the bodice. His eyes sought some part of Vivian Worth that could be viewed impassively. He found none.

She wore her raven's wing hair coiled low on the nape of her neck in a style that contradicted and bettered by comparison the fashion of the day. Her dark eyes were fringed by almost artificially long lashes, her nose was high-bridged and thin-nostrilled, her mouth was full-lipped and carmine.

They called her strange, these Eastern Shore people, because they could not decipher her. Her beauty, her bearing, her casual acceptance of their admiring glances, gave every man she met one idea of Vivian. Yet later, when this impression did not prove true, when these men grew to know Vivian and found her chaste, loyal to her husband, first amused and then quietly angered by their importuning, they sometimes laved their injured ego by deciding she was a frigid hussy who enjoyed leading men on and making fools of them. Because she came from London where a dissolute court was supposed to prize wantonness in women, many men named Vivian Worth a slut made cautious by her husband's jealousy. It irked them that she could be true to a husband nearly forty years her senior and some of them took their revenge for her disinterest by hinting at a vague ugliness that lay within that matchless beauty.

"Aunt Vivian," Jett was saying, "I think you know our neighbor, my friend, Task Tillman."

"Of course," Vivian said. Her smile was warming and her hand was cool in Task's. "We see too little of you here at Fairoverlea, Mister Tillman, for one who lives as close as you do."

"Task is bound so tight to Larkspur Hill," Jett explained, "that I had to argue like a lawyer to get him to come and dine with us."

"Why then I'm glad you're such a good convincer, Jett," Vivian smiled. She looked at Task again and he saw the luminous depths of her eyes. "And are you recovering," she asked, "from that fire that burnt your barns? It was a terrible night. Anthony and I watched the glare from our windows and I tell you truly we were both struck dumb by the horror of it. Fire is a dreadful, savage thing."

Task nodded grimly without speaking. Her eyes held his for a moment and then Vivian turned toward the table where the decanters were grouped.

"Do you suppose it would be most improper if I had a glass of brandy at this time of day?" she asked. "I've been gulping lemon shrub till my throat's demanding something honest. You'll join me?"

"We've both been waiting for a beautiful lady to join us and flavor our drinks with her presence," Jett said. "We thought you'd never come, we were that parched."

"Liar," Vivian said lightly. "You dare say that with two tumblers sitting there right before my eyes, just used? That laughing I heard in the hall came from no glass of water." She accepted the brandy from Jett and went on as her nephew splashed more whiskey into his tumbler and Task's. "What was that 'such a wonderful thing' and whom did it happen to?"

"That, dear Aunt Vivian," Jett said, "is a story that will have to wait for a day when you'll need a laugh to make you sparkle. You surely don't need it now."

The olive-skinned woman sipped at her brandy, her eyes moving from Jett to Task over the rim of her glass. She was smiling faintly as she lowered her drink.

"Then let me guess," she offered. "Had it something to do with a riding whip?"

"You listened!" Jett cried indignantly.

"Of course I listened. So would you if, say, you heard two women talking and laughing and you were as lonely for some company as I've been. But I knew that story, anyway; Anthony told me. And you mustn't tease your cousin with it, Jett, on your life."

She looked at Task, her eyes laughing at his discomfort.

"But why do we stand here in this stuffy place?" she asked. "Why not take advantage of the breeze on the porch? I'll have the things brought out there."

"We've got to see Uncle," Jett explained. "We—Task and I—have something to take up with him."

"Oh, Anthony's still down at the warehouses," Vivian returned. "There'll be time enough to talk to him when he comes back. Please spare a few minutes for a lonely lady, gentlemen."

"Lonely!" Jett scoffed. "Lonely, with what my uncle calls a troop of cavalry pounding up the drive all day?"

"Young men to see Gracellen," Vivian countered. "Who'd drop me a word or a glance while she's about? Oh, they pay their proper respects to that old nuisance, the chaperon, fairly pawing the ground to be gone, and then they desert me and leave me to my sewing or knitting or other granny pastimes."

It could very well be that way, Task told himself, and not because the young men wouldn't have liked to tarry close to Vivian longer than they did. Vivian's beauty, the way she dressed, the way her slender body moved, her low, intimate voice, could spell danger to many of the youngsters who came calling on Gracellen. And above all, Vivian was the wife of Anthony Worth; the young men feared The King as much as their fathers did.

"I think all the men in Talbot County have let their brains go to rot, then," Jett was saying. "Now, if I spent more time ashore you'd have me hanging around you so much you'd sicken at the sight of me."

Vivian's laugh came lightly as she swung her eyes toward Task. "You know Jett, Mister Tillman," she smiled, "so you know that any woman, even his aunt, sets his charmer's tongue to wagging at both ends. Let's to the porch and Jett can tell us of what's going on in my homeland, England."

"Hispaniola, Aunt Vivian. You mustn't forget that I've been nowhere near England on this voyage."

"Of course," the woman said and laughed again, softly. "Well, you can tell us then what's new in Hispaniola, especially on the Strand and Rotten Row."

The three moved to the porch and took chairs about a small table. A servant brought a tray burdened with decanters and glasses, together with a collation of biscuits and slivers of cold meats, fowl and cheese. To the west, puffy white clouds began climbing into the sky and the breeze freshened steadily.

"We're due a thunderstorm," Jett observed. "Perhaps it'll ease this heat. I hope so; I've been gasping like a stranded fish all day."

"You've been too long at sea to remember," Task said, "but it's usually hotter than this on the Eastern Shore in July."

"Too long at sea is it, exactly," Vivian said. "We see too little of him, Mister Tillman. He's hardly landed before we begin to bore him and then he's off again for months and months. I barely recognized him when I saw him this morning. He's more a stranger to his people here at home than he is to his lights o' love on the other side of the world."

"Blame your husband for that, Madam," Jett protested. "If I didn't know him better I'd think he was jealous of me by the way he sends me packing again before I've got my land legs back."

"Anthony, jealous?" the woman asked, her fine brows rising. "Good heavens, Jett, you know your uncle would laugh at a petty thing like jealousy." She turned to Task. "Are you one of the Dragon Footguards, Mister Tillman? Do you have one of the splendid uniforms Mister Rawlent wears when he comes calling?"

"No ma'am," Task said as Jett chuckled. "I don't find myself much time for such things."

"Task and Charley Rawlent don't see eye to eye about the

matter," Jett put in. "Charley's quite put out that Task won't drop everything and go marching up and down again while Charley bawls the orders."

"You mustn't laugh at them, Jett," Vivian smiled. "They all take it very seriously from what I've overheard them telling Gracellen and they do make a brave show when they parade. Anthony took me into Easton Town last week to watch them drill. It was all very exciting even if the young men did look a bit bloodthirsty."

"Children at play," Jett grunted. "Those drills give them a great excuse to strut around in fancy clothes and then guzzle at the tavern later till they all drop over." He looked about him as though realizing his cousin's absence for the first time. "Where's Gracellen?" he asked. "Out riding with one of her downy-cheeked swains?"

"She's somewhere around the house," Vivian said. "Leastwise, she went dashing upstairs and into her room a minute before you two rode up. She's resting, probably, or dressing."

"She's hiding," Jett said.

"Hiding? Whatever from?"

"Who knows?" Jett shrugged. "Perhaps she remembers a certain riding whip and a meeting along the road. Perhaps she—"

"Nay, Jett!" Task broke in sharply. "Gracellen's probably resting or—"

"She needs no rest, that girl," Jett said. "She can ride all day and dance all night and still have more spirit left than half a dozen men. Tough as alligator hide, is Gracellen-aleen. I'll just run up and drag her down here. We can't have her sulking in her room like a spoilt child."

"No need to fetch her, Jett," Vivian said. "Your boredom's about to be dismissed. I hear her coming now."

"Aye," Jett chuckled. "I thought she'd be pointing a big ear at what we're saying down here and come galloping as soon as I mentioned her name."

"And that's not so!" Gracellen flared from the hallway before she came into view. "I was coming down here anyway and your blatting wasn't needed."

80

She stepped through the doorway. Task's adoring eyes met her stormy glare for an instant before she abruptly switched her gaze to her cousin, grinning at her.

"And for your information," she said, "my ears are not half so big as your mouth and as for being tough as alligator hide—that's a pretty way to speak of a lady, I must say! What foreign doxy taught you that and was she black or white?"

"Gracellen," Vivian protested. "Really, child!"

"And I'm no child," Gracellen went on, "so please stop calling me one!"

"Your manners," Jett put in, "are hardly worthy of a child, at that. We have a guest, dear cousin."

Task was on his feet, shifting from one to the other, trying to find some place to put his hands. As Gracellen turned toward him, he assayed a bow and, for some reason, nearly lost his balance and lurched. It was not the whiskey, he swore silently; it could not have been the whiskey.

When he looked up, Gracellen's eyes were cold as they moved from him to the decanter-laden table. Her mouth was drawn down at the corners, her tall body was taut with disdain.

"Gracellen," Task attempted, "I swear I didn't mean to—"

"Pish-tush," Jett broke in. "Don't start out making excuses, man! Gracellen's the one to excuse herself for not giving proper greeting to a friend who's come to call."

"Not at my invitation, I'm sure," Gracellen said, icily.

"No, at mine," Jett said, equably. "I happened to meet Task at the inn at Easton Town and seeing with half an eye that the poor fellow was pining away for sight of you, Gracellen-aleen, I took pity on him and—"

"For the love of God, Jett!" Task burst out. "You said you'd smooth the way!"

He knew it was the wrong thing to say as soon as the words were out. Gracellen's chin came up a notch higher and her eyes burned with resentment, her mouth tightened to a thin line.

"So!" she snapped. "You two have spent the afternoon talking about me, eh? After you were thrown out of the inn taproom, no

81

doubt, you decided to come back here, if you could still stay on your horses, and you, my dear cousin, would plead your crony's case."

"Not at all, dear Gracellen," Jett murmured. "But go on, go on. I'm anxious to see just how completely wrong you can be this time—perhaps you'll set a new mark, even for you."

Vivian Worth spoke from her chair. Her deep, full voice cut off whatever hot words Gracellen was ready to throw back at her cousin.

"And I," Vivian said, "am anxious to have you two stop acting like a pair of ill-mannered children. Your father, Gracellen, would be very much displeased to have a guest at Fairoverlea subjected to such a disgraceful scene. Jett, remember you're a gentleman."

"But he—"

"But she—"

"I must insist," Vivian said, "that you two sit down and behave. Gracellen, will you have a glass of wine? Some brandy?"

Gracellen subsided slowly, her eyes still raging, her long-fingered hands clenched upon her anger. Across the porch from her, Jett Worth grinned openly at his cousin's wrath; he mentally chalked up another victory in the internecine warfare that had been going on between the two since Gracellen had been old enough to strike back at her teasing, bedeviling relative.

"Whiskey," Gracellen said, finally. "I know it's no lady's drink but then, I doubt that one, at least, of this fine pair is a gentleman. And I might as well get in their state as fast as possible if I'm going to stay here."

Vivian imperturbably poured out a generous splash of whiskey, added water and handed it to her step-daughter. Gracellen gulped recklessly, and coughed. Jett laughed at her behind his hand and wiped his face of the smile at Vivian's frown. Gracellen, with tremendous effort, smothered her choking and sipped again, as though the whiskey were the most familiar drink to her liking. There was a silence as the four sat in a rough circle, a silence that Jett, through deviltry, and Vivian through motives of her own allowed to persist.

82

Task Tillman sat on the edge of his chair wishing with all his heart that he was back at Larkspur Hill, even though the woman he loved sat not six feet away from him. He felt perspiration bedewing his forehead and he let it trickle, afraid to wipe it away lest the kerchief he used might have suffered too much from its day's usage. From time to time he stole a glance at Gracellen but her eyes did not stir from a fixed glare at some invisible object in the channel of the Miles River.

"Heat bugs" kept up their tireless whirring in the trees on the lawn. Inside the house there was the clink of china, the muted clash of silverware, signs that the long table was being set for dinner. The faint sound of a horse's whinny came from the stables; a dog barked down by the slave quarters. Jett began whistling a tuneless air under his breath.

What seemed an hour to Task, crawled by as his perspiration became sweat, despite the rising wind, and his tongue grew to immense proportions in his mouth. He knew he was acting like a bumpkin, a fright-frozen oaf, sitting there without a word to offer; he knew, too, that Jett, damn him, was not going to ease the situation nor was Vivian Worth, though why she would not was beyond him. As for Gracellen speaking first, better expect the skiff at the end of the dock to suddenly take off in flight like a brent-goose. He inhaled deeply and made the plunge.

"Gracellen," he said, and his words sounded thunderous in his ears, "I hope you've been well since I saw you last."

Damnation! "Since I saw you last" meant "since the day you tried to whip me and got kissed for your pains."

"I mean—that is," he blundered on, "I hope—no ill effects— I meant to say—oh, *God damn it!*"

The last explosive statement was wrenched from him by his inner torment. The curse hung there in the center of the circle. Then, crashingly, there was a peal of laughter from Jett, from Vivian—and good heavens, was it the drinks?—Gracellen.

The girl doubled over in her chair, her shoulders shaking, the whiskey slopping over the rim of the glass as her hand jiggled with her laughter. Before his astounded eyes, the girl he loved straightened, threw back her head and whooped with pure glee.

Jett was red-faced and gasping for breath. Vivian's eyes were moist with laugh-tears. As Task stared from one to the other, he felt anger rise on the heels of his consternation. True, he had been a fool, first stricken dumb and then shouting a curse like a drunken idiot, but these people—no, not even Gracellen—could sit there and laugh at him like this! He got out of his chair and made a rigid bow.

"Your pardon," he intoned sepulchrally. "I've just remembered something I have to do at Larkspur Hill. If you'll excuse me, I'll—"

"Oh, Task, Task," Gracellen gurgled. "Do sit down and stop acting like an outraged owl!"

"H-h-have another drink," Jett echoed. "Have two or three. Oh, Lord—the way you exploded! 'Twas worth a fortune to see your face!"

"I didn't mean—" Task began and then, suddenly, his anger fled. He saw himself as he had been, stuttering and stammering, swelling at the neck in his confusion, and then yelling the startled oath in a howl that must have carried to Kent Island. His laughter broke in a roar and he sat back in his chair, letting himself go as he had in the old days, the good days.

"I hoped the ice would break," Jett said when he regained control of himself, "but I had no idea 'twould be shivered so completely." He looked at Vivian. "And now, dear Aunt, you may show me those beagle puppies you spoke about at noon."

"Yes, take him somewhere, Vivian," Gracellen said, "or we'll be at each other's throats again. Dear Cousin Jett is a master at bringing out the worst in me."

Vivian arose, smoothing the green silk about her hips, touching her sleek hair, a faint smile on her crimson mouth. She took Jett's arm, looking back at Gracellen.

"Please call me, dear," she said, "if your father comes up from the warehouses before we get back."

Gracellen nodded without replying. Her eyes followed Vivian and Jett through the doorway into the main hall of Fairoverlea

84

before the red-haired daughter of Anthony Worth turned back to Task.

"She's lovely, isn't she?" she asked suddenly. "She's sweet and gentle and kind and I've been a perfect bitch to her ever since she came here. You know something, Task? She's never said one word to Father about the way I've treated her. If she had, I'd know."

Task groped unsuccessfully for words.

"And she's a wonderful wife to Father," Gracellen went on. "Oh, I know children are supposed to hate stepmothers but nobody could hate Vivian, though I've tried hard enough. When she first came to Fairoverlea I was so jealous of her that I used to sneak into her room and hide things; I tried to make her complain about me—and me a great big overgrown cow of a girl."

"Never that, Gracellen," Task said.

"No," Gracellen agreed. "Cows are gentle, aren't they, and I go about hitting people with my riding crop."

"Not hitting them—hitting at them."

She wrinkled her nose at him before she dropped back to her mood of self-reproach. Task waited; he knew this Gracellen as well as he could know any Gracellen. This was the remorseful Gracellen; a man had only to wait until the impulsive girl, or the rebellious, or the imperious, or the mischievous, or one of the other Gracellens would emerge.

"I don't know," she said, dolefully, after a long pause, "why anybody puts up with me. I don't know why you do, Task."

"Just say that I do and always will," Task Tillman said quietly, "and you have your answer."

She started to sip the glass of whiskey and water and drew back her head as its fumes came to her nostrils. She replaced the glass hurriedly on the table that sat between them.

"For heaven's sake," she said, "pour me some sherry. How you men can drink this is beyond me. Another sip and I'd be staggering around as you were when I first came out onto the porch."

"I wasn't—" Task began, and answered Gracellen's grin. "No, my girl," he said as he got up to unstopper the wine decanter,

85

"you're not going to bait me today. I'm feeling too good to wrangle with you this fine afternoon."

"Feeling too good on father's whiskey," she taunted, and then, as she saw his face stiffen, she stretched out a hand to touch his.

"That was the wrong thing to say, wasn't it, Task?" she asked, her voice rapid. "I shouldn't have reminded you that you were drinking Anthony Worth's liquor, should I?" Her hand knuckled her mouth. "Task, Task," she said brokenly, "why do you hate my father so?"

He dropped his eyes to the faceted ball of glass in his big, work-roughened hand.

"Why?" she cried. *"Tell me!"*

"Gracellen," he said, slowly, heavily, "I have not told you I hated your father."

She left her chair with the rustle of her skirts and her heels tapped across the porch to the top of the steps that led down to the drive and the sweep of lawn beyond it. She stood there, her hands clenched at her sides, her shoulders rigid, the setting sun painting a fiery halo about her head.

He carefully replaced the stopper in the decanter and took the three paces that brought him behind her. He put his hands on her shoulders and lowered his cheek against the soft and shining hair.

"Gracellen," he murmured, "nothing concerns us except that I love you and you love me. This—these other things needn't touch us; they're outside our love, Gracellen."

She twisted out from under his hands and turned to face him, her eyes bright with the tears that trembled on her lids, her red mouth uncertain.

"So you ask me to ignore them?" she said. "How can you think that I could ever turn my back on this—this evil thing that's betwixt you and my father? You say you love me yet you'd call my father—*my father*—a blackguard who would burn your tobacco barns! My God, Task, you ask a lot of a woman who'd love you, to think she must flirt her hand at a thing like this!"

She shook her head so sharply that a tendril escaped its pin and danced against her white cheek.

86

"I can't!" she said. "I won't! I love you, Task, but no woman could love a man that blindly! I know my father for a good man! Before I'd say different, even by keeping silent, I'd tear my heart out—as you will, Task, if you don't tell me you were drunk or mad when you accused my father!"

He stared down at her and her desirability swam up to him. She was there, close to him, where he had dreamed of her being for all these weeks and months. She would be gone forever if he did not hold her now by saying what she asked. He struggled with an old hate, with an old duty. Squire Wills' quiet words came to him clearly: *Cast out your devils, Task!* Where was the shame of an unfulfilled trust when the trust itself was imagined, as Squire Wills had proved? To serve a nightmare cause and lose Gracellen would be a sinful thing. The clamoring within him to hold true, *hold true,* was the voice of the devils he must cast out to win her to his arms for all time.

"I was not drunk," he said huskily, "but I must have been mad. I'll tell your father so when I see him. I'll ask his pardon for the wicked things I said."

She gave a low cry as she came to him. Her arms were about his neck, her cheek, wet with the tears that flowed at last, was pressed against his before she fumbled for his mouth with her lips. Her body moulded itself to his with an abandon he had never known in her before, with a straining urgency that mounted to the fringes of wildness.

"Task—Task," she mumbled. "If this seems a sacrifice to you, I'll make it up to you a thousand-fold. You speak of love—you'll never know what love is like till we're together. And soon, soon! Make me your wife, Task, as soon as you can!"

She wrenched herself free from his arms and half ran back to the chair she had left, crouched there trembling, with her hands to her temples. Task stayed where he was until the hammering of his blood subsided, the crimson haze of passion had faded.

The smile she greeted him with as he went back to the table was tremulous, her eyes starry.

"And so, Task Tillman," she said shakily, "you know what a

shameless wench you'll be marrying." Her voice firmed. "And lest some other damned barrier heaves itself up and separates us again, we'll ask my father—we'll *tell* my father this very night."

"When I ask his pardon—" Task began.

"No, Task," she cut in, shaking her head. "That'll be between you two men. This other affair I'll have to manage because he never yet has frowned for long on anything I asked him."

11

THE ROOM was low, smoky, stifling hot although outside drummed the rain that had brought relief from the day's heat and there was the muted sound of leaves thrashing about in the wind that had brought the storm.

The three men sat about the rough table, the lantern in its center painting grotesque shadows of the trio on the walls. Scraps of the evening meal lay on the plates that had been pushed aside; a demijohn squatted by the lantern and a pewter mug was in each man's hand, adding the redolent fumes of rum to the overlay of smells.

Tom Womble hunched closer over the drawings he was devouring and sniggered with a burble.

"Now here's one," he gloated, "I'd like t'try sometime. But where I'd find a wench who'd stand for it, even a black one, I don't know. Y'see, the man—"

"Oh, belay those damned prints!" Will Roan grunted. "Ever since you got 'em this mornin' you've been good fer nothin', shirkin' your work to have another peep at 'em."

"Lookin' at pitchers," Marsden sneered, "is all Fat-Belly has left to do."

"And you, I s'pose, are a ruttin' ram with the gals, eh?" Womble jeered. "Tell me, d'you take off that greatcoat when you have y'r yearly toss or do ye wrap another muffler 'round y'r neck for fear y'r strainin' will set up a draught?"

He drew a forearm across his glistening face.

"Fit t'bake a loaf of bread in here," he complained, "and Rattle-bones must have the doors and windows shut tight lest he ketch a chill."

"An you don't like it," Marsden growled, "go find y'rself another place to paw y'r pitchers. Go set with y'r nigger wenches—ye sleep with 'em so often y'r turnin' black in places y'rself."

Roan set down his mug with a bang.

"Will you two shut y'r clappers?" he roared. "Every night the same earachin' bickerin' betwixt the two of ye. How can a man think with you two clackin' at each other like a couple of hens?"

"Think, Will?" Womble asked, grinning. "Why spend time tryin' t'do somethin' ye never were intended to?"

Roan's little eyes, reddened now by rum, darted across the table, tapped Womble malevolently and swung back to the demijohn.

"Some day I'll end y'r clever talk for good," he said as he reached for the rum. "Some day I'll feed y'r carcass to the pigs, if they'll have it."

"Nay, Will," Womble chuckled. "Ye'd no more do that than I'd try to freshen my memory as to just what did happen in New Orleans."

"Nothing happened in New Orleans," Roan said and tilted his head back to gulp down the rum.

"Of course not," Womble nodded, and returned to his prints.

"But what I can't figger," Roan said as he put down his cup, "is what young Tillman is doin' here. You s'pose *The King* expected him and told me nothin' about it? And if he kept it to himself, why did he? I don't like it."

A moth flung itself against the lantern, dropped, rested until its strength returned and dashed itself at the light again.

"Has *The King*," Roan went on, "made his peace with Tillman, and why? And if he has, where does that put us? Has

Tillman happened across somethin' that brings him here to beard *The King?* And what c'ld that be?"

"He's found out nothin'," Marsden croaked. "Ye may lay to that, Will Roan. If Fat-Belly here had blundered somehow, as he always does, 'twould have been found out afore this."

Womble turned one of the pile of prints in front of him and squinted at the picture that was uncovered.

"Your Fat-Belly," he said, cheerfully, "never makes mistakes in that kind of a job. Else why was I picked to do both of 'em whilst you two sat at home with y'r fingers up y'r noses? Nay, I might not like heat like you, Rattlebones, but I can light me a pretty fire and be snug in my bunk by the time the first alarm cry is given. A genius, if I say so."

He guffawed, pointing a stubby forefinger at the picture.

"Now here's one for you, Marsden," he said. "Leastwise the man's a bundle of bones like you. 'Twouldn't work for a fleshy—"

Roan slammed his hamlike fist down on the table and the lantern guttered, then steadied again.

"Will ye listen to me?" he boomed. "This might be serious, you two! There's a reason for young Tillman's bein' at Fair-overlea tonight. Either *The King's* made his peace with him or Tillman's been made brave by some discovery. Either way, we've got to know what's goin' on at Great House."

"Why then," Womble said placidly, "ask Titus. He knows everything that goes on at Fairoverlea."

Roan's clouded face cleared and he looked approvingly at the fat man across from him.

"Sometimes ye show signs o' sense," he said grudgingly. "Go fetch him here."

Womble started an objection, saw Roan's eyes harden, and sighed. Carefully, he closed the folio of prints and, as carefully, knotted the tape that tied the two covers. He tucked his treasure under one arm, shoved back his stool and waddled to the door. The teeming downpour outside brought him up short at the threshold and he turned.

"Now I can't take my beauties out in that wet," he said

plaintively, "or they'll be ruint. And if I leave 'em here, Marsden will steal 'em and hide 'em from me. So—"

"Give the damned things here," Roan stormed. "Get goin'!"

Womble gave his prints over to Roan's keeping with a smirk at the sneering Marsden, then walked out, ducking his head against the wind-driven rain. Marsden, with a curse, got up to shut the door the fat man had left flapping behind him, shivering as a blast of cool, sweet air struck him at the opening.

"I hope he soaks himself into a fever," he said viciously, "though the chill can't reach him through that blubber."

Roan, busy at the demijohn again, did not answer. For years, ever since this trio had found refuge in Anthony Worth's kingdom, Marsden and Womble had wished each other an early end and Roan, their leader, had wished them both in hell. And still the three lived together and worked together, bound one to the other by the grim knowledge of what happened when thieves —and worse—fell out.

The fat man was not long in returning and behind him came Titus, the massive Negro who never was without his fearsome whip. The big black's position at Fairoverlea was an anomaly. He was a slave, yet his main duty was to lash other slaves. He lived apart from the other Negroes. He had no woman and had no need for one; a knife had freed him from all need for one. Titus seemed to find impassive joy in striping the backs of his brother slaves; he had to be watched lest he indulge in a lashing for the simple pleasure in it, and Anthony Worth must be given a good reason for every whipping.

Titus was feared as much as he was hated and this satisfaction seemed to make up for all the other things in life he had been robbed of. It was hard to tell definitely; the huge black's face was the mask of an obsidian image and he spoke only in answer to his white masters' questions.

As the Negro entered, Marsden left the table and went to a cabinet at the far end of the low-ceilinged room. The thin man rummaged in a coat hanging there and returned to his stool, carrying a long-barrelled pistol that he laid on the table in front of him. Marsden never allowed himself to be within reach of Titus' whip without a pistol at hand. Womble and Roan had jeered at him for this and had drawn only a sour, knowing sneer.

"Give him a sup of rum," Roan commanded Womble. The fat man poured a dram and handed it to the towering slave. Titus downed it with no sign of relish or distaste and stood waiting.

"Why is Mister Tillman at Great House?" Roan asked bluntly.

Titus' voice was high-pitched, flat, as hard as the clatter of sliding shale rock.

"Master Jett meet him Easton Town," he recited. "Bring him here. Talk in gun room, drink. Mist'ss Worth come, drink with 'em. Mist'ss Gracellen come. Master Jett, Mist'ss Worth go see little dogs. *He* talk Mist'ss Gracellen. Make love."

"Well, by Christ!" Roan breathed softly.

"Yes. Make love awhile. *De King* come f'm warehouses. *De King* don' like *he* bein' there but he don' show it Mist' Tillman. Shake hands. Talk little while, then *De King* and Mist' Tillman go gun room. Talk some more. Mist' Tillman say he wrong about barns. Ask pardon. Be friends."

The three men about the table uttered a simultaneous grunt.

"Yes. Shake hands again. Good friends, mebbe-so. They all go eat. They there now. Is all."

He closed his pendulous-lipped mouth and stood there, his gaze fixed an inch above Will Roan's head.

"Miss Gracellen and Mister Tillman made love," Roan pursued. "What d'ye mean by that?"

Titus spoke as though he had memorized everything he said.

"Talk love, kiss love," he explained. "She say she goin' marry him."

"*Marry him!*" the three white men exploded in one voice.

"Yes."

"Marry him!" Roan repeated. "Marry that man after what we did—" He stopped and looked up at the gigantic slave. "All right, Titus. That's all."

"Wait a minute," Womble giggled. He scurried to Roan's side and snatched up his folio of pornography, pulled the bow

93

knot and opened it. He trotted over to beside Titus, the folio open at a print.

"How'd you like that, Titus?" he burbled. "Ye'd like that, wouldn't you?"

"You God damned fool!" Roan grated.

Titus looked down at the print, stared at it for a moment and then looked at Womble. The white man slapped shut the folio and retreated to the table.

"Just a little fun, Will," he said, with an attempt at a laugh. "No call to raise an uproar."

"Ye'll raise one some day there'll be no stoppin'," Roan gravelled. "You and y'r damned tricks!" He gestured toward the door. "That's all, Titus."

The huge black looked once more at Womble, his face the same blank mask it always was. Then he turned and walked out into the rainy night.

12

ANTHONY WORTH sat at the head of the table in the panelled dining room of Fairoverlea, eating with an appetite that had not been blunted in the least by the presence of Task Tillman at the board.

This was not to say that Anthony was not puzzled, made wary, by Task's being there and by all that had happened before dinner; it was just that nothing, no matter how puzzling or troublesome, could dim his appreciation of good food. And the food at this table was good, always. It had better be.

He had been as unprepared as he ever was for the surprise of finding Task at Fairoverlea when he had walked into the Great House on his return from the warehouses. The first rain of the oncoming storm was falling when he had entered the house through his office to come upon Task with Gracellen, Vivian and Jett in the west drawing room. The sight of this ashen-haired young man, an enemy and the son of an enemy, sitting there drinking his whiskey had stopped him at the threshold of the room. For a half-second the scowl that leapt instinctively to his face stayed there, long enough for Gracellen to glimpse it, certainly, even if the others had not.

His daughter's voice had been swift.

"Father, we have a guest," she had said. "Jett met Task in Easton and persuaded him to pay us a long overdue visit."

That had been time enough for Anthony Worth to scrap the frown in favor of a smile, to stretch out his hand and speak calmly, not too heartily, not too coldly.

"Well, Task," he had said. "This is a welcome surprise."

For a second he had thought the fool was going to refuse his hand but Task had finally met his grip and Gracellen had beamed like a simpering schoolgirl, watching them.

He had wondered what was up, what lay behind all this, and his wondering had doubled a few minutes later when, prodded by both Gracellen and Jett, he had found himself going to the gun room with Task Tillman for a private talk.

What's the reason for this, his mind kept asking him; *what's behind all this?*

When Tillman had blurted out his apology for the harsh words exchanged six months before, he had had trouble playing his part, so overwhelming had been his surprise. He had scanned the other man's face for a sign of the nature of this trick but there had been nothing to be seen in the other's square face, not a single indication that there was anything in Tillman's mind that was not coming out of his mouth.

"And—and I guess my loss unhinged me," the fool had said. "I—I had no reason to speak so."

Stuttering and stumbling like a simpleton, he had been, and if there was anything that lay behind that strange apology, Anthony Worth had yet to pin it down. Still, there must be something behind it, a plan more crafty than he would have given Task Tillman credit for conceiving.

Now, hours after he had accepted the apology with an earnestness that had matched Tillman's well-masked insincerity (for such it must have been) he sat at the head of the table and reviewed this new twist to the situation.

Tillman had found a diary that had mentioned the vestry meeting. He had been clever enough to draw conclusions that had led him to the truth. Perhaps, if he had it to do over again, he, Anthony, would not have chosen the burning of the tobacco barns as the way to strike at this man who owned this dangerous truth;

it had been too reminiscent of the Larkspur Hill fire. But the cub of the old lion he had slain was getting too strong; with that tobacco sold he would have been firmly on his feet. The time to strike had been before Task Tillman got the money to pay his debts, threw off the yoke of the borrower, so he had ordered Womble to carry out the plan.

Now then. Tillman had known the fire had been Worth work, he had made that clear the day he, Anthony, had gone to Task to offer his sympathy and money to tide him over.

The offer had been a good move. For in this game, every die had to be looked over carefully on each surface before the cast was considered. The man who played recklessly was quickly lost. After the burning of the barns, the thing that had had to be done was for him to go to the man he had ruined and offer to lend him the money he needed to stave off bankruptcy. If young Tillman took the loan, means would have been devised to make it impossible for him to repay it; if he refused it as he had, the record still stood that Anthony Worth had been the first to offer help. When Tillman rejected the offer and showed he knew of the hate born at the vestry meeting so carefully noted by Randolph Tillman—and why did the old bastard keep a record of that, having been so completely cozened?—it had been his move to withdraw in martyred forbearance and bide his time for the next blow.

Time—it was the greatest weapon in any vendetta. A successful man in that kind of contest never watched the clock or the calendar. He had waited seven years before dealing Randolph Tillman his first blow, the burning of Larkspur Hill. Something had gone wrong there—all the Tillmans were supposed to have been burnt to cinders in that blaze—and so he had waited another year before taking direct means of disposing of Randolph Tillman. Then he had thought his work done—until Randolph's son had spoken of a diary that brought back all the danger, as close as it had been in 1788.

He reached out to pick up a slender silver goblet and sipped his wine. Jett was embarked on a story about the customs of some tribe of savages in the Caribbean Sea and the women and Task were fastened on his words. So, by donning a smile and a listening face, Anthony Worth could shut himself away from the others and rage within himself.

God damn Randolph Tillman and God damn his soul! God damn the day that Randolph had stood up in vestry meeting and exposed him. The words still lay imprinted in Anthony's mind as freshly as they had been the day they were thundered.

Lecher. Despoiler of the innocent. Disgrace to the parish. *Refuse cast up by the Boston sewers!*

How Randolph Tillman had learned about Boston, Anthony Worth never had been able to guess. Suffice it that he had somehow learned the whole shabby story of Anthony's beginning. Aside from that one purple-faced shout, Randolph Tillman had never sounded another word about Boston—*but he had known!* Knowing, he was dangerous. Dangerous, he had to be crushed and had been.

Now his son, this yellow-eyed Task Tillman, had learned the secret through that damned diary. Now he was dangerous. Now he had to be crushed, too, lest he bring stark terror again into Anthony Worth's life.

Aye, it had been terror, the only time he had felt fear. In the few seconds it had taken Randolph Tillman to shout those few words, Anthony had seen all that he had built, all he had worked for and fought for, all the position, the prestige that had come from his work and guile and ceaseless planning, brought crashing down about him. He had seen a gallows shadow cast across him.

He thought he had carried off that one moment of panic well. He thought he had tricked them all with his apology, with the hasty marriage of Johanna. He thought he had cozened Randolph Tillman completely with his "friendship" but the man must have been playing a waiting game, himself. If he had been, he had lost it; he had certainly lost it the night Roan and the others had dealt him his last card and left him by the roadside, the victim of a tragic accident.

But, his mind ordered him, *don't think of Randolph Tillman; think of the son and this new tack he's taken.*

He looked down the table and caught the glance that Gracellen gave Task Tillman and the look Tillman gave the girl in return and then he knew; he saw it all. The boy was a crafty foeman—or thought he was. He'd make no frontal attack in avenging his father; instead, he'd strike at Anthony Worth through the one who was dearest to him, his daughter. And the light in Gracellen's eyes showed him that Tillman had done his work well; the child was all put panting for him at the table.

Well, he knew now and he could beat that. He could—

"I'd not heard of that, Jett," he said easily, smoothly, as his nephew threw a question at him. "Where did you pick up that report?"

The talk swung in his direction and he slipped into it as neatly as though he never had been away from it. He laughed, he talked, he ate, he drank, and there never was a more charming host than Anthony Worth of Fairoverlea when he was in his element. He matched Jett's wit and outsparkled it, he brought ease and even loquacity to Task Tillman, he played the gallant to his wife, he made Gracellen's heart swell with love and admiration with his facile brilliance.

Within him, all this time, there sounded the triumphant shout: *I've seen through your pretty scheme and I can beat you now!*

He was in his office, an hour after they had left the table, when the rap sounded on the door. He knew the rap, Gracellen's. He frowned down at his quill, carefully replaced it in its tiny pot of birdshot. Carefully, he folded the letter he had just finished and, as carefully, he put it beneath a paperweight, a glass ball that enclosed a multi-colored whorl. Then he said quietly: "Come in."

He knew why they were there as soon as he looked at Task and Gracellen in the doorway. His mind clicked as with the sound of a pistol hammer being cocked. By God, Tillman was losing no time! His grey eyes calmly surveyed the couple at the threshold. Gracellen was wearing the look of a child caught stealing jam and Tillman was braced as though for physical combat.

This is your triumph, eh? You think I can't deny Gracellen what she wants.

"Sir—" Task Tillman began.

"Father," Gracellen broke in, "we—we have something to tell you." She looked up at Task and something within Anthony knotted and uncoiled. "Task—we—"

"We've come to ask your permission, sir," Task said, "for Gracellen to—to—"

"To marry Task," Gracellen said. "Oh Father, I'm so happy! All this time the two of us have been acting like a couple of simpletons and now we know it's—it's got to be the two of us or nobody at all!"

Anthony Worth sat at his desk, his eyes pinned on his daughter, his face rigid, his hands spread on the desktop in front of him. *So it was this close! He dared to bring her to me instead of spiriting her away in an elopement!* His heavy face was as white as its wind- and weather-burned skin would ever let it be, his teeth were clenched so tightly that muscles ridged his jaws.

"And so we came," Gracellen chattered on, "to do the correct thing and ask you for your blessing, and—Father!"

She stared at him, seeing him for the first time through the shimmer of happiness, noting his grim and steely glare. There was a silence and then Anthony Worth's voice tolled:

"I'd rather see you dead."

Gracellen's hand flew to her mouth as she recoiled from the hammer blows of her father's voice. Task Tillman's hand closed on her shoulder and she heard the hiss of indrawn breath through his teeth.

"Father," she stammered, "why—why do you say that? Task has told you he was wrong about—about the barns. He apologized and you accepted it."

100

"That!" Anthony Worth snorted. "I thought no more of his apologies than I did of his lying accusations."

"B-b-but you promised me that when I—when I chose the man I'd marry you'd never stand in my way. You did promise that!"

"Whatever I promised you," Anthony said with clanging emphasis, "had nothing to do with this dog."

Gracellen felt Task's body jerk as though the man had been hit heavily. His fingers bit into her shoulder deeply. She made herself speak before he could.

"Father—you've no right to say that!"

"No right?" Anthony Worth asked slowly, heavily. "No right to call a dog the man who now apes his dead and damned father in smearing mud on your mother's name, Gracellen?"

Task stepped past Gracellen, although her hand tried to hold him back. He walked up to the desk and looked down at Anthony, his hands balled into fists, his eyes glittering.

"Be careful," he warned, "about the lies you say about my father."

Worth's eyes came up to meet Tillman's. His mouth crooked in a grimace.

"No man," he said evenly, "ever called me a liar and lived long."

"No!" Gracellen cried. "No, Task! Father, no!"

She clutched at Task's arm again and he brushed her aside with a sweep of his hand.

"Then set your thugs on me, old man," he said, "because I say you lie if you accuse my father of smearing mud on any woman's name."

Gracellen was at his side, grasping at the big man, trying to pull him away from the desk, out of the room. Horror, piled so closely atop joy, made her incoherent.

"Don't—you must—" she gasped. "This can't be—he didn't mean it, Father—ah, God, somebody—"

"Let him go, Gracellen," Anthony said sharply. "If he must show you he's a younger man than me, let him. He means to throttle me to keep me from telling you the truth."

"The truth!" Task jerked out. "What would you have to do with the truth?"

"Then ask him, Gracellen," Anthony ordered, his voice a sudden roar. "Ask him here and now whether his father branded your mother publicly as my strumpet, not my wife! Ask him!"

The girl's panic-hazed eyes swung up to Task's. Her mouth dropped when she saw the dismay reflected there.

"No, Task," she whispered. "No!"

"And ask him," thundered Anthony Worth, "if he has not taken up the same slander! Ask him!"

Tillman shook his head in the motion of a goaded bull. Anthony's stab had come in under his guard. To try to tell Gracellen what had happened twenty-two years ago at a long-adjourned vestry meeting, to try to explain how he had repeated the details of that scene only to bolster his suspicions against Anthony Worth, would require hours, not seconds. And was there any explanation Gracellen could understand? Her mother had been called Anthony Worth's mistress in front of a group of men, true, but in pity, not in accusation. His father had been Johanna Igleway's friend, not her inquisitor.

"No," he said hesitantly, weakly. "No—I mean, it was not the way he puts it, Gracellen. My father laid no blame to your mother—I mean—"

"Laid no blame to my mother!" she cried in a stricken voice. "You mean your father did say that?"

"Wait, listen—"

"Aye, listen," Anthony put in grimly, "whilst he tries to find a lie to tell you. Hear me, Gracellen. This man's father, damn him, spread this filth about your mother years ago, before you were born. And why? Because Johanna would not welcome his advances. And—"

"God damn you!" Task choked.

"And I couldn't challenge Randolph Tillman because it would have dragged her name through the mud. So—"

"My father told the truth about you!" Task shouted. "For that, you murdered him!"

Anthony kept his eyes pinned on Gracellen's blanched face as he shrugged.

"You hear?" he asked. "Now he admits his father slandered your mother. Now ask him to admit the rest of it, that he has carried on with these foul lies where his father left off."

Task was dumb, made mute by the seething fury that blinded him, roared in his ears.

"I let the whelp come to this house," Worth went on ruthlessly, "because I was determined not to blame him for what his father did. The orphan neglected by a drunken sot of a brother —who would be less charitable to him? I even tried to help him when his barns burned. You know what thanks I got for that. Today, when he came to me with his fawning apology, I had trouble keeping from ordering him out of Fairoverlea, knowing he had taken up his father's filthy lies, but I didn't, though now I wish I had. When he left here tonight, you were to be forbidden to see him again and I was going to tell you why, as gently as I could. Now he dares insult you by asking to marry you, the daughter of the woman his own father's lies sped to her grave. Your mother, Gracellen!"

Gracellen stood near the doorway, her head bent, her body shivering. Task turned toward her, put out a hand.

"Gracellen," he said. "Believe me, not him! This is not so!"

The girl turned away from him and moved toward the threshold, draggingly.

"Gracellen!" Task cried. "Believe me!"

The broken cry reached her, made her turn. For a moment it seemed as though she would come back to Task and he arched his hands out from his sides, imploringly.

"And if you'd take this man's word above mine," Anthony Worth's voice crackled, "and if you'd turn against your dead mother's memory, ye'll still not have him! I said I'd rather see you dead; I meant it! But 'twon't be needed to go that far. Ye'll get to y'r room, Gracellen, and ye'll stay there, if I have to put Titus on guard at the door to keep you in!"

"You'd put that monster as a guard over me?" Gracellen asked in horror.

"I'd do worse than that to save you from your blindness," Anthony Worth said tonelessly. He reached for the bell-pull beside him. The ever-present Joseph entered. "Tell Madam Worth and Captain Jett to come here," Anthony ordered.

Jett preceded Vivian into the office. He moved his eyes from his uncle to Task and then to Gracellen. Vivian's distress at what she saw and what she guessed passed over her beauty in a faint cloud.

"Jett, take this man to the foot of the drive," Anthony Worth growled. "Call Roan and the others, if ye need them."

"But, Uncle—"

"You have your orders! He's not wanted here at Fairoverlea. If he sets foot on this place again he'll be shot as a prowler. Is that clear?"

"Anthony—" Vivian began in her soft voice.

"You'll take Gracellen to her room, Madam," Anthony whip-cracked. "Ye'll see she stays there. I told her I'd put Titus on guard if she tried to escape. I meant what I said."

"Anthony, Anthony," Vivian said quietly. "You don't mean that—your own daughter guarded by that creature."

"To keep her from throwing herself away on another creature, yes! Gracellen knows what kind of fellow this—this slime is. Don't you Gracellen?"

The girl's haggard eyes caught Task's for a fleeting moment, then dropped. Without answering, she went to Vivian and uttered her first sob against the dark-haired woman's shoulder. Vivian, with a last glance at her husband, put her arm about Gracellen's waist and led her from the room.

Task watched her go, his face dragged down by failure.

"As for you, Tillman," Anthony Worth went on, "make one false step and it'll be your last. So long as you stay away from me and mine, I'll let you live. Otherwise—"

"Uncle!" Jett broke in. "For God's sake, what's happened?"

"Your orders are to get this man off the place!"

Task found his voice and it was bleak and chill.

"Some day I'll kill you, Anthony Worth," he said impassively. "I'll kill you like the black-blooded toad you are."

Anthony's grey-green eyes held Tillman's tawny stare.

"Or I'll kill you," he rasped. "Now get out!"

Part Two

1

So Anthony Worth met what he saw as Task Tillman's thrust at him through his daughter, and he won that struggle, ruthlessly, as he won most of his battles. Gracellen's grief, the doubts that tormented her and made her a listless, pale and almost wordless woman, hurt Anthony but never to the point where he would comfort her with the truth.

"It's bitter medicine," he told Vivian when she protested, "but the cure is worth the pain, like the lancing of a fester."

"But Anthony," Vivian said, "the child doesn't eat. I've seen a light in her room at all hours so I doubt she sleeps at all. I worry for her health."

"I know Gracellen," Anthony said in a clipped voice. "A week, two weeks, and she will have forgotten all this."

"And that I doubt, Anthony," Vivian said quietly. "She truly loves Task. Is he really such a vile person that you hate him so?"

"Madam," Anthony Worth said heavily, "this thing goes back to a time when I did not know any Vivian Dangerfield of London. Gracellen is my daughter, not yours. You'll please me by keeping hands off this whole affair."

"I sometimes feel as though she is my sister, Anthony," Vivian said gently. "I'd be remiss if I didn't ask you to be kinder to her."

"When you give me a child," Anthony Worth rapped out, "'twill be the time for you to interfere in his upbringing. As for Gracellen, leave her to me!"

Vivian bowed slightly and left the room, her mouth tight. *When you give me a child;* Anthony had flung that at her more and more often in recent days and it was not fair—whose fault was it that she had not conceived? She had even descended, may God forgive her, to the use of the strange jujus her maidservant, Uley, supplied her, each one supposed to bring virility and fecundity to this strange marriage. She had prayed for children, mostly for Anthony's sake but in a good part because a child would ease some of her loneliness. Month after month she had approached her time with high hope, and the years had passed in a chain of disappointment.

She fought against blaming her husband's age for this; she resisted the hot reply to Anthony's blunt reproaches, the retort that a younger, more vigorous man would have given her a child long before this. She knew this taunt would wound Anthony beyond healing—and then, too, she feared his anger.

Was it fear or was it respect she felt for Anthony Worth? Vivian did not know and dared not examine her heart too closely. She knew it must be one or the other; it was not love—at least it was not the love she had felt for Sir Robert before Anthony had come into her life. Yes, she knew Sir Robert was unworthy of any woman's love, a cheat, a liar, a trifler, but she had loved him and his proven worthlessness had not done enough to wholly change her feelings for his memory.

Then there was her father—poor, grasping, shabby, shamed and faded Father; she could not blame him, either, for what he had done. She tried not to blame anybody for anything; this was life and a woman could weep but never rebel.

She mounted the stairs to Gracellen's room and tapped on the closed door, rapped a second time and got no answer.

"It's Vivian, dear," she called softly.

"What do you want?" Gracellen asked dully.

"To borrow some thread if you have it," Vivian lied. She

opened the door and walked into the room. Gracellen cast a brief glance in her direction and turned her eyes back to her steady, sightless contemplation of the boxwood maze that lay below her window.

"I thought I remembered seeing a spool of purple thread in your—ah, Gracellen!" Vivian moved to her stepdaughter's side and put a hand lightly on her shoulder. "You'll make yourself ill, child, this way. Come, it's not so final as all this. Give your father some time and things will come 'round your way, you'll see."

Gracellen gave a brief, mirthless laugh.

"You don't know Father," she said bitterly. "He'll never change."

"Well then, we'll hope for something to happen that'll change him, despite himself," Vivian said brightly. "Meanwhile, you're doing neither yourself nor Task any—"

"Don't speak of that man to me!" Gracellen jerked out.

"Why—"

"He must have said those things about my mother," Gracellen said in a low, hard voice, "else he'd have been here to press the truth on me in spite of everything Father could do."

"You know what your father threatened if he came back here, Gracellen."

"Hah, would that stop Jett if he were Task?"

"Well—well, Jett and Task are different men, Gracellen," Vivian said carefully. "Who'd gain by Task coming here and somebody being hurt, maybe killed, in a fight? Then your love surely would be blackened forever."

"No love, Vivian. I thought it was, I *knew* it was, but he's deserted me because he knows what Father said about him was the truth."

Gracellen abruptly left her chair and began pacing up and down the room, her hand to her mouth, her teeth closed over her thumbnail.

"You're right about the foolishness of pining," she told her stepmother. "He's not worth all this moping. Let him go, let him spend his time in the fields with his niggers—it's the place for him."

"Child—"

Gracellen whirled, her eyes blazing.

"I'll show him!" she flared. "I'll make him know he's not worth a snap of my fingers, the slanderous hound! Smear filth on my mother's name, will he? And he a bankrupt poseur with a high-sounding name and nothing else! If he expects me to—"

She broke off and swept across the room to a wardrobe, began pulling out the rainbow fragments that were her gayest gowns.

"The mourning's over!" she cried. "What's dead is dead and better buried deep! We'll have a ball, Vivian, that'll be the talk of the whole Eastern Shore. We'll fill Fairoverlea with a hundred people and dance all day and all night! And I hope the wind's in Larkspur Hill's direction so Task Tillman, the great Task Tillman with his rotten tongue, can hear it dinned into his ears and know I'm celebrating my escape from him!"

Vivian's eyes were deep and pitying as she watched her step-daughter's merry despair mount feverishly. She was remembering her own aching laughter when she had learned that Sir Robert had curtly jilted her, three months before their wedding day.

Task Tillman did not hear the music from the grand ball that was held at Fairoverlea that night and if he had it would have done nothing to either deepen or lighten the bitterness that burdened him.

He had not gone back to Fairoverlea to dare *The King* and his cutthroats to do their worst and his reason for not going back was never his fear of being killed. Task Tillman could not remember the time he had felt physical fear. It was not that his love for Gracellen had been dimmed because she had failed him when he had pled for her trust in him; Task spent nights of wide-eyed torture, seeing her face on his bedroom ceiling, hearing her voice in the wind off the Miles; after all these weeks there still were times when her vision rose to confront him in unexpected places and stab him with a pain so sharp that his breath caught in his throat, his hands trembled and the sweat broke out on his forehead.

He did not go back to Fairoverlea because he knew that if he met Anthony Worth in this black mood he would kill the man who was Gracellen's beloved father. And that would mean losing the girl he loved forever.

That was the strongest rein to check him each time he started for Fairoverlea. There was another. There was his pride, his inborn, adamantine pride that reminded him that even above the fact that Anthony Worth had branded him the reviler of Gracellen's mother was the fact that he had been ordered off Fairoverlea like a man caught cheating at cards.

A minor insult, compared with other calumny? It was not regarded so in 1810 on the Eastern Shore of Maryland, and by a Tillman.

The Tillmans had been an established leading family in Talbot County long before Anthony Worth had come out of nowhere with his insatiable ambition. A Tillman had been one of the early governors of Mary's Land; there had been judges and generals, ambassadors and bishops, who had borne the name of Tillman. Larkspur Hill, in its day, had been the gathering place of the famous and the fashionable; before Fairoverlea had raised its grandeur it had been the showplace of the Eastern Shore. An invitation to Larkspur Hill, in those times, had been a coveted thing, almost a command. Visitors from Baltimore and Philadelphia, Richmond and Charleston, had come and gone in a glittering stream.

The Tillman fortune had always been a precarious thing, forced to meet the demands of the Tillman position, but the Tillman name had been peerless in its ranking among the list of great families. And then, quite suddenly, as one Tillman after another died childless or without sons, as the Revolution cut down many a young Tillman who would have carried on the name, the direct line narrowed until it included only Randolph Tillman, William and Task. Now there was only Task.

With Larkspur Hill a weed-grown hole in the ground, with

113

the house that had been put up in its place a small, dowdy building, there remained to Task Tillman only the debt-burdened acres—and Task's pride in a name that once had been resplendent.

Then on that July day, Task had allowed his promise to Squire Wills and the persuasive tongue of Jett Worth, the man he had thought was his friend, to demolish his resolve to carry on the war against the man he *knew* had wrecked the Tillmans.

He had permitted himself to be cozened into eating his enemy's food, drinking his wine, laughing at his wit. He had let Gracellen's warm presence, the heating promise of her completeness, make him beg Anthony Worth's pardon.

He had begged Anthony Worth's pardon!

So, he knew now, he had met justice, swiftly and shamefully. He had seen the girl he loved believe the most vicious lies, deaf to his denials. He had been thrown off Fairoverlea like a horse-stealing gypsy. He had sacrificed his principles and his pride; he had met with his just desserts.

He loved Gracellen—he always would—but he never again would lower the sword against her father until one or the other of them died. He would not force a meeting with Anthony Worth; that concession he made to his love for Gracellen. But he would never seek a truce a second time.

2

THE SUMMER of 1810 passed and Autumn, then Fall, came to the Eastern Shore of Maryland.

Task Tillman got in his crops and paid something on his debt to the old Squire in Easton who had saved Larkspur Hill and had extracted an ill-fated promise. Squire Wills had been shocked, saddened, by what had happened that rainy night in the office of Fairoverlea, he had cursed Anthony Worth roundly as a liar, but he had not brought himself to believe what Task Tillman believed about the Master of Fairoverlea.

"Nay, Task," he had said, shaking his head, "the man proved himself a villain in his lies about your father but he did not prove himself a murderer, as you would have him. And—and he is fair daft over that daughter of his; it could have been his jealousy inflamed him so that he spoke wildly."

"As wildly as a rattlesnake," Task spat. "He spoke as though he'd planned each word and shaped it so I couldn't answer."

"Oh aye, he's clever with his tongue," Squire Wills nodded, "and he'd use his best wits to keep a man from taking his Gracellen away from him. But admitting that he lied, that his actions were of the basest sort, you cannot call him a murderer, the man who burned Larkspur Hill and your barns, on that account."

"I know," Task said, wryly, "that I can't shake your opinions, Squire. I'll hold to mine, then, and you hold to yours and we'll never speak of Anthony Worth between us. But my promise that I'd—"

"I release you from that, lad," the Squire interrupted. "I'd never ask you to demean yourself, even in the interests of peace between neighbors."

But Squire Wills was proved wrong, that Fall, in his contention that Anthony Worth was so jealous of Gracellen that he would fight any man who might seek to claim her. Gracellen's round of parties, balls, receptions, grew dizzier, more feverish by the week until it was climaxed by a grand ball at which her betrothal was announced on November seventh. To Charles Hilliard Rawlent of The Willows.

Vivian had held her tongue when Gracellen had announced —defiantly daring opposition—that she would marry Rawlent. Vivian had learned that there was nothing she could say to curb Gracellen's recklessness; her efforts to bring the girl back to disembittered ground had aroused only resentment in Gracellen and had brought rebuke from Anthony.

"He's handsome enough," Worth growled, "and he comes from a good family. If he's what she wants, let her have him."

"But she doesn't really love him," Vivian protested.

"Love—love!" Anthony scoffed. "You English women think there must be a swooning for love to make a successful marriage."

Ah no, Anthony, if you can call this marriage of ours a success. But she did not say the words aloud.

If Anthony Worth was disappointed in his daughter's choice of a husband, he showed no sign of it. He had laughed at Rawlent in the past, called him a coxcomb, a prissy idiot, but he raised no objection when Gracellen told him she had picked the beautiful young man as his son-in-law. Marriage to Rawlent, Anthony told himself, would be another blow at Task Tillman; it would close another port through which Tillman might try to attack. That thought balanced the realization of Rawlent's empty-headed foppery.

116

The betrothal party was a night-long affair, eclipsing anything that Talbot County had ever seen before. And Anthony Worth, usually the most cautious of tipplers, lost his grip on his drinks. He had prided himself on always being able to drink with any-one and everyone and keep his senses; he refused to admit that he was past the age for heavy drinking and night-long carousing. It was close to noon of the following day when he downed his last drinking opponent and staggered away from the shambles of the rout to make his way to his wife's rooms.

Champagne had fired Anthony Worth's mind; it had the opposite effect on certain laggard servants of his mind. Drunk, furious, shamed, suddenly frightened by the years that mocked him, he struck out at the patient woman who had endured his futile struggling, pitying him.

Anthony flung himself away from Vivian, rolled across the wide bed and stumbled to his feet.

"Christ!" he hiccoughed. "A lifeless hunk o' mutton! Man needs some fire, some spice!"

He fumbled his way across the room while Vivian's great eyes watched him. He reached for a bell-pull, missed it and nearly fell.

"Anthony," she asked from the bed, "what do you want? I'll get it for you."

He turned to survey her, blearily, waveringly.

"Ye'll get it for me, eh?" he repeated. "B'God, ye wouldn't know what t'look for. I want a little honest heat, that's what. And I know where t'get it! I'm sendin' for one of the wenches—maybe you can learn from her the proper way t'treat a man."

"Anthony!" Vivian scrambled from the bed and fled across the room to her husband, pushing aside the hand that reached again for the bell cord. "Anthony! You've had too much to drink! Anthony, you couldn't—"

He struck her and she reeled back, her hand going to the cheek that flamed under the back-handed blow. He peered at her foggily for a moment and then turned away from her, staggered to a chair and collapsed into it, sprawling.

117

"Don' scream the house down," he burbled. " 'M goin' t'wait awhile. Tired. Tired of everything. Tired of a hunk o' mutton f'r a wife. Barren. Can't have a child—oh, Christ, no—because she's too much the great lady to join her husband in . . . . . ."

He recited a list of obscenities.

"Anthony, please—"

"Ah, shut y'r simperin' mouth!" He lurched in his chair, flinging a hand toward her. "Barren as a jenny mule. Not my fault, b'God! I've swelled the belly of many a wench in the past year, but not yours!"

She turned her back on him in disgust. She told herself fiercely that Anthony was drunk, that he was half-crazed by the shame of his failure.

"Not worth a penny that I paid!" Anthony Worth was grumbling. "Not a shilling! And ye were s'pposed to be a fine brood mare!" He giggled. "Y'r father and y'r pretty sweetheart, that nancy-ann, Sir Robert, both pledged me ye'd be a fine brood mare before I paid 'em off."

Vivian turned slowly, her lips stiff.

"Before you paid *them* off, Anthony?" she asked quietly.

He laughed again and ended with a belch.

"Of course I paid for you," he said. "Y'r father needed the money f'r his debts. Oh, he asked a fancy price, the old skinflint, but—"

"I know all about Father," she interrupted in a monotone, "but you said you paid *them*."

"Aye, them!" Anthony roared. "Y'r young man, y'think he gave you up f'r nothin'? Oh, he needed guineas, too, to say he wouldn't have you! He was neck-deep in gamblin' debts. He came around to my way of thinkin' as soon as he saw the weight of my purse."

He slumped deeper in his chair as Vivian stared at him frozenly.

"I mind the first time I saw you," her husband sniggered. "Oh, ye were the high-and-mighty lady then!" His voice rose in weird mimicry of a woman's. " 'Oh, nay, Mister Worth; I'm betrothed to Sir Robert, y'know. We're to be married in the Spring.' Ye played y'r part well, woman! Ye made me hunger for you and raised the price I had to pay to y'r lover and y'r graspin' father!"

"You paid Robert to cast me aside?"

He nodded, his eyes heavy, his head beginning to loll.

"Oh aye, I paid," he muttered. "Too much—too much—y're not worth it f'r all the sons I get of you, y'lifeless hunk o' cold mutton."

She stood there, transfixed, as Anthony Worth's head rolled over on a shoulder and he began to snore. She made one gesture, a motion of a hand as though she were pushing the sight of him away from her. Then she turned and ran out of the bedroom, her bedgown half off her lustrous body, and went to the wardrobe of her dressing room.

She pulled on riding clothes with blind disregard for their arrangement. She hauled boots onto her slender legs, pinned a plumed hat to her disordered hair and half ran, half stumbled, down the hallway, down the stairs, through the littered lower hall out into the courtyard.

"Abraham!" she cried when she reached the yard. "I want my horse! I want to ride!"

The Negro Abraham, Vivian's own slave, hurried to saddle the roan his mistress used and threw a saddle on another horse for himself. His black forehead was furrowed by worry. Wasn't right for his lady to go riding like this, he told himself, when she was so far gone in wine. Or acted like it, anyway, though maybe a little different, somehow.

Task Tillman straightened up from the ledgers he had been working over and ran his fingers through his hair, darker now in November than it had been in July but still light enough to be called golden by the women who eyed it.

The crops were in and sold, Squire Wills had been paid what was due him, the Larkspur Hill land was safe for another year, at least. It had been a good growing year and Task's harvest had been the biggest, pound per acre, in Talbot County. Charles Rawlent and the others might sneer at him for working in the fields with his Negroes but the results had proved that any slave, no matter how loyal, did his best work when his master's eye was on him. It was not a question of shirking; the blacks' work tempo was naturally slower, more easily diverted, when he was untended than when the white man was over him and even, as in Task's case, working next to him.

"You'll lose your men's respect," people had warned him, "and the man a black don't respect won't get the work out of his hands."

Which had not proved true at all, at least at Larkspur Hill. With fewer Negroes than many a smaller place, Task had kept up with and ahead of his fields; the weeds, the corn-borers, the tobacco worms, had never gained a foothold in the Larkspur Hill crops.

He yawned and rubbed his eyes, stretched hugely. Book work,

to Task, was harder than hours spent with a hoe and he had been at these figures until they had started a dizzy dance under his tired eyes. But the totals were all added up now, the balances drawn; the ledgers could be closed on the harvest year of 1810.

He shoved back his chair and headed for the sideboard and the whiskey decanter that waited there. He poured a drink and sluiced it down his throat; he had been wanting it for hours but had been reluctant to take it for fear the figures would take to jiggling about more than they had without the liquor. He poured a second dollop and carried the glass with him to the front porch in search of some fresh air with which to sweep away the cobwebs left by the bookkeeping work.

The house faced the Miles River but no broad expanse of lawn swept down to the river's bank as had from the original Great House of Larkspur Hill and as did from Fairoverlea. Between this unprepossessing house and the water there was a narrow hayfield that rimmed a hummocky marsh, crisscrossed with muskrat runs. A zig-zag catwalk led from solid ground out to the short dock where Task's dory and skiff were moored. The boats were bobbing now in the wind that raised occasional whitecaps on the grey surface of the river.

He sniffed the wind appreciatively, a grower with his crops all in taking pleasure in the first smell of frost in the air. Already, the geese and ducks were beginning to crowd down out of the north in great flocks and with the book-work done, there would be sport to make up in some measure for the long months of drudgery and loneliness.

A buckeye was clawing her way up the Miles, tacking into the wind, and downriver a fishing smack was heading for Saint Michaels. Two Negroes in a dory were tonging the oyster bed that lay just off the opposite shore and the sight of them reminded Task that he must send Jobie out to scrape him up a bushel or so within the next couple of days. An oyster pie such as Tillie could fashion would be a toothsome dish on a chill November evening.

He turned at the sound of horses' hooves on the shell drive. Coming up the slight rise that sloped gently from the wagon lane was a Negro in livery—Fairoverlea livery, by God!—and he was leading a second horse in the saddle of which swayed and wavered the figure of a woman!

Task's heart gave a great leap and then settled again. It was not Gracellen nor had he any right to have hoped it would be; Gracellen would no more ride this way than he would ride to Fairoverlea. The woman was Vivian, Anthony Worth's soft-spoken, beautiful wife, and something was wrong with her.

He left the porch in a bound and ran down the drive. He was at Vivian's side when the woman's eyes closed, she gave a faint moan and slid gently down into his arms, fainted dead away.

"She hurt herself awful, Marse Tillman," Abraham groaned, grey-faced. "Hones,' suh, I di'n't have nothin' t'do with it, suh! She ride lak de Devil aftuh her, suh, and de hawss, he fell and th'ow her on her haid."

"Where was it?" Task demanded. "How long ago?"

"A ways back," Abraham jibbered. "Ah tried to make her go back to de house when she wake up but she say no, not thar. She ack like she outta her haid, Marse Tillman! Not thar, not thar, she holluh! So when she kin ride again, I brung her yere, suh."

Task looked down at the still face of the woman in his arms. There was a faint bruise on one cheekbone but no other signs of injury. He bore her into the house, a weightless burden, and laid her on the horsehair settee, yelling for Tillie. The old Negro woman's eyes walled at the sight of Anthony Worth's wife lying lifeless in the front parlor of Task Tillman's home and she muttered beneath her breath.

"Trouble," she said. "This means mo' trouble, a-plenty."

"She took a fall from her horse," Task snapped. "Do something! Get some water! Send Jobie or one of the others for a doctor!"

Vivian's thick-lashed lids quivered and then her eyes opened. "No doctor," she whispered, faintly. "I'm all right. Tired."

She closed her eyes again. Task doused a cloth in the basin of water Tillie brought and bathed her forehead and temples, brushing back the black hair from the smooth forehead. As he bent over her, Vivian's scent, as elusive as the understanding of the woman herself, drifted up to him. Her fall had torn the three top buttons of her riding habit away and the neckline gaped, showing him the curving beauty of her matchless breasts. Task stared, then looked away and hurriedly resumed his work with the wet cloth.

When she opened her eyes again, Vivian struggled to a sitting position despite Task's urging to lie still. She put a hand to her tumbled hair and pushed it back with a long-fingered hand. Her attempt to smile was weak.

"I'm all right," she murmured. "Must have fainted. I'm sorry, I—"

"You took a fall from your horse," Task explained. "Your boy brought you here to Larkspur Hill."

"I know," she nodded. "I couldn't go back. I mean, this place was closer." She started to get to her feet. "Thank you for—"

Task pressed her back to the couch.

"You've got to rest," he said. "I'll send word to Fairoverlea that you're here and—"

"No!" Vivian said sharply. "No!"

Task masked his puzzlement with quiet, reassuring words.

"All right then, but you must rest here till you get your strength back. Your boy said you had a bad fall. Do you feel that any bones are broken? I—ah—we didn't examine you—I mean—"

She smiled vaguely and shook her head.

"No," she said. "I—I was just a little shaken up, I guess. Could I have a glass of water, please?"

"Of course!" He cursed himself for a thoughtless fool. "Here—this whiskey'll serve the purpose better." He splashed some of the liquor into a glass and handed it to her, his fingers closing about her trembling hand to help guide the glass to her lips. She swallowed, gasped, and sipped again, then handed the tumbler back to him.

"Thank you. I feel much better now. I must be getting—"

"But you'll surely want to straighten up before you leave," Task said hurriedly. "I mean—well, there'd be bound to be questions if you rode home that way and—er—I take it that you'd rather not—"

"You come with me, Ma'am," Tillie said, "an' we bresh off yore dress and fix yore hair and sech."

Task's hand under her elbow steadied Vivian as she arose. Tillie led her from the parlor to a bedroom in the rear of the house. Task went to the porch to tell Abraham to take the horses around to the stable and water them.

"Your lady is all right," he told the black. "She must rest awhile before she starts back. If you're hungry, somebody in the kitchen will give you something to eat."

Abraham nodded dumbly. His greatest hope was that the folks back at Fairoverlea would never find out that his lady had ridden the way she had, like she was *looking* for a fall. Lucky for her, her neck wasn't broke, not that she looked like she cared much whether it was or not. Course it wasn't his fault at all that she was thrown but *De King,* he wouldn't listen to no excuses if he heard about it.

Task watched the Negro lead the horses toward the stable and then turned back to the house, frowning. Vivian, the quiet, low-voiced Vivian, the woman Gracellen had called the perfect wife for Anthony Worth, had been shaken by more than her fall from her horse. The first thought of a person who had met with an accident usually was to get home; Vivian had cried her protest when he had suggested notifying Fairoverlea that she was at Larkspur Hill; the Negro had told him she had refused to be carried back there when she had first come to.

That bruise on her face had not come from her fall, he was sure; it was on the other side from the cheek that was dirt-smeared. So it could well have been a blow that had sent her in flight from Fairoverlea in a ride so reckless that it had ended in her fall.

But who would strike Vivian? Vivian was Anthony Worth's wife and the person who touched Anthony Worth's wife would —*of course!*

"And now," Task muttered savagely, "he's added wife-beating to his other crimes."

He walked into the parlor just as Vivian, still chalk-faced, still trembling, returned, the dust and grime of her fall brushed away and her hair coiled neatly at the nape of her neck. Her step was uneven and Task sprang to help her across the room to the couch.

"I'm afraid," she said with an attempted smile, "that I'm still a little unsteady. Perhaps another glass of whiskey—with some water, please—would help my knees stop shaking."

"Are you sure," Task asked, "that you don't want me to send word to Fairoverlea?"

A pinched look came over her face as she shook her head again.

"No," she said in a low voice, "I—I don't even know whether or not I'm going back to Fairoverlea. Ever."

The questions crowded to Task's tongue and he swallowed them as he turned to the sideboard to refill her glass. Surely there was a bitterness in Vivian's voice, he told himself, that matched his own regard for Anthony Worth. More than a fist's blow had been dealt this woman to change her in this way.

He bent over her to hand her the drink and looked full into the great dark eyes of Vivian Dangerfield Worth.

"Task," she asked, suddenly, "am I so hideous—a hag—a—a hunk of cold mutton? Am I so worthless that a man could spend gold to buy me and yet prefer a Negro wench in his bed?"

The whiskey in the glass he held slopped over with his start.

"Vivian, I—you're distraught! No man could think such things! Hideous? Worthless?"

She nodded, slowly, rigidly.

"A hunk of cold mutton was what he called me," she said in a monotone. "Barren as a jenny mule. No fire, no spice, and he, the drunken—oh!"

Her head went down as the knuckles of her doubled hand caught at her mouth and her tears came in great, gasping sobs that wracked her slender body. The glass he was holding fell to the floor as Task went to her, sat down beside her. His arm went around her shoulders in a gesture of pure sympathy for this wounded creature, nothing else.

"Vivian, you mustn't," he said. "Why—why, you're lovely, beautiful! He must be mad to say things like that. I hate him, certainly, but I can't think that he'd mistreat you!"

Her tear-ravaged face came up from her hand, her tear-dimmed eyes gazed into his. Her mouth, swollen by her sobbing, twisted with her words.

"He—he bought me, Task, as you'd buy a slave in the market. He paid off the man I loved, paid him to drop me, and then he paid my father to order me to marry him. I knew about my father and I—I didn't care, because Robert was gone. But to buy me from Robert! Oh, I know he was weak in a lot of ways but I loved him! And he t-t-told Anthony I was a good brood mare."

"He never said that, Vivian! Worth lied!"

"And—and he called me barren while it's *him*, with his old man's body—and—oh Task, I'm so lonely! He hates me for his own faults! I'm a woman, a young woman. I want to be loved, not hated! So lonely! Task, Task, so—so alone and life's going by!"

The buttonless neck of her coat had been pinned but the pin did not hold as she turned to him and the gaping cloth brought her loveliness into view again. Her scent swirled up to him as he leaned forward. There was the taste of her salty tears in the kiss he pressed upon her mouth.

Here was an honorable young man and a chaste woman; here were two young people who had been thrown together in their loneliness and in their despair. Some strange alchemy fused them, some silent maelstrom sucked them into its vortex. All time stopped, all reason fled. Each grasped at surcease from pain they had not deserved; each found it in the other and its first calming balm gave way to frantic peace.

Blindly, gratefully, they gave themselves to each other, heedless of the thousand things that made this impossible. Their joining was sweet and right and stained with black dishonor. Her cry was a lilting paean of great joy after long suffering; his was a welcome of light after long darkness. Blended, they made a wail of agony at what their flesh had made them do.

And outside the house, tending the horses, Abraham heard those muffled cries of tortured ecstasy.

"Titus," he told himself, "he want to know 'bout this."

Part Three

1

Through the year of 1811 and during the first months of 1812, the United States moved steadily, inexorably, toward a war that half her people did not want and most of England tried to avert.

In Washington, Henry Clay worked his silvery tongue tirelessly; it seemed that he, the country's most articulate statesman, had some personal insult to avenge, some Clay account to settle with the mother country. Gathered about him were the younger members of Congress, the impetuous ones, the hot-heads, the men whose families and fortunes had suffered at the hands of the British in the Revolution and who saw a chance of retribution now. Also, there were men who mistrusted and even hated New England and who backed the war cause simply because the Federalists, headed by New Englanders, fought it.

Had the Federalist leadership been stronger, President Madison doubtless would have been able to skirt the crisis without a declaration of war. But the forces that opposed the War Hawks were poorly organized; they had no spokesman who could equal Clay in debate and their intra-party jealousies killed their chances of stemming the surge of the Congressional clique that cried for the conflict. Madison, no Jefferson or Washington, struggled manfully to preserve the uneasy peace but he could not stand alone; his advisors took their orders from Henry Clay.

Across the Atlantic, an England beset by her war with Napoleon, tried too late to make concessions that would satisfy the growing belligerency of the swaddled nation she had given birth to. The halls of Parliament resounded with the cries of some of Britain's foremost men, demanding that His Majesty's Navy leave off its mistreatment of American ships at sea, return to the United States every seaman who had been impressed from American vessels.

Cried the *London Statesman*: "In any war with America, England would have everything to lose and not one thing to gain. We have no quarrel with our cousins; we seek no fight with them; we pray them to be friends. And if war comes, how do we fare? America has a hundred thousand of the ablest seamen in the world. They can cause England great damage, harassing the sea lanes and even the Channel. No, England wants no war with America."

During the first week in June, 1812, England, as a last gesture, removed all restrictions against American commerce. American ships, she said, were free to serve any port in the world, even the French ports that supplied Napoleon, if they could run the blockade. American vessels stopped while trying to run this blockade, London promised, would be turned back but neither the ships nor their cargoes would be seized. In other words, according to the British concessions, the vessels would be free to try again.

The amazing offer, the most gracious ever made by mighty England, was buried in the avalanche of war spirit that had gained too much momentum to be stopped now. On June 18, 1812, Clay's forces struck for the Declaration of War. The House of Representatives voted 79 to 49 for war; the Senate, 19 to 13. And Governor Bowie of Maryland rode bareheaded to the State House in Annapolis at the news, to tell a throng assembled there that his "heart rejoices this day."

2

TASK TILLMAN was in Baltimore the day war was declared. He had accompanied Squire Wills to the city, though he could hardly spare the time away from Larkspur Hill, when his old friend had asked him to come with him on a business trip.

" 'Tis not only for selfish reasons that I ask ye, Task," the old man had explained. "I'd have you meet some men in Baltimore Town whom it might be of advantage to you to know some time in the future. I'd feel easier if you had other friends and advisors than me in your affairs and too many people around here are beholden to Anthony Worth."

"Between the two of us, we can take care of Anthony Worth," Task had grunted.

"Well, maybe, maybe," the Squire had smiled, "but I can't expect to be with you for many more years."

"You've got a score of years ahead of you, Squire," Task had protested. "Would to God I had your spirit and your sense right now."

But, in truth, the old man had failed during the past year; Task could not help but admit that. The war situation had weighed too heavily on Squire Wills; he had been tormented by his anxiety over the War Hawks' shrill yells for a fight. So deeply did he feel on the subject that he had left the comfort of his room at the Indian Queen to ride up and down the Eastern Shore, speaking at every opportunity in a plea for cool heads, compromise, peace. And the rebuffs he had met had hurt him; the loss of old friends in his one-man campaign had been a hard blow to Squire Wills.

He had been branded a traitorous coward on one occasion and by none other than Charles Rawlent, Gracellen Worth's husband since New Year's Day, 1811. That had happened at Oxford, where the Squire had gone to raise his lone voice at a meeting called to drum up more feverish opposition against the Federalist peace party in Washington. Rawlent, all military garb and supercilious scorn, had accused the old gentleman of "trembling at the prospect of losing some of his hoarded gold," had come close to the outright charge that Squire Wills was in the pay of the British "with the secret duty of dividing a united Maryland."

When Task Tillman had heard of that ugly incident he had started out to find Rawlent but had been restrained by the old Squire.

"As ye're grateful to me—aye, even have some love for an old man, ye'll not go brawling after Rawlent," the Squire had protested. "Ye'll not trounce him with your fists as ye did once nor call him out in any duel. I forbid it, Task—ye'll hurt others beside yourself if you do not let this thing pass."

What he really had meant and what Task had known he meant was that for Task to engage in any fight with Rawlent would be to loose a hurricane of gossip that would involve Gracellen. Though she had turned her back on him completely, though she had married a popinjay and proved to him and to everybody else that she cared nothing for a man's worth, only for his looks and his name, he could not do anything to touch her with scandal.

So, although at first he had fretted at the curb bit hauled on him by the one man in Talbot County he could call his true friend, Task Tillman had recognized the bitter need of letting Charles Rawlent strut. And when Squire Wills had asked him to sail him up the Bay to Baltimore in his skiff ("The coach would rattle these old bones to pieces and I'd have no confidence in any hand but yours at a tiller") he had been glad to agree.

Though it meant not seeing Vivian for the weeks he would be gone.

Yes, the dark-eyed wife of Anthony Worth and the broad-shouldered young Master of Larkspur Hill still saw each other although, perhaps, they fought against it. They had both agreed that the first delirious explosion had been a shameful mistake but one beyond their powers to resist; Vivian had sobbed her regrets when sanity had returned and Task had cursed himself for taking advantage of a distraught woman. They would never—no, never!—let themselves be caught in that flame-meshed web again!

But—Vivian was a woman, a young woman, a lonely woman, a woman who had lost her respect (or fear) of her husband, a woman who knew now that Anthony Worth had wrecked her chances for normal happiness by piling gold guineas in front of her weak lover, Sir Robert, until the coins had blocked out all sight of decency and honor. She had much to forgive Anthony and instead of pleading for her forgiveness he had reviled her as inferior to a black wench as a love-mate, a barren lump not worth the money he had spent to claim her. There was a motive of revenge in Vivian's return to Task Tillman. Just which was the more powerful motive, revenge or her need for forgetfulness in ecstasy, Vivian could not tell, herself.

As for Task, he was ripe for this affair. The demands of Larkspur Hill had virtually barred all social life to him; the woman he loved was lost forever, and Vivian brought him a tenderness, a companionship, which was not the least part of being with her. Nor the greater part, most certainly, because Vivian dropped her quiet restraint as she dropped her glorious hair, her whispering gowns, surrendered to unleashed desire as she surrendered to Task's arms.

Vivian Dangerfield Worth was Task Tillman's first woman, as he could be said to be Vivian's first man, actually. Task was no virgin when Vivian was brought to Larkspur Hill that November day; he had experienced the usual encounters with doxies and complaisant girls during his growing-up, but Vivian was the first to lead him, and be led by him, into such depths of passion as neither had dreamed were allowable to human beings. What she sought he gave to her in full measure and in her gratitude she discovered many things which she taught him, and found a fainting rapture in the teaching.

So, through those winter months of 1810 and 1811 and during all the next year they met and shared each other and although their guilt was heavy after each meeting it was not strong enough to prevent the next.

"Perhaps," Vivian told Task when he spoke of Squire Wills' request, "some time away from here—and me—will cool this fever in us both."

Now, in bustling Baltimore, Maryland's biggest city, the ship-building center that was rapidly outstripping the New England seaports in importance, Task found himself too busy to give Vivian more than an occasional yearning thought. He and the Squire had taken rooms at the Fountain Inn on Light Street, in the very center of things; they had walked the crowded streets, elbowing and being elbowed by excited men all flushed and babbling over thoughts of war. They had driven outside the city in a hired rig to view the work going on at the Federal Hill fortifications. They had seen the ramparts rising on the strongholds which were to be named Star Fort and Fort McHenry. They had watched as companies of militiamen and regulars tramped through the streets; they had heard the cheers that welled up as a uniformed man on horseback had ridden past the inn.

"Smith!" the crowds had yelled. "Sam Smith! Ye'll show 'em, Sam! Teach 'em their manners, Sam!"

And this man, they had learned, was the General who would win the land war in Maryland if the British ever had the temerity to land troops on Free State soil.

The news from Washington, the word that the city, the nation, waited for, came just at nightfall when a courier galloped into Baltimore on the Washington Pike, leaving behind him a wake of cheering. His arrival in the city was the signal for a celebration that might have attended a great victory. Bonfires flared everywhere, torchlight processions wound through the streets in snaking lengths of howling, shrieking, near-hysterical men. Cannon on Federal Hill boomed a salute to the conflict that was upon the nation.

Toasts were drunk to Clay, to Sam Smith, to Madison, to Governor Bowie, to General Dorsey, to Colonel Amey, to Captain Bunbury's Sea Fencibles, to Captain Evans' artillery, to General Stricker and to Colonel Bias' dashing cavalry.

The mood was one of wild exultation; there were few sober faces to be seen on the streets or in the taverns that night. The boasts were loud, the predictions were brave, the British fleet was sunk and the Lobsterbacks sent scurrying over a dozen slop-stained bars. Not many of the young men had put off joining a militia company but those who had pushed forward now to enlist with this officer or that who stood at street corners and in Court House Square, blurry-handed drummer boys beside them.

Task Tillman felt the pulse of the drumbeat's summons course through him as he and Squire Wills strolled back to the Fountain Inn from a walk through the fevered town. Each ruffle, each thump, seemed to be pounding out a call to him. The eyes of every uniformed man he passed seemed to be surveying him coldly, inquiringly, asking him what company he'd joined, what troop he'd fight with.

"You think it best I enlist with a company at Easton Town, Squire?" he asked. "Or maybe I'd do better, see action sooner, by joining a Baltimore company."

The old gentleman's eyes were shadowed by the tricorne hat he wore but the lines of his face showed his dejected weariness. The Squire paced slowly, leaning heavily on his long stick, not answering Task immediately but walking on, his head bent in deep thought.

"I'm sure the men could keep Larkspur Hill running," Task went on. "After a fashion, anyway. Of course, the harvest wouldn't be as big as last year's, 'cause I do say I can make 'em work, but the crops shouldn't suffer too much, sir. There'd be a fair return—"

A fierce gesture by the Squire's hand stopped him.

"Ye think I'm concerned about the loan?" the old man asked. "Nay, Task, it is not that. 'Tis only—all this merriment, when these men should be on their knees, asking God that an awful fate not overtake them and this nation. The churches, not the taverns, should be crowded. There should be prayers instead of all this braggadocio."

"But, sir, we'll beat 'em!" Task said excitedly. "First, we'll beat 'em on the sea and then, if any British transports should get through our Navy, why then we'll beat 'em on the land!"

He looked down at the ancient beside him and waited for Squire Wills' answering nod.

"Surely you know that's true!" he burst out when his friend made no reply. "Why, 'tis as plain as plain can be! There never was a Britisher could stand against an American on water or on land!"

Wills sighed heavily and looked up at Task, the lines of his face deeply etched by the shadows cast by a passing torch light.

"God knows," he said slowly, "there is no man who loves this country more than I do, no man ready to make more sacrifices in a just cause in her behalf. But I tell you, Task, I fear this'll always be a black day in our history."

"But—"

"They've called me coward and traitor, I know, for counselling compromise. Now that war's declared, they'll not hear me speak again against it. But I can tell you because we have grown close together in these past years; I ache in fear of what will befall this nation in this war."

He is very old, Task told himself. *The old are always over-cautious, seeing dangers that don't exist.*

"You—you would not have me join a company, then?" he asked aloud.

"Oh, aye," Squire Wills nodded. "You must do that; our country will need every man she can muster. But not in Baltimore, Task. To join a Baltimore company would keep you here, away from Larkspur Hill, when there'd be no real need to stay. And in

Easton Town there's the Fencibles and the Easton Militia Company and, of course, the Dragon Footguards which I don't suppose you'd care to join."

"Good God, no!" Task grunted.

"But the Easton companies have been drilling for some time now," the Squire went on, "and their ranks are filled, as I understand it. If I were you, I'd join a new company, such as Nicholson's at Queen's Town, the Queen Annes Militia. That's not far from Larkspur Hill and I doubt not that ye'd receive a welcome from them there."

"A welcome I wouldn't get at Easton?"

"Well, Rawlent has been talking, as I warned you he would after you thrashed him that day on the street. The officers of the Easton companies are all beholden to Anthony Worth in one way or another. I think your fortunes would be better served by joining Nicholson's troop."

"Which I'll do," Task nodded, "the minute we get back."

Now he was in a hurry to return to the Eastern Shore, to volunteer with Captain Joe Nicholson's Queen Annes Militia—and to see Vivian. The fever had not cooled in Task, at least; if anything, it had raged hotter with separation.

"We can get underway for Easton tomorrow—" he began, when Squire Wills' gesture cut him off.

"Nay, Task," he said. "Grant an old man further favor and stay in Baltimore for a time. We have not yet met half the gentlemen I'd have you see and know. They're all filled with this Declaration of War now but they'll get their heads back in a day or so. And they'll be important to you, Task. This war, pray God, will soon be over and then you'll have more need than ever for friends in bringing Larkspur Hill back to where it should be."

Thus it was that Task Tillman was still in Baltimore two days later when the *Federal Republican*, the Federalist newspaper owned by Alexander Contee Hanson and Jacob Wagner, appeared on the streets of the city with its virulent editorial condemning the war. Hanson was the writer and his pen was dipped in venom; his malice shocked even his fellow Federalists.

"By the Lord," Task exclaimed, his broad face darkening as he finished the seething article, "the man who wrote this ought to be strung up to the nearest tree! Of all the scrofulous dogs—"

"Gently, Task," Squire Wills said reprovingly. "We fought a bitter war with this England we'll fight again, to guard our freedom of the press."

"'Tis a freedom that's been mocked by this lying sheet!" Task shouted. "Where is the printer that turns out such a thing?" He searched for the address on the paper's masthead and reached for his hat, stormed toward the door of the inn bedroom.

"Where to?"

"To tell this man—these men—what I think of such base slander!" Task hurled over his shoulder. The slamming door cut off Squire Wills' protest.

Task Tillman was more than a block away from the printing shop when he saw that others had acted more promptly in their anger. A swirling, yelling mob eddied in front of the building where the *Federal Republican* was printed and, as Task shoved his way into the outer fringes of the crowd, there was a crash as the front door of the shop was rammed in. Tillman struggled with the others, caught by the fever of the rabble, trying to get into the shop, but he was barred by the press of sweaty bodies from getting closer than a hundred yards of the place. He found himself jammed up against a fat man with a crimson face and a gaping mouth that showed bad teeth and exuded bad breath.

"Kill the bastards!" the fat man was howling in a shrill voice. "String up the traitors!"

"Death to the spies!" squealed an oldster with sidewhiskers, a silver-knobbed walking stick held high above his head.

"Tar and feather 'em! Ride 'em out of town on a rail! Tear out their lyin' tongues, I say!"

Task's bulk enabled him to wedge himself a few feet nearer the shop. Over the heads in front of him he could see the gaping window of the place, its glass shattered, and he caught occasional glimpses of men inside, using sledgehammers and crowbars on the press, smashing type fonts, wrecking furniture.

"Burn the viper's nest!" came the chant of the mob. "Burn it to the ground!"

As if in answer to the clamor, a puff of smoke came whirling out of the crowded shop and behind it spilled the men who had been inside, tumbling over one another in their race to get away from the flames. The smoke thickened, rolling out of the door and window in thickening clouds and then there was a flare of orange flame, streaking the bellying smoke columns.

A roaring cheer went up from the crowd, a cheer that Task Tillman found himself joining with all the strength of his deep lungs. By God, that was the way to treat all lovers of King George! Axe and fire and ruin to the ones who'd try to discourage the men who'd win this war!

"This Wagner and the man Hanson," he screamed into the ear of the man next to him, "I hope they're inside!"

"Aye," the other grinned. "I hear they're tied to a pile of their own stinkin' newspapers."

"Good!" Task grinned back. "Oh, very good!"

The shop was an inferno now, flames shooting from the window and door to force back those in the front ranks of the mob with their heat. Sparks whirled upward with the smoke. From somewhere came the frantic clamor of an alarm bell.

"Don't let the fire brigade git to it!" hollered Task's informant. "Keep the fire brigade away—they'll ruin our fun!"

The mob turned to face whatever fire brigade might be coming to interfere, then recoiled in a collective backward step. No firemen were coming down the street. Instead, there marched a company of Army Regulars in their crossbelts and high, hard hats, headed by a young lieutenant who carried a bared sword in his hand.

The mob shifted uneasily. A mumbling growl spread, then died. There was a silence, broken only by the rhythmic tramp of soldiers' boots on the cobblestones, the hiss and crackle of the flames. Inside the printshop, there was the thud of a falling timber and a fountain of embers gushed out over the mob. Hands slapped frantically at sparks that showered the crowd. Someone in the very center of the throng yelped: "Down me collar! Down me collar!" There was a nervous, jerky laugh.

"Halt!" the lieutenant barked. The soldiers stopped, grounded their muskets. The two forces, soldiers and rioters, eyed each other tentatively.

"No sojer's goin' t'shoot us fer roughin' up a pair of spies," a man near Task muttered, unconvincingly. " 'Tain't right."

The lieutenant advanced toward the crowd. His face was pale beneath the peak of his shako, his body was held rigid against his nervousness. He stopped about a dozen paces from the outer rim of the crowd, cleared his throat and shouted what some regulation had taught him to say.

"Disperse!" he shrilled. "Go to your homes! Disperse, I sa-a-a-ay!"

His high voice held true until the last word. Then it broke into a womanish screech, soaring to falsetto heights in a scratchy trill.

It was what was needed to prevent the situation from becoming uglier. The mob, which might have been swung into a bloody clash with the soldiers by a wrong word or move, burst into a roar of laughter. Men who might have felt called upon to prove their personal courage in a reckless charge on musket and bayonet seized on the young lieutenant's choirboy note with relieved howls of glee. The officer's bright red face showed he would spend many a day trying to forget that moment but, had he known it, he had prevented an incident that could have been disastrous.

"Aw right, sonny-boy," a voice called from the rear of the crowd. "We'll all go home before you slap us."

"We're through here, anyway," another voice yelled. "Our work's done."

Slowly, and still whooping at the lieutenant's order, the crowd broke up. The fire inside the printshop crackled on, gutting the building. Owners of other houses and shops in the neighborhood (the printshop fortunately stood by itself in a sizable lot) were creeping from their gabled attic windows with buckets to snuff out embers that landed on their roofs, snarling down curses at the patriots who had put their properties in danger. Down the street behind the soldiers came a troop of volunteer firemen, dragging their cart with its ladders and buckets, the leader tooting on a blue tin horn.

"Let's git out," the man next to Task said, "before they press us t'carry buckets. Ye're liable to a fine if you refuse, y'know."

Task followed the man up a narrow alley between two houses on the opposite side of the street from the blazing shop, then turned down a lane which brought him, eventually, to Fayette Street. He headed back to the Fountain Inn and Squire Wills, brimming with his news, still caught up in the intoxication of mob lust.

He was almost at the inn when the reaction hit him. One moment he was hurrying along the brick sidewalk, afire with self-importance and the satisfaction of having helped do a good job well; the next instant he was stopped dead-still, the horrifying realization of actuality swamping him in a sickening tide.

What had he said to the man next to him as the flames had curled and eddied?

I hope Wagner and Hanson are inside!

And, when the other had said yes, they were, tied to a pile of their own newspapers, what had he said?

Good! Oh, very good!

His blood curdled at the memory. He had fairly licked his lips at the thought that two men, two men he had never seen, two strangers who were no enemies of his, were being burned alive before his eyes! This was Task Tillman who had done this and done it naturally, unthinkingly. Task Tillman, who had gone almost sleepless for a week, trying to save a colt with a broken leg rather than shoot it, had grinned at the thought of two humans shrivelling and blackening in a crackling furnace!

"What happened to me?" he asked aloud, from between stiffened lips. "Am I truly this foul?"

Two men passed him, turning to look at him curiously. A few steps beyond him, Task heard one of the pair laugh.

143

"I'll wager," he told his companion, "he doesn't make it to the next tavern, from the looks of him."

Task shuffled on to the Fountain Inn, mounted the stairs with leaden feet, pushed open the door of the room he shared with Squire Wills, and sank into the nearest chair, staring woodenly at the floor. Dimly, he heard the old man cross the room to stand beside his chair, hazily he heard the Squire's questions.

His tongue stumbled as he told the story of what had happened outside the printing shop of the *Federal Republican,* of his query to the grinning man and his ghoulish delight at learning that Wagner and Hanson were perishing with their office.

"I said," he told the Squire, "that it was good, oh, very good, and all the time—all the time—"

He covered his face with his hands and trembled at the horror of the thought. There was a silence and then his aged friend's hand gripped his shoulder. Wills' troubled voice sounded quietly.

"Don't put too much blame upon yourself, boy," the old gentleman said. "I've seen this madness affect the strongest men. Indeed, I've half a thought there'd be no great heroes if they weren't stricken by this very thing. It's a madness, like all war's a madness, and the best of us, it seems, have no defense against it when it strikes us."

He sighed and his hand left Task's shoulder.

"I saw it and a-plenty during the last war," he went on as he paced back across the room toward the window. "I saw friends of a lifetime at each other's throats, one with the cry of Tory and the other with the snarl of rebel dog. I saw decent men lose their wits and kill and burn and destroy from sheer wantonness and after their fever had passed weep like children at their own sinfulness—or strut like peacocks as they sought to cover their shame.

" 'Tis not war alone that brings these spells," he said, "but, oh, the damned disease does flourish in war! This is a part of war your speechmakers never tell about; this is the part your swashbucklers never admit. God grant you won't, Task Tillman, but I fear ye'll see much more of this and even be seized by the madness y'rself again if this new war they're all so merry about touches these shores."

The man who told Task Tillman that Jacob Wagner and Alexander Contee Hanson had died in the fire was wrong. Both editors had fled at the first roar of the oncoming mob and had ridden to Georgetown, outside Washington, where they took refuge with friends. In Georgetown, the two continued publishing the *Federal Republican* and if they had stayed there further trouble might have been avoided.

Hanson, however, could not endure the thought that he had been driven out of Baltimore. The more phlegmatic, more cautious Wagner was content to make Georgetown the newspaper's home but his partner harried him until he finally agreed reluctantly to return to Baltimore. A group of friends there pledged their support and Hanson and Wagner came back in July, bought a building on Charles Street and made the place an armed fort. Their friends, who included some of the city's leading Federalist citizens, garrisoned the place, muskets and pistols were handed out and Hanson, in effect, dared Baltimoreans to throw him out again.

The challenge was not long in being taken up. On July 26, 1812, another mob, bigger than the first, surged down upon the Charles Street shop and stoned the place. Someone fired a shot, a mobster screamed that he had been wounded, and the crowd scattered. But not for long; the gang was soon back and this time it trundled a small cannon.

The charge was rammed home, the ball followed, the glowing linstock was approaching the touch-hole when a cavalcade of city fathers galloped up, shouting the order to hold.

There was a parley between officials and leaders of the mob, then the city dignitaries entered the Charles Street printing house under a white flag. Hanson and his friends were pledged safe conduct from the besieged house to the jail, where they would be lodged temporarily under no charge. The Federalists accepted the proposal and left the house in a group which included General James M. Lingan and General Henry Lee, both veterans of the Revolution, John Thomson and Hanson.

The mob dispersed but fell into the hands of some rabble-rousers only a few hours later and, inflamed by the conviction that they had been cheated of their prey by trickery, swarmed down upon the city jail. The rioters smashed their way into the makeshift prison. This time, there was no stopping them in their insane fury.

When they slunk away, satiated, they left behind Thomson, tarred and feathered, beaten so savagely that he was close to death. They left General Lee crippled for life. They left General Lingan dead.

Hanson, somehow, had escaped without a scratch.

The next day brought a storm of protest from an outraged or conscience-stricken populace. Baltimore, which had been a hotbed of pro-war sentiment, abruptly became an anti-war city with a spirit that matched even the most peace-at-any-price town of all, New Bedford, Massachusetts. Now, it was down with the War Hawks who'd turn the country over to mob rule. Now, it was up with the Federalists and their sanity.

In vain, the war party swore that the whole sad business had been engineered by the Federalists themselves who had sacrificed their own men to fashion a *cause celebre*. Baltimore, in her shame, sought someone to do penance for her and she picked on the pro-war Governor at Annapolis, Robert Bowie.

Bowie was forced to resign and into his place stepped Levin Winder, one of the state's staunchest Federalists. So, with the war barely a month old, Baltimore had shown herself as the most loudly belligerent city in the nation and had changed her tune to a cry against the senselessness of any conflict with England.

She would change her tune, again and again, before this strange war was finished but when the final accounts were added up she would find she had done better than tolerably well in her nation's cause. And she would find that she had earned herself undying fame as the birthplace of another tune, a deathless one . . .

3

THE HERON was three days out of the Barbadoes, on her way home, when Jett Worth learned there was a war. It was His Majesty's Schooner *St. Lawrence*, thirteen guns, that imparted the information and in that Jett was a lucky man. His informant could as well have been a 74-gun ship of the line such as *Albion*, *Dragon*, or *San Domingo*, all of which were in those waters at the time, and even Jett Worth's skill at outrunning a pursuer would not have saved him then.

Heron was riding close to the water, making knots under a quartering wind, when the lookout shouted a sail, coming up on the starboard quarter. Jett was out of his cabin in a bound, the glass at his eye, before the lookout's wailing hail had drifted down the wind.

"A Britisher," he murmured, "and a schooner. But she's no merchant, from the looks of her."

He gave an order to the helmsman and *Heron* fell off several points to leeward. Jett saw the Britisher change course immediately and a frown creased his forehead.

"Now, here's a puzzle," he told his mate, Greer. "That schooner's mighty anxious to rub shoulders with us, I'd swear. Could be she's some sort of a decoy."

"Or bloody pirate," rumbled the short, stocky, full-bearded Greer. "Some damned buccaneer, perhaps, flyin' the handiest flag in the locker."

"Aye," Jett nodded. "Y'might be right, Mister Greer. Best take no chances with this cockerel, I think. All hands and best put a bit o' brass on deck."

The mate's bellow boomed. Below decks, the off-duty watches tumbled from their hammocks and came running topside. Mister Greer's orders were terse, the crew's work was smooth; this was not the first time these men had cleared the schooner's decks for action.

In *Heron's* bow, an orderly, if unusual, pile of gear was quickly cleared away to reveal a long bow-chaser, a sixteen-pounder. Aft, the bow gun's twin came into sight with the swift removal of a tented shelter which, had any Paul Pry at a visited port inquired about it, covered seedling orange trees which Jett was taking back to Maryland in the hope that they would flourish at Fairoverlea.

From the hold, block and tackle raised four blunt-snouted nine-pounders, little more than oversized blunderbusses but easily moved and effective at discouraging boarders when loaded with scrap iron and nails. The crewmen belted on cutlasses and looked to the priming of their pistols. *Heron* was ready for what might come.

Before this, Anthony Worth's *Heron* had been in three fights, twice with Barbary pirates and once with a buccaneer brig off the Dry Tortugas. All three brushes had been little more than gun practice; both Barbary lateens had veered off at the first shot Jett had flung at them and gone seeking tamer meat; the pirate had been poorly handled and, after scoring several times with his stern-chaser, Jett had run for it, leaving the brig to swallow his wake and fling futile shot after him.

This, Jett Worth told himself, promised to be different if the Englishman stayed as intent on closing as he now appeared to be.

He eyed the sails and the sky. *Heron* was not carrying her full canvas while—he squinted again through the glass—the Britisher, if that was what she really was, appeared to have cracked on everything she had. She was eager, that one, coming in close-hauled. Give the stranger another fifteen minutes, he calculated, and *Heron* would be within range with a sixteen-pounder or better, if the Britisher carried them.

The *St. Lawrence* did not wait out the quarter hour. Scarcely five minutes after Jett made his calculation, a puff of white smoke blossomed on the Britisher's bow. The shot was made at an impossibly long range; it could have been that the *St. Lawrence* thought she had an unarmed merchantman and sought to end the chase by showing her teeth and frightening the Yankee.

"Oh-ho!" Jett grinned. "Up goes His Majesty's ensign now. We'd best salute it, Mister Greer, with the stern pivot. But wait until I give the word, if you please. We've got no powder or ball to spend recklessly."

The *St. Lawrence's* bow-chaser puffed again and there was another splash astern the *Heron* but closer now. Jett shook his head, still smiling.

"He's in an anxious humor, this feller," he told Greer. "Not even an order to heave to before he starts throwin' shot. Now I call that most unneighborly; I really do! Ye'd think we were a Frenchie off Dover by the way—"

He stopped and his grin faded. His clenched hand pounded the rail beside him gently.

"Now, that's it, by God!" he breathed. "It's war, Mister Greer!"

"Y'think so?" the mate rumbled. "Y'think Madison's finally swallowed his fear and declared for it?"

"Aye," Jett nodded. "You can fair see it by the way that Englishman's closing. Before, even when they stopped and searched us, they went at it gingerly, knowin' that if they handled it poorly they'd get all hell from some admiral or other. But there's no doubt in this one. He's got no orders to tread lightly. He knows there'll be no blame even if he sinks us before he speaks us."

His grin returned and he clapped a hand to Greer's shoulder.

"Now this," he crowed, "is something like! Now we can show 'em how a schooner should be fought with no damned politics to worry us." He turned to bark at the stern pivot guncrew. "Lay it

149

on and lay it well, gunner!" he snapped. "I'd like the first to tickle him."

The *St. Lawrence* edged closer. There were twin blooms of smoke and a splash close by the *Heron's* stern. The second British ball passed over the Worth schooner, whurffling past with a chilling burble, and plunked into the sea on the port side.

"Too close," Jett murmured. "Fire when your gun bears, Stern."

There was a second's hesitation and then the sixteen-pounder thundered. Acrid smoke boiled back over the schooner, obscuring the sight of the Britisher for a moment until the wind whipped it away. A ragged cheer went up from the decks of the *Heron*.

It was a hit, as much by luck as by the gunner's skill. Jett's sixteen-pounder had scored on the *St. Lawrence's* foredeck, the ball crashing squarely through the bow-chaser's crew. The Britisher faltered and fell off. Jett whipped the wheel hard a-starboard to send *Heron* across *St. Lawrence's* bow.

"Bow gun!" he yelled. "When you bear!"

The bow pivot was on target as the Eastern Shoreman came out of the heeling tack and steadied. The sixteen-pounder boomed, the shot passing through the *St. Lawrence's* rigging with no more damage than a severed line or two.

"Take down those quoins, Bow!" Jett shouted. "Nine-pounders, touch her up!"

The two small guns in the starboard waist thudded as one as Jett put over the wheel again and *Heron* slanted off to port. *St. Lawrence* reached to starboard, spreading the distance between the two vessels, trying to come broadside to the American in the hope of blasting her with her six portside guns.

"Give me canvas, Mister Greer," Jett said calmly. "Crack on everything my sticks will hold, please."

"We could come 'round astern," Greer said wistfully. "She's carrying no stern-chaser I can see and—"

"And she's still got thirteen guns to our six," Jett broke in bluntly, "and four of ours mere toys. Nay, Mister Greer, we've bloodied this Englishman's nose and it's time to go. We've got Anthony Worth's cargo to look after on this voyage, sir. Another

150

time, with a bit more poison in our stinger, we'll give His Lordship a real lesson."

Greer sighed dolefully, then cupped his hands to bellow his orders for sail. Up went the flying jib, the staysail and the three studding sails; the *Heron* fairly leapt as she began a downwind run on a fresh tack.

St. Lawrence started to come about quickly enough but something, a line caught in a tackle block, a seaman's foot slipping on a wet deck, sent her yawing for one brief spell before she recovered and gave chase. She saw she had no chance to close in again after the first minute. The Englishman turned and sent one hopeful broadside billowing out over the water. The splashes marked the shortness of the try and the Americans jeered, spitting curses.

"Yaaah, lime-juicin' bastards! Learn to sail a vessel afore ye mix with us!"

Jett stood looking astern at the fast-diminishing *St. Lawrence*, his hands behind his back, his feet widespread. His heart was still hammering with the excitement of the brief fight; he realized now that his throat was tight and dry. But not from fear, by Heaven! He had not suffered a second's doubt, the least qualm, that his ship was a better ship, he a better man, than the Englishman with all his heavier guns. And, Lord, what a thrill it had been to look through the drifting smoke and see that splintered wreckage where his ball had ploughed the enemy's foredeck! That schooner had been no heathen Barbary lateen, no clumsy-footed buccaneer; *St. Lawrence* had been one of His Majesty's warships, one of the vessels that were supposed to be invincible, manned by the proudest officers in the world. True, it had been only a schooner he had outfought and outsailed but the Britisher had carried more guns, the *St. Lawrence* had had the advantage of surprise—an advantage which could have been murderous if the Britisher's captain had taken full advantage of it—and still the *Heron* had won.

"Give me a fast brig-sloop," Jett told himself, "and I'll take on anything they've got at sea and win." His mouth twisted in a grin. "Providing my luck holds good," he added, honestly.

4

ANTHONY WORTH was at his warehouses, checking the cargo just discharged from his schooner *Compass*, Elias Griffin, Master, arrived two days ago from South America. His heavy face wore a frown all out of keeping with the information the lading bills had offered him, his usual interest in the least detail of the business at hand was missing. Will Roan knew that something of no ordinary importance was eating at *The King*.

It had been like this for too long, the hulking Roan told himself, and damned if he could see why *The King* should be upset. Three of his four vessels, *Compass*, *Athena* and the old *Johanna*, had come in without trouble past the blockade England was trying to set up and even though *Heron* was still out, *The King* couldn't be worrying about young Cap'n Jett making it past the whole British fleet, if he had to, with his thumb to his nose. No, Roan said silently, a man must be sore put to find a worry if Anthony Worth with his bulging warehouses, his vessels all safe-harbored, his purse as heavy as an anvil, had searched one out.

Perhaps, Roan thought, something was going on at Great House; the red-headed filly might be kicking up her heels again. Marriage to that fool Rawlent hadn't changed her as far as he could see; she still went where she pleased, when she pleased, and more often than not the nancy-ann she'd married wasn't with her when she rode out.

For a time he had suspicioned that the girl was slipping off to see that Task Tillman again and he had gone so far as to query Titus about it. But the big nigger had said no, she hadn't seen Tillman since the night, two years and more ago, when The King had ordered him out of Fairoverlea. And Titus wouldn't hide a thing like that; Titus didn't give a curse for anybody. Matter o' fact, the whip would take pleasure in saying something that would bring ruin to man or woman. Even, he reminded himself grimly, Will Roan.

Damned devilish nigger; he'd met some brutes in his life but Titus was the first man he'd ever encountered who didn't have a single spark of humanness in him. Even the worst of the lot in that sweet little Florida nest, years back, had been human enough to cuddle a woman once in awhile, but not Titus.

Oh aye, he tamed the wildest stolen slave easily enough and kept them tamed, he could work a hand to exhaustion and beyond it, he made sure the secrets of the hidden part of Fairoverlea never leaked out through a slave's mouth, but Will Roan often wished that one of those mad tries to kill him had succeeded.

Well, if it wasn't the filly, then what was the reason for *The King's* mood? His wife? Hah, that could be it! The old boy was finding out that a young wife could be a pestering nuisance when she was bitten by the mosquito that couldn't be slapped and that Vivian looked as though she had a constant itching. Aye, a man might lord it over everybody all day long but there was one important servant who'd not take his orders that same night, even with the duty right before him, begging to be done. Not at *The King's* age.

Now, if that black-eyed bitch had a mind to look his way— Will Roan licked his lips and felt a stirring deep inside his mountainous body.

"That stuff there," he said, hastily, as though to cloak his thoughts from Anthony Worth's eyes, "ought t'bring a pretty price, now the war's on. Goods like them will be gettin' skeercer and skeercer with the damned Lobsterbacks' blockade."

153

Anthony came back from wherever his mind had carried him and shook his head, hunching his powerful shoulders.

"They'll find a ready market, right enough," he said, "but the prices will be pennies compared to what we could get for the stuff if England would put a real blockade against us."

"A real blockade, sir?"

"Aye. This show they're playing now can't be called that. The letters I get say not a port in Massachusetts or Rhode Island or New Hampshire has been closed by the British. That's a reward to the Yankees, you see, for holding off all support of the war. Beyond that, it's a bait to lure New England to secession."

"Them blasted Yankees," Roan growled. "They've soon forgot the time they hollered for help and all the rest of the country come runnin' to their aid, back in Seventy-six. Let 'em secede, I say; we'd be better off without the long-nosed codfish-eaters."

But Worth was walking away, not listening to what the hulking Roan was saying, his eyes fixed on the stacks of cases and piles of sacks but seeing little of what they scanned, his mouth pursed in the new expression he had worn so often lately. Roan looked after *The King* and raised a hand to push the frayed and dirty hat he wore back further on his head.

"Hang me," he muttered under his breath, "if *I* know what's pickin' at him. The day you can't get *The King* to join in cursin' New England, somethin's terrible bad around here."

Anthony circled a cluster of hogsheads and made for the wide doorway that lay beyond. It was barely noon and there was much work to be done here at the dock, where the *Compass* and *Johanna* were both moored. It had been too long since he had ridden through his fields to see how the crops were coming along; there were a dozen things that required his attention in Easton Town. Certainly, it was no time to be going back to the Great House unless he intended to attack the mountain of correspondence and ledger work that waited for him there—and he knew that was not what drew him up the lane toward the pillared mansion now.

No, this morning, like so many mornings and afternoons and

early evenings, he was dropping his work and hurrying to the house to satisfy some uneasiness, some suspicion that he could not name. Why had it become so much harder, lately, to keep his mind on the affairs that needed his attention; why was he scurrying back to the house at odd times, like a boy tip-toeing back to a forbidden crock of sweetcakes?

What did he expect to find when he got there, except the servants doing their work and Vivian directing them, if she wasn't reading or doing some embroidery or just sitting on the porch, looking out over the river? And was it Vivian who aroused this taunting restlessness in him or was it Gracellen? And why should either?

Gracellen was still Gracellen, changed not a whit by her marriage to Charles Rawlent. No man, he told himself, could change Gracellen; she would ever be a Worth, her father's daughter. That pipsqueak Rawlent—perhaps it had been a mistake to allow the girl to wed this nincompoop, but once married to even a jackanapes like him there'd be less chance of her running off with Task Tillman. When the children started coming, she would be separated still further from the big man she—aye, let's confess it—loved.

This Rawlent, now; did he in his silly vanity ever think Gracellen really loved him? Had he found out, had Gracellen told him yet, that he'd been chosen as a weapon to strike at Task Tillman? He, Anthony Worth, would have preferred Gracellen to have picked another husband to show Tillman he meant nothing to her but he had raised no objections for fear his opposition would send Gracellen flying off on another tangent that might take her back to Tillman.

Or did he really wish Gracellen had picked another, stronger man? He knew she did not love Rawlent; would he have allowed her to marry a man he thought she loved?

He shook his head angrily—of course he would!

And, by and large, it was a good match. Charley's family was a good one, an old one, though not too well situated now. Rawlent's father was in the Assembly and could prove useful.

Anthony had long been eyeing a tract of land the Rawlents were clinging to; when the time was ripe, he'd offer a loan through his son-in-law that could hardly be refused and, eventually, the land would be his.

As far as Gracellen's happiness with her husband was concerned, Gracellen was too much her father's daughter to ever be made unhappy by the man. If, as he suspected, she would never love another than Task Tillman, one bed partner would serve as well as another if she must have a husband, as she thought she must.

In fact, his mind ran on, it was better, perhaps, that his daughter's husband was such a witless coxcomb for another reason. A man of stronger will or sharper perception might interest himself too much in what went on by Peartree Creek. If Rawlent ever interested himself in that, the fool would give himself away so soon that steps could be taken before any damage was done.

He reached the side door which led to his office passageway, entered it and moved down its length to the oak door beyond which lay his desk. He paused for a moment, listening, and then snorted at himself—by God, he surely was stricken with the vapours if he had taken to listening for nothing before walking into a room! He moved through the office without a glance at the papers on his desk and went on into the main house.

It was what he had expected; Vivian was superintending the servants who were giving the west wing parlor a cleaning (though why it should be necessary to take down everything and put it back up every other day or so was beyond him), giving her orders in her low-pitched voice, quietly competent as she had been born and trained to be. He stood in the drawing room door, eyeing her slender back, the coil of glistening black hair that she wore low on her neck.

Vivian Dangerfield, third daughter of a threadbare British nobleman with an old and tattered title that had not been in royal favor since the days of the First Charles. Vivian Dangerfield, whom Anthony Worth had met at a London reception and whom he had instantly sworn to make his, whom he had determined to make his even after his headlong proposal of marriage had brought a sort of shocked amusement from the girl.

"Why, Mister Worth," she had smiled, her deep eyes wondering, "you Americans carry flattery to odd lengths."

"No flattery, Madam," Anthony had protested fervently. "I mean it. I've been fair crazy since I—"

"You're a stranger here, of course," Vivian had cut in, "or else you'd have known I'm betrothed and will be married in the Spring."

That should have made him smother this wild urge to possess the girl. Instead, it had served only to inflame him. Obstacles had always been challenges to Anthony Worth; this betrothal was no exception. Inquiry told him that Vivian was to marry a young and charming gentleman who wore a "Sir" before his name and who owned, or was possessed by, the immoderate conviction that his luck at cards was bound to change.

It had been a comparatively easy matter for Anthony to gain admittance to this Sir Robert's favorite gaming club and it had been easier still to get the young man several thousands of pounds in his, Anthony's, debt. This had not necessitated any double-dealing—or at least not much. The young man's blind confidence in his gambling talents, pitted against Anthony's abacus brain, had been quite enough.

Anthony had expected a fiery scene when he went to his young debtor with his proposition but the whole affair had been conducted in an atmosphere of complete understanding. Cancellation of the debt, plus a sizable sack of guineas, would do nicely as a substitute for the fair Vivian, thankee.

"I'm a hound for doing this, of course," Sir Robert had said cheerfully, "but I look at it as saving dear Viv from much unhappiness, married to a slave to fickle Dame Fortune."

Vivian's gaunt, seedy father had been even easier than Sir Robert to convince of the advantages of Anthony's plan. Worth's words were very persuasive, indeed, carrying with them as they did the echo of clinking coins in every syllable. His Lordship would not dream of selling his daughter; no, certainly not! But a fond father must look to his daughter's well-being and it was not hard for Vivian's father to see that this big man from Maryland was the ideal person to soothe the child's heart, sorely injured as it was by Sir Robert's inexplicable jilting.

Vivian herself, when Anthony had approached her with a second proposal of marriage, this time with the rival gone from the scene and with her father's passionately hopeful blessing, seemed only distantly interested in the whole affair. That her betrothed's abrupt dismissal had been a hard blow was visible in the shadowed eyes, the drooping mouth, but Vivian did her mourning out of sight and hearing if she mourned at all; outwardly, she was impassively resigned to the strange and sudden course of events; she accepted Anthony Worth's attentions almost listlessly.

"Of course, Mister Worth," she said when she finally nodded yes, "you know that I don't love you."

"I'll teach you to, my dear," Anthony promised. He was confident that he could, too.

So, in the end, everybody was better off by the fact that Anthony had met Vivian Dangerfield at that London reception. His Lordship was able to pay up his debts and cut quite a figure in circles he had avoided for years because they had been too liberally sprinkled with his creditors. Sir Robert had a run of good luck at the gaming tables before the cards and dice abandoned him so completely that, eventually, he disappeared. Anthony Worth had as his fourth wife the youngest and most beautiful of all of them. As for Vivian, she found herself mistress of the finest place on the Eastern Shore of Maryland, with an army of servants at her beck and call, with all the luxuries she could wish for, hers for the asking, and with a husband who was the biggest figure in that part of the country. And, as anyone could see, being married to Anthony was a much finer thing than being the wife of a handsome wastrel of her own years who doubtless would have caused her all kinds of misery. Oh yes, she was a fortunate young woman, was Vivian Dangerfield Worth.

The dark-eyed woman turned now, conscious of her husband's

eyes upon her back, and greeted him quietly. This expression she wore, Anthony told himself, had been often on her face since that unfortunate incident that had happened the morning after Gracellen's betrothal ball. It was as though Vivian knew the answer to the puzzling question of why her husband must see her at such odd and inconvenient intervals and found the answer amusing. Well, if she did, damn it, he'd be obliged if she'd tell him!

"Yes, Anthony?" she asked.

"Why—er—nothing, nothing," he replied, brusquely. "I had some things that needed looking to in the office and—and I thought I'd relish a drink, that's all."

To prove this, he moved to the sideboard with its array of decanters, poured something—it turned out to be sherry, which he detested—into a glass and gulped it. To emphasize his explanation, he poured another drink of the disgusting wine and swallowed it, repressing a grimace. Vivian watched him, her face telling him nothing.

Anthony set the glass down too hard on the silver tray and stalked, virtually stomped, into the office. He had made himself look foolish, he knew; Vivian and all the blacks within earshot had known he had not come to the Great House to attend to anything in the office. In a savage mood, he jerked a pile of papers toward him as he fell into his desk chair, and began studying them. They must have made sense else the people who had written them would not have wasted their time, but they proved so much gibberish to Anthony Worth.

He gave up trying to decipher them after a time and leaned back in his chair, his hands behind his head.

All this, he told himself, was some vagary that came with age—not that sixty-five was old, certainly. Or not very old. He was still a better man, mentally and physically, than most of the young squirts he met these days but he was tired. That was it; he was tired! He had worked ceaselessly since he could remember and his weary brain was playing tricks on him, confusing him with these doubts he could not put a finger on. Why did he keep remembering that drunken morning after the betrothal ball, for instance? He had been at his worst, yes, and he might have said some harsh things to Vivian, but what wife wasn't spoken to harshly on occasion; what woman didn't expect to see her husband in his cups now and then? Why was he always hearkening back to that morning? It was a whimsey, a vapour, that was all, and he must rid himself of it!

And he'd have to guard against all these fantasies that tried to distract a man when he reached a certain age. Being Anthony Worth, he could beat these whimsies just as he had beaten everything else that had tried to balk him.

Except that damned Task Tillman. The man was still at Larkspur Hill, still biding his time. Or had he been wrong in thinking that Task Tillman knew? No, he had been right—but, perhaps, he had put too much importance on—

"God damn it!" he muttered aloud. "Make up your mind!"

He had been right. Task Tillman knew everything and yet he did nothing except till his acres at Larkspur Hill. And good, productive acres they were, too; acres that would be well added to Fairoverlea.

Was Tillman afraid to make his move? No. Why did he hesitate, then, to force the issue, if he knew that Anthony Worth had burned Larkspur Hill, killed his father, burned his tobacco barns, turned Gracellen's heart against him with black lies? This last, he certainly knew, and yet he ploughed and planted like a clod; he had not made one move that might be parried to bring his ruin.

A man who waited, who took his own time, was the dangerous man; Anthony Worth should know that if anyone did. What was Task planning now, where would he strike and when?

It was enough to make a man look over his shoulder, listen for nothing as he had listened when he had paused at the doorway leading from the passageway to the office.

And was that why he had listened? Was his nerve going, his grip slipping?

He laughed and the laughter brought him no comfort. It lacked something that would have been in it not so long before. Before he had begun noticing Vivian's expression. Before he had begun listening outside closed doors. Before he had begun spending so much time wondering what Task Tillman was planning.

He brought his hands down from behind his head and pounded the desktop with both fists.

"No!" he swore silently. "No, it's not true! I'm still Anthony Worth, the one the niggers and a lot of white people call *The King*! I'm not old! I'm still strong! By God, I can still beat 'em all!"

There was a knock on the door to the main house and he jerked up his head, stared at the panelling. The knock sounded again and Anthony relaxed. He knew that knock; it was only Joseph.

"Come," he called.

The butler, Joseph, entered with a deep and polished bow.

"A gentleman to see you, sir," the slave intoned in perfect English. "His name is Mister Guthrie. He says it's important that he see you, sir, on a matter of business."

Guthrie? Guthrie? He knew no Guthrie. He waved an impatient hand.

"Show him in," he said, "and tell whoever looks after such things that the door knocker hasn't seen the polishing cloth in months."

"Yes sir," Joseph bowed, and disappeared. Anthony wondered vaguely if the knocker really did need polishing.

Mister Guthrie turned out to be a small man, dressed so conservatively that he seemed almost ministerial in appearance. He wore a dark blue coat with plain dark bone buttons, a grey waistcoat which showed no fobs or seals, a stock without ruffles or lace, grey trousers too loose to be in the mode and wrinkled where they had been stuffed into his boot tops during his ride to Fairoverlea. In his hand he carried a bell-crowned beaver hat that had seen better days.

His voice, when he spoke, was a delicate thing, flutelike and with exact enunciation.

"Mister Worth," he said, bowing, "it's very kind of you to see me, as busy as I know you must be. Permit me to introduce myself. Edward Guthrie, sir, at your service. Edward Guthrie of"— he looked Anthony Worth full in the eye—"of London."

5

"They're going at it all wrong, I tell you! The thing to do is not to wait till the British come at us; we should go out and fight 'em now! We ought to invade Canada right away; take their base at Bermuda. I tell you, Gracellen, if I were running things you'd see some action, not this do-nothing waiting for the fools in Washington to make up their minds!"

Gracellen looked across the second floor sitting room at her husband, nodded absently and returned her eyes to the copy of the Annapolis *Gazette* she was reading.

"And all these militia companies hereabouts," Charles Rawlent went on in his high, complaining voice, "they all ought to be joined in one regiment, I say. Under one command, the men could be drilled to fight as a unit; the way it is, they all have their separate ways of doin' things and none of 'em, save the Dragons, anything like right. Make one militia regiment, I say, and we'd be better off."

Gracellen lowered the paper again. Her voice was innocent as she asked:

"Who'd command this regiment, Charley? Somebody from the Fencibles or the Easton Militia, I suppose, seeing theirs were the first companies in these parts. Or perhaps Joseph Nicholson, over at Queen's Town."

Rawlent blew out his cheeks, his neck swelling beneath the tight collar of the claret uniform coat he always wore.

"Nicholson?" he demanded, his voice shrill. "Why, God's sake, Gracellen, he couldn't command a dog to heel! Have you ever seen Nicholson's company? Made up of any kind of person who'd enlist, I swear it!"

"While yours, dear Charley," Gracellen said softly, her eyes on her newspaper, "is a company of gentlemen, I know. No one admitted but the very best."

"Ah well," Rawlent nodded, smirking, "I guess you could say that, if you'd a mind to. We've been right careful who we've taken in. We want only the right people and those who'd attract favorable attention from Annapolis."

"I'm sure," said Gracellen in the same tone, "Governor Winder has his eye on you and your Dragons."

"Well, not too close an eye, I hope," Rawlent said uneasily. "I'd hate the Dragons to be called for service in the Regular Army. The company wasn't mobilized to serve under some nobody, y'know."

He left his chair and strutted into the adjoining bedroom, Gracellen's eyes following his exit. When he was gone she looked out the window at the boxwood-bordered garden below and permitted herself a sigh. Dear Charley; he was so good-looking, he had such beautiful manners—and he was such a fool!

Where, for instance, had he ever gotten the notion that he was a military genius; he, who had never handled a gun, not even a fowling piece, until militia companies had become fashionable? And did he think he was captain of his Dragon Footguards for any other reason than that he had near bankrupted himself outfitting the company before Father had come to his aid? Yes, knowing Charley Rawlent as she was coming to know her husband, Gracellen admitted that Charles doubtless did; he probably reasoned that he would have been chosen to lead the Dragons no matter who paid for those gorgeous uniforms and heavy muskets, the fifes and drums.

"Damn it, Gracellen," came Rawlent's voice from the bedroom,

"I can't find my sword again! What stupid, worthless wench has hidden it this time? I swear I'll—"

"It's by the doorway in here," Gracellen called with only a touch of irritation in her voice. "You said the handle had to be polished and so I—"

"Hilt, not handle!" Rawlent broke in. He came to the bedroom door, his face flushed by the exertions of his search for the sword. "Can't you ever remember the proper term? Handle, you say, when it's hilt and you call a musket a gun. It's a piece, I keep telling you, and a pistol is a sidearm. You spoke last night of Bayne Oliver as one of my men, yet you knew he's a lieutenant— he's one of my officers, not one of my men! Must I keep telling you—"

"Charles, dear," Gracellen said silkily, "I hate to interrupt your lecture on military things but one more word along those lines and I'll fling this footstool at your head."

She smiled widely at his apoplectic stare. Charles Rawlent's neck was swollen again but as she watched, his astonished anger began to fade, the crimson ebbed from his face and her husband began the spluttering that would end in an apology, as these scenes always did. She sighed again and went back to the *Gazette*.

"I'm sorry, love," Rawlent stammered. "It's—I'm so wrapped up in the Dragons that I forget my manners sometimes, I fear. I didn't mean to speak to you so bluntly. Forgive me, my dear."

She tilted her head to receive his kiss on her cheek, not lifting her eyes from the printed sheet in her hands.

"Of course, love," she murmured absently. "You'd best be off for Easton, hadn't you? You can't be late for the drill, you know."

"I do know, curse it!" Rawlent said. He moved toward the corner where the resplendent sword stood in its scabbard, propped against the wall. "You'd think a man's lieutenants could look after things if he's not there, but no! Unless I'm on hand to attend to every detail, the drill goes all wrong, I swear. The men"—with proud exasperation—"simply won't do their best for anyone but me."

He buckled on the basket-hilted sword, picked up the shako

that was never far from his reach and settled it on his head, fixed the strap under the point of his chin. Gracellen looked at him as he examined himself in the pierglass. He *was* a lovely sight, she told herself, even if she could not see him thus without thinking of a young girl preening herself in a new ballgown.

"Goodbye, love," he said as he tore himself away from the glass. "I don't know when I'll be back this evening. There's so much to attend to, y'know."

"I know," she smiled. "Poor Charles, kept from his home and hearth by this awful war."

He glanced at her suspiciously, was reassured by her expression and puffed more.

" 'Tis little enough to sacrifice," he told her solemnly, "beside what we all must do when the fightin' begins."

He left her then, a very heroic figure, an uncomplaining patriot on his way to do his duty though it meant leaving his beautiful wife. She kept her eyes on the empty doorway, hearing him clatter down the stairs, listening to his high-pitched bawl for his horse to be brought around. She wondered idly if she should go to one of the front rooms, to wave her kerchief at him from a window as he rode away, as tearful wives did in novels. She decided against it.

He would be gone, she knew, until well toward midnight and he would return full of brandy and boasting. Which would be all right if he didn't snore, later on when he fell asleep.

But—that was hours away and in the meantime there were a million minutes to occupy somehow. Ride? She was sick of riding; she had covered more back roads on horseback during the past months than she had ever dreamed existed. Go for a sail? No, she was tired of sailing the same old stretches of water. Order the "chariot" and go visiting? And who would she call on who'd not have a mouthful of vacuous chatter and nothing else? Her unmarried friends spent all their time talking around the question of what Charley had done to her the first night (as if some of them didn't know firsthand what was done) and the married friends all whined on and on about babies. No, she would not go calling.

166

If her father were free, she would ride with him, sail with him or even just sit and talk to him, but her father was caught up in some problem that kept him from enjoying the rides, the sailing trips, the talks they both had shared in other days. Anthony, in fact, didn't look too well, although there was nothing definite about his failing; it was just that his laugh was a little less ready, his thoughts had taken to wandering lately while he listened, there was always the impression that something weighty was bothering him, something that couldn't be discussed, even with Gracellen.

Oh well, she reminded herself, her father had been through these moods before and he had always done what had needed to be done and had come back to being his own self again after his victory over whatever troubled him. This spell would pass, too, whenever he found the answer to the puzzle that was claiming his thoughts these days.

If Jett were only home, the two of them could think up something to do; they could always make the hours fly if only by squabbling with each other. It was time the *Heron* was coming in, too; Father had told her several days ago that Filkey had begun his watch for the schooner. God grant that Filkey sight her and gallop the long miles to Fairoverlea with his good news again.

She wondered how Jett would get along with Charles during this stay at home. That one time he had been at Fairoverlea since she had married, Jett had been scrupulously pleasant to her husband but she had recognized the signs that had told her that his laughter was never far beneath the surface when Charles was in the room. And when Jett looked at her, it had seemed that his eyes were faintly mocking, as though asking her if she ever compared Charley with what Task Tillman would have been as a husband. He had had the sense, though, never to mention Task's name in anything he'd said to her.

It was almost impossible that she had not met Task face to face in all this time since Anthony Worth had said no, living as close to each other as they did, but that was the fact. She had glimpsed him three or four times but always at a distance; if he had seen her she had not known of it. They said he stayed close to Larkspur Hill and when he did attend any evening affair it was some stuffy men's meeting arranged by Squire Wills; he never accepted any invitations he may have gotten to balls or routs where he might meet Charles and her.

"Task Tillman?" was the inevitable answer to her careless question. "I haven't seen him in years, my dear. They say he lives a hermit's life."

"He's quite the woman-hater," one cat added. "But of course you wouldn't know why, dear Gracellen."

She had been half tempted to ask Jett if he had seen Task during that brief home visit between voyages of the *Heron* but she had not; she didn't know whether or not Jett had looked up his old friend during his week at Fairoverlea. She thought he would be sure to, ordinarily, but Anthony may have put his foot down on that, and Jett, for all his recklessness, followed Anthony Worth's orders.

Once again, Gracellen wondered what her life would be like now if she had believed Task, not her father, that night so long ago.

Not so comfortable—so empty?—as it was now, that was certain. If she had not listened to Father and had gone with Task, married him despite everything Father could have done, she would have doomed herself to a life of trouble. Or would Anthony Worth have forgiven her eventually? Doubtful, this; exceedingly doubtful. She knew her father well enough to know that he did not forgive easily, not even his own daughter. And he would have little mercy on a girl who would go to a man who had besmirched the name of her own mother.

(Why could she not believe Task and Task's father had done that? Father had said they did, hadn't he, and wasn't that enough?)

But if she had gone with Task, Anthony would have worked ceaselessly to break up the marriage, crush her husband beneath his heel and force her to come back to Fairoverlea on his own terms, which would not be gentle.

Her chin rose as she considered this. Did Father think he was strong enough to make her abandon Task? How wrong he was! She would starve with Task, live in a hovel—

Her brief laugh rang through the sitting room.

"You idiot!" she told herself aloud. "Next, you'll be having a litter of children by this dream husband of yours."

She left her chair and moved into the bedroom, sat down at the dressing table to unpin and brush her red hair. The strokes of the brush usually acted as an anodyne, guaranteed to shut off vagrant thoughts that pestered her. She brushed steadily, resolutely refusing to think of anything but the sting of the bristles on her scalp.

No, she would not think or if she had to think she would consider how much simpler, how much easier, how much more pleasant, really, was this life as the wife of Charles Rawlent than it would have been with—

She would list all Charley's fine qualities and prove to herself again that she had done the right thing in marrying him instead of—

She would plan the furnishings of the house Father was going to build for them when this war was over and trade was reopened with England (Anthony might magically furnish Fairoverlea during a war but that place was his; he had shown no inclination to summon the same magic to put up Gracellen's and Charles Rawlent's house) and think how different it would be from anything Task Tillman could—

She flung the brush to the floor, knocked over the chair as she stood up, her hands to her temples, her unbound hair streaming about her face.

"I'm happy, I'm happy, I'm happy!" she screamed at her mirror. "You hear me—*I'm happy!*"

6

THE United States had no Navy worth the name when the War of 1812 opened and her Army was nothing to boast about, but in the desperate situation she found herself in after the first heady flush of her Declaration of War wore off she searched for a weapon at hand and came up with a formidable one, the privateer.

One month after war was declared, there were sixty-five privateers ranging the Atlantic under the American flag and, as the *London Statesman* had prophesied, they "caused great damage, harassing the sea lanes and even the Channel." So great were the rewards of the first successful privateers that it was not long before the owners of virtually every seaworthy vessel of schooner weight or heavier were besieging the government for commissions and letters of marque, all hot to have a go at this rich, exciting game.

The privateering war against England brought some very dubious men out of hiding with loud cries of patriotism. Some of the gentlemen who applied for letters of marque had a suspicious resemblance to persons who had sailed under the Jolly Roger, regardless of the names they offered. The government could hardly afford to be too choosey at a time like this but it did insist that every skipper awarded a privateering commission post a bond of from $5,000 to $10,000, depending on the size of his vessel, to be forfeited if he ever fell victim to excessive patriotism and began hunting down ships bearing Spanish, Dutch, Portuguese or other such neutral flags. That these bonds were posted promptly and uncomplainingly was an indication of the riches the privateers saw waiting out on the Atlantic, or at least thought they saw.

According to the rules laid down, a privateer kept all English prizes seized, ships and cargoes, and furthermore was paid twenty dollars a head for each Britisher taken prisoner from a vessel of equal or larger size than the privateer, this qualification being intended to prevent the wholesale rounding up of the crews of Newfoundland fishing smacks at twenty dollars per man. Later, on March 3, 1813, Congress voted to pay a privateer half the full value of any British armed vessel she could sink. This was the dream of every privateering skipper, to somehow blow up a British ship of the line and retire with more money than a man could spend in a dozen lifetimes. A good many American schooners and brigs, dazzled by that lure, made fantastically foolhardy attempts to cash in on the offer and were sent to the bottom themselves but their fate never discouraged the others who came after them.

Although they scored no great successes against the seventy-four-gun British warships, the privateers exceeded all the brightest hopes of their effectiveness from the start. In two years and eight months of the war, American privateers captured or sank a total of one thousand six hundred and thirty-four British vessels of all classes and disrupted British commerce seriously, almost crippling it altogether.

The first of these privateers, the ships that proved how much money and glory was to be found in the service, were light schooners manned by eighty men or less, generally mounting nine twelve-pound guns. As England armed her merchantmen with guns and strengthened their convoys, these first privateers gave way to heavier schooners and brigs carrying crews of a hundred and twenty to a hundred and sixty men. Usually they were armed with long pivot guns of sixteen to twenty-four pounds, fore and aft, and either six or eight lighter guns, fourteen-pounders, in broadside.

The first months of the war established the reputations of some great privateering ships and captains and one of the greatest of these was Joshua Barney, later to become a Commodore of the Navy, and his *Rossie*. Between July 12 and November 10, 1812, Barney seized or sank four British naval vessels, eight brigs, three schooners and three sloops and captured two hundred and seventeen British seamen.

Close behind Barney came Thomas Boyle and his *Comet* and, later, his *Chasseur*. Boyle, a Marblehead, Massachusetts, man, was the boy wonder of the privateers, having been given command of his own ship at the age of sixteen. Then there were James Dooley and his *Rolla*, William Stafford and his *Dolphin*, John Murphy, who lost his luck when he gave up command of his fortune-favored *Globe* to take over the newer, bigger *Grampus* and was killed when a hail of British grape swept his new ship's quarterdeck. There was Robert Miller and his *Revenge*. There was Jett Worth and his *Lorelei*.

She was a beautiful lady, was *Lorelei*, with lines like a race-horse and the striking speed of a barracuda. She could find wind in a vacuum, she could take any gale and any sea with enough canvas aloft to make an oldtime skipper grow pale; she could run up on a victim and be alongside before her hapless prey could bend on another sheet. She could show her pretty tail to any vessel afloat, if Jett was so minded, or play in kittenish circles out of gunshot from a baffled man-o'-war.

Jett had wished for a brig-sloop after his encounter with the schooner *St. Lawrence* off the Barbadoes; Anthony Worth gave him a vessel that made the best brig-sloop seem a wallowing tub in comparison. Anthony turned over to Jett the fastest all-purpose ship afloat, a vessel of the design that had revolutionized all ship-building, which had confounded all critics, had given the United States a badly-needed advantage in these early days of the War of 1812.

Lorelei was a Baltimore Clipper, the sharp-prowed, lean-hulled, high-sticked queen of the seven seas.

Six days after Gracellen Worth flung her hairbrush to the floor and screamed her happiness, Filkey came pounding to Fairoverlea with his news that the *Heron* had been sighted by the southernmost of Anthony's relay chain of lookouts stationed close to the Virginia Capes. The following night, more out of habit than need, now that he did not have to elude revenue cutters, Jett made a dark landing at the Peartree Creek dock. Anthony Worth, Vivian and Gracellen were on hand to greet him; Charles Rawlent was left snoring in his bed, exhausted from a trying drill with his Dragon Footguards and the staff meeting at the tavern that had followed it.

"Uncle," Jett cried as he leapt to the dock, "it's war, isn't it?"

"Aye, Jett," Worth nodded. "It's been war since June and no way to let you know."

"I was given the word," the young, dark-skinned man grinned, "by a British armed schooner. She was kind enough to tell me by a foolish shot at a range a gull couldn't fly in a day."

"And you—"

"Oh, we gave her back her greeting with a ball into her bow and touched her up with the nine-pounders a bit before we took our leave. But now it's war, what about a brig-sloop, Uncle, that'll—"

"And must you babble about the war when we're here to greet you after all these months?" Gracellen broke in. "We've spent many a day wondering whether you were still afloat or food for the sharks and you scarce give us a glance before you plunge into talk about brig-sloops and British armed schooners. Impolite, I call it."

Jett turned to her, his eyes dancing in the fitful light of the lanterns and torches that illuminated the dock, and made a sweeping bow.

"My Lady Rawlent," he murmured as he straightened. "Forgive me, please. Truly, I didn't expect to find you here; a bride could scarce be expected to stand shivering on a dock in the dead

173

of night when back at Great House there'd be a warm bed and—"

"Oh, hush your leering talk!" Gracellen snapped, "and come and give me a proper greeting."

Jett walked up to his cousin, his hat in his hand, and bestowed a light kiss on the corner of her mouth, looking past her at Vivian.

"And my dear aunt," he went on. "This is a welcome, indeed." He moved past Gracellen to take Vivian's hand and bend over it with a courtliness that would have done credit to a French vicomte.

"Welcome home, Jett," Anthony Worth's wife said in a low voice. "We have all missed you."

"And your missing me has brought me back again, safe and sound," Jett said. "I swear, 'twas your good wishes that made that British schooner captain open fire when he was ten leagues away."

"A good voyage, Jett?" Anthony asked to break the tiny pause that followed.

"Good enough, Uncle," Jett nodded. "Of course I took your advice and stayed away from most of my usual ports of call. You read the backs of the cards right, sure enough."

"I had my sources of information," Worth explained. "My friends had ways of knowing the war declaration would be voted ere you got back to port. Some of my—er—colleagues were not so fortunate. They say the British seized a half-dozen American ships they trapped when the news of the war vote reached London. You spoke of a brig-sloop, Jett; I anticipated your—"

"And must we discuss all this standing here in this night mist?" Gracellen asked impatiently. "We'll all be croupy in the morning, breathing this damp."

"Aye, let's to the house," Anthony agreed. "We'll talk over our affairs in comfort, with a glass or two to ward off the damp the ladies fear so much." He threw an arm about Jett's shoulders as the little group turned toward the land end of the dock. "Ah, boy, it's good to have you back! I confess I've had my fears that

I did wrong, sending you out in a cockleshell armed with a few slingshots, knowing war wasn't far away. Had it been anyone but you, I'd have kept you ashore until I had a stronger vessel to put under your feet."

"I'll need one, Uncle," Jett said seriously, "before I sail again. 'Twas pure luck that I happened against a schooner and not a frigate out there."

"Aye, and a heavier ship ye'll be on when you raise sail again."

On shore, at the end of the dock, waited the three Worth henchmen, Will Roan, Marsden and Tom Womble, grotesque figures in the dark. Both Gracellen and Vivian drew their cloaks closer instinctively as they passed the trio, their heads bowed so that they might not accidentally meet the eyes of the brute, the scarecrow or the obscene Buddha.

The scar-faced Roan, his powerful shoulders straining the dirty jersey shirt he wore, stepped forward with a knuckle to his forehead as Jett approached.

"Fair landing, Cap'n," he growled, "and many of them, sir."

"Thanks, Roan," Jett smiled.

"And, sir," Roan went on with a rush, "now it's war, p'raps ye'd convince *The King* I'd be more worth to all concerned aboard y'r new vessel, sir."

"Why, scratch me," Jett laughed, "there's time enough for that when I get my ship."

"Aye, time a-plenty for that, Roan," Anthony rumbled. "Get busy dischargin' *Heron*."

Roan touched his forehead again, nodded, and went down the dock toward the stringpiece. Womble was the next member of the threesome to step up to Jett.

"My prayers were always wi' ye, Cap'n," he chuckled.

"And still I made safe landing," Jett said. "A miracle in itself! But I do thank you, Tom."

"Yessir," Womble said and cast a fleeting glance at Anthony. "And sir, did ye happen to—"

"Aye," Jett broke in. "An Indian carving, very rare. Mister Greer will show it to you."

"Thankee, thankee," Womble bobbed and waddled happily down the dock.

"What's this about an Indian carving?" Anthony Worth demanded. "What's Womble want with such stuff?"

"Why Uncle, he's quite a collector, in his way," Jett explained blandly. "Ye'd not think it to look at him but he has an eye for art, of a sort."

"And I can imagine the sort," Anthony growled. "I'd best look into this and—"

"Nay, nay, Uncle," Jett protested. "It does no harm and certainly the man must lead a lonely life, never leaving Fairoverlea that I can remember."

"And for good reason," Worth muttered. "He'd—yes, Marsden?"

"I only wanted to say greeting to Cap'n Jett," Marsden croaked from behind the scarf that muffled him to his beaked nose, "and say I'm happy to see him bring the *Heron* and himself safe home again."

"Thanks, Marsden," Jett said shortly and turned back to his uncle. "I'm fair parched for that glass you mentioned, sir, and the ladies are waiting."

On the path that led to the cart lane, he laughed again.

"So Marsden's happy to see me back," he said. "By God, that's the biggest compliment of all! If the man was ever happy, it must have been when he was a babe in arms, and I doubt even that. Roan, I can stand, for all his nightmare's face; Womble, I could even like though I'd never let him get behind me in the dark. But Marsden, that death's head—why do you keep him here, Uncle? He chills me with his buzzard's eye every time it lands on me and the ladies fair shiver when they have to pass him."

"He's useful," Anthony said briefly. "You care for your crew, Jett, and I'll take care of my men here."

"Aye sir," Jett Worth returned, feeling the sting of his uncle's words. "I didn't mean to question that."

In the gun room of the Great House and with the decanter

circulating, Jett told the story of his meeting with the *St. Lawrence* and dressed the story so that Gracellen and Vivian were laughing, while Anthony wore a broad smile.

"—and as she staggered out of the turn," the young captain said, "my Britisher saw us a-flittin' down the cowpath and so loosed all her guns, both starb'd and port, I swear, to dent the sea with a ton of shot and cheer the splashes. I've no doubt but she's back in Bermuda now, reportin' the sinking of an American frigate with all hands."

He looked across the small room and smiled at Vivian.

"Dear Aunt," he said, "I must admit I was amazed at your countrymen's sailing skill. What's this I've heard for so long about the Englishman being invincible at sea? The *St. Lawrence* was handled like a small boy's raft, I swear."

"Why, dear Nephew," Vivian returned, "I suppose the schooner was commanded by some relative of mine who must have recognized you for your derring-do and said: 'I'll not harm Vivian Dangerfield's favorite relative, 'pon my word.'"

"Then you'd best tell all the sea-farin' members of your family to fly some pennant so I'll recognize 'em when next I meet 'em in the brig-sloop I hope to have," Jett said. "I'd not do harm to any of your cousins from England, seeing the *St. Lawrence's* skipper was so kind to me."

"I'll post a letter off direct," Vivian nodded. "Anthony must have some way of seeing that it goes to England, eh, Anthony?"

The big blunt-faced man frowned blackly for a moment and then joined in the laughter.

"Oh, certainly," he boomed. "I have the direct ear of the British Admiralty itself. They've picked me to oversee this war, y'understand, much as a disinterested party presides at a duel, so name your wants of either side and I'll see that you get them."

"Then get me some action that'll win prizes for my brig-sloop," Jett said.

"But it's no brig-sloop," Gracellen cried. "'Tis a much finer vessel than any brig-sloop, Jett. It's—"

"Now, damn it!" Anthony Worth cut in with a growl. "Trust a woman to ruin a surprise!"

"Surprise?" Jett asked. "What's this?"

"Oh, Father thinks he has to play the whole show," Gracellen said, tossing her head, "even though we all had a hand in it, Vivian and I. We pleaded your case, dear Jett, when Father was all but convinced the *Lorelei* needed an older man in command. Didn't we, Vivian?"

"Now, 'twasn't me who raised that argument," Anthony protested. "The builders were the ones who set up that cry. I had it in mind that Jett would command from the start."

"Pooh!" Gracellen scoffed. "Had not Vivian and I pestered you, you'd have put old Griffin in her and—"

"Your pardon, please," Jett interrupted, "but if somebody would explain what this is all about, I'd be grateful. What or who is Lorelei? I take it she's a vessel but—"

"She's a clipper, lad," Anthony Worth said, "and the prettiest ship afloat, you'll see. Four hundred tons, built in Baltimore, and spoken for a dozen times before she left the ways, but I had friends who saw she came to me. Griffin's in Baltimore now, choosing the best crew from the regiment that's clamoring to sail aboard her. He should be finished with that task tomorrow or the next day and bring her down here for you to take command."

"A clipper ship!" Jett Worth breathed. "Now, by the Lord, we'll have ourselves a merry party! I've seen but one and that one off Cape Hatteras. She was a flying ghost of a ship, now here, now gone, and the beauty of her fair took my breath away."

"I don't know what clipper you saw," Anthony said, "but I'll wager my last dollar that she was not half so pretty as *Lorelei*."

"But must I wait till Captain Griffin brings her down here?" Jett asked. "Can't I take a skiff to Baltimore and board her now? 'Twould be but a day's sail and—"

"Nay, Jett," his uncle said brusquely. "I've given Griffin the job of shaping up her crew and attending to the provisioning and such. He ranks you in years of service with me—'twas a hard blow to him that I'm giving you the vessel. I'd not add insult to

178

injury by having you take command before his duties are finished. You can afford to wait a day or so before taking over."

"Aye, Uncle," Jett nodded, "but the waiting will be as hard as a bridegroom's waiting for his bride." He turned toward Gracellen. "And speakin' of bridegrooms, where's the worthy Charles? Don't tell me that his militia company's been called to the front, if there is a front."

Gracellen's chin jutted as the color tinged her high cheekbones.

"He didn't come home from the drill till past midnight," she explained haughtily, "and I did not wake him."

"Ah," Jett murmured. "The drill."

"Yes, and what's wrong with the drill?" Gracellen flared. "There's nothing for you to laugh at about a man's giving his time and effort to make his company the best, the readiest, on the Eastern Shore, Jett Worth! If it were not for—"

"Hold, hold!" Anthony intervened. "Nobody laughed at Charley's work with his militia company, my dear. Why must you be so touchy on the subject? God's love, let anybody say a word about the Dragon Footguards and you're flyin' at his throat!"

"There was a look in Jett's eye," Gracellen grumbled. "And something in the way he said: 'The drill.'"

Her cousin smiled at her benignly.

"You know, Gracellen-aleen," he murmured, "I'd rather blind both eyes and cut out my tongue than ever seem to make mock of dear Charles."

"I know what you think," Gracellen returned hotly, "and it's not so, in the least!"

"And then I'm wrong," Jett said imperturbably, "though I don't know what it is you know I think, exactly." He turned to his uncle. "Rather than risk another storm, sir, perhaps you can tell me what's the news these days? What's the war sentiment on the Eastern Shore?"

Anthony shrugged his heavy shoulders, looking down at the glass he cradled in both broad, blunt-fingered hands.

"Some blow hot and some blow cold," he explained. "The

young men seem distressed that the British have made no move in this direction—indeed, your brush with the *St. Lawrence* is the first real proof we've had that England is indeed at war with us. There was dirty business in Baltimore in July, some Federalists killed and beaten, and since then we've got a new Governor, Levin Winder, out of it. This Winder straddles the fence; he was a loud spokesman 'gainst the war but now he says he's bound to do his patriotic duty 'gainst the British. He'll do it, too, when the time comes, I'm pretty sure, but his idea of duty and the War Hawks' may not jibe."

He sipped at his drink and reached for a cheroot in the jar at his elbow.

"They're building a great fort at Annapolis," he went on, "and naming it Fort Madison. In Baltimore, they've got two new forts, McHenry and Star Fort, and also cannon on Federal Hill. At Easton Town they talk much of building some fortifications to protect the armory there but nobody can decide on where to put them, it seems, and so they're still unbuilt and probably will be until the British broadsides are bombarding the place."

"What of New England?" Jett asked. "Are the Yankees any more in favor of the war than they were when I sailed?"

"They're hotter than ever against it," Worth said. "You know the British have made no effort to blockade the New England coast, don't you? Their gesture has got results. I saw a newspaper not so many days past, the *New Bedford Mercury* it was, that said Baltimore was, as I remember it, 'a sink of corruption and the Sodom of our country,' because we're building clipper ships here. That'll give you an idea."

A frown creased Jett's forehead as he digested the news.

"Why then," he said slowly, "if New England deals with the enemy, as she seems ready to do, we're lost, aren't we? About our only hope was to cut England's supply lines with our privateers. But if the British have means of supplying their troops through New England's generosity, they'll be able to sustain themselves without supplies from overseas."

"And that," Anthony Worth said, "needs no Napoleon to figure out."

Jett muttered a curse under his breath.

"A devil of a mess," he said aloud. His eyes rose to meet his uncle's. "Britain will make every American who worked and fought against her in this war suffer if she wins it," he went on. Anthony nodded without speaking. "And seeing she must win it, where do we stand, Uncle?"

Anthony put a thumb to his lower lip and rubbed it gently.

"Why, Jett," he said, quietly, "you know me for the staunchest patriot in all Maryland. But speaking amongst ourselves, perhaps arrangements can be made to bring us out on top no matter which side wins this war."

7

IT WAS the night of the day after Jett Worth returned to Fair-overlea to learn of his new vessel that, five hundred leagues away, Sir Peter Porter yawned and heaved his arms wide in a tremendous stretch.

Sir Peter Porter was bored. Here he was, one of the youngest of the King's Vice-Admirals at twenty-six, in command of the frigate *Menelaus*, with his beloved England involved in two wars, and he and his vessel must gather barnacles at Bermuda while the Admiralty in London hemmed and hawed and did not a thing to send him into action.

Not that Bermuda was the most unpleasant place in the world to spend this winter of 1812 and 1813. The climate was fair wondrous, neither too hot nor too cold, and the eating was enough to give him a belly that didn't belong on a young frame such as his. The Governor gave superior balls and dinners and the ladies were most gracious; the native wenches were quite generous. But he was a fighting man; he needs must make some sort of a name for himself before this silly war with America was ended and the Admiralty, always so eager to use the pruning knife, retired him on pittance pay. And how in God's name could a man acquire a reputation spreading his butt in Bermuda, under the command of a drooling dotard such as Admiral Sir John Borlase Warren, the old goat?

Now if Cockburn had the fleet, he told himself, perhaps they'd see some fun. Admiral Sir George Cockburn fretted at this inactivity as much as he did. Sir Peter couldn't say he liked Co'burn much as a man, the fellow was too swinish at table, too much the guzzler, but at least he burned for action and would seek it out instead of spending his days at anchor as Old Warren did.

Aye, with Co'burn commanding, there'd be a chance for a frolic with the Yankees before the ragamuffins found out what they were up against and surrendered. As it was—

There was a knock on the door of his cabin and he bellowed a "Come in!" The corporal of his marine guard, spotless in his red tunic, opened the door and saluted stiffly.

"Admiral Warren's gig alongside, sir," he reported. "Sir John's compliments and will you please attend him on his flagship at your earliest convenience?"

"Christ, yes!" Sir Peter burst out. "Put that in the proper language, Corporal, and tell the watch officer to have the bos'n's mate ready my gig. And get Jones in here; I can't attend the Admiral in this uniform."

As he was shaved and dressed, Sir Peter Porter wondered at the summons. Coming at this hour, he thought, it could only mean that a dispatch ship had arrived in port with orders, though he had not heard the salute gun boom to mark the arrival. And if there were orders for the fleet to move, in what direction would that be; to join the French coastal blockade or to sail for America?

"America, I'll bet a month's pay," he decided. "I'll get that frolic after all!"

He fastened on his sword, straightened his hat, and hurried out of his cabin in the halfdeck under the quarterdeck, replying to the rigid salute of his marine guard. At the foot of the gangway, his gig waited, the oarsmen holding their long shafts upright. The officer of the deck saluted, the bos'n's pipe twittered, and Sir Peter scampered nimbly down the gangway and stepped into the gig.

"*San Domingo*," he ordered. "Look alive."

"Aye aye, sir," said the bos'n's mate in charge of the gig. "Shove off, starb'd, lively, lively!"

Porter found himself the fifth officer to arrive at Admiral Warren's cabin. Ahead of him had come Cockburn and his nephew, Captain Clement Vickers, Sir Sidney Beckwith of the seventy-four-gun *Albion* and Sir Charles Napier of the ship of the line *Dragon*. All these men except Vickers ranked Porter, he noted instantly, and Vickers couldn't be counted; he was Co'burn's pet, a captain before his time. He, Sir Peter, was the first frigate captain to have been summoned and that was a good sign.

After Sir Peter came the other captains of frigates, brigs and smaller vessels until Warren's cabin was crowded beyond comfort. Still, the old fleet commander sat in his chair in the corner, nodding briefly in response to the salutes of his subordinates as each entered, his almost toothless mouth working constantly as was his age-born habit.

And an inspiring commander he, thought Sir Peter Porter scornfully. The old fool was long past the year he should have retired and yet he clung to his command like a superannuated leech. He must have friends in the Admiralty, else he'd have been replaced a dozen years back; he had been sent to Bermuda to get him and his bungling out of the way and now that this new war looked as though it might make the Bermuda base important it was time London made a change in command. But, Sir Peter told himself gloomily, that was not London's way; the Admiralty seemed always to retire the able men and keep the fumbling figureheads in their commands.

The last captain had reported and there was a long, restless silence in the stifling, crowded cabin before Sir John bestirred himself.

"Er—aye, gentlemen," he said, in his quavering voice. He peered dimly about the cabin, for all the world as though he were wondering why it was so crowded. "Aye. Just so. Er-hemm." His wrinkled clawlike hand reached out for a rolled paper on

184

the table next to him. He unrolled it, peered at it dubiously. Sir Peter felt a yell bubbling in his throat and suppressed it. *Get on with it!*

"We have dispatches, gentlemen," Warren squeaked as the waiting came close to being unbearable. "The fleet—er—the fleet is ordered to move. Not all the fleet. No, a part, a squadron."

He looked down again at the dispatch and then at his officers. "Admiral Co'burn," his cracked old voice went on, "will command, on *Sceptre*. With him will sail Beckwith on *Albion*, Napier on *Dragon* and Adams on *Cressy*. In line will be the frigates *Menelaus*, *Marlborough*, *Narcissus*, *Loire* and *Severn*. Also . . . ."

Sir Peter did not listen as the old admiral recited the list of twenty brigs, brig-sloops and schooners that would make up the fleet. He was sailing at last, but where? The old man hadn't said and unless somebody, Co'burn for instance, reminded him he hadn't, he probably would forget to mention where this fleet was headed for. And this kind of command was supposed to maintain the British Navy as the finest in the world!

Sure enough, Old Warren was winding up with: "I believe that's all, gentlemen. You are or—er—ought to be ready to sail at dawn tomorrow. Good fortune, gentlemen."

There was a stir among the assembled officers, a rising buzz of muttering, and then Admiral Cockburn's harsh voice sounded.

"Your pardon, Admiral," Cockburn said with almost an open sneer, "but it's plain left my head where you said we were sailing for."

Warren's dim eyes swung in Cockburn's direction and rested on his second in command. The old lips pursed disapprovingly and there was the faint echo of the old bark Sir John must have owned at one time as he replied.

"Damme, sir," he said, "your memory serves you poorly, Sir George. I say again that the squadron will close the entrance to the Bay of Chesapeake, dispatching landing parties to take whatever fortifications and towns may be necessary."

Cockburn, the sneer still on his mouth, bowed under the ancient admiral's cackled reproof.

"I'll not be sailing with ye," Warren went on. "I'll follow later in *San Domingo*—there's much to be done here before I can leave. That's all, gentlemen. Sir George, will you stay behind the others, please?"

Sir Peter Porter's heart thumped with excitement as he stood at the head of the gangway, waiting for the officers who ranked him, the captains of the seventy-four-gun ships of the line, to board their gigs. His own boat, he noted with satisfaction, came up when it should have, immediately after the departure of Beckwith and ahead of the gigs of the other frigate captains whom he ranked. And it, by God, better had! Somebody would feel the cat for sure if his gig missed slipping into its rightful place and permitted, say, the master of the *Loire* or *Marlborough* to precede him.

Back in his cabin, he summoned his lieutenants and gave his orders. All watches to be turned out and the ship readied for sailing; all stores and armament to be checked and double-checked if it took all night; there'd be no last minute mishaps to embarrass him. Cockburn was in command now and Cockburn accepted no excuses for the slightest slip. He, Sir Peter Porter, was going to make sure there'd be nothing that would bring Old Co'burn's wrath down upon him. He, Sir Peter, was being given this chance to make a name for himself and, by all that was holy, he'd not muff it.

All that night the crew of the *Menelaus* labored at checking every gun, every powder keg, every signal flag, every brace, every halliard, every stay, every ratline, every cask of salt pork, every lancet in the surgeon's cabin. All night long the bos'n's long rattan cane thwacked the bare backs of the sweating sailors he suspected of shirking. Orders giving her position in the line reached *Menelaus* from Cockburn's *Sceptre*; Sir Peter's vessel was to lead all the other frigates, a good sign if ever there was one that he stood in the commanding admiral's favor.

"By heaven," Porter said as he stood on the quarterdeck that dawn, "this is my opportunity to get a ship of the line! I'll make it count or die trying!"

Signal flags streaked upward to *Sceptre's* mizzen top. Sails blossomed on the flagship and the seventy-four-gunner wheeled slowly out from her anchorage, followed by the hulking *Cressy*. *Albion* and *Dragon* fell into line and as *Albion* swept past, Sir Peter could hear the Marine band aboard pumping out the new air that had swept the fleet since the Yankees had dared declare war on England:

> *The wind and sea are Britain's wide domain;*
> *And not a sail but by permission spreads!*

Sir Peter Porter mounted the poop deck, a bos'n's mate at his side to relay his orders. Actually, the frigate captain knew, his directions were little more than a formality; his junior officers at their stations knew what had to be done and would do it automatically at the first sound of his voice. But when the time came to shake out his sails, give life to *Menelaus*, Porter was wrenched by a consuming thrill, as he always was when his ship got under way.

Damn all, there wasn't a finer ship in His Majesty's Navy nor one better handled than by this splendid crew! See how her sails caught the wind, feel how she sprang ahead as though she'd over-run her bigger sisters! Watch the smartness of her crew, the dispatch with which they did what had to be done! And when the fighting began, when those guns were run in and loaded and run out again, they'd all find out, Co'burn and the others, that he deserved a bigger command, a seventy-four-gunner.

So it was ho, for the Bay of the Chesapeake and let's hope the damned Yankees provided a frolic there before they were squashed!

8

"Right wheel! Left wheel! Company, halt! Ground arms!"

Task Tillman let the musket slide down his body until the butt struck the sand of the parade ground. It was late January, and the wind off the water was raw, but perspiration trickled down his face and neck, soaking the collar of his woolen uniform tunic. Captain Joe Nicholson had kept them hard at it for two hours without a rest and the ancient Towers musket had come to weigh a quarter of a ton in the past fifteen minutes. Nicholson was a hard-driving drill-master.

And to what purpose, Tillman asked himself. Since he had joined the Queen Annes Militia Company it had been a long, tiresome routine of shoulder arms, forward march, right wheel, left wheel, halt, ground arms. As a new recruit to the company, as a Talbot County man in a Queen Annes unit, he knew he had little right to criticize, but wouldn't it be more to the purpose to let the men fire their muskets at a mark so that if they had to fight they'd know how to aim their pieces? But Captain Nicholson had explained that there was a shortage of powder at the moment; in time the company might be able to draw on the stores at the Easton Armory and then there would be shooting practice.

Well then, shouldn't the company throw up some kind of

earthworks to protect Queen's Town in the event the British sailed up the Chester River? No, the Captain explained patiently, because if the Redcoats ever did come up the river they'd doubtless put landing parties ashore down below any fortification that might be built and circle the place, trapping the militia between them and the river. The militia's purpose, Task was told, was to act as a mobile force that could meet the British wherever they might land, unrestricted by any fortifications that would hold them to one place.

"You see, Tillman," Captain Nicholson had pointed out, "we know the land hereabouts and all the roads and lanes. The British don't and should they try to force a landing here we'd flank 'em right and left and send 'em back to their ships in confusion. If their warships try a bombardment of the town, we'll blast 'em with our cannon."

If Task was dubious about the ability of three nine-pound guns to blast a British ship of war, he kept his doubts to himself. Admitting that he knew nothing about soldiering, he proved himself a good soldier in Nicholson's Queen Annes Militia. He drilled as long as Nicholson called the orders, never falling out as many of the men did with the complaint of leg cramps. He took his turn at sentry duty, even though no British sail had yet been sighted off the Virginia Capes, well over a hundred miles away. He did not, as so many men in the company did, pester Nicholson for an officer's commission; he was quite content with his corporal's rating.

If Captain Joseph Nicholson wondered why Task Tillman chose to serve with a Queen Annes County company rather than with one of the closer Easton outfits he asked no questions, glad as he was to enlist Task's services.

For Tillman took his militia service seriously; too many members of the company regarded the drills as an excuse to get away from their work—or wives—and as a preliminary to a convivial evening at the tavern. As for sentry duty, Captain Nicholson had been forced to admit that more men strayed off their posts when the weather was anything but the finest than stayed where they had been stationed. Nicholson could always depend on Task Tillman to keep to his post, no matter how bitter the wind nor how wild the storm.

It is probable that if Task Tillman had been a native of Queen Annes County he would have been made an officer within a month after he joined Nicholson's company. As it was, the Captain had a hard time keeping peace with his own neighbors in parcelling out commissions; to have named an outsider a lieutenant would have been to invite wholesale desertions, if not outright mutiny.

Yes, a militia captain had to walk softly and carefully or find his command melted away overnight, deserters to some rival outfit. Other captains were on the watch for recruits just as he was and Nicholson knew that he had less to offer than most. He had not near as much, for instance, as that fool, Charles Rawlent in Easton, who was blessed with a father-in-law who was supporting the Dragon Footguards from a bottomless purse. The Dragons had everything; the new Baker rifles, the new triangular bayonets, two changes of dress uniforms and three of field uniforms and even two shakos. The Dragons were the swaggering possessors of six bright brass cannon, even if they did not know how to lay them on. The Easton Armory gave the Dragons all the powder and shot they needed for target practice; Anthony Worth had only to say the word and the Armory would have been turned inside-out for them.

Oh well, a man did what he could with what he had, so— Attention! Shoulder Arms! Forward March! Right Wheel! Left Wheel!

Task had almost reached the Larkspur Hill turn-off from the Miles River Road the following day, bending against a raw wind that swept over the bare, brown Eastern Shore, when Abraham stepped out of a clump of evergreens and silently held up a note. As Task took the paper from the Negro's hand, Abraham turned and faded back into the woods, quickly, effortlessly, bound back to the Fairoverlea that had never known he had left the place.

Task ran his eyes over the three words: *Tonight at eight.* There was no signature nor was one needed. It had been two months since Anthony Worth had been away from Fairoverlea for overnight and two months had been a long time without Vivian.

He stowed the scrap of paper in a pocket beneath his flapping cloak, his blood quickened by the thought of the night that lay ahead. There were things to prepare, arrangements to be made so that there would be no interruptions when Vivian reached Larkspur Hill.

He touched his spurs to Lucifer and the black stallion had just broken into a trot when Task's hand hard-reined him to a stop again. Around a sharp bend in the road came a carriage drawn by two handsome bays. In the carriage were Charles Rawlent and his wife, Gracellen.

Task cursed the chance that had brought about this meeting. The Rawlents, his mind said swiftly, must be bound for a visit up Queen's Town way; nobody from Fairoverlea used this road to go to Easton and for that he had been thankful. And the carriage would have to be hidden by that bend; given a straight stretch of road that would have let him see their approach and he would have jumped Lucifer over the fence and cut across the field at his right. As it was, he could not help but face them.

He saw the start of recognition Gracellen gave; he noticed Rawlent's lip curl at the sight of him. He pulled Lucifer over to the side of the road to let the carriage pass, keeping his eyes fixed on a point somewhere behind the shining barouche.

He heard Gracellen say a word to the coachman and there was the creak and jingle of harness, the blowing of the bays, as the carriage came to a stop beside him.

"Good day to you, Task Tillman," Gracellen said lightly.

She wore a heavy cloak of some soft grey stuff that was pulled close about her face and over her lap was thrown a heavy bearskin robe. The cold had heightened the color in her face, her eyes were glistening. Her wide-brimmed bonnet was banded by a strip of gay ribbon which encircled the crown, then came down under her chin, fastened by a large bow.

"Madam," Task bowed, a finger at the visor of his shako. He tried to make the one brief look he gave her cold, unadmiring, and then moved his eyes to meet Rawlent's. "Mister Rawlent," he said and this time he did not have to force the iciness of his tone.

"*Captain* Rawlent!" the man beside Gracellen corrected, haughtily. "I see you're in uniform—of a sort. You should know how to address an officer."

Task started to make reply, bit back what he was about to say.

"Oh, Charles," Gracellen laughed, "leave off the military talk a moment, do!" She looked up at Task again. "I haven't seen you in a long time," she went on. "How fares everything with you?"

"Very well, thank you, Madam," Task said rigidly. He looked at Rawlent again. "I'm very late with my congratulations, sir," he said. "I give them now and wishes for best happiness to you both."

Rawlent eyed him suspiciously without replying. Gracellen's laugh tinkled.

"Oh, good heavens!" she said. "You mean our marriage! It's been so long now, Task, that I had trouble deciding what you were congratulating Charley about. It's been—let's see—more than two years now. Think of it!"

Task's eyes drifted back to the woman and clung there, despite himself. The two years of marriage to Charles Rawlent did not seem to have changed her; outwardly, at least, she still had everything that had made him love her from the beginning. The thought had never been full-formed, but he had entertained the subconscious idea that Gracellen would lose her beauty, deteriorate, by giving herself to the caparisoned nincompoop who sat at her side in the carriage. What was it Jett had said the afternoon before that fateful night, "tough as alligator hide"? Aye, she might be that, to show no sign she'd been changed by letting this uniformed monkey-on-a-stick rifle the treasures he once had thought she saved for him.

And with that scrap of paper you carry beneath your cloak, Task Tillman, you have the right to condemn anyone at all?

He winced inwardly and swung Lucifer out a bit to pass the barouche and be on his way, out of sight of this girl in the grey cloak and beribboned hat who was as beautiful now—more beautiful—than when she had pressed herself against him and muttered choked words of love.

"We're on our way to a week's visit in Georgetown," Gracellen said, as though to block his flight. "The Ellingers. Perhaps you know them."

Task shook his head.

"And you, I see are on your way home from the drill," the girl went on. Desperately? "You have a green coat on beneath your cloak. What uniform is that, Task?"

"Nicholson's," Charles Rawlent grunted before Task could answer. "The Queen Annes Militia." He eyed Task's green tunic and buff breeches scornfully as the wind whipped Tillman's cloak aside. "Is it true what I hear, that you've filled your ranks with mill hands and farmers?"

"It's true we've picked our men for what they can do, how they can fight, and not how pretty they might look in a purple shift!" Task lashed back.

"Not purple, dammit, claret!" Rawlent shrilled, outraged. "And none of your insolence, Tillman! I could have you court-martialled for that—a common soldier speaking in that manner to an officer, a captain!"

"Suppose you make complaint to my captain, Captain Nicholson," Task said grimly. "I promise you he'll tell you just what you can do with your court-martial and even help you do it."

"Gentlemen, gentlemen!" Gracellen said, her voice shaken by laughter. "You forget there's a lady present. Stop bristling at each other, for goodness sake. You'll tire yourselves that way before you fight the British."

"Well, you heard him—" Rawlent began.

"Oh, Charles!" she commanded and looked up at Task again. For a second or perhaps much less than that, their eyes met and

193

locked in a manner that was familiar to them both; for a moment there was no Charles Rawlent huddled beneath the bearskin robe beside Gracellen. For that brief time, their eyes exchanged their old love message as openly as they had in the days before doubt had shoved trust aside and had squatted, scowling, between them.

In Gracellen's eyes there was an expression he could not read clearly. Was it an appeal for compassion, for generosity, a plea for understanding? Was she asking forgiveness—Gracellen? Was she trying to tell him that she had discovered the truth too late; that he had been right, she had been wrong? Was it perhaps possible that she—

"God's sake, Gracellen," Charles Rawlent broke in, "must we sit here and freeze with all this long trip ahead of us?"

The tenuous golden thread that had stretched itself unbidden between Task and Gracellen snapped. Task pulled Lucifer a step further aside, put his hand to his shako again.

"My last thought was to delay you, sir," he said. "I'm overdue now at Larkspur Hill. I'm uneasy for my house and barns every minute I'm away—as perhaps you can understand."

He saw Gracellen's grey eyes lose the light that had flickered there, saw her mouth firm. She cast him one flat glance, then turned to speak to the coachman. The whip flicked out to touch the bays and the carriage rolled on over the frozen road, Gracellen looking stonily ahead. Rawlent turned to cast one last sneer as he passed Task.

Tillman shifted in his saddle and watched the carriage until it rounded another bend. He turned back, shrugging, and clucked his tongue to Lucifer. If she had meant to flaunt her married happiness before his eyes she had fared poorly—but he could not make himself believe that had been her reason for stopping the barouche. She had been trying to tell him something, and what was there to say, now that everything between them was finished?

He moved in the saddle and the paper in his pocket, the note Abraham had handed him only seconds before he had met Gracellen, crackled. *Tonight at eight.*

194

Behind him was the woman he loved; that night he would hold in shame and exultation the woman who offered him relief from that love.

Revulsion swept him, as swift and biting as the wind that tore at his cloak. In the warm, moist, sweet secretness of Vivian he would find easement again that night from his love for Gracellen and the surcease would be earned at the cost of his honor. And Vivian, transfixed in his arms, would be crucified again on a rood of self-loathing and delight, her tears a mingling of sorrow for herself and overbrimming bliss, her moans an echo of blended agony and ecstasy, her fury born of hatred for herself and him and twinned with mad desire.

Vivian in rapture—he spurred Lucifer forward again.

Let the whole world, then, think of him as a blackguard without honor! But how could a man like Anthony Worth who was without honor himself be dishonored by the night that lay ahead and others and still others? That was not right nor ever could be right. What had Anthony Worth ever done to a Tillman that had been right?

(A young man's conscience is never without its blind side, say the wise old men. And this side, they add, swings uppermost in an almost physiological change at the touch of a warm and willing woman. The man's excuses which justify this phenomenon are always instinctive, limitless, and exceedingly convincing. Or so say the sages.)

9

Anthony Worth, Esq.
Fairoverlea Plantation,
On the Miles River in Talbot County,
Maryland.

Esteemed Sir:

This Letter is sent to you through the extreme kindness of Mr. Arnold Weems, who is Travelling to Virginia. I know you will show Mr. Weems every courtesy, for which, Sir, I will be most Grateful.

It is my Sad Duty to inform you that Mr. Matthew departed This Life last Friday, the 14th inst. He was found dead close to the Waterfront here in Boston. From what I learned from the Watchman, the Unfortunate Man must have been befuddled on leaving a Tavern and so missed his way back to his Lodging Place. He fell in a passageway between two Warehouses and was covered up by snow, there being a Storm that night.

I arranged a Decent Burial for him and if it is ever your wish to come here to Boston and visit his Grave I will direct you to his Last Resting Place.

*With Mr. Matthew's Death, our arrangement for providing
the funds you so generously gave him comes to an end. I
enclose a Statement of the Expenses of his burial, also a
Balance Sheet which shows the Amount on hand when he
Died.*

Believe me, Sir,

Yr. Ob't S'vt
Ephraim Dupuy
Att'y at Law.

Boston, Massachusetts,
January the 19th, 1813

"So he's finally dead," Anthony Worth muttered. He scanned
the letter once more, then smiled as he twisted it into a spill and
held it out to the wavering spire of flame that flickered in the
nearest lamp.

He watched the paper curl and blacken, burst into a bright puff
and send a tremulous thread of smoke toward the ceiling of the
office. The letter burned down to Anthony's blunt fingertips before the big man dropped the crisp corpse of the note to the floor
and crushed out its last sparks with a stamp of his thick-soled boot.

"So he's finally dead!"

He leaned back in his chair, his eyes brooding, his big-knuckled
hands brought up under his heavy chin.

He finally was dead; Matthew, his brother. And now there
was no need to fear that the drunken sot would ever break out
of the confines of his rum to make trouble. Now the story of
what happened that night in Boston so many years ago was buried
deep. As deep as Matthew.

Matthew had been a weakling from the start. When the two
of them had been boys, nameless catch-pennies scrabbling for
enough food to keep them alive from one day to the next, it had
always been he, Anthony, who had found the crusts and chop
bones while Matthew snivelled and leaked useless tears about his
lot.

And it had been he, Anthony, who had thought up the plan to waylay Merchant Shaw. Oh, Matthew had been the brave one when they had talked over their plan; he would do this and that—but when the time came and Old Shaw put up a furious fight for the gold he was carrying, Matthew had fled like the craven bastard he was. So it had been up to him, Anthony, fifteen years old and big for his years, to kill the old man to get the money he needed to make his start in life.

But he had been fair with Matthew; he had given his brother almost a quarter of what had been in Shaw's bulging leathern purse. And later, after he had made his way to Maryland and had begun to make his name, he had been most generous in the amounts he had sent to his brother in Boston. He had owed nothing to Matthew except the price of silence, but through the years that price had proved a high one.

When Matthew had married—Great God, what witless wench would ever tie herself to that worthless drunkard?—it had been Anthony Worth who had put out the money for their food (drink, for Matthew) and lodging, and at a time when he needed every coin he could lay hands on to finish Fairoverlea. Then, when the woman died giving birth to a baby boy, he had made the dangerous trip to Boston to rescue the starveling brat from the neglect of his staggering, haze-brained father.

And that was Jett, loved as the son the fates had never permitted to live to carry on Anthony Worth's name.

Since he had taken Jett, Anthony had made sure that his brother, Matthew, was provided for. Call it blackmail or call it what you would, the money was sent regularly to Boston to be doled out to Matthew by Lawyer Dupuy. Just recently, less than a year before, Anthony had almost doubled the amounts to be given Matthew.

That was after Dupuy had written that Matthew was a shivering, shaking wreck for whom there was no hope.

So he was dead at last, and Jett would never need to know that his father had been alive all these years. Jett would go on believing that Matthew Worth had died before the turn of the century and it was better so.

Jett was *his*, never Matthew's! The boy loved him as he never could have loved a reeling, puking creature on whom the mongrel dogs of Boston would scorn to lift a leg.

He was dead and the secret of an old murder had died with him.

Unless—

Anthony's square hand came down on the desktop with a pounding thud.

Unless Randolph Tillman's diary had given Task the whole story.

10

ADMIRAL Sir George Cockburn's fleet of four ships of the line, six frigates and twenty smaller vessels including brigs, brig-sloops and schooners, were sighted off the Virginia Capes on February first, 1813. Three days later, British landing parties under Cockburn's command gave the United States a sample of what was to be expected by a country that had the temerity to declare war against mighty England.

The scene of this first lesson was the little town of Hampton, Virginia, and in his sacking of that village Sir George Cockburn did something that all the American speechmakers had been unable to do; he welded a blazing and unyielding hatred of the British that never slackened, insofar as it was directed against him.

Sir Peter Porter, ashore in personal command of the landing detail from the *Menelaus*, saw the sickening spectacle from beginning to end. After it was over and he was back aboard his frigate, Sir Peter poured himself four jolting drams of rum and swallowed them, one after the other. The fourth did the trick; the shame raised by the scenes he had witnessed gave way to the reminder that this was war and war was never gentle.

But before those drinks—well, in the first place, the town of Hampton had offered no resistance to the British; its position on the James River at Hampton Roads certainly could never have been of such strategic importance in possibly hampering the British blockade of the Chesapeake that the village deserved destruction. It was just a place which Cockburn, as far as Sir Peter Porter could determine, had picked as a town on which to demonstrate British ruthlessness in dealing with Americans.

"Your men," the Admiral had told Porter, "will herd the women, all the women, up at that end of the village"—he pointed a stubby forefinger—"while Lieutenant Westphal's men off *Marlborough* will round up the men who haven't run off like the dogs they are. My own details will take care of the rest of the work to be done."

It was not, Porter thought resentfully, much of a duty for a ranking frigate captain. In fact this whole raid seemed to be of petty stuff. But later, when he saw what followed, he was glad he had not been ordered to do what Old Co'burn had taken upon himself to do.

As the Admiral barked commands, his men deployed through every house in the town and systematically looted them of every single thing of value. Chairs, clocks, beds, silverware, pewter, what little money was to be found, chests, clothing, foodstuffs, farm tools, wagons, livestock, even poultry, all were seized by the British sailors and marines and assembled in a great pile in the center of the town. Cockburn then pointed out the things that were to be carried off and freighted to the warships that rode at anchor offshore. These included the livestock which was slaughtered forthwith, the poultry, the foodstuffs, the silver and pewter, a few good clocks and a dozen or so beautifully carved beds and chairs. The rest, the farm equipment and the furniture that was not taken off, the pitifully worthless heirlooms and keepsakes, one milch cow too old and skinny to be butchered, the carcasses of six or seven dogs which had been shot when they had attacked or had simply gotten in the way of the looters, and other incidentals, were thrown in a heap that became a roaring, crackling pyre when Cockburn ordered torches put to it.

Sir Peter Porter swallowed hard and turned away as the women under his men's guard burst into a keening wail at the sight of the thick smoke rolling up from what had been their poor treasures, their meagre possessions. The men from the *Menelaus* stoically shoved back against the press of their prisoners' frantic bodies with their muskets; here and there a man pinked an hysterical woman with the point of his bayonet to keep her from breaking out of the makeshift stockade.

"Stand steady, all," the young Admiral said huskily. "Steady."

He found himself sweating profusely although the day was not warm. Cockburn, he kept reminding himself, was in command. Back at Bermuda, he had wished that Old Co'burn would take over. Well, Old Co'burn had and what was he, a girl to grow weak and sick at the sight of a few gewgaws being burned to teach the Yankees a lesson?

It was when the sailors scattered to the houses again, each one carrying a blazing torch, that the men under Westphal's guard went wild. They had endured the looting of their homes with comparative silence, cowed by the impressive display of strength shown by the British fleet that loomed close by, the impersonal machinelike efficiency of the sailors and marines who carried out their officers' brief orders. Their goods, their livestock, they could lose without showing resistance; when the flames began to curl about their houses and barns they forgot the hopeless odds against them and began to fight.

Screaming, they hurled themselves upon their captors, pummeling with their fists, kicking at British shins, scratching, biting, gouging. Westphal's men clubbed with their musket butts, stabbed with their bayonets. An American went down, blood pouring from a throat wound. The sight of his fall seemed to bring new fury to his neighbors.

"God damned swine!" howled a lanky farmer. "Butchers!" He stooped and picked up a rock, flung it full into the face of the nearest Britisher. The marine staggered back, his face a crimson mass as blood poured from a broken nose. A mate swung a heavy cutlass. The lanky man took the blow on a shoulder and an inhuman wail broke from him as he fell, sliced to the breastbone by the stroke.

Behind him, Sir Peter Porter heard the screaming of the women mount in chilling crescendo. There was a curse from one of his men and he turned to see the marine smash his musket butt into a woman's belly. She crumpled and fell, twisting on the ground, both hands pressed to her middle.

"Belay that!" Porter yelled.

"She bit me, sir!" the marine cried. "Bit me to the bone, she did, the ——— slut!"

"I said belay that!" Sir Peter snapped. "We don't make war on women."

There was a rattle of shots from the other side of the square. He turned back to see Westphal's men drawn up in an uneven rank, their muskets levelled. Three Americans were on the ground. One twitched jerkily. The other two were still, curiously shapeless lumps.

The drawn-down muskets choked off the Americans' uprising as quickly as it had begun. No man, no matter how enraged, could look down the barrels of those pieces and not shrink back. The Hampton villagers, bloody, bruised, despairing, huddled in a hopeless knot as the British sailors and marines regained control.

Sir George Cockburn, imposing in his dress uniform, stalked up to the line of guards, a grim sneer on his wide, lipless mouth. Arms akimbo, his thick legs planted wide apart, he thrust forward his bull-necked head and his voice rasped over the crackling of the flames and the sobs of the women behind Porter.

"And so we have some bully boys here, eh?" Cockburn grated. "Some choice heroes who'd dare oppose His Majesty's Navy! That old cock there, the one in the striped shirt—I marked him as the leader of this mob. Drag him out, Serjeant! I'd decorate him for his bravery, b'God!"

Marines hauled a diminutive old man out of the group of villagers. From where he stood, Sir Peter Porter could see that the man must be past sixty and a feeble grandfather at worst. The old man's face was chalky with fear, his eyes were staring, his mouth was twisted in dread.

"Sir—sir," he quavered, his voice surprisingly clear. "I did nary thing to anyone. I was but standin' here and—"

"Silence!" Cockburn roared. "I saw what ye did, ye damned, stinkin' colonial!"

From some disastrous font the ancient was revived by enough courage to straighten himself and jut his chin at the venomous Admiral.

"No colonial, by God!" the old man spat. "We've been our own masters since we whipped you Lobsterbacks out o' here and we'd rather die than bend a knee to your scurvy king again!"

Porter winced as the old man's words came to him, partly because the King had been maligned, mostly because he knew the oldster had signed his death warrant with his senseless defy. Damn these Americans, he muttered to himself, didn't they know when it was the time to keep their mouths shut?

Sir George Cockburn was speechless for a long moment, his thick body gripped by rage. His voice, when he spoke, came flint-hard through his teeth.

"Ye'd rather die, eh?" he asked. "Then die ye will and like the dog you are! Bos'n, bring y'r cat!"

The old man was borne struggling to the center of the village square and tied to a tripod quickly fashioned of muskets with interlocked bayonets. The bos'n, a burly man off the *Sceptre*, swung his lead-tipped cat o' nine tails experimentally while another sailor ripped the striped shirt (and what had prompted the man to don what obviously was his Sunday best this day?) from the thin shoulders and back.

"Twenty of the best," Cockburn grated, "and twenty more and twenty if this fine feller is as tough as his mouth."

From the knot of prisoners, a tall young man, one of the few young men rounded up in the raid, shoved past a guard and sprang toward Cockburn.

"Take me instead, sir!" he yelled. "My father meant no harm! He's an old man, y'must see that! I tell ye—"

"Shoot him!" Cockburn snapped after a bare glance at the youngster. A musket boomed, its report muffled by the fact that the muzzle had been held against the young man's side. The

American slewed sideways and sprawled, kicked a leg twice and then lay still.

Now Porter's women prisoners were silent, so stricken by their grief they could no longer wail. They kept their haggard eyes on the old man embracing the tripod of muskets. The wanton slaughter of the old man's son seemed only to deepen the shock that had carried them past vocal protest.

"At y'r work, Bos'n," Admiral Sir George Cockburn ordered, "and lay on."

The bos'n drew back his meaty arm; the cat's thongs whipped behind him, rose in a whistling arc and slashed across the white skin of their victim's back. The old American twisted against his bonds, arching his blood-striped body, straining his head back as a low, guttural cry came from his mouth. This cry was cut off as the cat slashed again. His head went forward; his body slumped against the muskets.

"Lose your senses, fool!" Sir Peter Porter murmured. "Faint and ye'll never feel the rest."

The cat rose and fell, each slicing thong shredding the skin, bringing the blood that first trickled, then flooded, down the doomed man's body, soaking the work-worn trousers and staining the ground under him. Beyond that first inhuman cry, the oldster said nothing; it must have been as Sir Peter had hoped and he had passed into blessed unconsciousness with that second blow.

Twenty times the cat hissed and clawed and at the twentieth slash the bos'n halted his grim work and looked toward Admiral Cockburn. It was Lieutenant Westphal, the *Marlborough's* captain, who spoke for the man.

"Sir, this fellow's quite dead," he said. "Twenty lashes were enough and more."

"Nay, Westphal," Sir Peter whispered to himself, *"that was a mistake, man!"*

Westphal must have realized it as Cockburn swung in his direction, his lizard's mouth curved in an ugly grimace. He eyed Westphal for a full five seconds before he spoke.

"I do not mind," he said heavily, "that I asked your advice,

Lieutenant. I do recall I gave ye the duty of guardin' this rabble and ye did y'r duty so clumsily that some of y'r men have been bloodied by these dogs. I'm not pleased in the least with y'r work till now, Lieutenant Westphal. Pray give me no more cause to wonder if you're a man fit to command a frigate."

Westphal, pale-faced, brought up a hand to salute his Admiral. He knew full well that in the few words he had spoken in an attempt to end this brutal scene he had doubtless spiked all his chances for a captaincy in the next promotion lists, if not forever.

Cockburn turned back to the man with the lash.

"Twenty more," he ordered stonily. "The beggar's shammin'."

The crowd, troops and prisoners, were forced to watch as the cat o' nine tails mutilated the lifeless body that still clutched the tripod in the embrace of death. When that gruesome count was finally finished, Cockburn turned away.

"Cut him loose," he ordered, over his shoulder, "and leave him where he falls."

He stalked back to a position between the two groups of prisoners and raised his voice.

"So now ye see, you scoundrels, what will come to every one of you damned connivin' Yankees if ye oppose His Majesty's forces in any way," he thundered. "And this is but sweet and gentle treatment beside what'll come to y'r pirate friends in Baltimore when we get there."

He turned to face Porter's group of women prisoners.

"You wenches," he went on, "are most fortunate because you're dealin' with a merciful man in me. Were I not so soft-hearted I'd turn the younger of you sluts over to my men, who've not tasted female meat in weeks and months. Then, I warrant, ye'd have cause to squeal and shriek—I've seen my hearties at their play. I spare you, but tell y'r slattern sisters what they can look forrad to when we pay our next call."

He made a grimace which might have been intended as a grin, turned back to cast an eye at the blazing torches that had been houses and outbuildings, and nodded.

"We're done here," he told his aide, his nephew, Captain

206

Clement Vickers. "Get the men back to their ships. Shoot any dog that tries to cause more trouble."

Sir Peter Porter, back aboard the *Menelaus,* looked at himself in his shaving glass and saw that his face had not changed, after all. There were no bestial lines graven in his smooth-shaven cheeks, no snout for a nose, no yellowed fangs in his mouth.

"You must be careful," he cautioned his image, "to make no mistake like Westphal's. You're an Admiral in the King's Navy and, by God, you can stomach anything that brute Co'burn proposes if it means your advancement to command of a ship of the line. Even another Hampton."

11

THE news of the sacking of Hampton raced up both shores of the Chesapeake Bay like fire through a hayfield. By the time it reached Easton Town the story was that all the women, from child to beldame, had been raped and then slaughtered after their torn bodies had been mutilated beyond unholy use; all the men had been shot out of hand—those of them who had not been thrown alive into the burning buildings.

So furious was the outcry throughout the country that, for the first time, Massachusetts, Rhode Island and New Hampshire, the Federalist strongholds that had persistently opposed the war, joined in. They sent their protests direct to London through the communications channels that still lay open between New England and the Mother Country.

England, even the Admiralty, was dismayed and angered. The British high command had hoped for and even planned on New England's secession from the United States; now Cockburn's needless savagery in a raid on an insignificant town appeared to have ruined everything.

Sharp demands for an explanation were sent to Sir John Borlase Warren as Cockburn's senior in command. They were biting enough to send the dotard sailing toward Hampton Roads to join Cockburn's fleet and take over active command. The old Admiral reached the American squadron early in March, 1813.

With communications what they were, it was not until the following July that Cockburn's version of the Hampton disgrace was made public. The British, said Sir George, had been unjustly accused. True, his landing parties had burned three warehouses filled with American military supplies. Some snipers had fired on a flag of truce and had been tried and executed in strict compliance with the rules of war. Aside from that, Cockburn lied blandly, not a chick nor child at Hampton had been harmed. The whole scandalous version given out by the Americans, Cockburn maintained, was an invention intended to whip up the flagging war spirits of the great majority of Americans who wanted only peace with England.

Cockburn's report, of course, was the one accepted by British officialdom and, in time, New England came to believe this version of the Hampton affair. But Maryland knew the truth and if she didn't then, she would have plenty of opportunity to witness first-hand the calloused inhumanity of the man, Admiral Sir George Cockburn.

With the British fleet closing the mouth of the Chesapeake, the towns along both shores of the Bay sent up a cry for help to Washington. Those patriots who had shaken dust from taproom rafters with their predictions of what they would do to the British if they came within gunshot were among the first to yell for protection.

"Where's our Navy?" was the popular complaint. "Where's our Army? Does Madison expect us to protect our ports with a handful of untried militiamen?"

Captain Rawlent, the Charles the Bold of Fairoverlea, was one of the loudest men in Talbot County with his protests.

"We've been deserted, b'gad!" he complained to Anthony Worth. "We've been left to die like rats in a trap whilst Madison huddles all his forces around Washington. If I had command, I'd—"

Anthony held up a hand and shook his head wearily.

"Now spare me that again, Charles," he said gently. "I've heard it all a hundred times, I know."

"But sir, you're uncommon quiet about the prospects," Rawlent said. "The British fleet, hundreds of warships, coming at us and you're not worried a whit."

"Why then," said the Master of Fairoverlea with a faint smile, "it must be because I've got the Dragon Footguards to defend me. I mind the time, and not so long past, when you were fair panting for a chance at the Lobsterbacks. Now that it's said the time is near, ye've changed your tune complete."

Rawlent flung out his hands, his bright sword swinging with the motion.

"I asked to meet them in fair fight," he whined. "I never said we were strong enough to fight the whole Royal Navy."

"Fair fight?" Anthony mused. "Y'mean the British should ask you how many men, how many cannon, you have and then oppose you with the same number?"

"Well, no, but—"

"Ye'll find out, Charles, that wars are not fought quite that way. And though I'd never complain about your command of the Dragons, I do mind that I proposed once that ye'd be less concerned about recruiting only those of fashion and enlarge your force with every able-bodied man who'd wish to join up. If you had, you might have more than a stylish handful to meet the British with."

Rawlent frowned, pursing his lips as he considered this reminder judiciously. Then he shook his head.

"Your pardon, sir," he said, "but my thought is that when the fighting comes, my Dragons will act as officers over the—er—workmen and field hands who'll be armed to meet the invaders."

Anthony's faint smile widened.

"You think they'll come flockin' to your banner, eh?" he asked. "When all you've done since you formed the company was to look down your nose at them because they weren't born gentlemen? I think, dear Charles, ye'll find out different. Of course I might be wrong."

"But—but, sir," Rawlent spluttered, "if what you say is true, what happens then to Fairoverlea, to all of us?"

"As to that," Anthony shrugged, "we'll have to wait and see—and trust in my good fortune in such matters."

"Good fortune," Rawlent said spitefully, "which might be helped by the visits of Mister Guthrie and the mysterious trips your vessels make, loaded with foodstuffs?"

Anthony Worth's eyes blazed as he lost his smile. His broad hands bunched themselves into fists and for a moment it seemed that he would smash at the man who was his daughter's husband. Then he relaxed and his voice was quiet.

"My good Charles," he said, "concern yourself with your Dragons and leave the rest to me. My advice is always good—heed it. There are those who have ignored it who've been sorry they did."

"I meant no offense, sir," Rawlent said with almost visible cringing. "I just wondered—"

"Wondering has done more harm than British bullets to some men! And now excuse me, I have these lading bills to study."

Rawlent started to leave the office and then paused at the door, turning.

"I beg another moment, sir," he said. Anthony raised his head, a faint frown over his eyes. "I wonder—I mean, would you oblige me by writing a letter to Governor Winder, asking him to strengthen the defenses of Eastern Bay and Easton Town?"

"I could write the Governor," Anthony said quietly, "but it would do no good. Even if he could send more cannon to these parts, which I doubt, he wouldn't, lest he'd weaken his precious Annapolis defenses, Fort Severn and Fort Madison. He thinks the whole war depends on him keeping the Capital—and his own skin—safe. He's spent most of his war funds in building his forts, letting the other Maryland ports, Baltimore included, more or less fend for themselves. Federal funds and public subscription accounted for most of the money put into Fort McHenry and Star Fort there; Baltimore got precious little from the State."

"And when we militia captains asked him for cannon," Rawlent added gloomily, "he told us there were none to be had. He had only one suggestion, that the Armory be removed from Easton so that the British might have no reason to attack the town."

"A good suggestion," Anthony nodded, "and one that might save us our homes." He smiled again. "Of course it's a damned poor way to fight a war, breaking up our defenses so as not to offend the enemy, but perhaps, as somebody has said, discretion is the better part of valor."

He turned toward the opposite doorway of the office and arose to bow at Vivian's entrance.

"Dull talk, my dear, I must warn you," he said. "We were deciding, Charles and I, how best the war could be won. Your own opinion is invited."

Vivian wore an Empire gown that enhanced the beauty of her smooth shoulders and bosom. Square-cut, the neckline revealed enough to fasten both men's eyes upon it.

"My opinion, Anthony?" she asked. "What would a woman be expected to know about war? Charles is the expert in such matters, isn't he?" Her dark eyes flicked at Rawlent, moved back to her husband. "Your pardon for this interruption, but I wondered if you still planned to go to Havre de Grace, as you said you might next month. There've been some invitations for the time you'd planned to be away and I must answer them yes or no."

Anthony Worth frowned, rubbing his lower lip with a blunt forefinger.

"I'd much prefer not going," he growled, finally, "but there's business there I must look after. What date is this? March twentieth? Aye, Vivian, best plan on me leaving here, say, a month from today. By then we should see what your countrymen plan to do as concerns this part of the Eastern Shore. I'd be here, certainly, if they take it into their heads to make a landing on the Miles"—he cast a sidelong glance at Rawlent—"to fight with Charles and his Dragons, though from what he's just told me I suppose I'll have a youngster like James Mulliken or Skipworth Jones over me as an officer whilst I march with the field hands."

"Nay, sir—" Rawlent began, his face crimson.

"Oh, let be, Charles," Worth smiled. "I was joking." He turned back to his wife. "What I was going to say was that I feel quite sure the British won't attack this part of The Shore, at least not till they've had their try at Baltimore. So I had best go to Havre de Grace as I planned."

"Then I'll accept these invitations that are for affairs before the twentieth next. And refuse those for—how long after that?"

"Two weeks, three weeks," Worth shrugged. "As short a time as I can arrange, be sure. I'd not like to be too long away from you, my dear."

"You think the British would mistreat one of their own country-women if they came while you were away?" Vivian asked idly.

"Nay, 'tis not the British I fear," Anthony smiled. " 'Tis the mischief that Satan finds for idle—and lonely—hands to do."

Vivian looked down at her fine hands as though examining them, then laughed in a sound barely above a whisper. She turned to Rawlent.

"There speaks the jealous husband, Charles," she said. "He flatters me—he, who knows full well my real worth."

12

At THE time Vivian Worth was speaking to Charles Rawlent, Task Tillman was being handed his commission as a lieutenant in the Queen Annes Militia Company commanded by Captain Joseph Nicholson.

"You've earned it, Task," Nicholson said gravely as he shook hands with his new officer. "You'd have had the commission a long time ago if you'd lived in this county but you know the feeling amongst the men and how I must be careful not to offend a single one of them."

"This promotion," Task offered, "I hope will not cause ill feeling."

Nicholson shrugged.

"To say it won't cause some would be foolish," he admitted. "I've no doubt but one or two might resign and try their luck with Captain Massey's company. But don't let that worry you, Task; most of the men have been plaguing me to make you a lieutenant and I've seen your work, myself. The ones who resign would be worthless in a fight, anyhow, most likely."

"You think the fighting's close, Captain?" Another shrug.

"It depends on how Co'burn will operate," Nicholson explained. "My own thought is that he'll strike right at Baltimore and the shipyards there. If he takes the place it would be a sorry blow for all of us; I doubt the nation could carry on the war for long without the clippers being built in Baltimore."

"He'll go directly up the Bay to the Patapsco, not bothering us?"

"That's my thought," Nicholson said, "but this Co'burn is a vicious hound. They say he can't sleep o' nights unless he has his daily fill of savagery. He might rage his way right up the Eastern Shore, raping and killing, simply as a frolic, as I hear the British called Hampton. There's word that Co'burn's sent messages to all the islands south of here that if they offer resistance not a person there will be left alive or a house above ground. This report may be another wild rumor but if it's true, Co'burn may be planning occupation of the whole Eastern Shore before he strikes at Baltimore. In which case, of course, we'll see our fill of fighting."

Task Tillman nodded solemnly, wondering what the fighting would bring. It was a far cry to the days when Task had clung fast to his childish conviction that one American soldier was worth a dozen Redcoats in a battle. The confusion, the bickering, the double-dealing, the incompetence and the plain laziness that riddled the company of Joe Nicholson was, he had come to know, common in all the militia companies thereabouts. To shirk a duty and get away with it, it seemed, was an occasion to boast about in the minds of the militiamen. For an officer to score a triumph over his captain in an argument over who should go where and when was more important to the officer than seeing his men were trained in even the rudiments of soldiering. True, the company had tightened up considerably with the news of Hampton and the threat of the British fleet's arrival off the shore of Queen's Town but, Task knew, the unit, for all its weeks of *halt, left wheel, ground arms,* was pitifully weak in discipline and even the basic elementals of battle conduct.

Task knew that Captain Nicholson realized this. Never, these days, was the plan of outflanking the British with the aid of the militia's knowledge of the terrain or blasting the British warships with the three nine-pounders mentioned. The captain's face grew longer and more glum as the days passed, the enemy drew nearer, and the company showed no improvement.

"Perhaps," Nicholson said in a voice that showed he did not believe what he said, himself, "the American fleet—wherever it is—will meet and drive the British out of the Bay before they can come up this far." He summoned a tired smile as he looked up at Task. "And perhaps," he added bitterly, "all the British warships will spring great leaks and sink with all hands before they come our way. Let's back to the drill, Lieutenant, and see if we can convince these men it'd be handy for them to learn how to use a bayonet."

The bayonet was a weapon which the militiamen of Nicholson's command eyed with deep distrust. In fact, most of the men put no faith in their muskets.

"These things," one soldier told Task, a few days after Tillman had been made a lieutenant, "might be all right for drillin', though they weigh a ton, but when the fightin' begins, give me a fowling piece loaded with buckshot. With that, I know damned well I'm goin' to sprinkle some Englishman good. As fer this pig-sticker—why, I don't aim t'git close enough to anybody to reach 'em with that thing."

"But if the Redcoats charge us," Task pointed out, "your fowling piece won't be worth a Continental after you've fired your load. With your bayonet—"

"Lootenant," grinned the bearded private, "when the Redcoats charge us, I'll be goin' in the other direction—fast!"

That, Task learned, was the attitude of most of the men and noncommissioned officers; they would fight at long range, possibly, but if the British launched a charge they'd scatter. *Stand up and fight against them fellers that's been weaned on war? Give me credit fer a little good sense, Lootenant!*

Tillman was forced to admit that position might have much to recommend it. Against an overwhelming force, only a fool would stand and die futilely. He had read somewhere among the military books he had studied since the start of the war that an orderly retreat in strength was almost as potent a weapon as an attack. The company, of course, had not been taught anything about retreating in good order; Nicholson was not alone among militia captains in thinking that any training in retreat would be a disgraceful confession of cowardice. The company, then, could be depended upon to break like a flushed covey of quail when the order came to retire—if not before any order was given. And where they would reassemble again, if they ever did, was left to chance.

Unbidden by the captain, Task Tillman tried to arrange some sort of rendezvous system among the members of the platoon given over to his command. His first mention of his plan to have the platoon withdraw from the firing line in squads on the order to retreat, one squad covering the other's retirement with its fire, met with a general snicker.

"My Gawd, Lootenant," somebody chuckled hoarsely, "when we retreat we don't want to be bothered about the next man, 'ceptin' he gits in our way. And anybody that gits in my way is goin' to be trompled."

A man with less patience (or perhaps stubbornness) than Task would have given up the idea as hopeless but Tillman stuck to it, explaining over and over that the men's own chances of escaping capture, or worse, would be improved by an orderly withdrawal, squad by squad.

"That way," he said, fighting down the exasperation that flared within him persistently, "we can take off our wounded. If any of you get a ball in the leg you won't want to be left behind while the rest take out, do you?"

It was this possibility that gave the men reason to pause. Like all soldiers, each man had considered the man next to him as the one who would be hit, not him. But, Task could see them pondering, if they *did* happen to be the one who took a musket ball in the leg (oh, just a scratch but a thing to hamper their running) it might be well to have some help in getting off the battlefield instead of being stuck there while the others took to their heels. So, at last, the platoon agreed to give the squad-by-squad withdrawal idea a try.

Once they entered the game they learned surprisingly easily and took pride, in fact, that they were the only platoon in the

Queen Annes Militia that knew how to leave a field like Regulars. Their way of retiring would have brought shudders to a professional soldier, perhaps, but Task was satisfied that he would have at least some semblance of a disciplined platoon when the order to give way came. That this disciplined retirement probably would leave his platoon exposed to the danger of being flanked and surrounded when the other units fled did not worry Task in the slightest; he did not know anything about that part of combat possibility.

Task was still perfecting his pet maneuver on the Queen's Town drill field the April afternoon when a horseman clad in the claret and white of the Dragon Footguard pounded into town and reined his sweating mount to a dust-whirling stop in front of Captain Nicholson.

"The British!" he cried hoarsely. "They're attacking along the Miles River! Captain Rawlent asks your help, sir!"

Task's throat tightened as he heard the courier's panted cry. The Redcoats were at Larkspur Hill, at Fairoverlea, and he was miles away instead of with the people who were fighting to defend the shores of the Miles. By now, the British were putting the torch to Larkspur Hill, looting the house of its few worthwhile possessions, carrying off the slaves. And Fairoverlea—Vivian—*Gracellen!* That fool, Rawlent, wouldn't hold off the enemy for as long as it took the British to walk ashore; his pretty-boy troop doubtless had fled without firing a volley, leaving the women to the bloody hands of the British who'd fall on them like wolves.

He left his platoon, every man dumbstruck and gaping at the messenger, and half ran to Nicholson, seized the captain's arm.

"Sir," he cried, "we must help! We've got to go to those people! If we double-time—"

Nicholson's cold eyes stopped his babble. He drew back the hand that gripped the captain's arm and brought it up in an abashed salute.

"Pardon, sir," he muttered.

"Ready your men for a quick-march," Nicholson snapped. "We're moving out at once for Easton Town."

From Queen's Town to Easton was eighteen miles and Nicholson's company made the march in three and a half hours. The creditable time was due as much to Task Tillman's sweaty urging as to any other factor. Captain Nicholson rode Lucifer as befit the commander of the company; Task marched with his men by choice, keeping up a running fire of encouragement, caustic taunts and biting threats to keep his men from dropping out of line when feet began to blister, muskets began to take on weight and muscles began stabbing their owners.

Task alternately watched his men and scanned the sky for the smoke that would tell him the British were laying waste to the Miles River countryside. He saw no heart-sickening columns of smoke, he heard no gunfire from the direction of Easton and the Miles. As the company trudged into the outskirts of Easton Town he met no panic-stricken refugees, no weeping women, no battle-stained and beaten soldiers. Instead, there were housewives at their windows, staring in frank curiosity, children waving, whooping and dancing along the road, men in the fields who watched the company's passing and then turned back to their work.

Captain Nicholson came riding down the column, a puzzled frown on his face.

"Damned if these people look as though the British were attacking on the Miles," he told Task. "That courier *did* say the Miles River, didn't he?"

"Yes sir," Tillman replied. "Perhaps—perhaps they were beaten off, sir. Perhaps they've left off the attack."

"Beaten off by Rawlent's dandies?" Nicholson scoffed. "I hope so but I doubt it." He eyed the weary Queen Annes Militiamen who practically staggered in their tracks. "Well, we'll go as far as Easton Town and inquire there. I begin to smell a rat in all this, Lieutenant."

At Easton, where the weary troops were told to fall out for a rest—and immediately collapsed, almost to a man—Nicholson, Tillman and the company's other officers went to that infallible source of information, the Indian Queen's taproom, to get the details of the British attack.

"I know nothin' about it, Cap'n," the barkeep said. "Gentleman was just in here said he saw one of Cap'n Rawlent's horsemen go tearin' up the old Queen's Town road but we thought nothin' about it—Cap'n Rawlent's always got his riders rippin' up and down the roads hereabouts."

"No sound of guns?" Nicholson asked. "No word of any British landing?"

"No sir," the barkeep replied, wagging his head. "If there was ye'd not find me here, sir, handin' out drinks. I'd be with *my* company, sir, the Fencibles."

Nicholson pushed his hat back on his head, then planted his hands on his hips. His dust-stained face grew stiff with anger and he cursed beneath his breath.

"We've been hoaxed, by God," he ground out, "and there's somebody that's going to pay for this fine trick before I'm much older. Where's Rawlent, barkeep—have you seen him in town?"

"No sir. Bein' as this is one o' their drill days, ye ought to find him at the field where the Dragons drill."

"And where's that?" Nicholson jerked out.

"I know," said Task. "I'll guide you there."

"You better had, Lieutenant," the captain nodded. "I'll hire a nag from the stables here and we'll ride together. You know this country better than I do."

The Dragons' drill field proved empty except for a small Negro boy who expressed the hazy thought that "the sojer gemmuns went down that-a-way, suh." "Down that-a-way" was in the direction of Fairoverlea and Task explained this to the captain.

"Lead on," Nicholson said grimly. "I'll run this fox to ground if it takes all day."

The Dragons were at Fairoverlea, dotting the lawn with their bright uniforms, surrounding a trestle table on which demijohns and decanters, a cask of ale and great platters of food had been set out. Nicholson reined in at the top of the drive and surveyed the scene bitterly for a moment before he turned to Task Tillman.

"Why it's an invitation to a picnic," he said with dangerous amusement. "Rawlent wanted to surprise us all so picked this novel way of bidding us to join the merriment." His jaw snapped shut and his eyes blazed. "Where is the cock-o'-walk whipper-snapper, Task; do ye see him?"

Task's eyes roved over the throng and picked out Charles Rawlent. He was standing beside Gracellen, a glass in his hand, laughing at some remark made to him by a stripling lieutenant who wore sidewhiskers that came close to touching the corners of his mouth.

"There he is, Captain," Tillman said, "over by that birch tree. The man next to the lady, sir."

Nicholson lurched out of his saddle with a grunt and Task dismounted. One of Fairoverlea's twin carriage boys had appeared out of nowhere and took the reins of the horses as the two green-jacketed Queen's Town officers walked across the carpet of grass toward Rawlent. They threaded their way through the crowd of Dragons without speaking, ignoring the few greetings that were directed at them. In their wake they left a spreading quiet as all eyes swung toward them.

Rawlent saw their approach when they were fifteen paces away and Task watched as a supercilious sneer replaced the smile on the face of Gracellen's husband.

"Ah, Nicholson," he called out as they walked up to him. "Sorry I had to bother you. 'Fraid you'll be disappointed if you expected a crack at the Lobsterbacks. Demmed affair turned out to be a false alarm."

"A—false—alarm," Nicholson repeated, breathing heavily.

"Yes," Rawlent went on in his superior drawl. "Y'see, a lookout did sight British sail and came to me with the alarm. I posted the Dragons instanter, of course. We were in position to repel landing parties in less time than it takes to tell. We move fast, if I do say it."

"My men marched—*marched at double-quick*—from Queen's Town—"

"Ah, yes," Rawlent sniffed. "Well, the British vessels, a whole flotilla, didn't turn in at Eastern Bay, after all. But by that time I'd sent word to you—just in case we might need some reinforcements, y'know. Called on you because the rabble at Easton won't cooperate in the slightest, y'see."

Task thought for a moment that Captain Nicholson was going to be stricken with apoplexy on the spot. His face was purple, cords stood out on his neck, his teeth ground and his hands were tightly clenched. After a struggle he regained control of himself, though his voice was not his own when he spoke.

"Your courier," he said with an effort, "told me the British were attacking along the Miles. Attacking!"

"I told him to report that," Rawlent nodded calmly. "Thought it would hurry you up, y'see."

"Hurry—us—up! And when you found the British weren't coming here, after all, you didn't send another messenger to countermand your call for help."

Rawlent shook his head, still sneering faintly.

"No," he admitted. "Y'see, I thought it would be a good chance to find out how long it would take your company to quick-march here in case we ever *did* need you as reinforcements. And I must say, Captain, that it took a little too long. Why, by the time you—"

Captain Nicholson's fist had started its blow when Task saw it. Tillman thrust out his hand and caught his captain's arm a split-second before the blow landed.

"Let me go!" Nicholson said in a hoarse, strangled voice. "Let me loose, Lieutenant."

"No, Captain," Task Tillman said. "'Twould be a dueling matter if you hit him and he's not worth it. The company, sir!"

"This ninnying fool—"

"Believe me, sir, I'd like nothing better than to flatten him again, as I did once, but there's the company. You'd lose your militia commission for dueling, you know. The Governor would call it back as soon as he got the word. Think of the company, Captain!"

"To hell with the company!"

"Well, think on this then, Captain," Task went on. "This— this gentleman says the British flotilla went up-Bay. What if they

222

swung in at the Chester River? We'd best get back in case they're aiming at Queen's Town, sir."

That warning erased the blind fury from Captain Nicholson's face. He turned toward Tillman, his face strained by a new emotion, fear.

"By God, ye're right," he almost whispered. "They could be headed there and my company on a fool's errand down here. If they've landed and sacked my town—come on, Lieutenant!"

He whirled and strode through the crowd, Task at his heels. He flung himself into the saddle and jerked his horse's head about to canter down the drive. Astride Lucifer, Task tarried only long enough to look back at Gracellen Rawlent. His eyes met hers and the scorn for the man standing beside her, the drawling, egotistical fool who had deliberately stripped the guard of an entire town to feed his vanity, must have shown in his stare.

Gracellen tried to lift her chin, meet his glare, and failed. He saw her bite her lip, then drop her head, in something that could be nothing but shame for her husband.

13

THE flotilla that had set Charles Rawlent screaming for help consisted of a ship of the line, *Sceptre*, a frigate, *Menelaus*, two brigs, a sloop and three schooners, each warship towing landing barges. The British did not turn into the Chester River nor the Sassafras, above it. All the vessels kept on their northward course until they were off the mouth of the Patapsco, a few miles down-river from Baltimore. There, they anchored.

Sir Peter Porter was summoned to Admiral Cockburn's flagship as soon as the anchors plunged into the water. He found the lizard-mouthed admiral in his cabin, being helped into his dress uniform. In a chair against the further bulkhead lolled the admiral's nephew and aide, Captain Clement Vickers.

"Ye're going with us, Porter," Cockburn said, with no preliminaries. "We're going to pay a call on the biggest dog in the Baltimore kennel, a man named Sam Smith who calls himself a General over this rabble."

"A call, sir?" Porter asked, puzzled.

"Aye," Cockburn grunted. "We'll go aboard the sloop and fly a truce flag. Oh, the Yankees will respect it, never fear. These yokels who play at soldiers know all the rules even though they can't fight worth a hound's lick of his arse."

"Aye, sir," the younger admiral nodded.

"And ye're wonderin' why I'm wastin' time instead of bringin' the fleet up and taking the cockroach nest?" Cockburn growled. "I could do that easy enough, p'raps, but I'd like to see just what we'll have to meet when we do. A visit to this Smith might give us the answers to all the questions I've got concernin' this hole."

He struggled into his boots, stood up and stamped them on the deck.

"So I thought we'd pay a call on Smith under a truce flag and offer him a chance to surrender," Cockburn grinned. "He won't take it, of course, but—"

"I'll wager he will, Uncle," Captain Vickers broke in in his indolent voice. Cockburn turned to glower and then smiled.

"Ye do, eh, Clement? Well, that binds it, 'cause ye've never won a wager yet—I should know, payin' y'r gamin' debts." He turned back to Sir Peter Porter. "No, he won't surrender but p'raps my peepers will disclose Smith's real strength and save us all time when we do come here to wipe out this den, eh?"

Without waiting for a reply, he stalked toward the door of his cabin, settling his hat on his bullet head.

"I want you with me," he hurled over his shoulder, "'cause two pair of eyes see more than one and Clement might sight a pretty lass and be good for naught. Look sharp, Porter, and see what you can see."

The sloop made its way upriver in wide tacks and Cockburn and Sir Peter Porter eyed the shore closely while above them fluttered the white flag that was their safe conduct warrant. Vickers lounged beside them, as idly disinterested in this venture as he was in most things.

"Looks like they've got some sort of a battery over there," Cockburn grunted. "Three pieces, looks like—not more than four. That vessel anchored there's a signal boat, that's plain. See, she's runnin' up her pennants now to tell 'em we're on our way. Is that another battery yonder, Porter?"

"Aye, sir," the young Admiral nodded. "Six guns, I'd say."

"Be cursed," Cockburn growled. "I'd heard the Yankees have been busy but I confess I didn't think they'd done this much.

What concerns me are those damned French seventy-two-pounders."

"Seventy-two-pounders?" Sir Peter Porter asked in surprise. "They have that big a gun?"

"Well, that's what I want to find out, damn it!" Cockburn snapped. "We've heard the Yankees bought a battery of seventy-two-pounders from France not long after the last war. Some say there were ten of 'em, others say only six. But six is enough, I'd say, to make it unpleasant for us if they're here. And all the numbskulls at the Admiralty can't find out where those big guns have been placed, confound 'em." He chuckled hoarsely. "P'raps our General Smith will get to boastin' and then we'll know."

The sloop's sails came down as the vessel edged closer to the ramparts of Fort McHenry and Sir Peter Porter's nape hair rose as he looked up from the longboat which carried him, Cockburn and Captain Vickers ashore. The staring muzzles of the fort's cannon seemed to be eyeing them hungrily. A white flag seemed at that moment to be almighty scant protection from the guns of these men who must hate Admiral Sir George Cockburn with all their hearts.

The squat Cockburn was completely at ease. As the longboat came up beside the fort's dock he leapt nimbly up onto the planking and straightened to face the American officer with gold epaulets who, Sir Peter decided, must be this General Smith. The two men eyed each other for the space of five seconds before Cockburn gave a grudging salute and received as cold an answer from Smith.

"General," Cockburn began, bluntly, "I'm here to give ye the chance to surrender this fort and the city to His Majesty's forces without bloodshed."

General Smith gave a slight bow, his face rigid.

"This fort and this city will never be surrendered," he said icily, "as was Hampton."

Cockburn grinned and waved a thick hand.

"That hamlet?" he sniggered. "They'd ha' been safe and sound if they hadn't treacherously fired on a flag of truce."

Smith started to speak, closed his lips firmly. Cockburn looked about him and Sir Peter Porter realized with a start that he was supposed to keep his own eyes busy, seeking out details of the American defenses.

"Ye have the idea this—this feeble trench ye've dug will hold us off when we determine to attack?" Cockburn was asking.

"I suggest," General Smith replied stiffly, "that the Admiral find that out for himself."

"And that I shall, that I shall," Cockburn nodded. "A few broadsides will prove the thing, quick enough."

There was no reply from Smith. Cockburn eyed the concealing parapets again. Sir Peter's gaze joined his admiral's. The guns whose muzzles were visible were heavy enough—probably thirty-six or even forty-two pounders—but there was nothing as big as a seventy-two to be seen. The Yankees, though, could have put sham parapets around them to hide them.

"Ah—I expect ye think those seventy-two's the Frenchies sold you will hold us off, eh?" Admiral Cockburn laughed. "Let me tell you about those guns, General. All Europe was laughin' when they heard you Yankees had bought 'em. Y'see the guns were not rightly forged. They're bound to blow up at the first shot."

General Smith's face tightened another notch.

"If it's information you seek, Admiral," he said frigidly, "I can save you all your searching questions. I'll tell you now that we've mounted the heaviest guns we have and we'll fire them at you and they'll not explode. I think that ends the need for continuing this parley. I bid you good day, gentlemen."

Cockburn hunched his thick shoulders, grinned humorlessly and turned away from General Sam Smith without a salute. Sir Peter, taking his cue from his superior, stopped his hand halfway to the peak of his hat, half-bowed and then followed the admiral and Vickers. He tried to keep his eyes squarely on the center of Cockburn's broad back but they kept sliding off to either side and he was uncomfortably conscious of the stark hatred reflected in the glare of the cross-belted, hard-hatted soldiers who lined the pathway back down to the dock where the longboat waited.

These men, Porter assumed, were American Regulars, although he was admittedly weak in his knowledge of Yankee uniforms. Certainly they seemed well-equipped and well-disciplined; not even a grumbling curse was heard from the soldiers who might have had relatives or friends at Hampton. The young Admiral wondered what Cockburn's reception under a flag of truce would have been if the situation were reversed and he was visiting a British fort after having laid waste to an innocent English coastal town.

With the longboat pulling back to the sloop, Cockburn dropped his sneering mask and replaced it with a black scowl.

"Damned impertinence!" he growled. "Treating me like an officer of equal rank, that Colonial who probably came out of some wilderness cabin and was wet-nursed by a she bear! And those seventy-two's; you didn't see anything of 'em, did you, Porter?"

"No sir."

"You, Clement?"

"Nothing, Uncle, except those thirty-sixes."

"They were forty-two's," Cockburn snarled. "Damn it, when are you goin' to learn a gun's weight by lookin' at it? There were some thirty-two's over at the far end and it looks like they've built a furnace for hot shot back of the ramparts. Aye, if they've got those seventy-two's hid someplace they're prettily fixed, damn their eyes."

He looked to port, surveying the raw mound of dirt that marked Star Fort on the other bank of the river.

"Too small for those French guns," he muttered. "It could be that the big 'uns are placed in some of those shore batteries we passed coming in—and if they are, we're lucky. We can silence those with landin' parties who'll encircle but"—his scowl deepened—"I must find out for certain where those seventy-two's are placed, if Smith has got 'em at all."

"He said he'd mounted the heaviest guns he had," Sir Peter pointed out.

"Which could well be the forty-two's," Cockburn grunted. "We needs must get some firsthand word as to just what they're armed with."

The ranking Admiral scrambled up the sloop's gangway with an agility that belied his squat bulk, Captain Vickers and Porter following. The warship's anchor was weighed, the sloop's sails filled and the vessel circled to begin its voyage back to where the looming *Sceptre* was anchored.

"Seein' we must wait on dependable word of what Smith's got at Fort McHenry," Admiral Cockburn rumbled to Porter as he mounted the poop, "I think we'll pay a call on some of the towns up the Chesapeake, just to keep the men alive. There's a ship-building yard at a town called Havre de Grace, near where Howe landed his forces in Seventy-six to capture Philadelphia. P'raps that'll be a good enough village to try our aim on, eh?"

"Yes sir," Porter nodded.

"I'm hot to try these new rockets 'gainst a fortified position," Cockburn went on. "The Admiralty says they're precious effective 'gainst ground troops. The fizzers are said t'kill 'em and scare 'em to death, both. And they're supposed to start pretty fires in a village."

He yawned, belched and dug under his ornate uniform tunic to scratch himself.

"It'll be Havre de Grace," he nodded. "The men will like settin' foot ashore and havin' themselves a bit of fun, good lads."

Sir Peter Porter kept his face immobile but a shiver coursed up his spine. To himself he said: *God help this town called Havre de Grace!*

Part Four

1

WHEN Sir Peter Porter breathed his silent prayer for the people of Havre de Grace, Anthony Worth was already on his way to the city that lay on the Susquehanna River, close to its confluence with the Chesapeake Bay.

The dust of his departure had barely settled down the lane before Vivian was sending a note to Task Tillman by the silent, dull-faced Abraham, the only one of Fairoverlea's slaves she could trust—and she never discounted the risks she took in trusting even him.

The Negro was her own personal servant, a slave given to her two years before as a birthday present and subject to her orders alone. She knew Abraham was envied by the other servants—Vivian was a kind, thoughtful mistress—and she presumed, she hoped, that he was grateful for the way he was treated. But she never could be sure; no one could ever be completely sure of what went on in the heads of the blacks. That obscene monster Titus, Vivian realized, had the power to wield more influence over Abraham and every other Negro at Fairoverlea than even Anthony Worth, himself. If Titus took it into his head to pry into her affairs she could never depend on Abraham's loyalty to hide her secrets.

But that was a risk that had to be taken if she would see Task Tillman. And during the passing months the need to see Task had become increasingly demanding. This longing for the tawny-eyed Master of Larkspur Hill had become a compulsion as strong as a tippler's need for his bottle or an addict's craving for his laudanum. This realization frightened Vivian but it did not deter her.

Vivian knew, too, that there was no excusing herself on any grounds that Anthony Worth had brought this upon himself. At the start there had been the underlying motive of revenge; now this flame that had consumed her had swept over that ground and left it behind, forgotten. Anthony's brutality on the morning after Gracellen's betrothal ball may have set Vivian on the dangerous path of reckless deception but now she rushed on her way in the pursuit of her own desires, shutting her eyes to the disaster that surely must lie ahead.

Alone, after a meeting with Task, she often wondered at herself and the change that the alchemy of Task Tillman had wrought in her. In England and betrothed to Sir Robert she had experienced only the mildest stirrings which any growing girl could have expected. In her despair which had followed Sir Robert's defalcation and her father's business deal, she had suffered herself to be used by Anthony Worth in a way she had presumed all wives were used, responding in the way she had been made to believe was her duty, no matter how repugnant.

And then, with Task Tillman's first touch everything had changed. There had been no question of love between them—indeed, she had hardly known the man—but all the blazing, dazzling brilliance of those few seconds when they were welded together in the parlor-office of Larkspur Hill had illumined shadowed corners of her life, her very being, to disclose beauty and transport as she had never dared dream existed.

She had read, or heard, that there could be no joy in union with a man unless there was an enveloping love that drew the partners out of their mundane selves. Vivian could give the lie to that conclusion—or could she?

Was it possible, she asked herself, that there was more to their feeling for each other than the mere need to satisfy their impatient

234

desires? Could there have been a love which, under different circumstances, would have blossomed into a fine, proud thing?

No. There was only Gracellen for Task and there never had been anyone but Gracellen. She must not demand love from Task to try to cloak her own wrongdoing. She was to blame for all of this. She had led Task, dragged him, along the way she followed, using strange and newborn wiles to urge him on when he was reluctant, ready to use tears and recriminations if he ever gave in to what must be his protesting conscience and sought to end this mad affair.

Was Task weak? Rather say that Vivian had been made stronger than a thousand strong men by her sudden discovery of the latent powers she had kept suppressed. She had been the chaste wife at whom so many sidelong glances had been cast by the men who had been misled by her beauty; now she was the complete wanton who showed all the world save Task a manner and mien grown frostier day by day as her competence in guile developed.

She knew an honest woman, a reasoning woman, a woman who was truly grateful to Task Tillman, would give him up, banish him from her life. She may have tried to do this but if she did she found she could not.

So Vivian Dangerfield Worth slipped along the hidden path that led from Fairoverlea to Larkspur Hill that night of Anthony's departure and on many of the nights that followed. To leave Fairoverlea without Gracellen or Rawlent discovering her absence was a comparatively easy thing; her rooms and Anthony's were in the mansion's east wing, the Rawlents' in the west. After the evening meal, when Anthony was not at home and when there were no guests to be entertained, Vivian went to her part of the house while Charles and Gracellen went to theirs. The two women had never been close enough for Gracellen to ordinarily drop in on Vivian in her rooms or for Vivian to seek Gracellen's company in hers.

The path Vivian used was a screened way and it twisted through a deep pine woods and skirted a marsh but Vivian had learned to fly over it without a light on the darkest night; she had walked back along it many times, more slowly, replete, through the swirling morning mists. She did not fear the dark. Indeed, she preferred night in her new self to blazing noon, the lowering skies of a storm-threatened sunset to the crystalline brilliance of a sparkling dawn.

"I surely must be a witch," she murmured to Task Tillman, one night, "for I can see as plainly on the blackest midnight as most people can by day. I'm frightened by none of the night noises in the deepest part of the woods."

"A witch you are," Task murmured drowsily, "and you've bewitched me past all curing. You've cast a spell I'll never throw off unless you bid me to."

"You want to cast off this spell?"

"Nay, Vivian. I want—I want—"

Vivian was most ready to fill his wants. Vivian was always ready to do that. And one of the nights when Anthony Worth was in Havre de Grace, she heard herself calling Task's name, heard her unbidden voice crying: "I love you!"

Task did not hear that cry, deafened as he was by the thundering in his ears, and Vivian was glad of that. She told herself it had been only a second's delighted hysteria and she assured herself that she would not repeat that mistake. But on another night she heard her cry again as she sank her nails deep into Task's shoulders and this time he answered her with the same words.

2

On the day Anthony Worth reached Havre de Grace, the clipper *Lorelei* was beating her way to the northeast off the coast of New Jersey, headed for Portsmouth, New Hampshire, with a prize in tow.

She was, Jett Worth had to admit, not much of a prize even though by strict definition she was an armed British warship. The captive vessel was the *Sprite*, a dispatch cutter that had been run down and seized on the Bermuda-Virginia Capes sea lane after a fight that had lasted only a few minutes.

"And I," Jett admitted to Mister Greer, the mate, "felt almost ashamed to grab her. 'Twas like a schoolyard bully picking on some undersized runt who didn't want to fight."

"Still, Cap'n," Greer said, consolingly, "she'll bring a fair prize value in port, if we get the right man to look her over. And half her full value's ours, remember."

"Aye," Jett said sourly, "and I'd had my heart set on seizing a frigate or a brig, at least, the first time my guns went into action. That would mean something, but this longboat—"

"P'raps the papers aboard her—"

"Mean nothing," Jett grumbled. "Her captain heaved overboard everything of any importance the minute he saw his vessel couldn't run away from us. All he left was his crew muster and a personal diary, as far as I've been able to find out."

"The diary—" Greer began again.

"Is his private affair," Jett finished. "Oh, I peeked at it but it's full of thoughts about some virgin maid—I hope she is—named Polly."

"Code?" asked the bearded Greer, hopefully.

"You've met our good captain," Jett laughed. "One minute's talk with him and you saw why that lieutenant was given command of a vessel the size of the *Sprite*. I doubt there's a code made that he could understand—but here he comes for his breakfast."

The *Lorelei's* officers not on watch arose as the skipper of the dispatch cutter entered the wardroom. Salutes were exchanged and the young British lieutenant, a sallow, long-faced individual with the air of superiority that the British Navy somehow engraved on all its officers, apparently during their servile days as midshipmen, took his place at the table.

"Good morning, gentlemen," he said in his admiral's voice. He glanced up at the scuttles through which the morning sun streamed. "Fair weather and a good breeze. This vessel is a smooth ship, I must say, Captain."

"Thank you, Captain," Jett returned with an acknowledging nod. "She was built to sail smoothly."

"Aye," the British lieutenant agreed. He accepted his plate of fried salt pork and the mug of coffee that was his breakfast. "I'll give you Yankees credit for your lighter vessels, such as this." He dipped a ship's biscuit in his coffee. "The *Sprite's* a wet-deck ship, even if I have to say it m'self. I've served her for more than two years and my locker was never altogether dry in all that time."

"Not Yankees, Lieutenant," Jett corrected, gently. "The Yankees are our neighbors in New England, where we're bound. We're all from Maryland, here."

"Can't keep you apart," the lieutenant—his name was Bean—apologized. "Thought all of you were Yankees. That song, 'Yankee Doodle Dandy,' y'know. And where is it we're bound, Captain?"

"One of the New England ports," Jett smiled. "You'll find yourself well-treated there. No Co'burn has been ravaging their coast and they're friendly to the English."

"Those stories about Admiral Co'burn," Bean said stiffly, "are mostly lies, y'know. A stern man he may be—aye, and I've reason to know that—but I can't credit these wild tales of looting and rape."

"Were you at Hampton?" Greer asked bluntly.

"Er—no, I was at sea when the village was taken," Bean admitted, "but I've talked with some who were there and they all say the taking of the town was carried out under all the prescribed rules of war. Those were the words of gentlemen, sir."

"And those who gave us our reports were not?" Greer growled. "Y'think a whole town burned itself to circulate an enormous lie, sir?"

"It's the word of an admiral of His Majesty's Navy against the word of a pack of nobodies," Bean said, without visible rancor. "Whose word could a thinkin' man accept, sir?"

"Gentlemen, gentlemen," Jett broke in. "We don't need to debate the thing in this wardroom, do we? I imagine they'll be arguing about the truth of Hampton for years to come. I say we drop the—"

Everybody at the board stiffened as the voice of the crow's-nest lookout came floating clearly through the scuttles.

"Sail ho!"

"Where away?" was the answering bellow of the watch officer aft.

"Port quarter and she flies the British ensign! Brig, sir, and she's bearin' down!"

There was the scramble of the *Lorelei*'s officers as they disentangled themselves from their benches. Jett paused with one foot on the coaming of the wardroom doorway to throw a word back at Bean.

"You'll stay below, Captain," he said briefly, "and in your cabin. Or must I post a guard?"

The dispatch sloop's skipper grinned back at him.

"A guard will give you one less man above, Captain," he returned, and so I think you'd better post one at my cabin."

Jett nodded, spoke a word to Greer and hurried up the ladder to the poopdeck.

Wilson, the clipper's third officer, already had given the order to the bos'n to shake out all watches and clear for action and the deck was a swift-moving, silent swirl of men going about their duties with an efficiency that brought a flush of pride to Jett Worth. These men had never felt the slash of a bos'n's rattan, they never had been forced to "kiss the gunner's daughter" by being bent over a cannon to be whipped, they were as apt to call him Jett as Captain when they spoke to him, they had little awe and certainly no fear of their officers; if they had a grievance they were quick to let their captain know about it; not a man amongst them was aboard the clipper against his will. It was a shipshape, fighting crew with a spirit that Great Britain never would understand.

Jett Worth, keeping his face impassive against the throat-jarring hammering of his heart, took the glass from Wilson and trained it on the speck of sail that grew larger as he watched. It was a brig, all right, and she was hot for a fight. She outweighed and outgunned the clipper by odds of five to three and the sensible thing for *Lorelei* to do was abandon the little dispatch cutter after transferring back aboard the clipper the prize crew that Jett had put on *Sprite*, and then run for it.

"Who's aboard the cutter?" he asked his third officer in a tight voice.

"Elwood, sir, second mate," Wilson answered. "Twelve-man crew, ten prisoners. The rest of the Lobsterbacks are aboard *Lorelei*, sir."

Jett frowned as he kept the glass on the brig. The prize he towed was a cockleshell that certainly was not worth risking *Lorelei* to keep. But, damn it, he *had* seized the vessel, it was his prize and *Lorelei's* first armed captive! To hand the cutter back to His Majesty would give whoever was in command of the brig a chance to strut and boast and shape some outrageous story.

"Signal *Sprite*," he rapped out, "and tell 'em to run for shallow water while we entertain our visitors! Cast off that tow line!"

240

"Aye, aye, sir!" There was jubilation in Wilson's voice. He moved to the signalman at the mizzen halliards. Jett looked up at his sails, spoke to Greer in a quiet voice that scarcely trembled with his excitement.

"Lay her on the port tack, please," he said. "Full and bye. We're going to engage, Mister Greer."

"Aye, sir." His deep voice boomed his orders the length of the clipper and a spontaneous cheer went up from the busy crew. Jett's mouth firmed into grim lines. Cheer they might now, but a clipper against a brig might bring more groans than cheers before this day was over.

On deck, men were scattering sand to protect the gunners against slipping at their work. The gunners themselves had scuffed off their boots so that no nail would strike a spark that might make flaming destruction of the powder they were handling. Beside each of *Lorelei's* eight broadside guns and the stern and bow-chasers was set a tub of water into which the gun swabs would be plunged after each shot and which also would serve in case of fire, should the oncoming brig use hotshot.

Around the mainmast were set more water tubs as well as slow-burning oiled wicks from which the gunners could rekindle their linstocks. Light carronades were trundled into place while the crews of the heavier guns ran their pieces in and out of their ports experimentally. The bustle of the preparation activities quieted and the men stood motionless in their appointed positions, waiting, ready.

The brig obviously had expected the clipper to run. When *Lorelei* cut across her bows on the swift port tack, the Britisher shortened sail and swung to starboard to intercept the American. She reckoned without *Lorelei's* superior speed. The clipper swept past before the brig's starboard broadside could be brought to bear.

Jett's own starboard battery thundered as the two vessels passed. The broadside was short, although both the bow and stern pivot guns had the distance but were astern the brig.

"Steady, steady!" Greer roared. "Wait till ye bear!"

The brig, H.M.S. *Unicorn*, answered the American's broadside with a blast of her stern guns. There was the liquid churning sound of balls passing overhead, the scream of ripping canvas, the twang of parting ratlines, as the missiles crashed through the rigging. *Unicorn* was striking at Jett's principal weapon, the sails that gave him his speed.

Scarcely had the boom of the Britisher's fire died before Wilson had his men aloft, bending new lines, lashing a tops'l spar that had been snapped, repairing the damage almost before *Lorelei* came about for another run at the brig. *Unicorn* came about smartly—aye, Jett grunted to himself, they knew their business—and plunged at *Lorelei*. The two vessels could have been tilting knights, each eager to get in the thrust that would destroy the other. On they came under full canvas, or close to it, and when it seemed that they must crash together, head-on, each fell off to port.

The two broadsides were as one. Flame-spiked clouds of smoke rolled out and met between the two vesels, surging up in a great, thick curtain that masked each ship from the other.

Unicorn's broadside had swept the clipper's deck with a devastating hail of solid and grapeshot. As Jett peered down the smoky deck he saw that half a dozen of his men were down and at least one gun was out of action. The Britisher had not tried for the sails this time; she had lowered her guns to deck level and she had scored.

There were some cries from the wounded men but not many and these were quickly hushed as the stricken sailors were carried below. The gun crews that had survived the blast were busy with their swabs, working as mechanically as though they were at target practice, showing not the least sign of panic at the swish of the deadly scythe that had passed over them.

Good men, Jett yelled without speaking. *Good men and brave!*

He turned *Lorelei* hard a-port while the British brig was still cloaked by the smoke of her own guns. He took the clipper running up close to the brig's stern and loosed his portside battery in a broadside that made *Lorelei* heel. Before the effect of that blow could be measured (indeed, Jett still did not know what his second broadside had done to *Unicorn*) he brought the clipper

242

in on another tack that put his damaged starboard guns to bear. There was another blast and Jett swung his vessel away.

Unicorn fired blindly with three or four guns. One heavy ball crashed into *Lorelei's* foredeck, flinging a shower of deadly splinters and felling all but two of the fore pivot gun's crew.

"Fire buckets here!" came the yell from forward and the fire details rushed toward where the glimmer of flames showed through black, roily smoke.

"Hot shot?" Jett asked from between clenched teeth. "Then we're done!"

"No sir," Greer rumbled. "Splinter friction caught some spilt powder, I'd say. Quickly out, sir, and—*look at the brig, Jett!*"

A vagrant wind had caught the brig and whirled away the masking smoke that had hung in a heavy haze over the Britisher. Jett looked and stared. A ball from one of his two heavy guns, the stern or bow pivot, had scored a hit that had splintered the brig's mainmast just below the lower main topsail. With the canvas *Unicorn* was carrying, the weakened mainmast had snapped, bringing down a tangle of canvas and lines that lay across the mizzen, effectively disabling the entire aft rigging. The brig's crew were frantically busy now, hacking at the lines, trying to unship the disabled mainmast and clear the mizzen. With only her foresail and jibs to move her, *Unicorn* floundered uncertainly before her captain tried to draw her off on a tack, out of *Lorelei's* range.

"Ah, no ye don't!" Jett roared. "Hard a-sta'bd!"

The clipper streaked in on her wounded foe. *Lorelei's* guns bellowed, raking the brig's deck with grape. *Unicorn's* answer was ragged and her gunners hurried their fire; most of the broadside was off the target. *Lorelei* danced away, came about "on top of her rudder," and darted in again. Again *Unicorn* shuddered under the impact of the broadside. Smoke from a fire below decks began seeping up through the brig's hatches. There was a bright burst of flame as a powder sack in the Britisher's waist flared.

The brig was in a desperate way and she knew it. Call it luck or superior seamanship, the heavier, better-armed vessel had been

243

practically put out of action, her striking power had been disorganized in the first or second broadside that had reached her. Still, doggedly, she lumbered about and tried to meet the next rush of the bedevilling *Lorelei*. In that, *Unicorn* made a mistake. Her only hope of escape lay then in evading the clipper's guns long enough to clear the clutter of the smashed mainmast, getting the mizzen back into action, putting out the fires that crackled between decks and in her waist, and bending on all possible sail to keep her distance from *Lorelei's* lighter guns while trying to reach the American with her twenty-four-pounders in a chase, if the clipper elected to follow her withdrawal.

As it was, the disabled brig was what Jett termed later a "crippled brent-goose" as she wallowed in to strike blindly at her tormentor. The clipper still had her speed and she had a target that was almost stationary. Her gunners were quoining with a true and confident eye. Nearly every ball, every merciless sweep of grape, struck home. The end of this fight was obvious a half hour after the first broadsides had been exchanged.

Still, *Unicorn* fought on, as hopeless as the outlook was, as brutally her punishment mounted. The fires aboard the brig spread and soon her lower gun deck was silent, her jib was in tatters. She lay helpless, the victim of the fortunes of war that had stripped her of her strength in the very opening of the fight.

"Strike, damn you," Jett implored as his guns thudded again and again. "Ye've shown you're brave enough. Strike, while you've still got a ship under you!"

As if in answer to Jett's silent demand, the brig's ensign came down in *Unicorn's* grudging surrender. A hurricane of cheers broke out on the clipper; sailors and officers waved their caps in the air, danced on the decks. And, Jett grinned, they had a right to celebrate; *Lorelei* had met and beaten her first worthy enemy.

"Next," he told the beaming Greer, "we'll bag us a frigate."

Later that day, with the fires aboard the captured brig extinguished, with the battered vessel jury-rigged and in tow with a prize crew handling her, Jett totted up the grim score of the battle. *Lorelei* had lost fourteen men killed, including Wilson, the third mate, and nine of the clipper's crew had been wounded or burned. Lieutenant Nicholas McComas of the *Unicorn* reported that his ship had lost thirty-one killed, six wounded so badly that they would soon die, and twenty-eight of his men less seriously wounded.

"And one of His Majesty's brigs," McComas added bitterly, "fallen into the hands of the Americans by my worthless command of her."

"I'd not say that, Captain," Jett protested. "'Twas a lucky hit on your mainm'st that did the trick. Nobody can say you didn't fight your ship as well as she could be fought, crippled as she was."

"I should've rammed you at the outset," McComas said inconsolably. "I had the heavier vessel, the bigger crew. I should've rammed you and boarded you before you got past your first broadside."

"And by rights," Jett smiled, "I should've picked up my skirts and fled when you raised us. I had no business engaging."

"That," McComas said sourly, "is the trouble with you Yankees. Ye're too new at this business to know the rules."

"Not Yankees, Captain, by your leave," Jett said softly. "I had to put Lieutenant Bean right on that score. We're all Marylanders aboard this vessel."

Lieutenant McComas was a thickset man whose grey temples showed he must have been passed over in promotion to still be captaining a brig with the rank of lieutenant, at his age. Now he summoned a faint smile to his fleshy lips.

"And there's another thing," he complained. "Who do we war against, the United States or Maryland? Before I cleared Bermuda I was told that more than a hundred of the privateers warring against us are Maryland vessels, whilst the other Colonies—or States, or whatever you call 'em—have sent out only a handful. Why do you Maryland men take on yourselves the full burden of this war, Captain?"

"Why sir," Jett explained, "it's 'cause we see our chance to prove to all America—aye, to the whole world—that there never was nor

245

ever can be a sailing man to match a son of Maryland. The Yankees have claimed too long that they were the best on any sea and now we're out to show they're only second best."

"And when Admiral Co'burn takes Baltimore," Lieutenant Mc-Comas asked, "what are you going to use for ships to prove your case?"

"Ah, Captain," Jett laughed, "askin' that question is like askin' what would happen if a gull's feather made a crack in a belaying pin. It's impossible to answer because it won't ever happen."

Lieutenant McComas raised his mug of rum and water to his lips.

"Co'burn a feather?" he asked. "By God, I'd like to see the tough old bird that feather moulted from!"

The *Lorelei* kept on up the coast after picking up again her first prize, the now insignificant *Sprite,* and sighted no other sail, friend or foe, on her way. She was off New Bedford, Massachusetts, when the clipper's surgeon, a young medical student gone to war, came to Jett's cabin.

"Sir," the surgeon said, "I'm badly in need of half a hundred items of supply. I've got our own wounded to care for as well as the men off the brig—their own surgeon was killed, you know, and his store of supplies ruined in the fire. Could I ask you to put in at the next port and let me go ashore to buy some medicines?"

Jett's brow wrinkled as he looked at the chart spread on the table in front of him.

"The nearest port's New Bedford," he said. "Can't you hold out till we reach Portsmouth?"

"I can if I must," the young man shrugged, "but 'twill mean a good many men will die or lie in terrible pain. Why not New Bedford, sir?"

"I doubt they'd welcome us there," Jett explained. "They hate us Marylanders in New Bedford like the Devil hates holy water, they say."

"But surely they won't refuse me medicines," the surgeon protested. "No matter how they feel about Maryland or the war they're human, ain't they? It'd be a brute, indeed, who'd say no to an appeal to buy medicines to relieve suffering men."

Jett shrugged. "We'll put in there," he said, "and you can try your luck with them. We should be off New Bedford by six bells, if this wind holds."

The three vessels, the clipper, the brig and the cutter, anchored off the Massachusetts port at dusk and the surgeon, together with Greer and Elwood, the second mate, were sent ashore in the *Lorelei's* longboat. They were back within the hour, foaming in their rage.

"The dirty scum!" the young surgeon shouted, his face livid. "They've refused to sell us a drop of medicine, an ounce of powders! I told 'em their own countrymen were dying and they sniffed their snotty noses and said *they* had nothing to do with that—*they* hadn't sent the men out to be wounded!"

"And I fair got on my knees to beg them!" Elwood panted. "They all but laughed at us! They told us if we wanted to fight a war for Maryland, let Maryland give us what we needed!"

"The cowards!" Greer boomed. "They're afraid if their British friends found out they helped us they'd leave off all this you-kiss-me-an'-I'll-kiss-you affair and shut off their flood of gold, that's what!"

"I feared it would be this way," Jett said stonily. "Ah well, we'll hope for strong winds to Portsmouth and God be kind to those poor devils who need the medicines."

His clenched fist struck the table in front of him with a heavy blow.

"Hear me," he said, "this country will never forget New Bedford and what she was, when this war's over."

The *Lorelei*, the *Unicorn* and the *Sprite* reached Portsmouth safely and there found the people willing to sell what was needed. But eight men died on the way who, the surgeon said, would not have died if the people of New Bedford had not hated Maryland so.

3

ANTHONY WORTH was in Havre de Grace when Cockburn's squadron struck at the city after wrecking little Frenchtown.

Just why Cockburn landed more than four hundred men from thirteen barges at Frenchtown and burned the place to the ground is still a mystery, unless, possibly, the British Admiral staged the landing as a rehearsal for the Havre de Grace action.

But land four hundred men he did and sacked the place to its last silver spoon. And thereby revived Maryland's hatred for his name. Then he swung his force back down the Chesapeake toward Havre de Grace.

If he had searched the charts, Cockburn could not have chosen a more insignificant target than Frenchtown. Even an attack on Elkton, across the Elk River from Frenchtown, would have been more understandable because Elkton was at least a fair-sized village. Frenchtown was nothing more than a stagecoach stop on the Philadelphia-Baltimore pike. There was an inn there, a few houses and that was all.

Yet Cockburn assaulted the place as though it was an American stronghold, personally commanding the landing of the relatively heavy force he put ashore. Later, in his reports to the Admiralty, Cockburn called Frenchtown a "heavily defended position and a key point in all travel between the northern and southern provinces of this country." As to the latter definition, stagecoach travel between Baltimore and Philadelphia was inconvenienced but not disrupted by Frenchtown's fate; the coaches were merely re-routed over a turnpike that lay further inland.

But the town *was* defended—by eleven stage drivers and wagoners who manned two ancient pre-Revolutionary War cannon which lobbed their shot a few yards out into the water, damaging only the placidity of the fish in the Susquehanna River. When the British barges touched land and the troops came ashore, the defenders fired a haphazard volley with a few fowling pieces and fled prudently.

Frenchtown was no Hampton as far as the murder of its inhabitants was concerned but it was as completely destroyed. All the village's few buildings were burned, all valuables were seized, all livestock was shot and left lying in the fields, all the small boats in the town's shallow harbor were sunk. When Admiral Sir George Cockburn recalled his men the place where Frenchtown had been was a scene of ruin, a town as utterly devastated as though it had been under a bombardment siege for weeks.

Anthony Worth watched terror sweep Havre de Grace as the news of Frenchtown reached the city on the Susquehanna. He saw men whom he recognized as the most fiery patriots in their speech scurry out of the town, deaf to the reassurances given by the commanding officer of the American Regulars, Brigadier General Henry Miller. He saw farmers drive their cattle and swine off into the woods. He saw shopkeepers overload wagons and carts with their goods and head for safety. There were others who buried their silver and other valuables, some who stayed themselves but who sent away their children, particularly the young girls. Still others refused to leave their homes, no matter what the threat.

There were many, too, who helped the Regulars and the militiamen throw up earthworks along the river front, who sweated at hauling cannon into place, who displayed a bravery and patriotism that impressed even the Master of Fairoverlea.

Because the base of its rampart had been made of earth-filled potato barrels, one of the gun emplacements was named the Potato Battery. It was presided over by a man named John O'Neil whose voice, when Anthony spoke to him, was hardly understandable through its thick brogue.

"I'm hopin' the divils will come," O'Neil said, " 'Cause there's minny a score I've got t'sittle with them fer w'at they did t'me and mine whin they coom through the Ould Country collectin' their taxes."

"You think," Worth asked, "you can stop the British with those guns?"

O'Neil turned to look at the two tiny six-pounders and the one nine-pound cannon that comprised his battery, wrinkled his long, sharp nose and turned back to grin at Anthony.

"It ain't what ye'd call McHinry now, is it?" he admitted. "But what I got here will give the best account of itself it can give, and no man or gun can do bettern'n that, b'gob!"

When he heard that the British fleet was heading for Havre de Grace, Anthony's first thought was to leave town and follow the other deserters and refugees to Baltimore. But, as he watched the preparations for the impending battle, he tarried, interested in the question of what these untried Americans could do against the mighty Royal Navy and the hated Cockburn.

Not that he intended to shoulder a musket or help serve a cannon, himself. No, his curiosity did not go to those lengths. But, he told himself, it would be an experience to watch the fight from some vantage point. Therefore, on May second, 1813, when the alarm that the British were about to attack sounded, Anthony Worth mounted a horse and rode out of Havre de Grace to a hill up-river, from which he could watch the whole affair through a spyglass.

Cockburn's flotilla edged up the Susquehanna that morning and dropped anchor out of gunshot of the shore defenses and out of range of the ships' guns on the town. There, while rumor followed rumor in Havre de Grace, while countermand came hard on the heels of command, the warships stayed, swinging lazily at anchor. Worth, through his glass, could make out the longboats busily plying between the giant *Sceptre,* the *Menelaus* and her sister frigate, *Marlborough,* and the other vessels, but there appeared to be no move to load the landing barges or even run out the ships' guns.

"A night attack," was the word at sundown. "Everybody stay at their posts."

They stayed, the Regulars and the militiamen, throughout a night that was featured by half a dozen false alarms. Patrols sent downriver to spy out any landing parties the British might have sent ashore returned to say there was no sign of activity among the enemy. The empty landing barges still trailed aft from the warships.

"A flag of truce," said the next rumors. "The British are going to give General Anderson a chance to march his men out of the town without a fight . . . They'll not harm the city if the cannon are surrendered . . . They'll attack at dawn . . . They see we're too ready for 'em and they've called off the whole thing."

Dawn came and still the men of Havre de Grace stood to their guns; still the British made no move. One by one, the militiamen began to slip away to get some sleep; the Regulars were relieved, all but a skeleton force, to rest. When the gun emplacements, the trenches, were emptied, when Miller had reduced his force to a dangerous minimum, the British fleet swept into action.

Sceptre, up-anchored and under topsails, opened fire first as she came in. The broadside was a volley of shells aimed at the town that lay behind the gun emplacements and the trenches. As the big ship of the line passed Havre de Grace, every gun on her port side bellowed. *Sceptre* came about gracefully, despite her bulk, and ploughed past Miller's position again, her starboard batteries thundering.

Next came *Menelaus,* with Sir Peter Porter snapping his terse orders to the quartermaster beside him. The frigate followed the same course *Sceptre* had taken, but *Menelaus* heaved solid shot into the fortifications where hastily roused men were now trying to scramble into some kind of organization.

Then came *Marlborough* and Anthony Worth saw in action the terrible new weapon he had heard about.

The second frigate in the line towed a squat scow astern and from this barge there streaked a hissing thunderbolt, spitting flame and sparks, leaving behind it a wavering dragon's tail of greenish-black smoke. It was a war rocket and as it thundered toward shore an involuntary groan went up from the Regulars and militiamen defending Havre de Grace.

The rocket struck the ramparts of a battery a glancing blow, ricochetted upward, then dived again to land among a company of Regulars drawn up behind the artillery. The men scattered in panic as the rocket writhed along the ground at incredible speed, still spurting smoke and sparks. Anthony's glass picked up one terrified soldier who turned squarely about and ran toward the rear in a straight line. A few steps to one side would have taken him out of the rocket's path but the man seemed bent on his own doom by keeping on a beeline. The spouting monster reached its victim, flattened him and passed over him without a second's pause, leaving behind it a blackened lump that twitched faintly for a moment and then was still. The rocket, meanwhile, kept on its way until it crashed into a frame house and erupted in a great burst of flame. The house blazed up like tinder.

While all this was going on, the barge attached to the *Marlborough* had fired half a dozen more rockets. Each one spread terror in the American lines. The weapon's effectiveness, Anthony Worth saw, was due as much to its frightening power as to its killing power. Men who doubtless would have stood up under even canister and grape winced, faltered and broke when they saw one of these strangely live-seeming serpents of death turn its hungry snout in their direction.

General Miller rallied most of his troops after that first panic and when *Marlborough* left off the rocket bombardment and sailed back to reload, the shore batteries began their feeble answer to the attacking ships. Miller, however, had no guns that could reach the warships or dent their oaken sides if they did happen to carry that far; the American General's only effective use of the guns he had at hand would have been to sweep the unprotected landing barges when they came in from their mother ships.

There was no telling the gunners that. The Americans popped away at the warships valiantly and futilely, their balls sending up splashes midway between the shore and the ships. Muskets began snapping in the trenches although the range was impossible; the defenders of Havre de Grace were uselessly expending ammunition they could ill afford to waste.

Nor, Anthony saw as he turned his glass on the town, would they have much of a city left to defend when the bombardment lifted. One of the ships, either *Sceptre* or *Menelaus,* was hurling hot shot, shells and bombs into the wooden houses behind the lines. Fires raged and spread in half a dozen places where the red hot cannonballs, the fragmentary missiles and the rockets had found a mark. The wind from the southwest carried the smoke down over the trenches and more than one militiaman looked back to see a twisting column of smoke marking his home.

The effect on the volunteers was definite and natural. Perhaps the man who saw his house ablaze had left his wife and children inside when he had come out to fight the British. His urge was not to stand by his cannon or his musket; he had to get home to see what had happened to his loved ones. A man dropped his piece and ran to the rear. Another followed; then two more. Somebody thought he heard the command to retreat and repeated it in a hoarse yell. Officers whipped at their men with the flats of their swords, then joined in the rout. Regulars, so contemptuous of the militia, were infected by the panic and fled. General Miller may have tried to get his troops to stand—later he was to be accused of having been the first to run—but if he did his attempt was hopeless. The defenses of Havre de Grace collapsed completely.

All, Anthony Worth's glass told him, except the Potato Battery; that was still in action. He saw that John O'Neil had three men with him at his guns, then one, and then he was alone, one man with three small cannon facing the overloaded landing barges that were being rowed ashore.

The man O'Neil was a marvel. Somehow, he skittered from gun to gun, swabbing, loading, firing. That he had no time to lay the guns on, that the Potato Battery's defiant outbursts had little or no effect on the British invaders was beside the point; John O'Neil had promised that his guns would do the best they could and he was seeing to it that they did.

Even a six-pound cannon is too heavy for a single man to turn and aim quickly and O'Neil had no time, no matter how much courage. The British, therefore, were able to open a clear alley for the one defending battery to fire into as they beached their landing barges and swarmed down on the Irishman from the right and left.

They did not kill him; they simply overwhelmed him. Worth caught a glimpse of O'Neil's legs and arms flying wildly before he was borne to the ground by the mass of Redcoats. Anthony could even imagine the squalls in brogue that the one-man battery must have yelled as he went down to defeat. When next Anthony Worth picked him out of the swirling scene on the beach, John O'Neil was stumbling along, his wrists lashed behind his back, a British bayonet prodding him toward a barge, a prisoner.

Then came the looting. Anthony had not believed all the story of Hampton; he could believe it now. The men, the Regulars, the militiamen, even the civilians who had not taken part in the grotesque defense of the town had fled but there were a few women, too panic-stricken by the rockets, too dazed by the destruction of their homes, or, possibly, too enraged by what the British had done to their city, who stayed. Some of these were young enough to please the eye of the British sailors and marines who spread through the town or perhaps the months at sea made a woman's age a trifling condition. Even Anthony Worth winced and lowered his spyglass, feeling a sense of guilt at merely standing by and looking on while such things took place in the prism of his telescope.

The raping ended when it had scarcely begun. Only a few women suffered the complete outrage although a score or more were manhandled, their clothes shredded from their bodies, their flesh prodded and poked and pinched while they shrieked or prayed or mercifully, fainted.

It was a British naval officer, tall and young and, by his uniform, a high-ranker, possibly even an admiral, who fell upon the rapists savagely, using the cutting edge of his sword, not the flat, to drive the woman-hunters off their prey. Anthony saw one British seaman, a great brute of a fellow who held a struggling naked girl over his shoulder as he headed for a shed, go down under the officer's sword and lie where he fell. This officer, Anthony thought grimly, was killing more British than the brave American defenders had been able to; as far as he had seen, not an Englishman had been scratched by the Regulars or the militiamen before Miller and his troops had scattered.

Once the women had been herded out of town, the systematic looting of Havre de Grace was carried out with disciplined dispatch. The houses that were not burning too briskly to be entered were emptied of all valuables before the torch was applied. Barges loaded with loot began shuttling between the shore and the warships in the river. Anthony saw even a coach, some rich man's elaborate affair, loaded on one barge and rowed out to the *Sceptre* to be hoisted aboard.

What Cockburn could not use he burned in a bonfire that sent flames roaring up fifty feet. All the boats in Havre de Grace's harbor were set ablaze or, in the case of the smaller craft, their bottoms stoved in. The town's warehouses and docks were ruined, the public buildings gutted; the nearest fields and vegetable gardens were trampled flat by squads of Cockburn's men who marched and countermarched over the young plants in orderly destruction.

The annihilation of Havre de Grace required the full day and when Cockburn drew off his landing barges and sailed his flotilla down to the mooring it had occupied the previous night, he left behind not even the corpse of a town but only its trampled, sered bones.

Anthony Worth wore a heavy, thoughtful frown as he slowly rode his horse back to the smoking ruins of the city. As he entered the ravaged outskirts, as he passed the weeping women and the white, shaken, shamed men who were trickling back into the town, he spoke beneath his breath.

"'Tis a risky thing I do," he muttered. "Should there be treachery in those promises of Guthrie's I would be ruined. But it must be done."

As the numbness of the horror that had visited them wore off, the men of Havre de Grace sought an excuse for their weak-knee'd exhibition. They chose Brigadier General Henry Miller as the one man to blame for all of it. The rockets had sent a chill of dread coursing through Anthony Worth, miles from the trenches, so who could blame a part-time soldier, a militiaman, for surrendering to panic while those devilish missiles hissed and roared and struck at him? But, because they were human, the bitterness was pointed away from themselves at Miller and loud were the accusations and recriminations.

"Coward . . . The first to turn and run . . . He ordered his troops to retreat before the British had fired a single shot . . . He should be court-martialed and strung up, the dog!"

They despised themselves for not having made a stand so their self-loathing poured out of them in streams of venom that swirled deeper by the minute, washing out the fact that the General had rallied his men after their first terror and had got them back to their lines, obliterating the fact that no one man, even a General, could block the headlong flight of nearly a thousand men made mad by their wild fear.

Anthony listened and kept his mouth shut. The temper of the town did not admit any defense of Henry Miller and he, Worth, did not intend to defend a man alone as John O'Neil with his silly Potato Battery had tried to defend Havre de Grace alone.

John O'Neil—Anthony made his way through the angry, noisy crowd until he found a man who wore the uniform of a lieutenant of militia, a man who cried louder than the rest that the militia could have broken the enemy's landing if the dogs of Regulars had supported them.

"I'm Anthony Worth, from the Eastern Shore," the Master of

Fairoverlea said briefly in introduction. "A civilian. An onlooker. One of your men, an Irishman who was in the Potato Battery, was captured. He manned those three guns alone, sir, till they charged him."

"I tell ye, Mister Worth," the lieutenant replied hotly, "we'd all have stuck to our guns if the goddam Regulars hadn't—"

"I know," Anthony put in. "What I'm asking is that you get me a boat somewhere. A small rowing boat will do and a slave to man the oars. I'd like to go out to the British ships under a flag of truce and see if I can't plead the release of this man O'Neil."

The officer stared at him, his adam's apple working in his stringy throat.

"Ye'd go out there?" he asked unbelievingly. "That's Co'burn out there, y'know."

"Aye," Anthony Worth nodded. "I don't think even Co'burn would harm a civilian who visited him under the white flag."

"But why? Are you O'Neil's good friend?"

"No," Anthony smiled. "I met him only yesterday or the day before. But he was a brave man, Lieutenant, and I'd not see him rot in the chains of a British warship's hold, to be eaten by the rats. I think Co'burn will listen to me and even if he refuses O'Neil's release, what harm can there be in trying?"

In the end and after considerable argument, the militia lieutenant agreed to Anthony's request. A rowboat that had escaped the British was procured and a black forced to handle the oars, his eyeballs rolling in dread as he propelled the tiny boat out toward the looming *Sceptre*. Anthony sat in the stern of the little boat, holding a hoe handle to which he had tied a big, spotless, linen handkerchief. The rowboat touched the side of the ship of the line at the bottom of the gangway and Anthony looked up at the hail of an officer who stood at the top of the ladder.

"What's y'r business?" asked the lieutenant crisply.

"Anthony Worth, sir, a civilian from another part of Maryland than this," Anthony called up, "to see Admiral Co'burn on the matter of the release of a prisoner."

The lieutenant's lip curled as his haughty voice came back.

"Admiral Co'burn's too busy to see you or any of the spineless curs who'd not even defend their own kennels."

Anthony rose slowly in the small boat, balancing himself with a hand against the planking of the *Sceptre's* hull. His jaw jutted and his voice boomed deeply.

"Ye'll take the word to Sir George that Anthony Worth's here to call on him!" he thundered. "I've no time to bandy words with young lieutenants!"

Anthony's bellow (at which the slave at the oars almost fell off his thwart) brought the lieutenant up short. There was a note of authority that made the watch officer wonder if he had been perhaps a trifle too hasty in dressing down this stranger. Certainly, the lieutenant thought, the man looked like a gentleman and, so he had been told, there were many gentlemen in America who were more sympathetic to England's righteous cause than to the Yankees. Perhaps—and this was a horrid thought—this Mister Worth was a personal friend of the admiral!

"Stay where ye are," he called down the ladder, "and I'll see if the admiral can see you—sir."

He was back at the head of the gangway in a remarkably short time and with him was a young officer Anthony thought he recognized—yes, he was the man who had killed the rapist.

"Come aboard, sir," Sir Peter Porter called.

Anthony mounted the gangway and found himself on the whitened, sanded deck of the man-o'-war. The young Admiral saluted.

"I'm Porter, sir," he said. "If you'll follow me, please, Mister Worth?"

The two moved toward the ladder that led to the admiral's cabin in the halfdeck under the quarterdeck. Anthony's eyes were busy with the scene. Everywhere, British sailors were securing the warship's gear, cleaning the twenty-four-pounders and carronades, coiling lines, wiping down brass and putting back into place the deckload that had been removed when the ship had cleared for action. It was a muted bustle with a minimum of orders. Anthony was struck by the efficiency of the crew; he thought again that these ships, these men, could never be beaten by anything America had to put against them.

"A pretty sight," he said. "Such order, such direction."

Sir Peter Porter turned toward him with a smile.

"They are good men," he admitted. "I must say that although, between the two of us, they're not half so lively as my own men. But you must not mention that to Sir George, I beg of you."

"This is not your ship then, Admiral?"

"Nay, Mister Worth. I chanced to be with the Admiral when the watch officer came with your request. I have the frigate lying astern, *Menelaus*."

They came to the cabin door guarded by its squad of marines and Porter knocked once and pushed his way inside. At his desk, which was slung to the bulkhead, crouched the man all America hated most, Sir George Cockburn.

He did not rise to greet his visitor, he did not acknowledge his presence with anything but a brief, cold nod. His lizard's mouth barely opened as he spoke.

"What d'ye want, Mister Worth? If it's damages to your privy in the shellin', ye're wastin' y'r time and mine."

"I'm not of Havre de Grace, Sir George," Anthony said quietly. "I come from the Eastern Shore, sir. Fairoverlea on the Miles River, with"—he paused and gave his next words emphasis— "Peartree Creek behind the house."

Cockburn's eyes glimmered once and then were cold again.

"I've come to ask the release of the one prisoner you took today," Anthony went on steadily. "A man named O'Neil."

Cockburn's lipless mouth twisted in a sneer.

"And what makes y'think," he asked, "that I'd listen to you?"

Anthony shrugged and spread his hands.

"I depended on your generosity, Admiral," he said. "I was told by a mutual friend of ours that you'd give ear to what I might have to ask of you."

"And what friend's this we both have?" Cockburn asked. "I've mighty few friends 'mongst the Yankees."

"His name," Anthony Worth said calmly, "is Mister Edward Guthrie—of London."

259

4

ADMIRAL COCKBURN's eyes narrowed still further for a fleeting instant and then he lurched around in his chair to speak to Sir Peter Porter.

"Find out where they've got this Yankee we picked up," he ordered, "and have him put ashore."

"Aye, sir," Porter said. He saluted the admiral, nodded to Anthony and left the cabin. Cockburn turned back in his chair and looked at the ledger in which he had been writing.

"So ye really are Worth, eh?" he asked conversationally when the door had closed behind Sir Peter. "Ye don't look like one of Guthrie's agents."

"I'm not, exactly," Anthony said. He glanced around the cabin, looked squarely at a chair in the opposite corner and waited. Be damned, he told himself, if Anthony Worth could be kept standing by anybody, even a titled Admiral of His Majesty's Navy. Cockburn raised his head at the silence, noticed the direction of Worth's stare and waved a thick hand impatiently.

"Oh go ahead, sit ye down," he grunted.

"Thank you, Admiral," Anthony bowed. He seated himself carefully, drawing the skirts of his coat forward to keep them from wrinkling. As carefully, he drew a leather case of cheroots from an inside pocket and offered them to Cockburn. The squat admiral shook his head and, as Worth raised his eyebrows, growled: "Go ahead; I don't use the weed. Be careful of the sparks, if y'please. There's a might of powder aboard this vessel."

He leaned back in his chair and regarded his visitor, his piggish eyes curious.

"Our Guthrie," he said, "finds some strange birds to fly for him. I'd never take ye for a spy and a traitor, Mister Worth."

Anthony looked at the end of the kindled cheroot.

"And I," he replied, "would never take you for a butcher, Sir George."

There was a dull, ugly flush on the admiral's face, a cold flickering in his eyes as Anthony raised his. There was a taut second. Then Cockburn rasped out a laugh.

"Ye've got a good opinion of y'rself, Mister Worth," he rumbled, "if ye think ye're safe to say such a thing to me aboard my own flagship. What's to prevent me from flingin' you below in chains —or worse? P'raps y'r doughty countrymen ashore?"

"No, Sir George," Anthony smiled. "Let's put it that we're both gentlemen of honor—in our own way. There's a certain amount of—er—trust that it would benefit us to put in each other, perhaps. And also there's the matter of the supplies some British-minded gentleman on the Eastern Shore has been getting to your fleet."

"At a fancy price."

"But not too dear when paid for with confiscated gold."

Cockburn flung out his hand again.

"Enough of this quadrille," he growled. "Was it really the man O'Neil you wanted to see me about?"

"I did want to see him let free," Worth nodded, "but more than that I wanted to meet you, Sir George. I have the idea we're in the nature of being kindred spirits."

Admiral Sir George Cockburn, titled officer of His Majesty King George the Third, the blind, mad King who writhed helplessly in a strait waistcoat while his rakish Prince Regent, "The First Gentleman in Europe," schemed and fought for the throne of the father he always had hated, looked at Anthony Worth, born of God only knew what parentage in a Boston slum, his fortune foundationed by murder, his power kept intact by more murder.

The two men bored deep into the other's eyes and it was

261

Cockburn who knew he was looking at the more dangerous man.

"Well," he grumbled uneasily, "that may be, that may be. And now ye've met me, what else?"

"I wanted to make sure we've both got a clear idea of the situation," Anthony said easily. "Did Guthrie get word to you about Peartree Creek?"

"Aye," Cockburn growled. "Ye've got a militia company all y'r own to guard that part of the Miles for you. These men are commanded by y'r son-in-law, Guthrie said, and the man's a fool."

"Who's been prying into our affairs, Sir George?"

"So? Well, when we are ready to take Easton Town and the other village, Saint Michaels, we're to make a landing at night in y'r Peachtree Creek—"

"Peartree Creek, Admiral."

"—with no bother from y'r son-in-law's militia company, which you'll divert. In return, we'll spare your houses and all your buildings and your livestock and your slaves and harm nobody on y'r place."

Anthony Worth leaned forward in his chair, his hands clasped tightly.

"That was the first plan, Admiral," he said. "I've changed it."

"Changed it? Y'mean—"

"Certain things have come up since I talked to Mister Guthrie," Anthony cut in. "The landing's to be made, of course, but—"

He glanced toward the cabin door.

"Ye needn't be afraid of bein' overheard," Cockburn said.

"With the landing," Anthony Worth went on, "there'll be certain things that I'd have done—oh, to your advantage, sir." He puffed at his cheroot and nodded. "Very much to your advantage, Sir George."

"Come, come—let's hear it!"

Anthony told him. And when Cockburn had digested the new plan and when he had recovered from his fit of hoarse, admiring laughter, Anthony Worth supplied him with all the information the British Admiral needed about the size, strength, disposition and effectiveness of the American militia forces up and down the Eastern Shore of Maryland.

Part Five

1

THE DAY before Anthony Worth returned from Havre de Grace to Fairoverlea, Task Tillman had a visitor he never had expected to see again at Larkspur Hill, Gracellen.

He was in his fields when she came riding up the drive alone and it was the clang of the big brass bell wielded by Tillie that summoned him. He muttered a curse; there had been too many interruptions in recent weeks to let him get more than a third of his tobacco planting done. Nicholson, at Queen's Town, was getting more and more nervous. He was forever sending couriers to fetch Task, usually to a staff meeting that produced a great deal of talk and nothing else.

With all this lost time, the Larkspur Hill crops had suffered. Task had been willing to make his share of sacrifices to the cause and Squire Wills had urged him to give all his time, if necessary, to the militia, foregoing all planting this year. The needless trips to Queen's Town, though, annoyed him. All the futile talk about forgetting differences and jealousies between the Eastern Shore's militia companies and building a united force that could turn back the British was to him so much waste time.

"And now, I suppose," he grumbled as he made his way to the house, "Nicholson's got a new idea about stretching a boom across the Chester River. Twenty different plans and no boom yet."

He stamped into the house through the kitchen door, dusty, sweaty, in a surly mood, and walked down the hallway to the front parlor. He stopped at the threshold, his mouth dropping in frank amazement.

She was standing by the fireplace, clad in a russet corduroy riding habit, the plume of her hat curling down behind her shoulders, her short crop held in both hands in front of her, her booted feet braced as though she were fighting herself to keep from running out of the room. Her face was pale and high. Her eyes held full on Task's by what must have been a mighty effort.

She grew more beautiful every time he saw her, he thought instinctively. Today she was more regal, more Anthony Worth's daughter, than he had ever seen her in her most imperious mood.

"Gracellen!" he burst out when his tongue unlocked. Then, remembering, he bowed and murmured: "Madam."

"I didn't want to come, Task Tillman!" Gracellen said without preliminaries. "But I was afraid not to come! I have no reason to care what happens to you—to either of you—but I'll not have my father be made a murderer by you!"

Task stared at her. The shaken violence of Gracellen's voice silenced him for a long moment and then he found a husky whisper.

"Your father a murderer?" he asked. "He's been—I mean, what do you say, Gracellen?"

"I suppose 'twouldn't be counted as murder," the tall, red-haired girl at the fireplace went on. Her voice was flat, mechanical; she seemed to be reciting a well-rehearsed speech. "A duel over this couldn't be called a murder, but"—and her imperiousness crumpled—"oh, Task! He'll surely kill you!"

She took three steps from the fireplace and dropped into a chair, her knuckles at her mouth, her head bowed. Task Tillman crossed the room to her side and placed a hand on her shoulder.

"What does all this mean, Gracellen?" he asked. There was a dryness in his throat and his heart thumped achingly. He knew.

He knew! But still he must ask the questions. "Why did you come here to warn me 'gainst your father?"

She jerked her shoulder from under his hand and her eyes came up to meet his, flaring hotly.

"I don't know!" she cried. "There's no sense to it! You'd both deserve anything my father would do to you! I ought to stand back and let him do his worst! Sneaking, crawling—neither of you worth a word to save you! *She'll* get no word from me but you can tell your—your bawd, if you must!"

Task Tillman drew back, his face rigid, his mouth set.

"You speak wildly, Madam Rawlent," he said coldly. "You must be out of your wits."

"Oh, I have my wits, Task Tillman!" Gracellen stormed. "I've wits enough to know the two of you face ruin. I know! My father knows!"

She looked down at her lap and a tremor went through her straight body.

"And it's what Father will do that frightens me," she went on. "I don't care a whit what becomes of her—or what happens to you, either! No, I don't! But—but it was the bitch who led you into this, Task! I'm sure of that! She has her ways. Oh Task, why did you let her corrupt you—you who were always so honorable?"

Tillman turned his back on the girl in the chair and walked toward the windows. He looked out over the drive, saw the horse Gracellen had ridden being held by Jobie, saw the larches with their spring gowns of dainty green, saw beyond the marsh the dark cedars through which wound the path Vivian used.

Who always were so honorable.

Gracellen's words dislodged an avalanche of guilt that swept down over Task Tillman, delayed this long time and doubly crushing now. He had been an honorable man, all the Tillmans had been honorable men, and Vivian's mouth and Vivian's deep-shadowed body had wiped out all sense of duty to the name of Tillman and to his own honor. He had lain with the wife of another man and though he might hate that man, although Vivian's

267

husband might be without honor, himself, he had betrayed his right to bear the name of gentleman.

But to blame Vivian for all of it—no, that was not right! He was the villain of this situation. Vivian had come to him, yes, but she had been a woman made half-mad by her husband's brutality. Another man, an honorable man, would never have taken advantage of Vivian's predicament. He had. And granting that that one explosion could have blasted its silent, white-hot paroxysm with no real blame to either of them, he had let her come back, again and again, until the inescapable bonds had been forged.

Now, though they had both tried to shun it, there was a love of sorts between them, something more than the driving need to forget themselves in each other. Or name it some strange companionship between a man and a woman who had been cursed with the loss of the ones they had really loved, a companionship that made them tender with each other while they played their dishonorable game.

His voice was low and tight when he spoke to Gracellen, not turning.

"These words puzzle me, Madam Rawlent," he forced himself to say. "Bawd—corrupt—bitch—I'm at a loss."

She left her chair and walked up behind him, her voice breathlessly hurried.

"Then carry on your role," she told him bitterly. "But hear me when I tell you what you pretend you cannot understand. Vivian's manservant, the slave Abraham, was caught stealing from the smokehouse yesterday by my—my husband, Charles. He didn't tell Vivian. Instead, he handed Abraham over to Titus to be lashed. Then Charles told me."

She caught her breath and then her rush of words Niagaraed.

"I knew it wasn't right of Charles to have Abraham punished without telling Vivian. I ran down to the—the place where Titus has his whipping post and I got there before Titus had laid the whip on Abraham. I told Titus to let Vivian's manservant go."

Task turned to look down at Gracellen's drawn face.

268

"I don't know why you tell me this, Gracellen," he said. "What that brute Titus does to Vivian's Negro, Abraham, hasn't the least concern with me."

"It has! It has! Listen! I've always hated Titus and he's hated me as he hates everybody. That great—ugh, I shudder every time he's near me. I had to stand there while his—his evil eyes looked at me and through me. And then he told me that if my father were there he'd order Abraham whipped till he was dead. He— he told me that Father intended that Abraham *should* die—soon. I asked him why. And—and Titus told me in that awful voice of his that Abraham had been helping Vivian meet you here while my father has been away from Fairoverlea. He told me that he'd told Father this a few days before he left for Havre de Grace. He almost smiled when he told me that my father bade him be silent; that he'd take care of matters when he returned from his trip."

Her hands went out to seize his arms in a grip that marked his skin beneath the shirt he wore.

"He'll kill you, Task, and Vivian, too!" she cried. "Believe me, I know my father! He—he knew about you and Vivian and still he could kiss her goodbye and ride off without a hint he knew she was an adulteress. He'll kill you both, Task, and— and may God forgive me for saying it—he'll have his revenge in a way that—"

She could go no further. She sobbed into her hands, cupped over her face.

"You mean he'll set his precious cutthroats 'gainst me?" Task asked, his voice steely.

She nodded, the hat's plume bobbing, and then, suddenly, she was against him, her head on his chest.

"Either by Roan and the other two or in some other way," she whimpered, "he'll kill you both while—while he smokes a cheroot and never moves a muscle of his face to show he knows what's being done. Oh Task, get away! Don't try to be a hero—this is no time to show your courage! Go to Baltimore or Philadelphia —anywhere! As you love me, get away while you can!"

She stiffened, realizing what she had said, and drew back, her tear-stained face working.

"I—I didn't mean that," she faltered. "I know you don't love me but—but for Vivian's sake then, if it's her you love. Take her with you—both of you escape! He'll not follow her, I swear it! Or if he does, he won't be able to do the things to you in some other place that he can—he can devise here in Talbot County. Oh Task, believe me! Your life's in danger!"

"You counsel me to steal your father's wife in an elopement?" Task asked.

"Anything," Gracellen answered brokenly, "to keep Father from taking his revenge on you." Her voice dropped to a whisper. "I—I could not bear to see you harmed. You see, I once loved you, Task Tillman."

"And now?"

She took a backward step, lifting her chin.

"And now I am Charles Rawlent's wife and a faithful one. My husband has all my love. This visit here's but a—a move to keep my father from staining his hands with your murder."

She added fiercely:

"Don't think that I was prompted by any other thought! For all I've said, for all the foolish things my concern for my father has made me blab, I've told you this for Father's sake, not yours or Vivian's. For all I care, the two of you can burn in Hell!"

She swept past him before he could put out a hand or even speak. Her bootheels rang in the hallway and there was the faint squeak of a hinge that needed greasing. The door slammed behind her and Task Tillman did not move his sightless stare from the fireplace as the hoofbeats of Gracellen's horse faded down the drive.

2

VIVIAN came to Larkspur Hill that night, although Anthony Worth's return to Fairoverlea was long past due. Her husband had sent a letter by coach to Easton, explaining that the sack of Havre de Grace required him to stay in those parts longer than he had intended, trying to get some order out of the mess in which the British raid had left his affairs there, but that he should be home by the end of May. This was early June and Vivian risked her husband's arrival at Fairoverlea when she went to Larkspur Hill.

Or perhaps it was no important risk at all. If Titus had told Anthony Worth of Anthony's wife's unfaithfulness before he had cantered off to Havre de Grace, he might find Vivian *in flagrante delicto* on his return without its making much difference in the plans that the broad-shouldered, greying-haired Master of Fairoverlea certainly had already made.

Vivian knew of Titus's revelation to Gracellen even though her step-daughter had not told her, nor had Abraham. The black grapevine at Fairoverlea was as efficient as on any other Eastern Shore plantation—indeed, more efficient than most—and word of what Titus had told Gracellen had streaked through the slave quarters up to Great House and, by devious ways, to Vivian. It was from her maidservant, the mulatto named Uley, that Vivian had received the word that she was doomed.

There was no sign of fear when she faced Task Tillman that evening. There was only an acceptive fatalism, the look of a woman who had just been told that she was suffering from an incurable disease. There was even a faint smile on her lips as she took the glass that Task offered her silently. There was no tremor in the hand that raised the drink to her full lips. Her eyebrows rose slightly as Task slopped whiskey into a tumbler and downed it in a gulp. Quite evidently, it was not the first drink Tillman had had that day.

"You'll find no answer in that jug, dear Task," Vivian murmured. She shrugged her slender shoulders. "But on second thought perhaps there are as many answers there as anywhere."

"Vivian," Task asked hoarsely, "what are we going to do?"

"Do? What can we do? Unless Titus is lying—and he's not human enough to lie—all the plans we might make have all been foreseen and well taken care of by my husband."

"But he'll—I'm only thinking of you!" Task blurted.

Her strange smile widened as her dark eyes held his with a discomforting search.

"I am!" Task insisted. "I know—I know I should have something prepared, some faultless scheme that would confound Worth. But—but I'm not a clever man, Vivian. I never claimed to be. I'm slow-witted, dull, but I'm not the complete coward. I can take care of Anthony Worth and all his cutthroats—it's you I fear for."

Her eyes stayed on his for a time and then dropped to the glass in her hands.

"I believe you, Task," she said in a low voice. "I do, truly. And I thank you for it. But in this—this mésalliance of ours we've never said a word of any protection one should give the other when trouble came. You say you can deal with Anthony—why then, I hope you're right. Perhaps I have my own ways of dealing with the man, who knows?"

"I—we could go to Baltimore or Richmond or some such place," he offered. She shook her head, still smiling.

"A gallant thought," she said evenly, "but you must know that's

272

not possible. I couldn't go anyplace in this whole great country and escape what's set out for me unless I found refuge with the savages west of the mountains." She looked at the silk of her dress, a jeweled ring on her finger, and her mouth crooked. "And I doubt that I'm suited for a deerhide shirt and a redman's hut."

"No, listen," Task said, his voice rising. "There are places in Georgia and Ohio where Anthony Worth couldn't reach us. His power would mean nothing there. Why, Gracellen herself told me to take you—" He broke off his words.

Vivian's dark eyes rose to meet his.

"So Gracellen's made a plan, eh?" she asked. "I wonder if it's fair to guess her father put it up to her."

"No—not Gracellen!" he protested. Vivian leaned back in her chair, her eyes half closed. "She wouldn't do that!" Task kept on. "She—she rode here to warn us, Vivian!"

She shook her head, her lashes drooping.

"Not us—you," she said. "The girl would never help me, and why should she?"

"But no matter who she came to help, she said we ought to—"

Vivian's hand rose from her lap as she shook her head again.

"No, Task," she said quietly. " 'Twould do no good for us to run. I know it. Even if we did escape I—I know you'd hate me for making you leave this place, your home."

She opened her eyes and looked across the room at him.

"I'll take whatever's coming to me," she said slowly, "and there'll be nobody to deny that I deserved it. But you—you haven't earned what Anthony plans for you, not really."

"I can take care of myself against Anthony Worth," Task said. "It's you—"

"And here we sit and say no you, no you," Vivian smiled, wearily, "when we well know that what's to happen will, when Anthony Worth decides it's time to happen. And if I say this has been all my fault I suppose you'll argue it."

"The fault was mine," Task said instantly. "If it'll do any good, I'll make Anthony Worth know that."

273

"No, Task," she said. She rose from her chair and moved toward the door. She stopped and turned back to him.

"No, we've met up with what was bound to come. You say you can take care of yourself against Anthony—God grant that you can. I'll try to take care of myself, too, and perhaps the fates will be kinder than I deserve. We've reached the fork in the road, Task. From now on we'll deal with what comes, each for himself."

"But—Vivian there were times when you—you said you loved me," Task said hesitantly. "A man and a woman in love don't turn their backs on each other in time of trouble."

Vivian threw back her head, her throat arched. Where there had been quiet resignation in her voice before there was a lightness, a gaiety in her laugh now.

"I said I loved you?" she asked. "Ah Task, I must have cried a lot of things when we were together and there was nothing in all the world but the feel of you. Perhaps—who knows?—you said you loved me, too, in those wild minutes. I think no judge could ever blame or praise a woman for what she might cry out at a time like that."

"That's all it meant?" Task asked in a low voice.

"You thought it was more than that? Oh Task, you are a serious one, always reaching for some deep meaning in the slightest thing. Of course that's all it meant. That's all it meant, too, with the others. You're just unfortunate in being the one that's been discovered."

"The others?"

She rose and smoothed her skirt, her smile set, her voice trembling with mirth.

"You didn't think you were the only man, did you?" she asked. "You must have known I was a woman who needed a great deal of affection—more than you or any other one man could give me."

"I—didn't—know."

"Well, now you do," she said, tilting her head, her dark eyes mocking. "And now I suppose, between what you've just learned and what's to come, you want me to leave without our usual tête-a-tête?"

274

He stared at her, his eyes dead, his mouth wrenched into ugly lines, disgust starkly etched on his face. She waited, then summoned the smile again as she turned back toward the door.

"Goodbye Task," she said softly and went out.

She did not weep until she reached the densest part of the path through the pines. And though she sought it hopefully she could find no solace in her performance at Larkspur Hill that had made an embittered, disillusioned enemy of her one lover who might have felt called upon by gallantry to thrust his head into Anthony Worth's noose by coming to her rescue.

3

Anthony Worth came back to Fairoverlea with his echoing laugh, his ease of manner, his clear grey eyes, unchanged. He dropped from his horse and walked up to Vivian, picked her up in his arms and told her he had missed her before he kissed her, warmly and prolongedly, for everybody to see.

Watching her father, Gracellen felt the quick catch of her breath in her throat. That he kill his whoring wife would have a certain justice to blunt the crime; to hold her thus, smiling into her watchful eyes, and kiss her was wholly wrong.

"And ye've missed me, too, dear Vivian," Anthony said, his voice light. "The shadows about your pretty eyes tell me that plainly."

One arm about his wife's waist, he mounted the steps to place the other around Gracellen's shoulders as he dropped a kiss on her cheek.

"And now I have my own two sweethearts again," he said. "And after the things I've seen whilst I've been gone, homecoming's doubly precious. But I've got an inch of dust in my throat and at least two inches on the rest of me so I'll have a drink—several drinks—and a bath before I tell you all the news about the British sack of Havre de Grace."

He dropped his hands with a last affectionate pat to each of the women and strode into the house, his spurs clinking. The two men on the porch heard him humming a tuneless air as he mounted the stairs to his rooms in the mansion's east wing.

The women's eyes moved from the empty doorway to meet each other's and lock in a level stare. No words passed between Gracellen and Vivian but the question screamed silently between them: *Did Anthony really know?*

It was Gracellen who broke off the welded stare. She lowered her head with a muffled sound that might have been a sob and, with a hand to her mouth, hurried through the doorway and up the stairs to her rooms. Vivian watched her flight, her mouth curving.

"Aye, does he know?" she asked herself under her breath. "I've been his wife for all these years and I can't tell, for sure. Perhaps Uley and the others all lied. Perhaps Titus never told Anthony. Perhaps Abraham never told Titus. And perhaps there is a Heaven and a Hell and I'm sure to go to Heaven—'tis as unlikely as thinking he doesn't know. Aye, he knows! It amuses him to think he is tormenting me, waiting for the thunderbolt to strike. And so then, I must spoil his pleasure and, pray God, put some doubt in his own mind as to whether Titus told the truth."

She played her part well in the days that followed. She did not overdo it; she was careful to guard against the slightest change in the Vivian Worth who had been before that fateful ride that had ended at Larkspur Hill. She was quiet, her calm unshakable, the perfect foil to her husband's facile wit, a hostess who graced Fairoverlea with an ease of hospitality that few of the great houses of Maryland's Eastern Shore could boast.

And all this time she lived with the sharp shadow of a sword at her throat. There was not one unlighted passage in her own home she could walk through without forcing herself to keep from cringing under the expectancy of hard hands about her neck, a knife in her side. She could not descend a stairway without feeling the presence of some shapeless figure behind her, ready to snap her neck before she hurtled down the steps in a lamentable accident. She could not put a bite of food in her mouth without wondering whether this dish had been poisoned. She could not ride with Anthony without expecting to be brought back to Fairoverlea a limp bundle that had been thrown from a horse. She could not sail with her husband without thinking that this was the day he had picked to drown her.

She did not crack, although there were times when she crouched behind the bolted door of her room, trembling uncontrollably, close to screaming aloud. She kept her smile, her rigid calm, though there was only the sleep of sheer exhaustion for her and that populated by the most horrid dreams. She forced herself to eat although the food stuck in her throat. She made herself curtsey, dance, chatter nonsense, lower her eyelashes at a man's compliment, keep table talk circulating, dress herself in gowns that set off her dark beauty—and when the evening's gaiety was finished and she was blessedly alone, she ofttimes staggered across her bedroom and flung herself limply across the bed, drained of all her strength, too weary of her struggle to care whether or not Anthony walked in and found her thus, with her defenses levelled.

This, Anthony never did. When he was not at work or playing host to some sparkling gathering, he kept to his room. In all the weeks that followed, he made no visit to his wife's bed, even though his goodnight kiss was as warm as it ever had been.

Vivian waited.

4

Task Tillman waited.

He made Larkspur Hill an armed camp with guards posted each night to watch for prowlers. He never went anywhere without a pistol stuck in his waistband and a knife sheathed to his belt. When he rode at night along the narrow lanes that led to Easton and Queen's Town he died a hundred ambushed deaths and suffered nothing more than the scratched face he gave himself the time he pulled Lucifer off the road into a thicket at the noise of an opossum's scuffling.

No night riders came to Larkspur Hill, no torch was put to Task's house or barns. Task met Anthony Worth face-to-face in Easton one day and the Master of Fairoverlea merely looked at him and through him, blankly, and passed on.

Task almost convinced himself at times that Titus had lied to Gracellen. Task knew that no other man alive could have stayed his hand from the enemy who had cuckolded him, could hide the vengeful hate that was Anthony Worth's. Task also knew that Anthony could stay his hand, hide his hate.

Task had reason to know that the silence, the inaction, meant nothing except that *The King* was choosing his own time to strike.

That time might be in the next minute or in the next year. In his father's case, it had been nine years between the time Randolph Tillman had made Worth hate him and the day he had died. And Randolph Tillman had not—no honorable man had—given Anthony Worth such just cause to hate as he, Task Tillman, had.

Task Tillman waited.

His first instinctive motion, then, was toward his pistol the day a rider came cutting across the fields, his horse lathered, with Captain Nicholson's word that the British were moving up the Sassafras River just north of the Chester and might strike at Queen's Town.

Task flung himself into the saddle and spurred Lucifer toward the town where his command awaited, some twenty miles away. He could see that this was no false alarm set off by Charles Rawlent. As he galloped through Easton he saw the Easton Fencibles mustering and the claret-jacketed riders of Rawlent's Dragon Footguards hurrying to their own rendezvous. Along the road to Queen's Town he saw families leaving their homes and heading for Easton, gangs of slaves being herded out of the fields and put to work loading wagons with furniture and other valuables. Each man he passed yelled some question at him: where were the British, how soon would they be here, had Georgetown fallen?

Nicholson's company was drawn up in ranks when Task thundered his black stallion onto the parade ground. The captain, his face reflecting all his misgivings, returned Task's salute.

"They've asked for help at Fredericktown and Georgetown, across the river," he said in a clipped voice. "We're moving out at once. I'll ride the stallion, by your leave."

The company's rollcall showed at least a third of the men missing, either out of reach, sick, or mysteriously disappeared. Task's platoon made the best showing of the company's six and none of his men was stricken with the sudden illnesses that hit the other units when the men learned that they were going to march to battle. Tillman was proud of his men as the company swung out onto the highway and began the quick-march to Frederick-town and Georgetown.

They had covered three-quarters of the distance when Task first heard the dull thudding of the guns. The distant grunt of cannon struck a chill through him. He found his mouth dry, his armpits and loins dampened by a cold sweat, his heart fluttering, as he trudged forward. Behind him he heard the mutter of the troops in their double file.

"Steady!" he called out. "Keep in line, boys!"

They marched on, Task's platoon in the van, the position of honor, the best-trained of the company, the men who knew the rudiments of bayonet drill. *Bayonet drill!* Good God, Task told himself, of what use was the bayonet when the British, so the news from Havre de Grace had been, had a new rocket weapon that chased a man until it caught him and then burned him to a crisp? Of what possible use would this handful of militia be against the thousands of Redcoats who were pouring ashore from the British fleet? Better that they had all stayed at Queen's Town and built some defenses against the Lobsterbacks in case they followed up their raid on the Sassafras River with an invasion of the Chester River shores. He had half a mind to tell Captain Nicholson that this was a senseless expedition, to bid him let the Fredericktown and Georgetown people look out for themselves instead of crying for help from other companies.

"Steady!" he called back again. "Steady, men!"

It was a quarter of a mile further on that they met the vanguard of the refugees from Fredericktown and Georgetown and their greeting was loud and virulent.

"Goddam militia!" squalled the first old man they encountered. "Goddam cowards!"

"Ye come now when it's all over," screeched an enormously fat woman, brandishing a skillet. "Now ye're the brave heroes, after the British have had their fill!"

"Go back where ye came from!" howled a boy with a bandaged arm.

"Ye're runnin' the wrong way!" jeered the lanky driver of a

mule cart loaded with household goods. "Keep on the way ye're goin' and ye'll run into the British and ye don't want that!"

Captain Nicholson, his face impassive under the torrent of abuse, halted his company and rode Lucifer over to the thin man on the cart.

"Hold your filthy tongue," he said quietly, "or by God I'll have you shot and thrown to the hogs as a traitor."

The skinny man blanched and slid along the cart's seat away from the captain.

"I ain't no traitor, Cap'n," he whined. "I just got so goddam mad at seein' those yeller bellies of a militia run just now that I—"

"Have the British taken the towns?" Nicholson snapped.

A dozen voices answered his question.

"An hour ago . . . They didn't meet no trouble doin' *that* . . . The militia just took up and run . . . They didn't fire a shot, hardly . . . Look at the sky up there and you'll see."

Heads turned to follow the gnarled forefinger of the old man who had goddammed the militia. Task felt his hopelessness swell within him as he looked at the towering, twisting cloud of black smoke that reached up over the horizon. The firing had stopped; if what the refugees had said was true and the towns had fallen to the English an hour before, the booming Task had heard must have come from guns hurling hot shot into the village to start fires after the looting had been taken care of.

Captain Nicholson turned back to the civilians, his face set in bleak lines.

"Do you know where the militia retired to?" he asked.

"I dunno where they *retired* to," the old man cackled harshly, "but they was runnin' in all directions the last we see of 'em. Left their cannon, they did, and just took off."

Nicholson turned Lucifer and rode to where Task Tillman waited, summoning the other lieutenants with a wave of his arm. The troops began firing questions at the file of refugees as they passed down the column.

"Ye better turn back," somebody shouted. "It'll save ye a lot of runnin' if ye turn back now."

"Get on your way!" a lieutenant of the Queen Annes Militia roared. "We take no advice from a rabble that dirtied their britches at the first sign of a British sail."

A volley of jeers and curses came from the refugees. The militiamen hunched their shoulders and shifted their feet uneasily, eying the calamitous sky ahead.

"My idea," said Captain Nicholson when his officers were gathered, "is to cut across country to behind Georgetown. We're too late to try to save the town so perhaps we can reinforce the Georgetown defenses for a counter-attack."

"We'll probably be too late for that, too, Captain," put in the lieutenant who had roared at the civilians, a middle-aged mill owner named Johnson, "if these people are right. Looks like the Georgetown men have scattered."

"We'll try it, nonetheless," Nicholson rapped out. "There's a side road on a little further that'll take us to behind Georgetown in a matter of minutes. Get the men closed up and keep the double quick-step moving, gentlemen."

There were growls among the ranks as the platoons formed up again. It was a reluctant body of men that moved toward the side road to Georgetown and all the lieutenants were kept busy ordering back into line the soldiers who tried to fall out with complaints of cramped legs, diarrhea and dizziness. Some men did manage to slip away, screened by the dust the column churned up, but the desertions were comparatively few after some men felt the whack of a sword flat across their buttocks.

The road the Queen's Town men took dwindled into a lane and then a cowpath and the troops were forced to go into a single file through some dense groves and thickets that had them peering fearfully at the shadows on each side.

"We c'ld be massacreed like Braddock in this place," one grumbled. "Ain't even a clearing big enough to run in."

"I think the damn officers is lost," another ventured. "Prob'ly lead us right into Old Co'burn's hands, they will."

283

"Aw, squeeze y'r knees together," scoffed a third. "Whatcha feered of, just gettin' kilt or stobbed with a bay'net?"

"They git close enough t'me," a teen-aged boy muttered, "and it'll be them that gits stobbed."

"Hooray fer Willie Parsons!" came the jeer. "Gonna stob hisself a Lobsterback before he gits kilt."

"*Silence!*" Task Tillman yelled.

The company's spirits lifted some, not much, as the cowpath broadened again into a lane. But whatever rise in morale that change accomplished was soon dispersed by the sound of gunfire ahead, the hollow bang of an occasional fowling piece punctuating the hard rap of musketry.

"By God!" Captain Nicholson ejaculated, "our boys are holding them!"

The captain's optimism held for a moment, but only for a moment. The firing was coming toward the Queen's Town company much faster than the militia's approach warranted. The Americans, indubitably, were in retreat.

"Fall out!" Nicholson ordered. "Form a line on each side of the lane along that ridge. Let our men through and then pour it on the British, boys!"

The Queen Annes Militia, for all its rebellious muttering, went into line along the ridge without a pause. Task, his heart thumping, knelt behind his sprawled men, his pistol in his hand. His voice was rusty with excitement when he spoke but the fear he had almost acknowledged earlier was gone.

"Remember," he called along the line, "be sure it's a Britisher you're aiming at. Let our men get through."

The firing ahead died to an occasional shot, then broke out in renewed fury. There was a crashing in the brush in front of the ridge off to the right of the road and the first Georgetown militiamen burst into the clear, scrambling through the briars and honeysuckle with frantic disregard to the knifing slashes of the briar thorns.

Task saw at first glance that they were close to panic. Their eyes were wide and staring, their mouths hung loosely. Their faces were smudged with powder stains through which the trickling sweat had washed grey channels. Most of them had thrown away their muskets and many of them had ripped off their jackets for greater freedom in their flight. All were hatless; their trim shakos that had looked so impressive on parade had proved useless encumbrances in the wild retreat.

"Rally! Rally, men!" Nicholson cried. "There are reinforcements here!"

"Rally, hell!" a rat-faced militiaman with a long scratch across one cheek squealed. "There's a million Britishers behind us!"

A few of the retreating men heeded Nicholson's command; the others barely hesitated in their gallop. Still, ahead of the ridge there was the ebb and flow of musket fire. Some remnant of the Georgetown company was keeping its formation.

They came into view with a rush, a force of about three squads which still kept their discipline intact, who still fired their muskets and shotguns back at the hidden enemy. They were led by a lieutenant in a uniform from which a sleeve somehow had been ripped from its shoulder, a gaunt man who never gave a command but who somehow held this group together despite the panic that flowed about it.

"Reinforcements, Lieutenant!" Captain Nicholson yelled. "Drop back behind this ridge!"

The hollow-cheeked man flung one disbelieving glance in Nicholson's direction before he turned back to fire his pistol at the brush through which his unit had come.

"Y'heard that, men," he drawled. "The hull damn Yew-nited States Army is right back of us. *In*-cluding artillery. Let's git behind the ridge and rest up for the next dance."

The retreating militiamen wearily dragged themselves over the ridge and down to the hollow behind it, there to drop to the ground in exhausted heaps. The one-sleeved lieutenant wobbled over to Captain Nicholson and attempted a salute.

"Lieutenant Mason, Cap'n," he said. "Third Platoon, Georgetown Militia. We just got the hell whupped out of us, Cap'n."

"How many British behind you, Lieutenant?" Nicholson asked.

"Dunno, Cap'n," Mason twanged. "Ain't so many as I'd guess, noways. Just a detail to run us down, I think. They want prisoners and we looked handy."

"How far behind—"

"I see one!" a militiaman on the ridge howled. His musket banged.

Task swung his eyes back from watching the captain and Mason and peered over the crest of the ridge. The bushes over to his right were moving. He levelled his pistol and then waited; it could be a Georgetown straggler. There was a brief flash of crimson in a tiny clearing and Task Tillman's hand jumped as the pistol cracked. A ripple of fire broke out along the entire line.

Task reloaded with trembling fingers, dividing his attention between the pistol and the bushes ahead of him, from which he expected a regiment of King George's finest dragoons to burst, bayonets levelled, at the next instant.

The fire of the Americans died for lack of targets. Thinning powder smoke drifted slowly in the idle wind. Overhead, a turkey buzzard wheeled in wide circles, eying the ground for carrion. A fly lit on Task's cheek and he slapped at it frantically before he realized what it was; his nerves were so keyed up that the insect's touch had jarred him like a blow.

He did not take his eyes from the front as somebody lowered himself to the ground beside him, breathing heavily.

"D'you suppose they've retired?" Captain Joseph Nicholson asked. "Maybe our volley told them the Georgetown men had found reinforcements."

"I don't think so, Captain," Task said, shaking his head. "I think they're spying out our position, seeing if they can flank us. They wouldn't retire without—"

From just ahead of them in the thick brush came a high yell. *"Vive l'Anglais! A bas les Yonkee!"*

Tillman started in astonishment and turned to Nicholson inquiringly.

"Those damned *Chasseurs Britannique*," the captain explained. "Frenchies captured in Boney's war. The English gave some of

286

'em the choice of fighting for them against us or rotting in prison." He spat disgustedly into the tall grass beside him. "Co'burn's supposed to have over two thousand of 'em—our noble allies in the last war. The British have got a regiment of blacks, too, from the islands. They say those niggers are hell when they get close enough for knife work."

The front stayed quiet. The cicadas resumed their interrupted conversations. From some distance came the lowing of a cow.

"What're they doing?" Nicholson fretted. "You think we ought to send out patrols to see what's up, Lieutenant?"

"Not yet," Task returned. "I think they want us to come down off this ridge after them. The more rest our men get, and the Georgetown boys, is all to the good. We can't save the town now so let's not lose our company by a rash charge."

The Americans waited as the silence deepened. The prone Queen's Town troopers, emboldened by the enemy's refusal to advance, began raising their heads and yelling toward the thickets in front of them.

"C'mon and get y'r belly full of American lead . . . Y'ain't fightin' no Havre de Grace milishy now . . . We don't squat to pee, we don't . . . M'father whupped you at Princeton and we'll whup you here, you vomit-eatin' dogs . . . Is y'r crazy King out o' Bedlam yet?"

The taunts and jibes volleyed out, swelling in volume, coarsening in context, until at length a British officer's temper snapped under the strain of listening to comments about his King, his country, his antecedents and his own curious sexual habits.

"At them!" his high-pitched voice cried. *"En avant, les Chasseurs!"*

The British force crashed out from their cover with the command, the French mercenaries clad in blue tunics marked by white crossbelts. They were led by a scarlet-coated Dragoon officer. They made splendid targets as they came into view. The Americans on the ridge waited for no command from Captain Nicholson to send a roaring volley sweeping down the incline.

Three Chasseurs dropped like toppled scarecrows. Half a dozen others yelped with pain as the American bullets struck them, clutching at shattered arms, shoulders and legs. These men, though, had been trained in the finest army the world had yet seen, Napoleon's, and the ranks of the unit sent out to harry the American retreat and capture prisoners stood firm. A red-tunicked officer snapped a command and the muskets came up, there was another word and the hollow below the ridge was filled with smoking thunder.

Task ducked his head and heard the belly-tightening whine and burble of the British bullets going over, the smack of lead plunking into tree trunks, the witch's wail of the ricochets slanting off rocks.

"Bayonets!" cried the Dragoon who commanded the British detail.

"Let us in here, you-all," drawled the Georgetown Lieutenant, Mason, from behind Task. "We had ourselves a little rest and we're loaded—you ain't."

The Georgetown men of the Third Platoon scrambled up the slope to wedge themselves between the men of Task's command, bring down their muskets and fire a volley into the smoke that hovered in front of the British force. It was a blow that struck the enemy hard. The British commanding officer obviously expected no more than a scattering fire from the Americans—to reload a musket took more time than he was going to give them before his bayonets reached the top of the ridge—and Mason's volley broke his front line and reached his few reserves. He had no way of knowing how many men had come up to support the Georgetowners; he had only heard Nicholson's shout, "Reinforcements here!" His duty, that of keeping the Americans from sniping at the looters of Georgetown and taking a few prisoners, had been completed; he could not risk his detail of Frenchies in any pitched battle on this terrain.

The British commander ordered a retreat. It was the first time in the War of 1812 that a British force had given ground before the fire of the American militia.

Ironically, none of the Americans on the ridge knew that they had beaten off the British. When the smoke in the hollow grudgingly lifted, they saw that the dead and wounded had been carried off but they expected a second assault and a third and as many as would be necessary to dislodge or overwhelm them.

"Not meaning to take command, Captain," Task Tillman said, "but there's a place about half a mile back that's better to defend than this spot. Here, they're right on top of us before we can see them. The place I have in mind would give us a clean sweep of about a hundred yards."

"I mind the position," Nicholson nodded. "We'll drop back to there."

Task's platoon was assigned to cover the retreat, a dubious honor if the British discovered the retirement but one that brought a flush of pride to Tillman. The four American wounded—none hurt seriously—were helped off the brief battlefield, the five other platoons followed and Task's unit dropped back in short sprints, turning to cover their rear at every hundred yards. There was not a shot sent after them.

At the new stand, where a sand pit gave them a high position with an unobstructed view, the Americans dug in again and waited for the British advance. Over the tops of the trees they could see the smoke of burning Georgetown and Fredericktown but even this sight failed to dim the spirit of the men of the Queen Annes Militia who had met and, at least temporarily, held back the British.

The waiting stretched out into an hour, an hour and a half, and still there was no sign of the enemy. Nicholson sent out half a dozen scouts chosen from among the teen-aged boys in his company. They returned to tell him that the British had marched back to Georgetown.

"They're goin' aboard their vessels, sir," said one carrot-topped youngster. "It looks like they're through here."

Cautiously, the militia company and the remnants of the Third Platoon, Georgetown Militia, followed the lane toward the burning town. By the time they reached the outskirts of Georgetown they could see the British sails moving back down the Sassafras toward the Chesapeake. As they entered the town and looked across the river at Fredericktown, they were given grim evidence that the British had been as thorough as usual in their destruction. Brick buildings were shells with staring, soot-rimmed eyes that looked down reproachfully at the troops that had failed to save them. What had been frame structures were smouldering piles of charred timbers and glowing ashes. Everywhere were pieces of furniture smashed into kindling by musket butts, shattered clocks, garments and household linens that had been wantonly slashed by bayonets and knives. A dead hound lay in a pool of its own blood. Squarely in the center of the town's main thoroughfare there was a mule that had been hamstrung, braying plaintively in its agony. A piglet that somehow had escaped the general slaughter dashed about crazily, bleeding from half a dozen deep slashes, squealing hysterically.

The buzzards were thick overhead, eying the provender supplied by the British raiders, waiting for the humans who moved so dazedly about the village to leave the scene so they could dine.

These Georgetown people, Task discovered, had none of the vituperative anger at the militia that had marked the refugees. Instead, they went about in hopeless silence, their resigned grief much as it would have been if their city had been swept by a natural disaster such as a flood or a hurricane. They had seen their militiamen try to stop the British and they did not blame their men for retreating against hopeless odds. The British, they reasoned numbly, could never be stopped; they had only to choose the towns it would please them to wipe off the map of Maryland's Eastern Shore.

The pall of despair, the utter hopelessness of the Georgetown people, had more effect on the men from Queen's Town than had the British lead that had whizzed over them. Looking about them at their first-hand evidence of Admiral Cockburn's brand of warfare they all, from Captain Nicholson down through Task Tillman to the youngest recruit in the ranks, knew that for all their drilling, for all their uniforms and muskets and their three puny cannon, Queen's Town would be a smoking ruin like Georgetown and Fredericktown when Cockburn's ships elected to sail up the Chester River.

Dispirited, their tongues paralyzed by what they had seen and the thoughts of what lay ahead for their own village, the company marched back to Queen's Town. So grim, so inevitably desperate was the outlook that none of the militiamen, not even the loudest braggarts, lay any claim to a victory over the *Chasseurs Britannique* at the ridge. They threw away their chances to become local heroes; they deliberately turned their backs on the pages of history from which they could have emerged as victors of a major battle, men who broke the vaunted British line.

5

ALTHOUGH the Eastern Shore's militia could never hold off the attack on Queen's Town, scurvy and the dreaded "ship fevers," dysentery and typhus, did.

Cockburn's fleet—actually Sir John Borlase Warren's fleet but always called Cockburn's by the Americans, most of whom never knew that the fumbling old man who stayed aboard the *San Domingo* off Cape Henry was technically in command—was riddled by an epidemic that spread through virtually every British vessel in the Chesapeake. The admiral's ship's surgeons warned him bluntly that unless his jammed sick bays could be emptied and their patients put ashore, and soon, the whole expedition faced disaster.

Cockburn, on July 27, 1813, moved on undefended Kent Island, that beautiful stretch of creeks and farmlands that lay between the Chester River and Eastern Bay, and landed more than three thousand sick men there in a hospital camp. The squat admiral held his warships offshore, except for a few brig-sloops, schooners and one frigate, *Menelaus*, which he sent down the Bay to raid the Chesapeake's islands, Sharpe's, Poole's, Tilghman's and Poplar, for provisions.

Admiral Sir Peter Porter was in charge of these minor operations and, therefore, the islands were not ravaged as they would have been had Cockburn taken personal command of the raids. Porter, in fact, did the incredible; he paid for most of the things he seized, thereby nearly emptying the chest of gold pieces supplied him for this purpose instead of following Cockburn's system —and the system of most British admirals of the day—of pocketing the guineas and juggling the accounts.

"Ye're a damn fool, Porter," Cockburn said sourly when the younger admiral made his report. "When the war's over and the Admiralty cuts the fleet, ye'll wish ye had the money you threw to the Yankees. There'll be mightly little for you to play at Brook's with on y'r peacetime pay. And y'r haughty distaste for honest lootin' has kept y'r pockets near empty, that I know."

"Aye sir," Porter nodded. "It's just that I can't convince myself it's right to take something besides war stores."

Cockburn's little eyes gleamed wickedly.

"Y'blame me, then, f'r helpin' m'self to a few Yankee baubles, Porter?" he grunted softly.

Porter's narrow face flushed under the urging of the answer that must not be given unless he wanted to see his career garroted.

"No sir," he forced himself to say. "I know that it's always to the victor that belong the spoils, Admiral."

"Aye," Cockburn croaked, "and it's time you found out that you can't be lily-livered in this business, Porter. You sail a good ship, I'll give ye that, and you follow orders, but you haven't found out yet that this is no quadrille we're engaged in here. We've got the word to break the Yankee spirit entire and you can't do that by doffing y'r hat to 'em and beggin' their pardon f'r usin' their wind and water. You have an idea of what this puny fight might end in?"

"You think we'll take back the colonies, sir?"

"Aye. Mark my words, I say the Americans are about ready to come back to English rule, to save themselves from more punishment. Hell, half the country's achin' for a return right now. A few more towns burnt, Baltimore crushed flat, these skulkin' privateers driven to ground, and England can move in and take over where she left off back in Eight-One. And unless I miss my guess we'll be rewarded handsomely for what we did to bring the rebels back to where they belong—a governorship or some such opportunity to line our pockets, eh?"

"I hope you're right, Admiral," Sir Peter Porter said dubiously. "But—well sir, in each of the towns we—er—visited on the islands I summoned the village officers together and told 'em what you told me to say: Leave off this war, vote for your Federalists, or we'll return and burn your places to the ground. And not once, sir, did those people give me any promise. They listened and they eyed me like I was a polecat and when I was finished talkin' they walked off without an answer of any kind. They did not seem to me like men who were anxious to surrender their cause, no matter how badly their affairs had gone."

"They'll change their tune," Cockburn said grimly. "They'll be pushin' each other aside to wave their white flags, once I'm done with 'em. When the men get rested and this sickness leaves us, we'll take Queen's Town and Easton Town and Saint Michaels and every damned town we can reach. And if they've cursed me for what happened at Havre de Grace and Hampton, they'll think those were but gentle reproofs compared with what I've in store for 'em."

Sir Peter Porter nodded dutifully. He had come to loathe his superior in the days that had followed the fleet's departure from Bermuda but he could not let his tongue, his eyes, his whole expression, give the least hint of his loathing. The Royal Navy was his career; he loved his life except for the things Sir George Cockburn made him witness; he was bound that some day he would command a ship of the line, a fleet, and wage war against England's enemies in a way that would be civilized and yet victorious beyond Cockburn's greatest accomplishments.

Until he reached his goal he would keep his mouth closed, his protests stilled, his memory cloaked against the scenes of horror he had looked upon, beginning with the sack of Hampton.

"Aye, sir," he told Admiral Sir George Cockburn as he saluted and left the captain's cabin aboard the drowsing *Sceptre*.

The entire British fleet drowsed that night; the lookouts, cursing the bos'ns who had posted them to the needless duty, dozed in the crows-nests of *Sceptre, Marlborough, Menelaus* and the other vessels. But even if they had kept alert they probably could not have seen Jett Worth's *Lorelei* slip silently into Eastern Bay in the dead of a moonless night, pick a way by a combination of instinct and long experience up the channel of the Chesapeake's pocket and slide neatly into the hideaway fastness of Peartree Creek.

It was a daring, if not foolhardy, venture. The clipper was no *Heron*; her length and beam were enough to make her an easy victim if she was caught in the narrow, twisting waters of the creek or even in the inner part of Eastern Bay, unable to make the full sail reaches that made her so elusive at sea. Jett had had to slip past Warren's blockade of the Virginia Capes, although this had not been half as difficult a maneuver as it would seem; Jett had been slipping by American cutters for years and he knew the channels over bars and reefs that never had been marked on a chart; he knew where to hide by day and how to sail by night without a spark of light aboard or a pale star to guide him.

He had come up the Chesapeake hugging the western shore, knowing that any of Cockburn's vessels abroad would be almost sure to be along the eastern shoreline. Opposite Eastern Bay, off Herring Bay, he had come about and had streaked across the Chesapeake under full canvas, moving into Eastern Bay just below the last ship in Cockburn's line. He made a black landing in the cove off Fairoverlea and jauntily stepped ashore from his longboat under the flickering light of the lanthorns held by Anthony Worth, Roan, Womble and Marsden.

"Jett, ye young idiot!" Anthony burst out as his hands reached for his nephew's shoulders, "Ye'll tweak the Devil's beard just once too often some time! What do ye do here?"

"I was homesick for sight of you and the others, Uncle," Jett laughed, "and when I thought of the coach trip I'd have to make to get me here from Charleston, I decided I'd take the chance."

"And risk *Lorelei* doing it," Anthony growled. "After the fine record ye've made, ye'd throw the vessel away in a crazy scheme like this?"

"Nay, Uncle. We knew that by the time Co'burn roused himself out of his sleep and cleared his eyes of fog we could be back down through the Capes again." Jett's voice sobered. "The reason I'm here, sir, besides the need of seeing all of you again, is that my crew needs rest, good men, and *Lorelei*, too. I vowed I'd head for home—the men's home, too, most of them—after the next prize, and when we took a fat West Indian merchantman off Bermuda I headed back. With your permission, sir, I'd like to give the crew a week or so at home whilst the shipbuilders you know how to summon here patch up a few rents and rips in *Lorelei* and make her a tidy ship again."

"Why—why, I don't know whether that can be arranged, Jett," Anthony said. Jett looked up quickly at his uncle. Worth's face was gloomy, his brow wrinkled.

"You don't think it can be arranged?" Jett asked. Since when, he queried himself, had Anthony Worth ever doubted that he could arrange anything to his satisfaction? The surprise on Jett's dark face obviously nettled the older man.

"Good God, Jett, I'm no wizard!" he said. "Matters are in a devil of a mess hereabouts, as you've not heard, having been at sea. Co'burn's whole fleet is at our doorstep and there's no doubt he'll hit us—and soon. Your vessel would be surely taken if he came this way and, most probably, Fairoverlea and all of us made to pay for sheltering a privateer as famous as you've become."

Jett started to speak, then reminded himself of the presence of Roan, Womble and Marsden behind his uncle, as silent as three roosting birds of prey. He forced a lightness to his voice that he did not feel.

"Well, we'll speak of this up at Great House," he said. "At least my men can come ashore and feast themselves on a change from salt meat, can't they?"

"Of course," Anthony said heartily. "Roan, you and Marsden and Womble see that the men from the ship get everything they want. I'd take them to Number Five Warehouse, that's empty now, and be sure there's blankets hung at the windows and doors. We don't want to make the Lobsterbacks too curious of what's goin' on should a patrol boat come peeping around these waters. Jett, let's to the house and you can give me all the news. We hear nothin' in this place except the British are monsters that can't be beaten."

"And I can tell you that is wrong," Jett said earnestly. "We've met our weight and more than our weight in Britishers and we've beat every one."

"Yes, the brig *Unicorn* and the sloop-of-war *Dart*. Fine prizes, those, and the little *Sprite*, besides the merchantmen. Ye've made yourself rich, boy, and all your crew. Your name's as well known as Barney's all over Maryland and, I vow, the world. Barney's a Navy Commodore now, you know. I wager he wishes he never got that commission. He'll never get wealthy in that job and the government gives him no decent vessels to fight with. He's never completely recovered from his disappointment at not gettin' the *Constitution* that was built here, the ship that took the British frigate *Guerriere* last August."

"Our biggest victory at sea," Jett nodded. "I wish I could meet a frigate with *Lorelei*."

"Nay, lad. The brig's enough for you to rest your laurels on. Your vessel was never meant to fight out of her class, Jett."

"I still could do it, I think," Jett said earnestly. "I really think so, Uncle, with the crew I've got."

The two men were nearing the rear of Fairoverlea, the great bulk reared against the moonless sky.

"And about the crew, Uncle," Jett went on, "they really ought to have rest. Y'know we've scarce paused to draw a breath since we sailed out of here. Whenever we put in with a prize we needs must fill up our water casks, hurry aboard some fresh provisions, patch up our dents and bruises, and rush out again lest the British find out where we are and lay a trap for us."

Anthony nodded somberly, a hand pulling at his chin.

"Another time than this," he said, "and I'd tell ye to stay here till this war's over, if need be, but—but I'll tell ye frankly, lad,

I've means of knowin' something of what's going on in Co'burn's mind; never ask what means. I know as truly as I know my name that he's aiming at us as soon as he's able to move again. First it'll be Queen's Town, then Saint Michaels and Easton, and if he strikes at Easton we can expect him to land along the Miles. I've run *Heron* and *Johanna* and the two other schooners over to the western shore where they're well hidden. The same anchorage won't take a vessel of your draught, Jett. I know of none save Peartree Creek that could accommodate you. You see my predicament."

He opened the side door that led to his office passageway and stood aside to let Jett enter, put a hand to his nephew's shoulder as the younger man passed him.

"But it shouldn't be too long before the coast is clear," he added. "Tell the men not to feel their disappointment too deeply. Another two months—three—anyway before winter sets in—and they ought to be able to come home to stay."

Jett turned in the dimly lit passageway and eyed his uncle's face, his own graven deeply by shadows.

"You mean we will have won by winter?" he asked.

"I mean somebody will have won," Anthony Worth said heavily. "Whichever side, there'll be an end to all this trouble."

"But—but if the British win—"

Anthony laughed softly.

"Fight them at sea, Jett," he counseled, "and take their ships as prizes but there's no need to think of the British as fiends from Hell, y'know. If they do carry this war I doubt not ye'll agree that things will be better run by them, all our affairs better administered, than by that pack of yapping dogs in Washington."

Jett started to reply, then held his tongue again. Silently, thoughtfully, he preceded his uncle down the passageway to the office, brightly lit by several lamps. He moved to a chair in a corner and dropped into it, his eyes troubled, his mouth drawn down at the corners. Anthony hauled at a bell-pull and the black face of Joseph, the butler who never appeared to be more than two paces from where he was wanted, appeared at the door.

"Rouse the ladies' maidservants," Anthony directed, "and bid them tell their mistresses that Cap'n Jett is home on a surprise visit. And bring something to eat and drink here."

There was a brief silence after the butler left as Anthony went to the chair behind his desk, sat down and reached for a long, thin, black cheroot. When it was alight and sending its acrid clouds ceilingward, Jett spoke from his corner in the shadows.

"You really think, don't you, Uncle, that we have no chance to win this war?" he asked, simply.

Anthony shrugged and held his cigar out from his lips, regarding it instead of the man who had asked the question.

"I'd thought you'd be one of the first to admit that, Jett," he said. "You never were a taproom patriot, as full of fiery speeches as of rum. I'd counted on your level head to show you the truth; I thought you'd recognized it long ago. Nay, Jett, we have no business fighting a first-class power and you know it. We've proved that our ships and the men who sail 'em can meet anybody and give a good accounting of themselves; on land we've proved we are not soldiers nor ever will be. I saw Havre de Grace—"

"But weren't the troops there disorganized by the new rockets?" Jett put in. "So I heard in Charleston."

His uncle shrugged again.

"To me, they looked as though they were seeking some excuse to break and run," he replied. "The rockets but provided the excuse. The things are frightening, yes, but they're all fizz and smoke—I don't believe they're half as deadly as a charge of grape or a bomb."

He put the cheroot back between his teeth and spoke around it.

"Or if you blame Havre de Grace on the rockets," he went on, "what do you say about Fredericktown and Georgetown? There were no rockets used there and still the American militia fled like whipped curs. 'Twill be the same at Queen's Town and at Easton when the British get around to those places, you'll see."

"Haven't the militia companies made a stand at all?"

Anthony Worth grunted a harsh laugh.

"Can you see a company such as the one Gracellen's precious husband leads makin' a stand against anything?" he asked. "Nay, Jett, if you'd pick a winner in this war, don't look to the militia or even the Regulars. They stand no chance."

He looked at his nephew, a frown descending his wide forehead.

"But why are you so put out?" he asked. "I told you once that I'd see that we made out all right, no matter which side won, and that still holds. You're rich, no matter what, so why scowl, Jett?"

The young clipper captain's words came hesitantly from the corner where Jett sat, staring at the carpeted floor.

"I—I don't know," he faltered, "but—well, I suppose you're right, as you've always been right in everything. But—my men aboard *Lorelei*—d'you know, Uncle, the prize money they share means nothing to them compared with their faith in their cause? Every man-jack of them is *sure* America will win this war. They'd fight their guns just as hard, I know, if there wasn't a penny in it for them."

"Oh well," sniffed Anthony with a flirt of a heavy hand, "you know sailormen!"

"Aye, but"—and the words came in a rush—"*I* feel the same way, too. Uncle, I'd rather go down with *Lorelei* than ever trim my sails to take advantage of my country's defeat."

Anthony tapped the long grey ash from his cheroot. He kept his eyes on the silver tray and if Jett Worth had been able to see those grey eyes he would have seen that they were masked, curtained. The clock over the dead fireplace ticked noisily as he kept tapping his cheroot against the edge of the tray. A minute passed, another, and then Anthony cleared his throat.

"I take it then," he said quietly, "that you count me a traitor for looking ahead to what I think's inevitable."

"Nay, Uncle," Jett said quickly. "I have no right to blame you for anything you might think or do; you know that! I'd never call you traitor, sir, no matter what stand you took! Perhaps I'm all wrong in all I feel and America would be wise to surrender a hopeless cause now. But sailing a ship like *Lorelei*, knowing the spirit of my crew, I'd be something less than human if I didn't fight to win, with never a thought of defeat. Why sir, if you'd but take one voyage aboard her and see—"

"The ladies," Anthony Worth broke in, his voice harsh.

The two men rose, Anthony crushing out his cigar, as Vivian and Gracellen entered, both in voluminous dressing gowns, their hair about their shoulders. Behind them, yawning openly, was Charles Rawlent in a silk dressing robe, his face puffed by sleep, his hair frowsy, his mouth rubbery. Jett saw that Rawlent had grown heavier, softer, in the three years he had been married to Gracellen. Too many nights spent in taprooms after the Dragons' drills was robbing him of much of his looks. He was scowling now, blinking his eyes against the lights, obviously provoked because he had been hauled from his bed.

"God's sake," he muttered as he entered the office. "Couldn't this wait till a man has had his sleep? I've been with the troops till—"

His complaint was drowned by Gracellen's welcoming cries as she rushed across the room to clasp her cousin and press her lips to his.

"Dear Jett!" she exclaimed. "We've had the news of all the wonderful victories you've scored 'gainst the Lobsterbacks—they say Co'burn himself's afraid to stir out of the Chesapeake lest you take his whole fleet!"

"I'm here to entertain his plea for terms," Jett said gravely. "Would you prefer a frigate or a ship of the line as your own personal souvenir of this war, Gracellen-aleen?"

"Just give me the Admiral, himself," the red-haired girl said vehemently. "I've got my own ideas of how that precious villain should be treated."

"And my dear Aunt Vivian," Jett said, moving toward Anthony's wife. "More beautiful than ever, I'll be bound." He kissed her lightly, briefly, and turned toward Anthony. "Uncle," he said, "if I were you I'd be the most jealous husband on all the Eastern Shore, with a beauty like Vivian for a wife."

For a second, less than a second, there was a stark, shocked, silence in the room. Vivian, Gracellen, even Anthony Worth, were transfixed by a spear of mute astonishment at Jett's abrupt stripping of the cloak from the dread secret that ruled Fairoverlea. The instant's hush was broken by a cavernous yawn from Rawlent and the Dragon captain's peevish voice.

"Where's Joseph with a drink?" Charles asked. "I've got a mouth that's wrinkled like a prune and filled with sawdust."

The irritable question broke the aching tension and Anthony Worth's full laugh boomed.

"Now was there, Jett," he asked, "ever a day when I had to worry about the young cockerels of these times? Your Aunt Vivian knows the better man when she sees him and I've no cause for a moment's worry about jealousy." He eyed his wife fondly and placed a hand on her shoulder. "When you decide to marry, Jett," he went on, "you must let me pass on the young lady—I can tell just by looking into her eyes whether or not she'll make a dutiful wife."

"And that," Jett bowed, hiding his puzzlement at that pregnant pause behind his smile, "is what I'll do, Uncle, though marrying's a long way off for me."

"And again I ask, where's the—ah, there you are, Joseph," Rawlent whined. "Did this stuff have to be distilled, for God's sake?"

Jett switched his mind from the question of what had sent that lightning flicker of revealment forking through the office and fastened on his dislike for Charles Rawlent. How, he asked himself, could his uncle maintain his tolerant smile in the face of that coxcomb's complaints? If he, Jett, had ever used such a tone there'd have been the swift and biting lash of Anthony Worth's tongue to remind him that Fairoverlea was Anthony's and no one but he might criticize the way it was run. Had his uncle's love for his daughter made him accept Rawlent completely? Or had Charles been given a role in some plan still to be carried out and

302

Anthony must bear his son-in-law's nerve-jangling presence until the role was played?

And how, he asked himself further, did Gracellen stand the man? Three years as the wife of a jackanapes like Rawlent must be enough to wreck the temper of a less highly-strung girl than Gracellen; unless she'd completely lost her fire she must be close to tearing her red hair out by the roots now. Most likely it was her pride, forbidding her to admit by single word or look or action that she had made a grievous mistake when she had taken this complaining fop for a husband.

Now with Task Tillman—Jett cursed again the fates that had wrecked the love between his cousin and his friend. He still did not know why his uncle hated Task so and he did not know why Task hated his uncle, but if there was one thing he would have done if he were able to make magic, it would be to clear up the feud.

He still remembered Task's rage-twisted face the night he had hurled himself out of Fairoverlea. He, Jett, had tried to say something to express his sympathy. In return he had been given a snarl and nothing more. He had stood there on the back steps of the west wing, watching his friend ride out into the black rain, and he had wondered if that was the last he would ever see of Task Tillman. He had the idea that it was.

He accepted a glass from his uncle and let his palate revel in the delicate taste of the fine brandy.

"You're home for a long stay, Jett?" Vivian's low voice was asking.

"I'm afraid not," Anthony Worth answered for him. "I've explained to Jett the danger that his ship is in if he tarries here long. God knows which way the British will move next—the dark of the moon he needs will be gone soon—"

"And I think 'twas a foolhardy thing to come here at all!" Charles Rawlent's irritating voice broke in. "Here we're trying to keep this section from the enemy's attention and Jett makes the childish gesture of sailin' his ship right up under the enemy's nose. Y'know how they hate clippers, Cousin. Y'must have known you'd bring danger to Fairoverlea, comin' here."

Jett's hand tightened about his glass but he kept his voice smooth.

"I thought, dear Charles," he purred, "that the brave Dragons were hot to fight the enemy, not fearful of attracting their disapproving attention."

"Well, we are getting ready to fight," Rawlent replied, "but any expert in military affairs will tell you it's senseless to provoke a battle till you're fully prepared."

"Not ready yet?" Jett asked, shaking his head wonderingly. "Ye've had the Dragons thumping around for years and still ye're not ready? What d'ye lack, a proper gallery to applaud when you lead the charge?"

"Now, damn it—" Rawlent began, his voice furious.

"Enough, enough!" Anthony Worth broke in. "Jett, I endorse what Charles says, for once. Your vessel here at this time might bring the ruin of us all. I bid you take the *Lorelei* out tomorrow night."

Jett stared levelly across the room at his uncle, then dropped his eyes to his glass.

"Aye, sir," he said. "An order is an order. My men, bless 'em, won't grumble but they'll be sore disappointed."

"Tell 'em I'll bank a bonus for each man," Anthony rumbled. "The extra pay will soothe their disappointment."

"But sir," Charles Rawlent protested, "you turned me down when I asked you for—"

Veins bulged in Worth's forehead and his old roar thundered.

"Aye, and I'll turn ye down again if ye ask for another penny for y'r troop of carpet knights!" he boomed. "Don't dare compare that company of yours with the crew aboard the *Lorelei*—those men are men!"

"You have no right to speak like that to me," Rawlent said stiffly. "Two can make accusations, if that's your wish, sir."

Anthony's eyes narrowed as he leaned forward over his desk.

"What d'ye mean?" he asked ominously. "Out with it! All these half-statements of yours I've heard of late—what's behind them?"

Charles Rawlent held his eyes locked with Anthony's for a moment and then dropped them.

"Nothing, sir," he mumbled. "But you cut me when you spoke so harshly of the Dragons."

"Well, where were your fine Dragons when the British raided Georgetown and Fredericktown?" Anthony kept on relentlessly.

"We were on guard against a landing on the Miles."

"Aye, and left the fightin' to the troop ye've always sneered at, Nicholson's. The Easton Militia marched, I notice, even though they moved too late to help."

"Father," Gracellen put in, "you know you agreed the Dragons' place was here. You even financed the company with the understanding they'd protect this part of the county."

"Well then, it won't be long," Anthony Worth grumbled, subsiding, "before I'll find out what kind of investment I've made."

There was an awkward silence broken only by Charles Rawlent's aggrieved under-breath murmuring. Jett finished his drink and stood up to replenish his glass.

"So Nicholson's company was engaged, eh?" he asked absently. "That's the one Task Tillman joined, isn't it?"

Again there was that vivid silence, again the breathless hush that had dropped over the room with Jett's laughing mention of Anthony's reason to be jealous. Realization struck Jett with an almost physical blow even as Gracellen hurried to say something, anything, to break the pause.

So that's it! Jett told himself. *But, good God, not Task Tillman!*

". . . and the Queen Annes Militia reached there after Georgetown was taken," Gracellen was rattling on, feverishly. "Nobody knows whether they stopped the Redcoats or the British broke off the fight of their own accord."

"Of course the British broke it off," Charles Rawlent said in his querulous voice. (*Thank God*, Jett's mind whispered, *for a fool to take us past this dangerous place.*) "Nicholson's men haven't got the training or the weapons to turn back a single squad of British troops. Now, the Dragons . . ." and he was off on a meandering discourse, disjointed and boastful, about the quality of his own company. Nobody seemed eager to shut off the recitation.

Jett sat in the office, listening and talking, answering questions and asking them, but if he had been ordered to recount what he had talked about he would have been unable to recall a single word. His brain was whirling under the impact of the stunning discovery that Anthony Worth had been given cause for jealousy and that Task Tillman, of all people, had been the one who had supplied the reason.

Task—honorable, conscientious Task Tillman; the role of wife-stealer never had been made for him! Even in the old days at Saint John's College in Annapolis, Task had always hung back from the students' forays on willing town girls, he had invariably suffered conscience pangs that had been hooted at by the others. Aye, Task would be the last man Jett could imagine as Vivian's lover, the one who had fixed the horns to Anthony Worth's head—but there it was, as plain to see as though Vivian had boasted about the affair.

And, he told himself, it must have been all Vivian's doing; she must have seduced Task as completely as a rake deflowering an innocent maid. He, Jett, had suspected that fires burned beneath Vivian's calm; there had been more than one occasion in the past when he had felt the urge to break the calm and warm himself by the heat.

But he had warded these temptations off; Task had not! The Task who had been his friend since childhood had splattered the name of Worth with slime by dishonoring the uncle who had been the only father Jett had ever known.

For which, his mind whispered, *he'll have to pay!*

As he left the office for his room, Jett was conscious of Gracellen's anxious eyes following him, of Vivian's veiled stare, of his uncle's searching glance that showed in the old man's eyes for an instant before Anthony's buoyant: "Goodnight, lad, and have a good sleep in a steady bed." He thought dimly that they all must know he knew—all but Rawlent, of course, and he did

306

not count in this. He wondered if any of them would try to stop him from doing what he had to do and he told himself fiercely that not even *The King's* order would keep him from giving Task Tillman his due.

He was pulling on riding clothes when the door of his bed-chamber opened and Vivian Dangerfield Worth walked in, her shadowed eyes made deeper by the uncertain light of the candles on Jett's highboy. He watched her reflection in the glass, not turning, as she came across the carpeted floor toward him.

This was a new Vivian, her impregnable self-composure torn from her, her quiet placidity given away to a haggard pallor, her soft eyes strained and bleak, her deep, full voice a hoarse, dry whisper.

"Jett," she murmured huskily.

"Madam," Jett said coldly, "you must have mistaken the room."

The woman's reflection jerked a hand impatiently as Vivian shook her head.

"Nay Jett," she whispered, "listen to me. Jett—Jett, help me!"

"Help you, Madam?" he jeered. "You take me for a fool or a traitor or both?"

Her hands caught his arms from behind, gripping him just above the elbows. He stood there, stiff and unyielding, his own hands at his stock.

"Have a bit of mercy," the woman said dully. "Aye, I'll confess to anything you'd have me, but listen! He's going to kill me, Jett! He's going to murder me! Tonight or tomorrow or—oh Jett, this waiting is more than I can bear!"

He turned and her hands fell away from him, dropped limply to her sides.

"Why then," he said, his voice flat, "why didn't ye seek protection from the man who brought you to such straits? That tow-headed bastard no doubt would have been glad to run with you like the rat he is."

She shook her head again, dumbly, despairingly.

"Or has he cast you off?" Jett went on ruthlessly. "Don't tell me he has another strumpet who pleases him better!"

Her head bent and she twisted her long-fingered hands against her bosom. Her burdened whisper was scarcely audible.

"Do only this for me, Jett," she muttered, "and call me what you will, do with me what you will beyond that. Let me hide away aboard your vessel when you sail tomorrow night. Get me away from Fairoverlea, Jett! Once clear of here you can land me anywhere—put me adrift in a boat. I'll take my chances with the British."

Her hands went to her face and a whimper broke through her trembling fingers.

"I thought I could brave it through but I can't," she moaned. "I said I'd never run but now I must or go mad! I beg you, Jett, help me as you'd help any miserable woman!"

Jett looked down at the sleek hair, smelled the fragrance of Vivian's perfume, missed the warmth that always had flowed from her body and which now was gone, giving way to a dank and corpselike cold. Pity edged its way into his mind but it could not endure against the bitter anger there. This woman had brought heartache and disgrace to Anthony Worth in his declining years; she had repaid kindness and gentleness and an abject love with treachery and cuckoldry, answered his wistful appeal for her heart by whoring with his enemy. Now she feared the just deserts that Anthony could never steel himself to give her—Jett knew his uncle would never harm even this woman who had betrayed him—and, tortured by her guilt, she flung herself at the son Anthony never had and begged him to betray her husband!

"Get out!" he told her tonelessly. "Get out before I forget you're a woman and beat you out of here with my riding whip. I can't give you what you deserve but I can deal with your bed partner in this stinking affair, and I mean to do it. Now!"

"Not him, Jett, your friend!" Vivian cried brokenly. "No blame to him—I swear it!"

Jett barked a hoarse laugh as he brushed off her reaching hands and stalked to the door, the grip of the pistol in his belt gleaming dully in the flickering candlelight.

"It was another man!" Vivian shrilled. " 'Twas never Task Tillman! I swear to God it was another man!"

Jett banged the door to shut out Vivian's last, despairing wail. He made no effort to soften the pound of his footsteps as he hurried down the hallway; no one, not even his uncle, could stop him now. He heard Gracellen's cry, his uncle's rumbling command, and he did not hesitate. At the stables and with the help of a goggle-eyed slave, he saddled the same chestnut mare he had ridden that day he had met Task outside the Indian Queen Inn, so long ago. He was hauling at the saddle girth when Anthony Worth, his nightshirt stuck into his breeches, his hair disheveled, came running up.

"Get back to y'r room, Jett!" Anthony commanded. "Damn ye, I'll not have you interferin'!"

"Don't try to stop me," Jett said levelly. "I warn you, I'll not be stopped."

Anthony's iron grip caught the lighter man's arm and swung Jett around. The older man's scowl glared down at him witheringly, Anthony's voice pounded sledgelike.

"Ye *will* be stopped!" the big man boomed. "Ye'll be stopped from this crazy venture if I have to club ye senseless—if I have to call Roan and the others to stop ye! Now, listen to me!"

Jett struggled to free himself and the older man's grip tightened cruelly.

"I'll kill the hound!" Jett panted.

"Stop!" Anthony bellowed. "Ye'd spread this thing the length and breadth of Talbot County? Listen, ye young fool!"

He thrust his face close to Jett's and lowered his voice.

"Ye'd make me a laughing-stock, Jett!" he said urgently. "There'd not be one of my enemies who wouldn't guess why ye called out —the man ye're bound to see! Ye'd bring disgrace to the whole family! Think of Gracellen, man, if ye'd not think of me!"

"I'd—I'd insult him somehow! Nobody'd know—"

"They'd all know, ye idiot! Ye think they'd not guess why ye'd knock up—that man at dawn, you just in from a voyage, and

309

pistol him? The word would be all over the county by breakfast
—oh, a meaty morsel it'd make for them that hate me, Jett!"

The younger man's struggles to free himself quieted.

"The *Lorelei*, Jett! Think of *Lorelei* and her crew!"

"The ship?"

"Aye," Anthony Worth rumbled. "A scandal and the British
w'ld be sure to hear you're home—Co'burn would strike like a
snake to seize a clipper! Your men—they'd be caught and hung as
pirates, Jett! If you don't care about me or Gracellen, think of
your crew, lad!"

Jett Worth drooped wearily in his uncle's hands. The truth of
Anthony's words struck through the haze of rage that had enveloped his brain. The ship, the crew, his uncle, Gracellen—
they all stood to lose by his rashness. His pistol ball must not be
the one to drill his false friend, Task Tillman.

"Leave this thing to me," Anthony was counseling. "I told you
once that there were certain things ye musn't concern yourself
with—this is one of them. Let this thing rest. Trust me to take
care of it in my own way, and in my good time."

"They—they must be punished," Jett said drearily.

"And so they will be," Anthony Worth promised. "Aye, Jett,
so they will be!"

6

GRACELLEN RAWLENT returned to her sitting room after she heard her father and Jett come back to the Great House. The two men did not see her standing at the top of the darkened west wing stairs; they turned up the opposite stairway, Anthony's arm flung about his nephew's shoulders. Gracellen heard them go down the hallway to Jett's room and close the door behind them.

She walked slowly across the sitting room and dropped into a chair near the windows, leaned back her head and looked up at the ceiling. She was only half aware of her husband's snoring in the adjacent bedroom, she did not hear the first cock crows that anticipated the coming dawn. Her ears still rang with the cry that had come through the panelling of Jett's door, Vivian's shrill plaint.

"I swear to God it was another man!"

Gracellen shivered. That wail had echoed through the quiet house like the shriek of a damned soul. It must have been ear-piercing to her father, in his rooms so close to Jett's.

So now her father knew, if Titus had lied and he had not known before. But surely he must have known; in the office when Jett had mentioned jealousy and then Task Tillman, her father's face had stiffened with a black expression that had made itself seen in the split-second before his smile had come back.

And if he had known for all this time, why hadn't he moved, why had he held his hand? Was it that he was so enamoured of this high-born English wench that he could even forgive her adultery? No, Anthony Worth, whom many called *The King*, would never do that! Then why had he waited; what was he planning?

She had told herself that she cared nothing about what happened to Vivian and yet, if she would admit it, her mind dwelt constantly on her stepmother's fate. She had witnessed her father's ruthlessness in dealing with certain business matters; she had never allowed herself to believe the rumors of his vindictiveness in other affairs. Those stories that had made their way to her had all been the lies of people who were jealous of Anthony Worth, of that she had assured herself. Now she found herself wondering whether all those rumors had been so highly colored, after all, and if they hadn't, what lay in store for Vivian Dangerfield Worth?

"She deserves whatever it is," she whispered aloud. "Nothing could be too bad for a woman who'd betray Father."

Still—Vivian had never truly loved Anthony Worth; Gracellen had known that from the day her father had brought his fourth wife to Fairoverlea from London. Anthony never had told her the details of his wooing of the dark-haired English girl, Vivian never had permitted her the slightest confidences, and yet Gracellen knew well that Vivian had not gone to the altar with Anthony Worth through love. And her father had spoken often of Vivian's titled father; Vivian had never mentioned his name. That, Gracellen decided, told the story. Vivian had been forced into this marriage by her father and for what reason? Untitled and with only the family name he had built himself, years older than the girl, Anthony Worth had had only one thing to offer a British nobleman and that was gold.

"I must stop thinking along this way," Gracellen reproved herself now. "I'll end up by sympathizing with her against my own father."

Let Vivian, then, take what was coming to her and forget

what might have contributed to her ruin. And what of Task Tillman?

Gracellen felt a quick ache at the thought of Task as she had last seen him, in the shabby parlor of Larkspur Hill, silhouetted against the windows and then, as his face caught the light, looking at her with tortured eyes. There had been shame in his stare, shame at the truth of the accusations she had flung at him, but beyond the shame there had been a sort of hopeless bewilderment, a look of wondering how he could have floundered into this depthless quagmire he now found himself in. Her impulse then had been to reach out and help him. She had come close to telling him she loved him still, as deeply as she ever had; she had caught herself at the last minute and had told him that she loved him—once.

Once? Gracellen had loved him always and loved him still; Gracellen, the wife of the empty-headed fop who snored in the next room! She had been a headstrong child when she had waited for Task to sweep her up and carry her away from Fairoverlea as his bride, when she had been stung by his failure to sword-slash his way through all her father's henchmen and capture her. She had still been living a story-book dream when she had taken Charles Rawlent as her husband; there had been some vague thought that her marriage would move Task Tillman so that, in some way, he would simply turn back the pages and arrange new chapters for a happy ending.

She had grown up in these past three years and now she knew that marriage, even marriage to a vain fool, was more than a spiteful whim to bring a dismissed lover back. The first night Charles Rawlent had come to her she had forced herself to bite back the cry of: "I didn't mean it! I didn't mean it!" As time passed, she had come to accept Charles with a kind of detached resignation. When she was alone with Charles and unless he talked too much, she could half convince herself that she had not made an impossibly bad choice; it was when he was brought into comparison with Task that she realized what kind of husband she had so recklessly chosen.

313

And all the time, although she tried to deny its existence, there was the insistent yearning for Task.

Now there was no doubt that Anthony Worth knew everything, had known it for months, and Task Tillman faced a danger made more threatening by her father's delay in acting. It must be an elaborate plan, well studied to extract the last drop of venomous revenge, she told herself, to take so long in being readied. Well then, perhaps there still was time to save Task in spite of what had happened this night.

She had gone to him once and had accomplished nothing; she knew she could not convince him in a second visit. Task would think it cowardly to try to escape now that he knew Anthony Worth had discovered everything. No, tow-headed mule, he would stand his ground and suffer what was coming unless somebody—*somebody*—could persuade him that his course, his *duty*, was to save himself.

Jett could have done it, perhaps, but she had just seen Jett's face twisted by a rage against the man who had been his friend; she had watched Jett being led by Anthony Worth back to his room after having started out to shoot Task down. She herself— no, Task would never listen to her. Vivian? If Vivian could make Task believe that he owed it to his paramour to take her out of Anthony Worth's reach, he might scrap his principles again and go with his doxy.

She left the chair, moving across the sitting room swiftly and silently, and let herself out into the long hallway that stretched to the top of the stairs. On tip-toe she fled down the steps and up the opposite stairway. Silently, she made her way to Vivian's door and, as silently, let herself into her stepmother's room.

The pale light of the halfdawn filtering through the window was enough to show Vivian huddled on her bed, her hair tumbled, her lined face so unnaturally pale as to make her deep-shadowed eyes enormous. Vivian's mouth was loose, her hands were raised to her throat as though she sought to protect her soft neck from the cruel fingers she felt reaching for her.

The two women looked at each other silently as several seconds ticked past before Vivian moved her stiff lips.

"What do you want?" The woman's voice was dull, dispirited. The hands that had flown to her throat at Gracellen's entrance dropped limply to her lap. Gracellen moved to the side of the bed and sat down on its edge. She kept her voice low but it screamed its urgency.

"Vivian," she said, "we—we haven't any time to spare!"

Vivian's eyes were pinned on Gracellen's, fearfully, calculatingly. Her tongue went out to moisten her dry lips.

"Did Jett—" she began and groped for words.

"No, Father brought him back to the house. They're in Jett's room now." She reached out to grasp Vivian's arm. "You've got to go to Task! You've got to get him to take you away from here!"

"Task?"

"He'll do it if you tell him you're in danger, Vivian! He must! After what's happened tonight there's no telling what my father will do. You've got to get to Task somehow!"

Vivian shook her head, slowly, stubbornly.

"It wasn't Task," she said doggedly. "I swear it was somebody else."

Gracellen's hand moved in an impatient gesture.

"That's no good," she snapped. "No better than if you said there was nobody. Father knows it was Task—he's known it for some time."

"Because you told him!" Vivian spat.

"It wasn't me and you know it. Did you ever hope that you could keep a secret from Father in this place? You thought they called him *The King* for nothing?"

Vivian lay back on the high pillows, her eyes wary now.

"Why do you want to help me?" she demanded in her raspy whisper. "You must hate me."

"It's not you, though I—I'd feel sorry for a slave wench who was in your trouble."

"Task Tillman, eh?" Vivian asked. Her eyes glared and her lips curled. "You still itch for him, don't you? You've never given

315

up your hope of getting him, have you, even though you married—"

"Be still!" Gracellen burst out. "Never mind my reasons, I'm here to help you get away from Fairoverlea and get to Task. It's up to you to convince him he must take you away. I can't do it all."

Vivian's tortured face moved into ugly, crafty lines and a grating parody of a laugh spilled from between her lips.

"You can't do any of it," she snarled. "Not one part of your scheme."

"Scheme?"

"You take me for a fool? You think I don't know you've been sent here by your father? You'll help me escape, you say—escape to what? Don't you think I can see through your precious plan? Oh yes, you'd help me—help me run for Task—and die!"

"Vivian, I—"

"You're not as clever as your father, Gracellen." The words were flung out now with utter disregard of who might overhear. "He'd have better sent another to bait the trap. Dear, gentle Jett, f'r instance, who begged my kisses and turns on me now."

"You lie!"

"You think I lie?" Vivian sneered. "Sweet Christ, we've enjoyed many a tumble when he's been home and laughed at your father's trust in him while we clipped and kissed!"

Her inhuman laugh rang through the room and she rolled on the bed in her frenzy. Her words were fevered by the sickness of her mind. With all lost now, her madness sought to daub everyone within reach with the muck of the sinkhole into which her own life had been plunged.

"And Jett was not the only one here at this fine house," she shrieked. "There was Roan and Womble and—and half a dozen blacks! Oh, aye, I diddled the great Anthony Worth with any man who was at hand, time after time!"

Gracellen's hand flashed out and there was the stinging crack of a slap. Vivian's wild eyes cleared, her head dropped to her hands and her shoulders heaved in muffled sobs.

"Help me," she mumbled. "For the love of God, help me, some-body."

"You must keep hold of yourself," Gracellen said swiftly. "You have no hope if you give way like this, if you fall apart in hysteria. Now, my plan's this. We'll—"

She stopped as she saw Vivian's head come up, her eyes move to look beyond her shoulder toward the door. Stark fear sprang back into the glazed eyes and her hands went to her throat again.

"Gracellen, child," said Anthony Worth in his deep rumble. "Whatever do ye here?"

She turned, rose and walked swiftly to her father, one hand outstretched as though to block his path to the bed where the disheveled wretch huddled.

"Father, you can't—"

His smile was easy, benign, unforced.

"Girl," he said, "you should be in bed, getting some rest. We're all wrought up by this night's mad misunderstandings." He looked toward the bed from which Vivian's hollowed eyes glared. "Poor Vivian," he said calmly. "It's regrettable she had this—this attack at a time it couldn't be kept secret."

"Attack?" Gracellen asked numbly.

"Aye." Anthony shook his head sadly. "There've been others but I've always managed to keep 'em from the rest of you. Her father warned me that she had these seizures as a girl but I thought she'd outgrown them—and they *are* scarcer these days. I prayed she would—"

"He lies," Vivian croaked from the disordered bed. "He lies to make you think me mad. Gracellen—"

"Now Vivian," Anthony said gently, "everything is all right, my dear. A sleeping draught and you'll forget these nightmares."

"Poison!" Vivian bleated. Anthony's grey eyes held Gracellen's and the girl could read the deep, pitying concern for Vivian in their depths. He sighed heavily and shook his head again.

"I hoped 'twould not be needed," he said in a low voice, "but I fear we'd best call a doctor to look after her. I'd thought this—this sickness could be hid from the gossips but—"

He broke off, looked down at the floor, his clubbed, grey-streaked, rusty hair moving from side to side in helpless sorrow. Gracellen took a backward step, horror rising in her throat. Her father did not know, had never been told, what Titus had said to her. Her father believed she had been kept out of the evil secret of Vivian's guilt, and Task's, and now he worked to make her believe that Vivian was mad so that whatever dark development might come could be blamed on her insanity.

"Father," she whispered, "no! No, Vivian's not mad! I know—"

"Of course she's not," Anthony broke in. "I've always held she's not." His hand touched Gracellen's shoulder and she almost flinched. "Get to bed, dear," he said. "I'll see to this; 'tis my duty, not yours."

"Gracellen!" Vivian squealed from the bed. "Don't leave me! He'll kill me!"

Gracellen turned back to look at the woman lumped against the wall, her eyes gone animal in their fear. She looked back at her father.

"You—you won't harm her?" she faltered.

Deep hurt showed in Anthony Worth's blunt features as he gazed back at his daughter. One of his big hands caught up hers and held it in a gentle grip.

"My dear," he murmured, "don't you know your old father better than to have to ask that? What d'ye take me for that you think I'd harm a poor sick woman who's my beautiful wife?"

Gracellen's free hand came up to cover Anthony's in a fervent clasp.

"Then promise me," she said hurriedly, "as you love me, Father, that you'll not hurt her or—or frighten her. And promise me, too, that—that nobody else will suffer by being named in Vivian's —hallucinations."

Anthony's eyes were somber as he looked down at his daughter although there was a quirk at one corner of his mouth that was unreadable.

"I think I know the one you mean," he said gravely. "She—she's cried his name before when the sickness was upon her. Dear

318

Gracellen, if I'd been fool enough to believe her poor raving, d'ye think I'd have tarried a gnat's heartbeat to settle the score?"

She searched for some flaw in the sincerity of his voice. She could not find one. This man was her father; it was impossible that he could look at her like this and calmly, quietly, lie. The others all were wrong—Titus, Jett, Vivian—she herself had been far wide of the truth through all this. Vivian *was* sick, her ranting about taking blacks as partners in her sin proved that. And Task—Task had never spoken a word admitting there ever had been anything between him and Vivian and that must have been more than a gentleman's silence.

Belief in her father's goodness, the throwing off of the burdens of doubt, came with a rush. With a low cry, Gracellen moved into the shelter of his arms, nuzzled her head against his shoulder as he put his face against her hair, a blunt-fingered hand stroking her gently.

"There, there, my dear," he murmured. "You're worn out—we all are. Go get some sleep and forget all this that's happened here. Trust me; it will come out all right."

From the bed, Vivian whimpered: "You're blind, like all the rest!"

7

JETT WORTH sailed *Lorelei* out of Peartree Creek and down the Chesapeake the next night after having spent the day aboard the clipper, not returning to Great House before he cleared. No doctor was called for Vivian; Anthony told Gracellen that the seizure had passed and his wife, rational though very weak, had decided to keep to her room for the next few days. The black shadow that had cloaked Fairoverlea that July night was dissipated by the passing hours until, to Gracellen, it seemed like some remnant of a bad dream.

When Vivian did reappear she seemed more her old self. True, she showed the effects of her illness, her face was sallow, her eyes haunted, her gestures fitful, her movements lacking her old grace, but she did not break down completely again. Not ever in her life did Vivian Dangerfield Worth break down completely again.

July sweated out its days as the British fleet stayed at anchor off Kent Island, Cockburn detailing only an occasional vessel for patrol to send the fishing boats scurrying back to their home ports. One of these British patrol vessels, a brig-sloop, missed the channel in Annapolis Roads in a fog and went hard aground on The Spit, a bar built up by the tides at the mouth of the Severn River, directly under the guns of Governor Winder's Fort Madison. The townspeople of Annapolis gathered on captain's walks and atop roofs to watch the fort's guns blast the enemy ship to kindling.

They watched, their disbelief growing, while Fort Madison's guns remained silent. They watched, their muttering becoming a rumbling roar, as a second British warship sailed up, unhindered, and helped free the brig-sloop from The Spit. They watched, with bitter curses, as the two Cockburn warships placidly sailed back down Annapolis Roads again and still Fort Madison was dumb.

Governor Levin Winder made no effort to explain this odd incident. Perhaps the glowing letter he received from Admiral Sir George Cockburn, complimenting the people of Annapolis and particularly the heroes of Fort Madison for acting sensibly and "in the best interests of the city," plugged his ears against the howls of "Treachery" that echoed from one shore of the Chesapeake Bay to the other.

Admiral Cockburn's fleet bestirred itself on August 1, 1813, when the sick men who had recovered enough to return to duty were brought back aboard their ships. On August 6, the anchors were weighed, the sails unreefed. On the seventh, Cockburn moved toward Queen's Town.

Task Tillman had hurried to his post with the first warning that the British flotilla was getting ready to move. He was with Captain Nicholson's Queen Annes Militia when a breathless rider reported that British sail was moving up the Chester River.

"And now," said Nicholson grimly, " 'tis time to see what we can do."

Cockburn's forces moved leisurely. The British admiral, thanks to Anthony Worth, knew exactly what he had to contend with and he was not unduly impressed. He knew the militia were entrenched behind makeshift breastworks close to the town; very well, he would flank the breastworks, rout the farmer-soldiers, and proceed in his own good time to burn Queen's Town to the ground.

Because his men had been inactive for so long, Cockburn decided to make Queen's Town more of a land action than had been any previous engagement in this one-sided war. Therefore, the British admiral put ashore fifteen hundred men in forty-five landing barges, nearly three times the number of troops he had used in the razing of bigger, more important, Havre de Grace.

The heavier detachment of these British troops went ashore at Blakeford Plantation, upriver from Nicholson's little fort. A smaller body landed below the Queen's Town trenches and moved in on the Americans from that direction, driving the militia pickets before them. Aside from a brief skirmish at a place known locally as Slippery Hill, near the Blakeford landing, there was no opposition to the British pincer movement.

It would be fine to be able to say that the Queen Annes Militia, sparked by Task Tillman, fought heroically and routed the British, or even that they put up a bitter defense before retiring. It would be fine, splendid, but the story of Queen's Town was no story of American heroism; it was a dreary tale of frustration and defeat.

The Slippery Hill pickets were later blamed for what followed but actually there was no need to blame any man or group of men; Cockburn's force was overwhelmingly superior; the outcome would have been the same if every American militiaman had died fighting at his post.

Task Tillman was in the hastily constructed fort when the first of the Slippery Hill pickets came running to Captain Nicholson. To his last day, Tillman remembered the man although he did not know his name or ever learned it. He was a gaunt individual with a squint in one eye and a mouthful of pitted teeth, the perfect harbinger of bad news.

"Cap'n, sir," he gasped when he stumbled up to Nicholson, "there's thousands of 'em—thousands! We met 'em at Slippery Hill and we fought 'em till they was too many fer us."

His voice was shrill and it carried to the men in the trenches, the men standing by to serve the ridiculous nine-pounders.

"We can't stay here, Cap'n!" the gaunt man yelled. "I tell ye, they're still comin' ashore, thousands of 'em. We ain't got a chance!"

"Quiet, you fool!" Nicholson roared, but the damage was done.

The picket's hysteria was a contagious thing; the men under Task had been nervous enough before this; now they were afraid.

Task fought the fright that streaked through his own mind and found his voice surprisingly strong as he barked his order.

"Stand steady! Are you going to let a scared rabbit's wild tale turn ye into frightened children?"

The picket turned on him with a snarl.

"Scared rabbit, eh?" he yelled from where he stood by Nicholson. "By Gawd, you'll see who's the scared rabbit when them British come down on ye! Thousands of 'em!"

"Silence!" Nicholson cried. "Shut up or I'll shut you up!"

There was a sudden silence as the picket glared at the captain and the men in the trenches and at the cannon stared at both and at each other. The quiet was broken by a sullen boom and the *willa-willa-willa* of a heavy British cannon ball churning the air over the heads of the militiamen as it arched over them into the town. Cockburn had opened his bombardment.

Almost at the same time, the popping of muskets rattled on Nicholson's left, on the opposite flank from Slippery Hill. As all eyes swung in that direction, the green-coated figures of the militia pickets showed over a rise, running for the tiny fort. A serjeant smeared with clay where he had slipped in his wild dash, flung himself at Nicholson.

"A big force, sir," he panted. "Must be close to a thousand of 'em."

Harrumppp! Whee-ah-wee-ah-wee-ah! Whoomp! Willa-willa-willa! Cockburn's ships standing out in the river stepped up their fire. In the town behind the trenches something, a house, a barn, began to burn.

Joe Nicholson was as brave a man as the next. He had spent months, years, trying to prepare for this day, trying to whip together a company that could defend the town he loved, and now he found that all those laborious hours, all the work and disappointments and frustrations, had gone for naught. So far as its worth was concerned at this moment, there might as well never have been a Queen Annes Militia. For all Joe Nicholson could do that day, all the drilling, all the uniforms, all the solemn appointments had been part of a game played by adult children who should have found a worthier use for their time.

He stood there, the bowed-shouldered figure of despairing defeat, looking first to his right where his Slippery Hill pickets were streaming in, then to his left where the outposts of his other flank were dodging their way to the fort, and then at the river where Cockburn's warships were decorated with the cotton bolls of cannon smoke.

As Task watched, Nicholson shook his head slowly, then drew the back of a hand across his eyes. He made a brief beckoning gesture that brought Task and the other lieutenants to his side.

"It's no good staying here," the captain said dully. "We'll drop back to Centreville." He looked around the circle of lieutenants, unashamed of the tears that stood in his eyes. "Myself," he went on with no hint of apology or braggadocio, "I'd stay here, but the men—get your platoons ready to march, gentlemen."

Silently, dispiritedly, drained of all emotion except the bitterness of complete, inevitable defeat, the Queen Annes militiamen slogged down the sandy road to Centreville. Two rattling farm wagons carried the five men who had been wounded in the Slippery Hill skirmish and brought in. Behind the column trundled the three little cannon that had never fired a ball in anger.

Task marched beside his platoon, his eyes on the road, his sword slapping his leg with every other step. The bile of failure rose in his throat, the nausea of impotent defeat wrenched his belly. Hail, the brave hero, the man who had dreamed of one day leading a charge against a British bastion!

"There was nothing else we could do," he told himself fiercely.

You could have stood and fought, his mind snickered.

"And be massacred," Task argued.

Your men know the bayonet, his nagging brain reminded him. *You taught them yourself.*

"Bayonets! Against thousands of Britishers!"

How do you know there were thousands? Did you wait to find out? No, you're running with the rest.

"Orders."

You welcomed them. Coward!

"The next time—"

Ah God, the next time! It will be the same the next time and every time.

"And next," Admiral Cockburn was telling his officers, "we pay a visit to Saint Michaels and Easton Town. Now, in connection with the attack along the Miles River—where's the chart? Ah yes. In that action, there are some things to bear in mind. See, where m'finger's pointin'. That place is to be . . . ."

8

BRIGADIER GENERAL PERRY BENSON sat his chestnut horse and looked over the five hundred-odd men he had with which to defend Saint Michaels. They were, he decided privately, a motley crew in their vari-colored uniforms and mufti but it was possible that their temper was such that he could prevail on them to stand and fight.

It was not much for the General to depend upon but the gloomy succession of defeats, the contempt with which the American militia was coming to be treated by the British and their own people alike, the acid of the men's own self-reproach, might, he thought, have stiffened the spirit of these Eastern Shoremen.

Saint Michaels and Easton were to be the final test. If the British took Saint Michaels, Easton must fall and if the enemy levelled Easton as they had every town they had attacked, they would claim the whole territory between Elkton and Cape Henry as their own. If the Eastern Shore fell without a single American victory or even a creditable defense, all Maryland's support of the war would be in danger of crumbling. Without Baltimore, the most stalwart, loyal port on the Atlantic seacoast, the entire war effort surely would shrivel and the cause be lost.

Benson hoped that these men realized this. He had explained it all but he must tell them again. He rose in his stirrups and his voice rolled out over the massed troops, gathered in a field out-side Easton.

"We've been given the chance," he boomed, "to clear the record of our past mistakes. Till now, we've done little to merit praise and much to bring blame down on us. Now we can give the answer to the question of what kind of soldiers we really are. Are we the cowardly dogs that Co'burn calls us?"

There was a fierce, bitter *"No!"* from the troops.

"Or are we men who can fight and win, never breaking for rockets or bombs or shells, never fainting before the worst of the tricks the British devils might try against us?"

The *"Yes!"* thundered back at the General. Benson nodded, quieted his horse as it danced nervously.

"We've got the best prepared positions we've ever been able to put up against the Redcoats," he went on. "We've got the best force we've yet put in the field to face the invaders. Let's beat 'em, boys, and beat 'em so bad they'll never come back to this part of the world!"

The cheers that went up were not the raucous whoops with which the militiamen had answered other high-sounding speeches; the men growled their yells in reply to Benson now. They knew what they faced this time; there was no illusion about what lay ahead. Many of them had been at Georgetown and at Queen's Town; they had seen the strength, the precisioned excellence of the British ships and men, the disorganization and lack of dis-cipline that had wrecked American chances time after time. They also had seen those towns after the British had dealt with them and they were resolved that this would not happen to the last important town on their beloved Eastern Shore.

General Benson turned his horse and walked it back to the group of officers who made up his staff, dismounted as an orderly took the reins. His voice was clipped as he spoke to the men he commanded.

"Has the boom been stretched at Saint Michaels harbor?" he asked.

"Yes sir," a captain answered. "Tight and strong it is, between

327

Parrott's Point and Three Cedars Point. It'll hold back a ship of the line, sir."

Benson shook his head grimly.

"It won't hold them entirely if they risk ramming it," he said, "but I'm hoping it'll slow 'em up within range of our shore batteries." He looked up at the gloomy skies. "We're due for rain," he continued, "and probably fog. Which is to their advantage. All positions must keep a sharp eye out for landing parties in dirty weather; with fog they'll be able to creep ashore almost anywhere. Lieutenant Dodson?"

"Yes sir." The lieutenant was a young man, scarcely more than a boy, and he was visibly nervous as he saluted the General.

"I bid you especially to keep your men alert at all times, Lieutenant," Benson said, gravely. "The way I see it, when the British hit that boom they'll try to land a force at Parrott's Point to unanchor it there. How many cannon have you, Lieutenant?"

"Two nine-pounders, sir."

The General frowned and shook his head slowly.

"I wish you had more, sir, but we have to make do with what we have," he said. "Load with grape and hold your fire as long as possible and perhaps you'll be able to do some damage."

"Yes sir." By the set of his jaw, Lieutenant Dodson showed that he realized just how long two puny nine-pounders could be expected to hold off the British if they attacked in force. General Benson looked at his young officer for a long moment and then turned his gaze back to the captain of the Queen Annes Militia, Joseph Nicholson.

"Captain," he said, "you say there's a full company already in position at a vantage point near Peartree Creek?"

"Yes sir," Task's commander nodded. "The Dragon Footguards, sir. Captain Rawlent commanding."

"They did not muster here with the others?"

"No sir," Nicholson explained. "A courier brought word that they dared not leave their positions for a minute, expecting an attack at any time as they were."

The General grunted.

"Unless Co'burn moves faster than usual," he said, "the British are some hours away from here. But it's good to know that the creek's defended, in any case. Is the battery at Fairview ready?"

"Yes sir," another captain put in. "Manned and ready for action."

"Fairview," General Benson said thoughtfully. "This Fairview isn't the big place on Peartree Creek, I take it."

"No sir. Fairview's upriver from Fairoverlea on Peartree Creek. Fairoverlea is Anthony Worth's estate, where the Dragons are posted. Captain Rawlent is Worth's son-in-law."

"Why then," said General Benson, "his troops ought to fight that much harder." A drop of rain struck his hand and he frowned up at the sky. "Aye, there's the rain and better today than tomorrow. Maybe this weather will clear in time to give us a good view of the British."

He forced a smile to his weathered features.

"You all have your orders, gentlemen," he said quietly. "I'd suggest you get your men in position and ready in case Co'burn uses the weather in a surprise move." His hand went up in answer to the salutes of his staff. "Good fortune, gentlemen. Let us give America a victory."

Task Tillman moved his platoon out under the command of Lieutenant Dodson. There were gaps in the ranks of his unit; a good many of the Queen's Town men had not journeyed the miles to help in the defense of Saint Michaels and Easton; some of the militiamen who had seen their own town devastated without any aid from Easton had refused to risk their lives to protect the larger town.

But, Task knew, the men he could be depended upon to do their best, from Willie Parsons, the red-haired youth who had announced his intention to "stob" a Lobsterback at Georgetown, to the middle-aged mill owner, Johnson, who, having been unable to persuade a single man of his own platoon to join the Saint Michaels defenses, had resigned as a lieutenant of the Queen Annes Militia and had joined Task's platoon as a private soldier.

"Though I do wish," the older man grumbled in an aside to Task, "that we were under the command of a grown man and not that infant, Dodson. He looks like he's just out of his napkin, that child."

"I think he'll fight," Task said seriously.

"Which the oldsters have yet to do, eh?" Johnson asked, smiling faintly. "Well, I hope you're right—we'll soon know."

The rain was falling hard by the time the detail reached the lane that led to Parrott's Point and, as General Benson had feared, there was a mist rising on the river. Dirty weather was certainly on the way and the fog favored only the British.

The Parrott's Point defenses were a strong position for their size and armament. There were the two gun emplacements, set low so that the grapeshot would sweep the expanse of beach that surrounded the anchor of the boom. Facing the river and behind the guns was a crescent-shaped trench, reinforced by thick pine logs. In back of the trenches was a series of lookout posts, each holding four men, that dotted the perimeter of the position as protection against an enveloping movement from the land side.

The two nine-pounders rested on plank platforms and could be swiveled readily to cover a considerable stretch of the shoreline. And, most important of all in Task's opinion, nearly all of his men's cumbersome, slow-loading muskets had been replaced by fowling pieces, as familiar to these duck- and goose-hunters as their own hands.

"Loaded with buckshot," Dodson told Task, "those duck guns should play hell with a tidy lot of our visitors."

Dodson did not make the mistake that had been made at Havre de Grace; he did not keep his men at their guns until they were asleep on their feet and then relieve his entire force to eat and sleep. Instead, he divided his company into three watches; the men who were off guard slept—if their soaked blankets allowed them to—within reach of their weapons.

Task could not sleep. When he went off guard he huddled his rain cape about him and sat down with his back against a tree, his head lowered on his arms, folded across his knees. The hot-breathed excitement that had stirred him when the little army had mustered, and during the march to Parrott's Point, slowly waned under the pelting rain and gave way to bleak reverie. A great many things went through Task Tillman's mind, a great many black regrets crowded in on him to be reviewed, too many thoughts of what might have been danced tauntingly across his memory.

Vivian—Gracellen—Anthony Worth—Jett—Squire Wills—his father—they spoke out of all the yesterdays and there was nothing but reproach, recrimination, in what they said.

He had done nothing right; where there had been a right way and a wrong he had always chosen the wrong. He had failed to avenge his father. He had lost Gracellen. He had muddied his honor in Vivian's arms, all the time trying to convince himself that it was not wrong to cuckold Anthony Worth.

No one to blame but yourself, his inner voice told him. *No one but yourself—and an old diary.*

His father's diary of 1788—it had twisted his life ever since he had found it. One page, written nearly a quarter of a century ago, had sparked hate for Anthony Worth in him and because of that hate and what it had brought him, he, Task Tillman, crouched beneath a dripping tree without the memory of one thing well done to warm him on this, the day that could well be his last on earth.

And perhaps you pray that it will be, Task Tillman, the silent voice mourned. *Perhaps you hope a British musket ball, a piece of shell, finds its target in you and so brings retribution for all your failures, all your blunders, all your sins. For what have you to look forward to but a final end to heartsickness?*

9

THE FOG rolled in, thickening by the hour, shrouding Eastern Bay and the Miles River with a dense cloak of mist that blinded the watchers along the shores long before the early dusk descended.

Charles Rawlent, glass in hand, stood in the west parlor of Fairoverlea, stuttering a protestation made almost incoherent by outraged vanity and brandy.

"I tuh-tell you it's demmed disorderly," he spluttered, "and I won't have it! You pickets can't come in, y'know, till I order you to! Not soldierly, that's what!"

The parlor was crowded with Dragon Footguards in various stages of uniform. They had marched out that morning to their positions along Peartree Creek, a brave sight in their claret tunics and white crossbelts, their spotless trousers and shining boots, their gleaming shakos and the white gloves swinging in perfect unison as the drum tapped out the beat. Then, as the rain poured down and the fog swirled in, Charles Rawlent's blue-blooded militiamen had left off cursing the weather and had straggled back to Fairoverlea, singly, in pairs and by squads, to fortify themselves with Anthony Worth's hospitality.

Rawlent, dry and comfortable in the Command Post he had set up in Fairoverlea's gun room, had fortified himself, too, to the point where he was finding it difficult to stand without wavering or talk without stammering. His fleshy face was bright red now and the sweat trickled down his full cheeks as he tried to make himself heard over the rumble of voices, the clattering laughter, that hammered through the room.

It wasn't right, dammit; it wasn't right at all! He was captain of the Footguards, wasn't he? Hadn't his money, what little of it there had been before Anthony Worth, the old pirate, had loaned him what he needed to fill the bill, paid for those uniforms, the swords, the sashes, the carbines and all the rest?

He drained his drink and recovered from a dangerous sway.

"Attention!" he bawled.

The yell resounded through the crowded room, ricochetting off the walls. The talk was silenced, the laughter died in mid-whoop. The Dragons, most of them stripped down to their sodden pantaloons, swung their eyes toward their commanding officer. Charles drew himself erect, steadied himself with a hand on the sideboard.

"Every one of you," he told his men, "go back where you were till I relieve you! Every one!"

There was a stunned silence and then somebody laughed. It was not a friendly sound and there was an exposed challenge in it.

"Go lie down, Charley," advised somebody at the other side of the parlor. "You'll feel better in a minute."

"Who said that?" Rawlent roared. He lurched in the general direction of the voice and slammed into a man—was it Mulliken or Rickard?—and caromed off. He tried desperately to hold his balance and fell, jarringly, his sword hilt grinding into his hip.

Hands were raising him to his feet and there were waves of flat laughter all around him. He fought the man who was helping him and found his arms pinioned. He kicked out with one foot and a slender table went over with a crash.

Now, God damn it, they couldn't do this! He was Captain Charles Rawlent and he was commanding officer of the Dragon Footguards and if they laughed at him, if they refused to follow his orders, he'd have 'em all court-martialled, every one, and shot! He'd paid for this company and they had to listen to him!

"Now, all right, Charles," a deep voice was telling him, over and over. "Now, all right. You need a little rest, that's all. A half hour or so will fix you up like new."

He turned his head to see the face of Anthony Worth swimming in front of him. Anthony was smiling at him and his hand on Charles' pinned arm was the pat a man would give a nervous horse.

The great Anthony Worth, eh? Well, he, Charles Rawlent, could tell things he knew about that big bastard if he had to. And he would, unless they all treated him with a little more respect.

"A little rest," Anthony kept saying gently. "A little rest, Charles. You've had a long day and—"

"A little rest, my arse!" Rawlent shouted. "These damned mutinous swine—I'll show 'em what happens to men who come in off duty without bein' ordered in! Shot—that's what they ought to be!"

Somebody—his face was too clouded by Rawlent's own fog to be identified—staggered forward and thrust himself against the wavering captain.

"Shoot me, will you?" he bellowed. "By God, you'd better aim straight, you Split-britches, when you shoot at me, else I'll put a ball down your gullet that'll—"

There was a confusion of bodies jostling Rawlent as he dragged his pistol from his belt. A hard hand on his wrist turned the cumbersome piece's muzzle toward the parqueted floor and then he was being hurtled out of the crowded room while behind him arose a roar that was evenly divided between laughter and curses.

Rawlent, struggling, kicking, swearing and sobbing, was shoved out of the room and down a hallway. Ungentle hands threw him through a doorway. He pitched forward, his hands outstretched, and landed on a carpeted floor, the pistol slithering out of his hand and sliding out of sight.

"Lay still, damn ye," grunted a voice, "or I'll kick y'r teeth in. Tom, get the weapon."

"Oh, let the nancy-ann try to use it," burbled a fat-lipped voice. " 'Twould be interestin' to see if he really knows how to shoot one."

"Get the pistol!"

"Oh aye, Will," the oleaginous voice whined. "No need to get so 'roused about it. I was just havin' me a little joke."

Charles Rawlent shoved himself up from the floor and looked about him. There were three men in the shadowy room with him. One was tall and broad, one was thin and peering, the third was round and chuckling. Roan, Marsden and Womble. Rawlent shook his head, trying to free himself of the nightmare. Dimly, he heard the subdued murmur of the men in the west parlor of Fairoverlea, the Dragon Footguards who had laughed at him when he had tried to assert his authority. They had flouted his orders but they were still the Dragons, beholden to him. Whatever else had gone wrong, they'd rally to him when he called for help. He opened his mouth to yell and was dealt a back-handed slap by Roan that knocked him over on his side.

He put a fumbling hand to his cut mouth and looked stupidly at the crimson knuckles as he took them down from his flaming lips. He stared up at Roan and shuddered before he turned his eyes away. The twisted mouth, the scarred face, bespoke death.

Womble was smiling cheerily. Womble looked as though he were about to share a priceless joke with the man on the floor. Womble, as he bubbled another laugh, smeared a fat hand over his pendulous mouth in a gesture that was more obscene than any of his carvings or his prints. Marsden was a cloaked skeleton, standing against the wall with his long, white face glowing faintly in a luminescent sheen that went with his graveyard garb.

"The King," Charles Rawlent choked. *"The King* will skin you alive for this!"

Tom Womble giggled as Roan bent over the man on the floor. "Whose orders d'ye think we serve?" the big man grunted. "Who had ye brought here? Who'll send you where ye're goin'?

335

Ye've pried too much, my pretty lad, and ye made the mistake of lettin' *The King* know ye pried."

"I'll not tell!" Rawlent cried. "I swear I'll never tell a soul!"

And Womble giggled again.

Rawlent felt his sword at his side. If he could roll out of their way to draw it and—

He groaned and turned over. Another roll and he'd be out of the way of Roan's heavy boots. What was it he had heard somewhere? A man should thrust the scabbard straight out in front of him, swinging it as he drew the blade. He doubted that a person could draw a blade from a scabbard while it was moving; it was hard enough to free it to return the salute of the platoons that passed on parade. And if he missed, Roan would be at him with those thick-soled boots thudding into his face and his groin.

And Womble would—

And Marsden would—

If he had had warning that he was going to weep he might have stopped the tears. As it was, he had no chance; he found himself lying there under the three pairs of soulless eyes, hiccoughing and choking as the tears flooded his face.

"No gentleman—" he managed to say before the dim room whirled and he slid down into black nothingness.

Tom Womble trotted over to the disheveled officer on the floor and nicely aimed a kick at his middle. When the body jerked but did not make a sound he nodded happily at Will Roan.

"Fainted away," he chirruped. "Makes it that much easier."

"Aye," Roan grumbled, "but where's *The King*? He said we'd best—"

"Behind you, Will," Womble nodded.

Anthony Worth looked old, drawn, in the pale half-light of the office. His wide shoulders were stooped and his step dragged as he moved to beside Charles Rawlent's limp form. Marsden moved wraithlike along the wall to shut the door behind Anthony, cutting off a burst of song from the parlor.

"Ohhhh, God bless King Gee-orge,
  And reform him,
  And take him!
'Cause we don't want him any lo-o-o-onger!"

"Light another candle!" Anthony said, his voice clipped. When Womble handed him the tapered silver candlestick he bent over the captain of the Dragon Footguards and studied the blood-smeared face of his son-in-law. Satisfied, he straightened.

"You know what to do with him?" he asked Roan. The hulking overseer nodded.

"Ye said to wait till they came," he reminded Worth.

The Master of Fairoverlea shrugged and turned away from Gracellen's husband. He crossed the narrow room to a window and looked out at the mist, tinged orange by the glow from the west wing's windows. He held his hands clasped behind his back, his feet spread wide, his chin upraised.

"Ohhh, the Devil take King Gee-orge,
  And roast him,
  And toast him,
'Cause we don't want him any mo-o-o-ore!"

"Ain't it time, sir?" Tom Womble asked. "Y'said they'd be here by midnight."

"This fog," Anthony Worth said, without turning. "Is Titus at the landing?"

"Aye, sir," Will Roan answered. "The ladies are ready, sir?"

"They'll be ready," Anthony said bluntly.

He pulled a watch from his pocket, bent to consult it, and shook his head. If Cockburn did find this fog too thick, all the plans would have to be changed and that would be a pity. Conditions might not be as perfect the next time, with this fool, Rawlent, playing directly into his hands and the Dragon Footguards so drunk they wouldn't see anything strange about what was going to happen, or remember it if they did.

The rain and fog that had driven in Rawlent's pickets had

done away with the need for Anthony Worth's first plan, a flask of brandy liberally laced with laudanum for every outpost on Peartree Creek. Now there wouldn't be the risk of some busybody wondering.

He turned from the window and walked back to the center of the small room, casting a cursory look at the still figure on the floor.

"I'll be in the parlor with the others," he said briefly. "Let me know when they come."

"If they don't come soon," Roan said slowly, "they ain't comin'. And what do we do with him, him knowin' what he knows?"

Anthony Worth paused on his way to the door to fling a glance back over his shoulder.

"If we have to," he said casually, "we can always have him wander out into the swamp, drunk."

He closed the door gently behind him. Tom Womble breathed gustily.

"Now there's a man," he said, "that's after me own heart."

Anthony Worth donned his smile at the parlor doorway, clapped the nearest man on the shoulder and led him to the sideboard.

"You'll not be riding home tonight, Lieutenant," he told James Mulliken. "We have plenty of room here for you if you don't mind sleeping three or four to the bed. And a good soldier shouldn't find that too rough, should he?"

"N-n-n-nossir," Mulliken said. He debated with himself and arrived at a weighty conclusion. "Damn fog spoiled a good battle, didn't it, sir?"

"The fog will lift," Anthony said reassuringly, "and we'll still get our chance to send 'em running."

"I had a platoon around somewhere," Lieutenant Mulliken said owlishly, "but the last time I saw 'em they were all asleep."

"They'll be ready when the time comes," Anthony laughed. "Ah, there, Mister Harrison. Join me in a drink. We old men are envying your youth. You're going to be the heroes tomorrow

338

when the British come and we'll be the oldsters who just looked on."

Harrison took his drink and stared down at it. His saturnine features grimaced.

"Heroes?" he repeated sourly. "Hell, if a boatload of British Regulars landed anywhere on the Miles River tonight they could have the whole place for the asking. Who's to say nay to 'em?"

"Why, the Dragon Footguards, of course," Anthony protested.

Harrison looked around the room, slowly, deliberately, and Anthony's eyes followed the taciturn serjeant's. Men were asleep in chairs, on settees, on the floor. Those who were still awake reeled and staggered. Through the open windows came the groans of those whose stomachs had rebelled. Sword belts and bayonet scabbards, pistols and carbines, littered the room. Open cartouches spilled their contents on the carpeted floor; bullets were strewn about, thrown there by some drunken trooper's fling.

Harrison turned back to Worth, his voice quiet.

"You think the Dragon Footguards are able to defend anything at all, sir?" he asked.

Anthony waved a hand.

"Certainly you don't expect a British attack this late on a foggy night, do you?" he asked.

"I do, Mister Worth," Harrison's steely voice rapped back, "and I have been wondering just why you are so complacent about your plantation's position. The British are at your doorstep and still you spend your effort, it seems, getting the militia expected to defend it drunk, sir."

Anthony Worth looked down at his glass and reached inside to pluck a drowned greenfly from its surface. He turned to pour his drink into a slopjar and splashed amber brandy into the crystal glass, filled it to its brim with water. He sipped the drink, nodded, and then turned back to Harrison.

"As for my complacency, as you call it," he said, smiling, "I'm what I expect you'd call a fatalist. If the British are coming to Fairoverlea, why then they're coming; if this place of mine has

339

to suffer their outrages, why then it does. A long face and a head full of worry won't change what happens a whit. I've never been much of a man to worry about what I couldn't help, Mister Harrison."

He looked about the noisy, smoke-clouded room.

"As for my getting the Dragons drunk," he went on with a shrug, "I'm not in command of your troop. Would you have me lock my bottles up when a houseful of guests is at hand? All any of these gentlemen had to do was to refuse, sir, when I did what any host would be expected to do. And you'll pardon me? I have something to attend to."

As he walked away from the frowning Harrison, Anthony Worth made a mental note that somebody would have to make certain that a serjeant by the name of Harrison had no chance to voice his strange suspicions after this night's work was done.

10

"Easy oars, easy all," murmured the bos'n. Sir Peter Porter hunched the greatcoat about his shoulders and wondered again, more dismally this time, when His Majesty's Admiralty would devise a raincape that was not made out of wool thick enough to turn back an Arctic blast. This was—let's see, what was it?— August the tenth and the heat of this Eastern Shore of Maryland was enough to make a Portuygee faint.

If Old Co'burn ever found out that he had taken personal command of this landing party there might be hell to pay, Porter told himself, but, on the other hand, the Admiral hadn't said he should *not* go ashore with the men.

"*Menelaus* will land a hundred men at this Peartree Creek," was all Old Co'burn had said. "Draft some from the vessels not going into action if y'need to."

The landing party properly should have been in charge of one of his lieutenants but it had been too long since he had been ashore, far too long since he had seen any excitement of any kind. Boredom was a worse enemy than the Yankees and so he had seized on this opportunity to take over the detail himself.

And eerie business it was, too, this creeping along with muffled oars, five crowded barges strung out behind this one, making up a creek that twisted and turned like a stepped-on serpent, with the trees growing almost together over the middle of the waterway. The fog was a blessing in one way, a curse in another; it made slipping in without being seen incomparably easier but at the same time it meant picking one's way along at a tiresome pace, blundering ashore time after time with the following boats lumbering aground like obedient sheep after a bellwether.

The damned tree frogs or whatever they were made a ferocious din, enough to add a knife edge to nerves that were already none too quiet. A loud splash close at hand, a heron or a muskrat, sent his hand flashing to the butt of his pistol and then he relaxed, laughing at himself.

Co'burn had said that a clipper ship used this creek as a hideaway at times but the old boy must be wrong in that. The only clipper Sir Peter had ever seen had been a saucy wench named *Lorelei* that had shown her neat behind to *Menelaus* near the Virginia Capes one day when the frigate had tried to chase her down. *Lorelei*, he knew, could never use this trickle for more than to fill her water casks.

He peered ahead into the foggy nothingness, straining to pick up the light that Co'burn had told him would be flashed for him to signal a safe landing. There was no light, only the dim figure of the bos'n's mate who was trying to steer the boat. And if there was no light, it would mean that Old Co'burn's arrangements had gone all wrong.

"In which case," the Admiral had told him, "the detail will make a landing at the best place and destroy every building down to the smallest pigpen on the plantation."

Admiral Cockburn had seemed pretty sure there would be a light and that was strange. Usually, Old Co'burn was a suspicious devil; it was odd that he trusted this situation so completely that he'd order a hundred men into a creek like this, where they could be ambushed and slaughtered. Whatever arrangements he had made with this Yankee turncoat must have carried a solid guarantee with it.

Sir Peter wondered idly why this Yankee, Worth, was doing this, betraying his own people this way. What prompted a man to

342

turn traitor, anyway; love of money, a sincere belief that Britain was right and America wrong, a fear for his own skin? Cockburn had told him that this place, Fairoverlea, was not to be damaged in any way unless things went wrong so Worth probably preferred to sell out his country than see his property go up in smoke. He must be a timid fellow, Porter decided; a place way out here in the country would hardly be in danger from Old Co'burn. The Admiral put his torch to towns.

Sir Peter wondered just how he should deal with this Worth when he talked to him. He hoped he could hide the loathing that the sight of a spy or a traitor set up in him but if he couldn't, he thought, it would make little difference; Worth must be a cringing sort of swine to be engaged in this business in the first place.

And about—

"Light ahead, sir," the bos'n hissed. Sir Peter looked up to see the faint blob of yellow light glow once through the mist and then disappear. From beneath a thwart, Porter pulled a signal lantern, a heavy brass affair with a sliding shutter, and stood up. He balanced himself and drew the shutter, snapped it shut, opened it and closed it three times more. There were two answering lights from ahead.

"Head for the light," the young admiral ordered. "Ready with your arms, men."

There was a stir and rustle in the boat as the Marines in the lead craft looked to their carbines. Sir Peter freed his own pistol, loosened his blade in its scabbard. He did not like this. He began to wish he had not impulsively taken command of this party; there was a crawling along his spine at the thought of moving blindly through this fog toward a light that might mark the place where an ambush had been set.

Porter's boat edged in toward the place where the light had shone, the other's following. The silence was broken only by the subdued splash of the oars, an occasional muffled noise from one of the following barges. The deathly stillness screamed in Sir Peter Porter's ears. He was not, he decided, made for this work; he craved a poopdeck with its bawled orders, the rattle of lines through their blocks, the eternal creak and mutter of a heavy vessel at sea. This skulking about in the foggy darkness was not for him.

Suddenly, impossibly close, the light blazed again, blinding his straining eyes.

"This way, sarrh," piped a high, harsh voice. "Over this way."

There was a smothered curse from one of the Marines in Porter's boat and the oars churned aimlessly for a moment before the bos'n rapped out the orders that brought the longboat up to a dock. Sir Peter was the first on the pier's planking, his pistol in his hand.

The man holding the light, he discovered, was the biggest Negro he ever had seen, a black who must have been seven feet tall, if an inch. In the foggy darkness there was not much to be seen of him except his eyes and they glimmered a full twelves inches above Sir Peter Porter as he stared upward.

"De King," said the Negro, "bids me tell you he ready foh you at de house, sarrh."

"King?" Porter demanded sharply. "What do you mean, The King?"

"Mistuh Worth, sarrh," Titus explained in his incongruously high voice. "'Round here he call De King."

"And why isn't this Mister Worth here to meet us?" the young admiral asked. "Why does he have to send word by you?"

"He fixin' things," Titus said simply. "Ever'thing ready fer you when De King fixes 'em. You follow me, please, sarrh."

Porter considered. This whole expedition bordered on the fantastic and now he was being expected to follow a Negro giant with a woman's voice somewhere off into the dark, blank fog to meet a man known as The King. Better, he thought, to have the whole force land and march to meet this "king" at the head of them, in case of trickery—but Old Co'burn had told him to follow Worth's suggestions in this matter and to put the whole party ashore and thus upset whatever preparations Worth might have made would bring Co'burn's wrath down upon him. He had grappled with and boarded a French man-o'-war without a qualm

344

but he never had been able to think of meeting a purple-faced Cockburn without a shudder.

"How far is it to this Mister Worth?" he asked.

"He up yonder at de house," Titus said. "Not far. I show you. You kin hear it from yere."

Porter listened and heard, from what seemed a great distance, a snatch of a song.

"—for we don't want him any mo-o-o-ore!"

"That de Dragons, Marse Rawlent's sojers," Titus explained. "They all drunk. You come with me."

Well, strike him dead as a madman, Sir Peter Porter told himself, but this was an adventure nobody would believe when he tried to describe it. Here he was, set down in the middle of God only knew what kind of swamp, with a nine-foot nigra who spoke soprano telling him a king awaited him in a house that was full of American dragons! The whole thing was so unbelievable that he laughed and nodded.

"A moment," he said, "till I get some men to go with me and we'll go see this king of yours."

Above him, inhumanly tall in the uncertain light, Titus shook his head.

"*De King* say only one gennelman come," he squeaked. "Only one gennelman, de off'cer in command, he say."

"Then, dammit," Sir Peter Porter barked, "nobody's coming!"

Titus shrugged unconcernedly. It was obvious to the young admiral that the huge black had orders and beyond those orders he could not be threatened, coaxed or cajoled. He looked into the depthless fog beyond the giant and shivered slightly.

"All right," he said after a pause. "I'll go along to meet this king. But I warn you, no tricks!"

And what, he asked himself, would he be able to do against this monster if there were tricks?

He turned over his command to the lieutenant whom he had superseded as leader of this fogbound sortie, ordering him to post sentries up and down the banks of Peartree Creek to guard against an attack (there was nothing else he could do, dammit;

the landing party was neatly trapped if this was treachery), looked to his pistol and followed Titus up the steep bank that led from the landing.

The wet bushes clung to him as though imploring him to go no further; his boots grated unpleasantly on the marl and sand of the lane, a trickle of water ran down inside the neck of his cape and coursed down the small of his back. War ashore, Sir Peter Porter decided, was a damned sight more unpleasant than war afloat.

He asked himself if he had completely taken leave of his wits, following this man alone into what certainly must be a nest of American militia. He was no Old Co'burn, certainly, but the Yankees, starved as they must be for any kind of triumph, would welcome the capture of a junior British admiral and, so far as he knew, this overgrown slave was arranging just that.

But Old Co'burn had arranged all this and Old Co'burn often boasted that he never made the same mistake twice.

"P'raps," Sir Peter murmured to himself, "that means he won't be taken in by any Mister Worth a second time. Meanwhile, though, what about me?"

The two men made a turn around a clump of cedars and Porter caught his breath at the immensity of Fairoverlea, dimly impressive in the fog. The lower floor of one wing of the mansion was ablaze with lights; there was the babble of voices, broken by shouts and scraps of song, coming from that wing. Porter caught the sound of crashing glass and a hurricane of laughter.

"A ball," he mused, "but what do the Yankees have to celebrate?"

Titus led the way across the courtyard toward the small door set in its niche between the kitchens and the main part of the house. The two men were halfway between the stables and the door when a figure lurched out of the rainy fog and descended on Sir Peter Porter.

He froze, his blood standing still, as he cursed himself for walking into this trap like a simple-minded child. He wondered, in the space between his first sight of the man and the thump

346

of hands on his shoulders, what Old Co'burn would do about
this. The fool who was seizing him, though, should have known
enough to watch his hands beneath the cloak because now the
pistol—

"Friend," wheezed the man who leaned on him, his breath a
horrendous swirl of brandy fumes, "where's the privy? Lost the
goddam privy somewhere. Saw it a minute ago but it's clean disappeared. I sh'ld think—"

He drew back, his eyes focusing on Porter.

"Say," he said thickly, "you're no Dragon. Who are you, anyway? Say, that uniform makes you look like—"

He went down like a horse shot in the ear. Titus stepped back
and lowered the club—no, b'God, it was the butt of a whip!—
he had used on the drunken man's skull. Unceremoniously, the
big black hauled the Dragon Footguardsman across the court's
cobblestones and, as unceremoniously, lifted him to fling him
into the boxwood border of the garden. Sir Peter watched with
wide eyes as his erstwhile brandy-drinking friend pinwheeled
through the air like a petulantly tossed doll and disappeared
with a crash somewhere in the fog-blanketed garden.

"This way, sarrh," Titus said, as unconcernedly as though the
brief incident never had happened.

Porter hitched his cape more closely about him and followed
his guide toward the house in which these Dragons, whoever
they were, caroused. The Negro's swift disposal of the privy-
seeking American reassured him slightly; at least if this was a
trap it would be sprung with some kind of delayed-action fuse.

He paused at the door beside which Titus waited. He brought
the pistol out from beneath his cloak and waved it toward the
doorway.

"You first," he ordered. "And remember, I'm right behind you
with this pistol."

Titus looked down at the weapon in Porter's hand, seemed
about to smile and merely shrugged. The big black bent his
head to step through the doorway and Porter followed, closing
the door behind him. He found himself in a narrow passageway,

347

beyond the wall of which the roar of the militiamen at play thumped and thundered.

The Negro padded ahead of the admiral down the passageway to another door on which he knocked, twice, once more, then twice again. There was the sound of a bolt being drawn and light filled the passageway as the door opened into a small room.

"Come in, sir," Anthony Worth bowed. "Welcome to Fairoverlea."

11

GINGERLY, Sir Peter Porter stepped into the room, brushing past the gigantic Negro who had led him here. He looked around to discover that this was an office with its desk and ledgers, its bookcase filled with tape-wrapped papers.

Besides Worth, he saw, there were three men in the room and a more ill-favored trio he had seldom seen, even aboard ship where beauty was rare. He kept his grip on his pistol butt, held himself balanced on the balls of his feet—as though that could make any difference.

"Mister Worth?" he asked coldly. The tall, broad-shouldered old man bowed again. "Admiral Porter, sir, here on the order of Admiral Sir George Co'burn of His Majesty's Navy."

The other man smiled as graciously as though he were welcoming Porter on the front steps of his home.

"I recognize you, Admiral," he said pleasantly.

"We've met?"

"Only for a few minutes which I doubt you'd recall," Anthony explained. He turned to the villainous trio who stood against the wall, their eyes pinned on Porter. "You post yourselves at the end of the pasageway," he said in a clipped voice. "I'll call you when I need you."

The three men touched their foreheads, cast another curious

glance at Porter and filed out. The towering slave who had led him to this place, Sir Peter saw, had disappeared silently while Worth was giving his greeting.

Anthony shot the bolt on the hallway door, then strolled back to behind the desk, waving his hand at the chair against the opposite wall.

"Make yourself comfortable, Admiral," he said. He gestured toward a decanter on a nearby table. "A drink? No? I thought not, though I imagine ye'd relish one on a wet night like this. The fog gets through to a man's bones, don't it, and a little brandy—"

"No brandy, thankee," Porter broke in. "I'd like to finish up this business as soon as possible. I have no liking for the whole affair, to be blunt, sir. If Sir George hadn't said you were to explain the final arrangements, you'd not find me here at all." He nodded his head toward the wall through which filtered echoes of the whooping crowd in the west parlor. "I don't think the Admiral had any thought you'd place his emissary in such a risky position, sir."

"Those fools?" Anthony shrugged. "You have nothing to fear from them, Admiral."

"I did not say I feared them," Sir Peter said stiffly, "but at the same time, all this is against common sense. One of those Dragon fellows met me outside and if it hadn't been for your black breaking his skull with the whip he carries I'd have had to shoot him and so raised the alarm."

"That man shouldn't have been allowed back there," Anthony Worth frowned. "Somebody slipped up. I'll find out who it was and take steps."

"Devil take steps," Sir Peter said impatiently. "What I want is to hear what you have to say and get on with it."

Anthony Worth kept his smile intact with an effort. He was not accustomed to being addressed in the tone this young British admiral was using. Years before, he had told Jett that he could put up with British arrogance, even British contempt, when it served his purpose; he did so now.

" 'Tis quickly explained, Admiral," he said. "You have your men?"

"A hundred of the best," Porter jerked out, "sitting in the fog in that tiny creek of yours, as easy a target as—I mean to say, well protected 'gainst any trickery."

Anthony Worth nodded. He hunched forward over the desk, his broad hands clasped in front of him.

"Then here's the plan," he said swiftly. "Those three men who were just in here will guide your party to a favorable position near the creek. You can be assured there'll be no trickery in any of this, Admiral. At the proper time, your men will set up a fire— have 'em shoot in the air. The alarm will be sounded here and, I promise you, it'll be all confusion. Those fancy dress ball soldiers in the next room are completely befuddled."

He hunched further over the desk.

"Now," he went on, "my part will be to rally these drunken fools and have 'em led in your direction. The position I'll send 'em to will be hopeless but they'll be too drunk to see that till it's too late. It'll be up to your men to take advantage of the gift of a full company of militia—or those of them who won't be too besotted to stagger into battle."

Sir Peter Porter scowled openly at the man behind the desk, his loathing open in his eyes. To betray one's country by giving away secrets to the enemy, as Old Co'burn had told him Worth had done, was one thing; to deliberately lead a company of countrymen into a death trap was another, viler crime. He drew his sodden cape about him closer as though he feared contamination by his very presence in the same room with this villain.

"And if this plan's successful," he forced himself to say, "what do you expect in return, Mister Worth?"

Anthony smiled and shrugged, spreading his hands.

"A mere trifle, as balanced against the advantages I've given you," he said. "Once the Dragons are—er—eliminated, your men are to stay away from Fairoverlea, keep their hands off what is mine."

"No command of mine is a looting command, sir," Porter rapped out. Anthony shrugged again.

"Your pardon, sir," he said negligently. "In any case, it will appear that your attack was directed at Fairoverlea and that it was beaten off by the heroic defense of the Dragons. Oh, those of 'em who are left won't dispute that, you may be sure. Nor will they be inclined to spread the word about their own drunkenness. So in the end, all the little—ah—side affairs I've planned will all be linked to this battle I've—hee hee—arranged."

The young admiral shifted impatiently in his chair.

"I must tell you," he burst out, "that I've little stomach for this kind of villainy, Mister Worth!"

Anthony's eyes grew cold, his voice hardened.

"Then I must say, sir," he retorted, "that your nice scruples do not interest me. I've explained this plan to Sir George and it has his full approval. If you faint at the thought, why then perhaps 'twould be best for you to take your men and go back to your ships and tell Admiral Co'burn that you disapproved his plan."

His smile was icily ironic now.

"I doubt that he'd exactly jump for joy at the news," he went on. "I chance to know that he is depending on this diversion here at Fairoverlea in his general plan of action against Saint Michaels and Easton Town."

He leaned back with a flirt of his hand.

"Which plan," he purred, "he no doubt would be happy to see fail because of your qualms, Admiral."

Sir Peter Porter bit his lip. Damn it all, he told himself, for having elected this choice bit of back-stabbing as a chance to lead a landing party! What the devil sitting behind the desk had just said was true enough; Old Co'burn would slit the throat of his career without a second's hesitation if the whole Easton-Saint Michaels move was spoiled by a breakdown at Fairoverlea. If only he had stayed on *Menelaus* and left this night's work up to the lieutenant who had been supposed to lead this detail in the first place—but he hadn't.

"Go on, then," he told Anthony brusquely. "We ambush these Dragons, we leave your place alone because, to all intents, we are beaten off. What then?"

"Why then," Worth smiled, "you follow Sir George's orders and strike at Easton along the road from here."

"I know all about that," Porter said, "but I had the impression there was a favor or two we'd do for you, personally, before we struck out for Easton. Sir George told me that the commander of the party would get your explanation of these favors when he talked to you."

Anthony's hand came up to stroke his chin, his eyes thoughtful.

"Oh aye," he said in a soft voice, "but I don't believe Sir George expected you to lead the party, Admiral. And seeing that you do, I think I'll leave those favors Sir George spoke of to other hands."

Sir Peter Porter nodded his relief. He had no idea what these favors might be but Old Co'burn's leer, plus the nature of the toad that sat behind the desk, convinced him that they were no pretty things. He had enough black-hearted work ahead of him, as it was, he told himself, without carrying out God knew what things as the balance of this unholy bargain.

He arose, settling his cape about his shoulders. Another burst of laughter, another off-key belch of song, thudded against the wall that separated this room from the Dragon Footguards in the west wing parlor.

"I'd best get back to my men," he told Anthony in his clipped voice, "and have your people guide us to this ambush you've planned. They know what time we're to begin shooting?"

"Aye," Anthony nodded. "They've been well coached in this and they can be depended on."

He got up to precede Sir Peter to the passageway door, drew back the bolt. The young admiral paused at the threshold and looked over his shoulder at the Master of Fairoverlea.

"I need not tell you," he said, with disdain stark in every word, "what will happen to you and this fine house of yours if Sir George Co'burn finds that he's been falsely dealt with."

353

"And I might remind you," Anthony said evenly, "that my neck would not be worth one of your farthings if the details of this little—er—arrangement were made public, now or at any time in the future."

Porter grunted and turned to walk down the passageway, Anthony Worth behind him. Outside the outer door waited Womble, Roan and Marsden, each with a lanthorn. Wordlessly, the three men started across the courtyard toward the lane that led to the landing. Sir Peter Porter followed them. Anthony Worth stood for a moment, looking after the four men until their lights winked out as they rounded the clump of cedars. Then, smiling gently, he closed the door.

There were many things to be done.

12

Task Tillman paced up and down the platform on which squatted the two nine-pound cannon which defended the Parrott's Point anchor of the log and chain boom stretched across Saint Michaels harbor.

The rain still drizzled down, tirelessly, endlessly, drearily. The fog still swirled in from the river although it seemed some lighter, not much. The night hours crawled past, each one a year of waiting, and still there was no sign of the British.

Nor, Task told himself, was there likely to be in this weather. Even Cockburn would think twice before he'd risk sending his warships into the Miles in a fog so dense that a miracle would be needed to keep a vessel from going aground. Still, the man was a devil; Beelzebub might bring his forked tail aboard Cockburn's flagship to act as steersman for one of his good servants and it would never do for the Americans to drop their guard one second.

It was dull work, this waiting. In clear daylight at least there would be the excitement of watching the river for sight of British sail. In this muck the enemy could be a dozen yards offshore and nobody the wiser.

The passing hours had brought their share of rumors. Somebody had said that the people of Saint Michaels had hung lanterns

355

in the tops of trees behind the town while fixing blankets over the windows of their houses in the hope that the British would pick out false targets should they try a night bombardment. Another story was that there had been a fight somewhere along the nearby Tred Avon River and that the British had been driven off. Still another report was that the whole British fleet had up-anchored and sailed, either north or south, toward Baltimore or the Virginia Capes, depending on who had the "exact information."

Lieutenant Dodson lay under the tree where Task had sat in grim reverie. The young commander of the Parrott's Point position had been on his feet since the detail had reached the Point, inspecting the outposts, checking on the men's weapons, going over the cannon, supervising the apportioning of the food that had been sent out from the town, talking to the men at their posts, until Task had seen him waver with weariness and had urged him to rest.

"There's nothing to be gained, sir, by wearing yourself out," he had told Dodson. "We'll all need our wits about us when the British come."

So now Dodson snored the sleep of the exhausted while Task took over the command. Beyond making sure that the pickets stayed awake and seeing to it that the men protected their ammunition against the weather, there was little to do and he found himself fighting drowsiness that crept up on him from time to time, usually when he least expected it.

He routed the latest threat of nodding and went back to the fire that struggled to survive by gnawing at wet wood. A large coffeepot sat on a flat rock beside the fire but Task had found out that its contents were barely warm and tooth-jarringly bitter. He wished again for a drink of brandy and told himself again that even if he had brought along a flask he would not dare uncork it, not this night.

One of the gunners off duty, a man Task knew slightly as Phelps, from Easton, gave up trying to sleep and left his soaked blankets to walk up to the fire, yawning and scratching his head.

356

"How long till dawn, Lieutenant?" he asked Tillman.

"A couple of hours," Task replied. Phelps nodded and leaned over to pick up the coffeepot, splashed some of the thick black stuff into a tin mug and drank a swallow. He grimaced and threw the rest of the coffee on the ground.

"Must've been brewed by a British spy," he observed mildly, "who's tryin' to poison us all."

He sat down beside Task and took a stubby clay pipe from his pocket, packed it with tobacco and reached out for a smouldering twig with which to light it. The smoke was strong and rank but Phelps seemed to relish it.

"So here we set," he said conversationally as he leaned back, puffing, "waitin' fer His Everlastingly Damned Lordship, Sir George Co'burn, to come and gobble us up. And as fer me, I been wonderin' just why I'm settin' here."

He grinned at Task around the pipestem.

"Oh, I ain't goin' to desert, Lieutenant," he went on, "I'll be here as long as the rest of you are, but just the same I can't help wonderin' about my bein' here instead of home in a nice dry bed."

"A good many of us are missing our nice dry beds," Task smiled, "and still we stay out here in the rain."

"Uh-huh," Phelps nodded. He puffed thoughtfully and then reached up to take the pipe from his mouth and point its stem at Task. "And there's the wonderment of it, Lieutenant," he said. "Take a lot of men with ordinary good sense and the only time they'll go through misery like this is when they're huntin' or soldierin'. Now in huntin', a feller expects t'git somethin' fer his trouble, a bag of geese or a good chase with his coon hounds or somethin' like that. Soldierin', all he can expect—the best he can expect—is t'git away with a whole skin."

"Well," said Task slowly, "he can say he's doing his duty, soldiering."

"Duty?" asked Phelps. "Well, maybe so. But I ain't sure I can see where my duty comes into it, exactly. Look, sir; I've got a little farm the other side of Easton. I was doing all right, gettin' along, when all of a sudden somebody tells me there's a war on and we're

357

goin' t'fight the British again because they're no-account bastards that need a whuppin'."

He puffed again at his pipe.

"Well, now maybe they do need a whuppin'," he nodded, "but not on account of anything they did to me, Isaac Phelps. They never cheated me out of nothin', they never laid hands on my ox or my ass or my wife, as the Bible says—I think. They don't know Isaac Phelps is alive and never have. So what's my argument with them, Lieutenant?"

"Your argument with them is over what they've done to us, the towns they've burned, the Americans they've killed."

"I suppose you're right," Phelps said dubiously, "but I can't help thinkin' that it was Americans, Henry Clay and that bunch, that dared them to come over here and burn our towns and kill our people in the first place. Oh, I suppose the dirty Lobsterbacks did impress some sailormen off our ships but they wasn't botherin' *me* none. No sir, they wasn't botherin' me half as much as the man who holds the mortgage on my farm, Anthony Worth at Fairoverlea. Now if somebody was to come to me and say we're goin' t'war over what Anthony Worth done, why I c'ld see some sense to settin' out here in the rain."

He glanced over at Task, his eyes narrowed.

"Not," he added hastily, "that I'm complainin' about Anthony Worth, y'understand. He's treated me fair and square. I guess it's just that you look at any man that holds your paper the wrong way, huh Lieutenant?"

"I guess so," Task said briefly.

"I wouldn't want anything I said t'git back to Anthony Worth, y'understand, Lieutenant," Phelps said earnestly. "I remember you live over his way."

"You needn't be afraid of my saying anything to Anthony Worth," Task said heavily. "No matter what you think of him, I think a hundred times worse of him."

"Well, now," Phelps said uneasily, "I don't know as he's such a bad—*hark!*"

Task Tillman had heard it and was on his feet in a bound.

358

Around him, men were flinging aside their blankets, running for their posts. Dodson came scrambling down the bank from where he had been asleep. From the outposts came the voices of pickets yelling back and forth. The cannoneers scuttled up to the fire for fresh linstocks. There was the click of shotgun hammers being cocked. All eyes strained in the direction from which had come the sudden burst of musket fire that had shattered the dripping quiet of the night.

"Upriver," Dodson said. His voice was charged with excitement, his breathing was rapid. "Sounded like it was quite a ways away, didn't it to you, Tillman?"

"Halfway to Easton, I'd say," Task nodded. "Somewhere around—"

Realization struck him in mid-sentence, cutting off his words with the knife of dread.

Somewhere around Larkspur Hill!

"Fairoverlea, I'd say," Dodson supplied. "Must be Rawlent's company is engaged and if it is, God help the men he commands, the fool!"

The rattle and pop upriver died away and there was a silence.

"Soon over," Dodson grunted after a pause. "Rawlent and his high-class friends are probably high-tailing it for safer parts now, if they didn't start running at sight of the enemy. Aye, the British will find that part of the river easy pickings if Rawlent's company is all there is to stop 'em."

He turned suddenly to Task and put a hand on his arm.

"Damn it," he said, "I'd forgotten that your place is right next to Fairoverlea, isn't it?"

Task nodded dumbly, unable to put voice to the fears that crowded in upon him. Any British landing party gone ashore at Fairoverlea could hardly be expected to content itself with the destruction of that one place; the Redcoats probably were swarming through the countryside around Fairoverlea now and their next target was almost bound to be Larkspur Hill.

And Gracellen—what of her? Anthony Worth could be counted on to do all that he could to protect his daughter, cer-

359

tainly, but this attack must have come without warning, before he could get Gracellen and Vivian away. Get Vivian away? If Worth knew his wife for the faithless clutchjohn she was—and Gracellen said he did—he'd take little trouble to save her from the British or any other danger.

Which would serve her right! She had stood there with almost a smile on her lying face and had mocked him, that last day, for thinking that he had been the only man with whom she had betrayed her husband. The worst the British could do to her would be no more than—*ah, no!* Whatever she was, he could not revile Vivian in his own mind. He hoped she would be safe if the British really were at Fairoverlea.

"I probably misjudged it," Dodson was saying lamely. "Thinking on it, the firing sounded as though it came from somewhere closer than Fairoverlea. And it was but a scatter of shots, in any case—perhaps some of Rawlent's Dragons saw ghosts in the fog and fired at nothing."

He turned again to peer into the opaque blankness that was the river.

"But if it was a British force," he went on, "that means they've sailed past us and are attackin' Easton direct, not stopping at Saint Michaels. General Benson was sure they'd hit here first, to clear their rear, before going on to Easton Town but—"

He stopped as the firing broke out upriver again. This second outburst was a general exchange, much fiercer than the first rattle that had come to the listeners at Parrott's Point. Sustained volleys crashed out, heavy though muted by the distance, and between the fusillades there was the constant hammer of musketry.

Amazement showed in Lieutenant Dodson's eyes as he turned to stare at Task.

"Rawlent's fighting, by God!" he cried. "I take back all I said about him if he's making a fight of it, and he must be! Who would have thought he had it in him? Listen to it, man! It must be a pitched battle and hooray, I say, for the Dragon Footguards!"

Task listened with growing disbelief. Whatever was taking place upriver certainly was no shoot-and-run affair. The Dragons, then, were confounding all expectations about them; from the

360

sound of the action they were making a stand; the fighting seemed to be in one spot which must mean that Rawlent and his claret-tunicked men were holding.

"And I," he told Dodson, "gladly eat all the words I said against Charles Rawlent."

"Which goes to prove," Lieutenant Dodson began, "that—"

"*Halt!*" squalled an outpost. "*Halt, I say!*"

Both officers whirled and stared.

There they were, emerging from the fog that had cloaked their approach, up to the very ramparts of the Parrott's Point position. There were the British, led by a young, high-ranking officer, coming at them, silently, grimly.

Task was the first of the two officers to shake off the paralysis that gripped them both. His hand went to his pistol, he wrenched it from his belt and levelled it at the British officer. His hand jarred under the explosion and smoke mushroomed. Through the haze he saw the officer drop his sword, clutch his belly and turn slowly, his knees sagging, before he sprawled.

"British!" Dodson was screaming. "Fire! Fire!"

The man named Phelps, the farmer who had told Task Tillman that he wondered why he was sitting in the rain that night, was the one who swiveled one of the little nine-pounders around until its muzzle stared into the faces of the Britishers. It was Task who somehow had grabbed a glowing linstock from somebody and touched it to the cannon's touch-hole.

Swiftly, expertly, Phelps worked while the British ran at him. He may not have known exactly why he was there but he acted as though this, helping loose thunderous death at the British who were almost upon Task Tillman and him, was the most natural thing in the world for him to do.

He did not wince, although Task did, as the charge of grape, delivered at murderous range, slashed across the foremost Britishers. He did not blanch, though Tillman did, when he saw the body of one young soldier, a youngster with an open mouth that meant he must be shouting, split into two sections, head, shoulders and trunk going one way and the wildly-kicking legs whirling off in the opposite direction.

361

13

WHEN Anthony Worth shut the door on Admiral Sir Peter Porter's departure, he went at once to the second floor of Fairoverlea and rapped on the door of Gracellen's room.

"It's me," he called softly, when she answered. "I've got to speak with you, my dear. At once."

She was in her nightdress over which she had thrown a wrap of some light blue stuff that did nothing to hide the fine lines of her body.

Aye, he thought, she is a beautiful woman and but yesterday she was a child I held in my arms. She must not be touched by any of this night's work and she won't be; my plans are too carefully fixed for that. They might think Anthony Worth is an old man, past his prime, a man who can be cozened by a lying bitch of a wife, but they'll find out different. Anthony Worth's still clever enough to shake the whole world apart, if he must, to get what he wants without leaving the littlest trace for the people who laugh at him to put a finger on.

"I don't want to alarm you, my dear," he smiled, "but I think you'd best dress and pack whatever you'll need to leave here at once."

Her eyes widened for a moment and then she answered his smile. She stood aside to let her father enter the room and closed the door behind him, shutting out the noise of the Dragon Footguards below.

"The British are on their way here, then?" she asked quietly.

He shrugged. "There are rumors and reports," he said, "and nothing proved. But 'tis likely they'll be here soon, if not tonight, then maybe tomorrow. I'd feel easier if I knew you were ready to go the moment we know for sure they're on their way."

She gestured toward the sounds of revelry.

"They don't sound as though the British were anywhere near," she pointed out. He hunched his shoulders again, still smiling.

"Perhaps I'm an over-anxious old man," he explained. "The Dragons have all their outposts set and they've reported nothing. But I've got the uneasy feeling in my bones that we might have a visit from our red-coated friends ere long and that's why I ask you to get ready. I'm having a carriage harnessed for you and Vivian; it'll be waiting in the yard. At the first sign of any trouble, I want you to go directly there. You'll both be driven to your sister's in Chestertown; it should be safe enough there."

She nodded, her eyes pinned on him.

"Vivian's getting ready to go now," he continued, "and I must not delay you further. For all we know, you haven't much time."

"Where's Charles?" she asked slowly.

"Inspecting his outposts, the last I knew," he told her. "I must say, Gracellen, he has surprised me by the workmanlike way he's handled his troops tonight."

"From the noise," Gracellen said wryly, "I thought different. It sounded like a rout from here."

"A lot of noise," Anthony explained, "but the men are in good shape, I think. They're all on edge and inclined to hide their nervousness with loud talk and song. And now, you'd best get ready. Remember, at the first sign of danger or when I tell you to, go straight to the carriage. Don't tarry for anything."

"And Vivian will meet me there?"

He nodded as he turned toward the door. He paused with a hand on the knob and smiled back at Gracellen.

"And if aught should go amiss tonight," he said, almost apologetically, "remember that I've always loved you more than life itself."

"Oh, Father!" she cried as she went to him. "I want to know—I mean—oh, do be careful! Stay out of harm's way, for my sake!"

He held her close for an instant and then dropped his arms.

"I am a fool, perhaps," he said, "for worrying you needlessly. Chances are the British will not stir in this fog. But better to be prepared, eh? And I will take care of myself and Charles, too, if I can."

"Oh yes, Charles," Gracellen said. "Tell him—give him my love and tell him to be careful. Perhaps I can see him before—"

"No, my dear," he cut in. "Remember, he'll have a thousand things to do if the British attack—you'd but add to his problems. He bids you go straight to the carriage, as I told you. And he sends you his deepest love and all his prayers. Those were his words."

She started to speak, then held up, frowning slightly. Anthony knew he had made some slip in quoting Charles Rawlent; that vainglorious fop would never say a thing like that.

"Or very near what he said, in any case," he added. "Now goodbye, Gracellen, if this is goodbye. Goodnight, if all these precautions are foolish ones."

He kissed her on the forehead and left the room. He returned to the office in time to answer a knock at the passageway door and drew the bolt to admit Will Roan.

"The Redcoats are on their way to the place," the scar-faced man said. "They should be there in twenty minutes."

Anthony nodded briefly. "You know what's to be done with Rawlent," he said. "Plant him down by the lane and make it seem he died a hero's death, the craven ninny. Also, I'd have ye pay strict attention to a man named Harrison. Ye know him?"

"Aye," Roan growled.

"If the British don't get him," Anthony said in a matter-of-fact voice, "he must be disposed of by one of you. He's not been drinking and he has a curiosity I don't like. Also, the British admiral spoke of one of the Dragons meeting him in the courtyard and being dealt with by Titus. He must not be able to tell anyone what he saw."

"He's been cared for. A knife can make a hole like a bayonet when it's twisted properly."

"Good," Anthony nodded, then hesitated. "There's one more thing, Roan, and this I trust to your hands alone. I had planned to have the British care for this work but that admiral—he is a finicky young gentleman not fitted for the task at all."

"What's to be done, sir?"

"It's a delicate matter, my good Will," Anthony said. "As touchy a bit of business as I've ever asked you to care for. It involves my wife."

If Roan was surprised he did not show it.

"Aye," he said tonelessly.

"She has—er—displeased me. She has wronged me in such a way that the punishment must be strict. You understand?"

The bulky Roan nodded.

"This punishment must be complete and still it must be carried out so that no one, least of all my daughter, can ever think other than that the British were to blame, as they would have been if my first plan could have been carried out."

"Ye want her dead?" Roan asked bluntly. Anthony shook his head.

"Not killed and planted with the rest," he explained. "Even Co'burn wouldn't shoot down a beautiful woman and a countrywoman of his, at that. No, my good Will, I want her carried off by the dastardly British—carried off or run away with the Redcoats. I want her disappeared, at any rate."

Roan's forehead was wrinkled in a doubtful frown.

"Carrying the lady anyplace would be a risky thing," he said slowly. "She'd have but to cry out and all this night's doings would be spoilt."

"She could be carried as far as the swamp," Anthony Worth said lightly, "and I doubt her cries would attract too much attention."

Realization dawned in Roan's brutish face. He nodded slowly.

"Ah," he said, "now I see. It'll be easily done. Though it seems a pity—" He broke off. Anthony's eyes hardened as he stared at Roan.

"What seems a pity?" he asked sharply. "A pity that a cheating whore gets what she deserves? God's sake, I had planned worse for her and still I couldn't come close to what's coming to her. I had planned to have her taken aboard a British warship and fed to the crew, passed from man to man till she had her fill, for once! Nay, there's no pity due her. She's fortunate that admiral came here tonight and so dealt her a quick end."

Roan nodded silently, his little eyes averted from Anthony's hot glare.

"So I'll deliver her to you here when the Dragons have left and you'll deal with her as you know how to so well," Anthony went on. "When you lead the Dragons to the place their reception waits, return here to get her. Now, have the carriage harnessed."

Roan touched his forehead and left. Anthony returned to the howling throng that jammed the west wing parlor. The Dragons were in full cry now; even the men who had been comparatively sober when Anthony had left the room were beginning to reel and stagger. The songs had lost all semblance of tune, the oaths were more obscene, the laughter was more jarringly senseless, the litter of castoff uniforms and equipment was more disorderly. Anthony had told Gracellen that Charles Rawlent's company was in good shape; he chuckled inwardly now at the thought that the Dragon Footguards were in the best possible shape for his purposes.

He was nursing a weak mixture of brandy and water when the first shots cracked out in a ragged volley from the place where Sir Peter Porter had been directed to post his men.

The effect was as Anthony Worth had expected. First, there was the deathly hush of the drunken men in the parlor, then a storm of shouts and curses, a confused rush for jackets, belts, shakos, guns. Men shoved and elbowed, staggered and fell, as they scrambled about in a melee of wild disorder.

"Where's m'boots, God damn it? Where's m'boots?"

366

"That's my coat, you fool!"

"Stop pushin' or I'll deal you one, by God!"

"Where's Rawlent? Anybody seen Rawlent?"

"Drunk, he is! Fine captain, *this* troop has!"

They spilled out of Fairoverlea, disheveled, carrying carbines with no ammunition, cartouches with no weapons. They milled about in the fog, slipping and sliding in the mud, as aimless as a panicked herd of sheep, until Anthony Worth's voice boomed:

"The British are on the road leading up from Peartree Creek, lads! Here's my man, just come from there! They're down by the creek, men!"

Beside Worth stood Roan, pointing.

"A small party," Roan yelled. "Not more'n ten or a dozen, I'd say!"

"Then let's at them!" a Dragon howled. "Let's carve ourselves a slab of British beef!"

"Where's Captain Rawlent?" somebody cried.

"He's down there now," Roan bellowed. "Him and a couple of others are fightin' the Redcoats!"

"Let's get to him, men!" a reeling lieutenant shouted. "What're we standin' here like this for, for God's sake?"

They were off in a shouting, scrabbling rush, flushed with their liquor and the confidence that they were five to one at least over this little party of Britishers. They left behind only those who lay in a drunken stupor and these were the lucky ones, though not a man of them would ever admit that he had not been with the others when they boiled down the lane into the death trap that had been so carefully set for them.

Anthony watched them go, then half ran through the house to the courtyard in the rear where the carriage waited, a groom at the head of the two horses that jerked and fidgeted, made balky by the shooting. The man on the box leaned back on the reins, rolled his eyes at Anthony as he ran up.

"Miss Gracellen?" Worth cried. "Has she come yet?"

"Here, Father," Gracellen answered from the doorway. She

strode toward the carriage, her cape billowing behind her, carrying a small portmanteau. "Where's Vivian?"

"I can't find her!" Anthony cried wildly. "I bade her stay in her room but she's gone! Perhaps she had her horse saddled and rode off at the first shot. I'll check. You go on, Gracellen!"

"I'll not leave without Vivian!"

"You will!" he told her. He seized her arm and pulled her toward the carriage. "I tell you, you will! I'll find Vivian if she's still here. She was very scared—she may have bolted in spite of my orders. If she's about, I'll find her and send her after you with Abraham. But you go now!"

"Father, I—"

He lifted his daughter and flung her into the carriage.

"No time to argue!" he panted. To the driver he shouted; "Get going and don't stop for anything till you get past Tunis Mills! Whatever Miss Gracellen says, don't stop or turn back or ye'll have Titus to deal with! Now, go!"

The driver touched the restless horses with a flick of his whip. The two animals lurched forward with a clatter of hooves on the courtyard's paving. The groom flung himself aside in time to escape being run down as the carriage whipped past him, out of the courtyard and down the curving drive that led out of Fairoverlea.

Anthony Worth turned back to the house, the elation of complete success swelling within him. From the direction of Peartree Creek came a blast of fire that meant that the Dragons had tripped their trap; they had plunged into the hollow that would expose them to the murderous cross-fire of the British that lined its rim.

"And all be heroes," Anthony grinned as he paced through the lower hallway of Fairoverlea, "with their wives and sweethearts and mammas fair burstin' with pride as they weep over the graves."

He took the steps leading to the east wing's second floor two at a time—and what younger man could do that so nimbly?—and went down the hallway to the door of his wife's bedroom. He pushed it open unceremoniously and looked across at the bed.

Vivian lay there, watching him. Her eyes shone in the light of the small whaleoil lamp on her dresser, her hands bunched the sheet at her bosom. She met her husband's stare from the threshold and she knew that all the weeks and months of waiting were ended, at last.

Her fear that had betrayed her into shameful panic on two occasions, with Jett and with Gracellen, would not overwhelm her a third time. She knew that death was walking into her room but whatever form death took, whatever agony Anthony Worth had prepared for her, could not be worse than what she had already suffered. Nor could it be worse than she deserved for having submitted to her body's hunger—for that was what it had been and all it had been.

That was all it had been! She would not seek excuses for herself now and call it love. Love was some dainty, ephemeral thing she was too coarse to realize. Love was not for sluts who cast themselves at a man, bare-breasted and knees atremble, as she had cast herself at Task Tillman.

But oh, my sweet, you are so dear to me in these last minutes!

Anthony Worth walked slowly up to the side of the bed. Through the windows came the spiteful bark of gunfire. He did not heed it, she noted, and that meant he must have arranged it, somehow, for purposes of his own. She had lain there, listening to the uproar on the lower floor, hearing the comings and goings, the murmured voices, in the courtyard, the traffic along the passageway to Anthony's office, and she had known that the night was brewing some crisis at Fairoverlea. Now it was here and she was part of it.

Anthony walked slowly to the side of the bed and looked down at his wife, his wide mouth crooked, his eyes holding a lambent glimmer.

"And so, my dear," he said smoothly, "it's time you were up and on your way."

"To where?" Vivian asked bravely. He snorted a laugh.

"To where?" he mocked. "How would I know, any more than I knew where you ran those nights I was not here to watch you? To Larkspur Hill, mayhap, to let your lover wallow in you as be-

369

fore, though I doubt it. Let's say, dear Vivian, you're on your way to Hell."

His face twitched and his voice rasped viciously.

"Get up, bitch!"

She looked at him and saw that he was suffering beneath his deadly rage. Anthony Worth, the man some called *The King*, was at the height of a triumph he had engineered; he was flushed with a success that he had brought about; he was on the verge of realizing a revenge that was long past due him. He was an old, old man, knowing now that what should have been rich meat and heady wine was proving only ashes and vinegar, and she pitied him.

She threw back the sheet and slipped out of bed, stood up and confronted him. The points of her breasts thrust against the fine cambric of her nightdress as she firmed her shoulders. To Anthony, she was more beautiful at this moment, the hour of her ruin, than she ever had been. Her great eyes were luminous, her mouth was a poignant flower, damp-petaled as she moistened her lips with a flick of her tongue. Beneath the sheer cloth her slender body showed all the warm curves that had enticed him when first he had scanned them, half-hidden beneath the ballgown she had worn at the London reception.

He gazed at her, the old fires flickering dully at the sight of this woman he had bought and had thought he possessed but never had beyond the mere entrapment of the flesh. She had never told him but he knew now that Task Tillman had been given what he, Anthony Worth, had never had. His eyes were sick with longing for what that must have been and he roughened his voice to a low growl.

"Ye'll not be needin' clothes where you're goin'," he said. " 'Tis meet I cast you naked out of this house."

His big hand grasped the neckline of the gown and ripped downward; there was the faint scream of outraged cloth and she stood there, unshrinking, in her beauty. And still she would not cringe or cry out. She had expected it to be a struggle to steel herself against her fear but now she found a strength she had not dared believe she owned.

The hand that had violated her bedgown reached for her hair, twisted its thick fingers in its luxuriousness and pulled her forward as he turned and stalked toward the door. She stumbled, nearly fell, and lurched out into the hall with her husband. The pain of her scalp brought tears to her eyes but they were the only tears Vivian Dangerfield Worth shed that night.

Halfway down the stairs to the lower hall she lost her footing and went to her knees. He hauled her upright with a curse and she hurtled through the disordered, littered rooms to Anthony's office. He flung her to the floor there and she huddled in a corner, fighting to keep her consciousness against this horror. She heard a door flung open, her husband's bellow; then there were heavy footsteps coming across the room toward her and she raised her eyes to meet the evil glare of Will Roan.

Desperately, she tried to cover her nakedness with her hands, then gave up the attempt as Anthony dragged her to her feet again. She stood there with bowed head and her lips moved in the fragments of a prayer she called back from her childhood—as though He would listen to one who had sinned as joyously as she!

"Take her!" Anthony Worth commanded. "Get her out of sight! Get her away before somebody comes!"

Roan licked his lips, his eyes glowing as they played over Vivian.

"Sir," he said huskily. "Sir—"

"You have your orders! Get 'em done! Take her away!"

Roan stepped forward and clutched Vivian's wrist, whirled her in front of him. His other paw clamped itself over her mouth and she felt herself lifted, flung over a shoulder and borne toward the passageway door. She did not struggle for she knew that all her struggling would be futile. Her doom was upon her in its terrible finality and she could but endure until death—God send it soon—made no more need of hopeless courage.

There was the rush of damp night air bathing her skin and the darkness of the court as Roan bore her swiftly across the yard, past

371

the stables and onto a narrow path. The wet leaves stroked her, not ungently, as she was carried into the blackness.

Behind her, Anthony crashed shut the passageway door and leaned against it, breathing heavily. His head swam, there was a dull ache in the pit of his stomach, his whole body was trembling with a weakness he could not fend off.

Staring at the floor, he croaked triumphantly:

"So she learns what happens to all who'd betray Anthony Worth!"

14

THE BANG of Task's pistol and the boom of the cannon at Parrott's Point had barely died away before all the men of Lieutenant Dodson's command were at their posts, their shotguns and muskets thumping and yapping, streaking the foggy pre-dawn with stabbing flames.

The cannon blast, delivered at point-blank range, had shredded the first British attack. In front of the low parapet of the Parrott's Point position lay the crumpled figures of eight Redcoats, ripped by grapeshot, and the body of the officer Task Tillman had shot. Beyond them were the Britishers who dropped under the buckshot and pistol balls that rained down on them as the Americans recovered from their surprise and went into action.

Task, crouching on one knee, fired his pistol again at a vague figure in the mist, saw his target lurch as though hit and stagger back into the concealment of the fog. His fingers shook devilishly as he reloaded; he cursed himself for a quaking girl as he missed the pistol barrel with the ball and reached down to pluck it out of the sand.

Beside him, Lieutenant Dodson was yelling commands to his little force.

" 'Ware right flank! Watch 'em through that marsh grass there! Get that cannon to bear, gunners! Again with the grape!"

The nine-pounders thudded, one-two, and the grapeshot whined out again into the fog, searching for targets in the mist that hid all but the shadowy, furtive outline of the enemy.

The British fell back, regrouped, flung themselves at the Parrott's Point bulwark. The Redcoats had lost their commanding officer to Task's pistol ball; they answered now to the commands of a subordinate who may have been unnerved by that disastrous charge of grape that had greeted their stumbling upon the American position. In any case, the British hardly acted like seasoned troops; they came at the Americans in a way that offered Tillman and the others the best possible targets.

Again, the militia's fire swept out in a wave that riddled the British ranks; again the Redcoats drew off without firing a shot. It was only then that the officer in charge of the landing party collected his wits enough to order a volley flung at the American position. The muskets and carbines crackled, the leaden wasps buzzed and stung along the American line.

Lieutenant Dodson's men wavered at the first British reply. The old curse of militiamen, unreasoning terror under fire, struck at the farmers, the fishermen, the coopers and millwrights who made up the little company. A man threw down his shotgun and turned, crouching, to run. Task Tillman was on him with a bound.

He did not spend time arguing; he lashed out with his fist and sent the panic-stricken man sprawling in the sand.

"Damn it!" he shouted. "We've got this fight won if you don't turn cowards now!"

"Pour into 'em, boys!" Dodson screeched. "Another minute and they'll be taking to their heels!"

The dangerous moment passed. The militiamen turned back toward the enemy, the familiar thump of their shotgun butts jarring their shoulders satisfyingly. One of the nine-pounders boomed again. When the next British volley whistled at them from the fog not a militiaman did more than duck, pressing himself flat, before he brought his piece back up into firing position and blazed away.

"A charge," Dodson yelled at Task, "and we'd sweep 'em off the beach!"

Task shook his head.

"We'd run onto their bayonets," he said. "Let 'em come to us."

Out on the river the fog was brightened by bursts of orange flame and to Task's ears came the hollow *crrrumppp* of a ship's big guns. The British fleet was opening fire on the town of Saint Michaels, back of Parrott's Point. Faintly, he heard the whurffle of the balls sailing into the village; then the ship, or ships, delivered another broadside.

"We've got to keep that boom anchored here!" Dodson cried. "So long as those vessels have to stay outside the boom they've got to guess their targets in the fog."

If Dodson knew the boom must be maintained, the battered British landing party knew they must dislodge the Parrott's Point defenders and cut the boom. Again, and the effort could be almost called suicidal, they smashed at Task Tillman and the others.

This time they nearly gained the trench. Task fired his pistol at a Britisher who loomed up in front of him, then reversed the weapon in his hand and clubbed with its butt. The Britisher flung up an arm to parry the blow and fired his carbine with the other hand. There was the searing breath of the explosion, bright white and black specks blinded Task, and he flailed out with the pistol butt again. He missed and pitched headlong, carried off his feet by his swing. Directly over him a shotgun whoomed. A man yelled in a shrill, ear-piercing squall.

Task scrambled to his feet, blinking away the dazzle in his eyes. He remembered his sword, wrenched it from its scabbard and looked for an enemy to take its slash. The parapet was free; the Redcoats had been beaten back again.

The Americans reloaded, crouched, waited. Dodson and Task walked up and down behind their men, muttering words of encouragement, praise and caution. In both men's mind there was one grim thought uppermost; if the British ships out on the river turned their guns on the little fort the position would be hopeless.

No man could be expected to stand under the fire of the twenty-four-pound cannon hammering on the decks of the warships.

But still the fog-hidden vessels pumped their missiles at the town, still the British landing party held back from another assault on Parrott's Point. The minutes ticked past, the Americans shifted uneasily in their positions, looked at one another with their unspoken questions: Why the lull? What are the Lobsterbacks planning now? Where will they strike from next and when?

Then, amazingly, the British ships broke off the action. The flash and thud of the cannon outside the boom stopped; dripping silence descended over the whole area. The Americans at Parrot's Point heard the rattle and creak of ships' gear, the sound of orders ringing from quarterdeck to waist to forepeak, the grind of windlasses and the clank of anchor chains, the twitter of bos'n pipes.

"By God," Dodson half whispered, "I do believe they're giving up the attack!"

"You mean," Task Tillman asked dazedly, "you mean—"

"I mean we've won, man! I mean we've beat the British!"

And, as dawn brought a wind that swept the fog away, as a sun struggled to break through the morning's overcast, Dodson's exultant shout was proven true. The roofs and spires of Saint Michaels glistened in the weak sunlight; no smoke wreathed a scene of desolation such as Havre de Grace and Georgetown and Queen's Town and Hampden. A place had come under Admiral Sir George Cockburn's fire and it had survived. Saint Michaels was saved and by her survival had saved Easton. The Eastern Shore was not yet Cockburn's. Maryland had reason for fresh hope and with Maryland, Baltimore, fired with new courage, new resolve, by the news from Saint Michael's, the war was not yet lost to America.

15

ADMIRAL SIR GEORGE COCKBURN was in a black rage. He stumped up and down his cabin aboard his flagship, *Sceptre*, while his fleet officers stood at uneasy attention, waiting for his wrath to strike.

"By God," Cockburn raged, "this mess stinks! To think that you, with all your men and fire power, let a handful of Yankees make fools of the lot of you!"

The admiral's face was purple, the veins bulged on his forehead, his mouth was wrenched in a snarl that had been there since the moment he had broken off the attack on Saint Michaels.

"The whole damned town," he said now, his words accented by the thud of his fist into the open palm of his other hand, "the whole damned town wasn't worth that boy's life, I tell you!"

Sir Peter Porter shifted from one foot to the other, repressing a grimace of resentment. Old Co'burn, he told himself, could send a hundred other men to certain death without a quiver and yet, when his favorite nephew, that darling Captain Clement Vickers, had run into a pistol ball, the admiral had been so shaken that he had dropped his whole plan of attack on two important towns and had sailed back to Kent Island to grieve and blame his officers for what he had done himself.

"Arnold!" grated Cockburn, whirling, "tell me what happened

once more! I cannot believe—I cannot think my nephew would make a mistake so raw."

A young lieutenant, pale with the knowledge that his career probably had been wrecked by the stroke of ill luck that had placed him second in command to Captain Clement Vickers in a landing party, began a recitation he had repeated several times before.

"Captain Vickers," he said, "directed the landing at a place close to Parrott's Point. He led the men off in the fog. I was in command of the second detail that stayed in reserve, by the boats. We heard a shot and then a cannon. Then there was a sharp burst of fire. Some of Captain Vickers' men ran back to me and reported that because of the fog the captain had stumbled directly upon the Yankees before he knew he was so close to them. The pistol shot, the first shot fired, cut down the captain, sir."

"Impossible!" Cockburn snarled. "My nephew couldn't have made that kind of mistake! There's been treachery somewhere!"

The young lieutenant, Arnold, opened his mouth to speak and then closed it again. Sir Peter Porter risked a glance of sympathy for the youngster; everybody in the fleet knew that Vickers had been the kind of fool who would do exactly some such thing as bumbling into an enemy position, but there was no saying that now.

"Go on, go on!" Cockburn barked. "Or are you prettying up your fanciful tale?"

"Sir, I took command at once," Arnold said tonelessly. "We assaulted the American position three times and three times were repulsed with heavy losses. I had understood the position was weakly garrisoned; I found it was much stronger than we could hope to take with our force. I therefore broke off the action and returned to the vessels and reported to you. I thought that with fire from the ships, the Yankees would be forced—"

"Aye, you thought, you thought!" Cockburn raged. "You thought to save your own skin, that's what you thought! You were assigned to take that position and ye didn't. The boom kept us

378

off from any effective range while ye diddled away our chances for success!"

He turned away from Lieutenant Arnold with a snort of malignant disgust.

"Porter!" he grated.

Sir Peter took a step forward, his face set, his chin outthrust. Damme, he said silently, if Old Co'burn's going to lay the blame on me for what he did on his own; I don't care if he ships me back to England under a cloud.

"Sir," he said to Cockburn.

"Where was your party from *Menelaus* while all this was goin' on? Attendin' a ball or mayhap catchin' up on y'r sleep?"

"Sir," Porter retorted, "I commanded the party myself. We went to that place, Fairoverlea, by your order and there dispatched almost a full company of American militia—though I can't say I liked the way the thing was done."

"What you like means nothin'," Cockburn sneered.

"Aye, sir," Porter said with what he hoped was hidden contempt. "When that was finished I took the force along the road laid out in your plan, Admiral, and halted at the place marked on the chart. My orders were to wait there till Saint Michaels was taken, then move on Easton Town as the ships—"

"I know the orders!" Cockburn bellowed. "By God, I planned them, didn't I?"

"Aye, sir," Porter's clipped voice replied. "When I saw the ships retire from Saint Michaels I withdrew my force to the landing barges on Peartree Creek and returned to my ship."

"Without a single pass at Easton," Cockburn growled.

"Without a single pass," Porter nodded. "With the fleet moving out of the Miles River, without any support and surrounded by Yankee militia, it would have been senseless to attempt any strike at Easton. We were lucky to get away as we did, I'd say."

Cockburn's eyes narrowed as he stared at the younger admiral.

"You'd say, eh?" he asked with an unpleasant twist of his lips. "Sometimes I think you say too much, m'lad."

Porter kept his eyes fixed on his superior. *Damn you and your*

379

rotten schemes that trap a company of besotted fools, he thought. Damn you and your Mister Worths.

"So this is the end of all the planning," Cockburn was muttering. "My nephew dead and no town taken. He was worth more than the whole war, I say—worth more than every one of these stinkin' United States."

He looked down at the deck, then up again, his face contorted.

"By God," he cried, "they'll pay for this! They think I've been hard, eh? Let me get another town in my fist and I'll show 'em what a hard man's like."

"We go back to Saint Michaels and Easton, sir?" Porter asked boldly.

For the first time since he had known him, Sir Peter saw Cockburn's eyes shift, saw indecision in the blunt-snouted face.

"Devil take that river," Cockburn grumbled. "We'll find another place to visit."

16

Tom Womble and Marsden walked through the thinning mists toward Fairoverlea as the first pale rays of the sun struck a feeble light on the upper windows of the great mansion that looked out over the Miles River. The tall, lanky Marsden drooped with weariness; Womble trotted along as blithely as though he had not spent the night in work so foul that it would bring nightmares even to his soulless sleep.

"This," he chuckled, "has been a night and no mistake. *The King* sure outdid himself in this. How many o' them pretty-boy sojers you figger are layin' around, Marsden?"

"Enough," the muffled scarecrow beside him croaked. "Enough to feed a flock o' buzzards for a fortnight. There'll be a deal of weepin' and wailin' when the news gets back to Easton Town, if it ain't already."

"Sure, sure," Womble burbled. "A couple of them got away, certainly, but most of 'em won't do no more arse-switchin' drill on this earth, noways."

"Includin' Rawlent," Marsden nodded, his voice hollow. "Of all of 'em it give me the most satisfaction to lay him out all pretty, with his tin sword in his hand and a hole in his head. The bastard always looked at me like I was dirt—well, now we'll see who feeds the worms first."

"Aye," Womble said. "Y'know, I wonder why *The King* put on this show, Marsden. What does he stand to gain by all o' this?"

Marsden shrugged unconcernedly.

"Plenty, you may be sure," he said. He pulled the muffler higher about his skull's face. "F'r one thing, the British won't burn Fairoverlea 'cause they're in debt to him f'r handin' over the Dragon Footguards. 'Course I don't think they would anyway, 'cause of the way *The King's* been supplyin' 'em, but if they come here and burned every other place, people would wonder, wouldn't they? Now *The King* has proved to everybody he was no friend of the Lobsterbacks—it looks like they tried to grab Fairoverlea first of anything, don't it?"

"And was beaten off by the Dragon Footguards," Womble snickered, "at a turrible cost."

"The way them that escaped will tell it," Marsden intoned, "'twill be just that."

"Aye, but it seems an almighty expensive way to prove he's no traitor, just the same," Womble said thoughtfully.

"What expense to him?" Marsden gravelled. "He's rid himself of a cock-o'-thumb son-in-law he didn't want, he's proved himself a ravin' patriot, he'll end up a hero that fought with the sojers, and he's not lost more than a night's sleep."

"And maybe not that," Womble grinned. "I'd not put it past *The King* to have stretched out for a nap at the height of things. Aye, he could sleep whilst we three did all the work."

"We two," Marsden corrected. "Will Roan disappeared early in the doin's, seems like."

Womble frowned, pursed his rosebud mouth and nodded.

"That he did," he agreed, "and that's not like Will. You suppose somethin' went wrong and he took a ball in the guts, too?" He laughed happily. "Now there's a thought! 'Twould be funny if Will Roan was mistook for a Dragon Footguard and—"

He stopped at Marsden's hand on his arm. The tall, skinny man nodded toward the Great House and at the knot of horses in the courtyard.

"That'll be folks from Easton," he croaked, "and *The King* bade us to stay out o' sight till he explained everything. Best slip down this way, Tom, and cut over behind the sheds to that little place in the swamp."

"Damn all," Womble said peevishly. "I'd set me heart on a warm, dry bed with a wench and now a pallet on the floor's the best I'll get."

He followed the swathed skeleton, Marsden, around a corner, still grumbling. The two men clung close to the far side of the sheds that hid them from the Great House and plunged into a thicket through which ran the barest trace of a path that wandered toward the swamp beyond Peartree Creek.

They had reached the morass with its shoulder-high cattails, its hungry quicksand, its black muck and its grisly secrets, when both men stopped in their tracks. Womble turned round eyes on his companion.

"Y'hear that?" he breathed.

Marsden nodded, his murky eyes fixed on the thick growth of evergreens ahead that marked the place where the shack was hidden.

"Aye," he said slowly, "I heard it, right enough."

"It sounded like a woman."

"Perhaps," Marsden offered, " 'twas a rabbit, caught by a hawk."

" 'Twas a woman, I say," Womble argued. "And what would a woman—"

He broke off and his jaw dropped, his eyes glinted.

"Roan!" he burst out. "That bastard's been gone since the shootin' started. He's in the cabin and he's got a woman with him! Whilst we wore our legs out doin' what had to be done, he's been dallyin' with a wench down here! Now, by God—"

Marsden frowned, shaking his head.

"Roan won't touch a black wench," he said. "You know that. Then where's he goin' t'get a white woman to come into this swamp on such a night as last? Unless—" He pulled at his lower lip, then shook his head again. "But that's not possible," he murmured.

"Possible or not," Womble giggled, "let's tiptoe up and see what

383

rabbit Roan's caught, if you say 'twas a rabbit we heard. He'll not have this all to himself, whatever it is!"

The two men advanced noiselessly on the sagging, weather-beaten shelter that sat among the pines on the small firm-grounded island in the very center of the marsh. Womble and Marsden moved from grass hummock to grass hummock, silently yet carefully, knowing that a misstep meant plunging into the bottomless sand.

Womble was the first to reach the island and he crept up to the shack's one unshuttered window as Marsden stilted his way ashore gingerly. The merry little fat man raised himself inch by inch and peeped inside. Marsden saw him start, grow rigid and then turn away from the window, his round face white.

"Jesus!" Womble squealed. His dimpled hands flapped as he gestured toward the window. "Look there, Marsden, look there!"

From inside the shack came a roared curse and the thick body of Will Roan filled the doorway, his scar livid, his pocked face twisted. His knife glittered as he rounded the corner of the cabin and made for Womble.

"Spyin' on me, are ye?" he thundered. "I'll learn ye, ye snivellin' sneak!"

Marsden's rusty voice stopped the big man before the knife could swoop.

"Hold, Will!" the scarecrow creaked. Roan whirled and glowered, his shoulders hunched, his cropped head thrust forward on the bull neck. Womble cowered behind the trunk of the cedar he had scrambled around, an inch ahead of the bright knife. His face was drained of its perpetual flush; both his danger and the shock of what he had glimpsed inside the shack made him pallid.

"Hold," Marsden said again. "What's this, ye'd knife a friend, Will Roan? After tonight, we'd best stick closer together than ever before unless we all want a rope around our gullet."

Slowly, Roan lowered the long blade, his tiny reddened eyes fixed on Marsden as the thin man advanced up the slope of the island bank.

"Get back to where ye belong," Roan growled. "Leave this t'me."

"Aye," Marsden nodded, "but we can't go back right now. Fairoverlea's crawlin' with people come to find out what's happened and *The King* bade us make ourselves scarce."

"I care not what *The King* bade you," Roan said bluntly, "this place is mine. I'll not have ye pokin' in here."

"Look inside," Womble quavered from behind his tree. "God's sake, Marsden, he's got—*he's got The King's wife there!*"

Roan turned toward the fat man with a rasping curse and Womble squeaked as he danced over to behind another tree. The big scar-faced man took a couple of steps toward Womble, then turned back quickly as Marsden edged toward the cabin's door.

"Stay away from there," he warned. "Put one foot inside and I'll slice y'r guts, Marsden."

The skinny, cloaked Marsden fingered his long chin thoughtfully.

"The King's wife, eh?" he asked in his raven's voice. "I've long eyed that chunk o' meat and wanted some. I'll not ask how ye came by it, Will, but ye'd not begrudge me a few slices, would ye—when you're done with it, o' course."

"Ye'll get none of it!" Will Roan grunted. "Now get ye gone from here, the two of you!"

Marsden spread his long, knob-knuckled hands in a deprecatory gesture.

"Now Will," he mourned, "that's not friendly! Surely there's enough for three in that fine package and we'd not complain if it was a bit used afore we got to it."

"*I said no!*"

Marsden's long face grew bleaker. He shook his head sadly.

"You disappoint me, dear Will," he said. "If 'twere me, why, I'd say—"

"It ain't you, so get out!"

Marsden sighed and turned to go. Over his shoulder he cast his last word.

"Mayhap I'll ask *The King* about this," he said. "I'll ask him why he throws his sweetmeat to you and not to all three of us. I'll ask him what you've done that gets you all the reward and poor Womble and I get nothin'. I'll ask him —"

His foot slipped on the rain-slicked ground as he tried to dodge. He twisted with a last desperate effort, knowing that he, Marsden the close-mouthed, had let the thought of Vivian Worth's lush loveliness wag his tongue past the point where Will Roan could let him live.

He fumbled in the pocket of his flapping coat for his pistol but the gesture was hopeless from the start. His bony fingers had barely closed over the butt of the weapon before the knife struck him, driving upward under the ribs. He felt the blow, the searing fire, and knew that he was dead even as the rank green grass rushed up to meet him.

It was cold lying there on the ground and he tried to move away from the icy confines of his helplessness. He pushed himself to his elbows and the cold grew more bitter. He tried to curse Will Roan with his last breath but the rush in his throat—*warm, at last he was warm*—choked him and he died silently.

Roan straightened and glared about him, searching for Tom Womble. He saw the cattails waving violently, halfway toward the shore opposite Fairoverlea and his boots gritted in the sand as he started to give chase. He stopped at the edge of the island.

Womble was gone and there was no hope of catching him; the fat little devil could outrun a deer when he was frightened. Slowly, Roan turned back to the shack, stepping over Marsden's body on his way to the doorway. Time enough to get rid of that body later, time enough to fix some story for *The King*. Now, inside the cabin, there was a soft and fragrant thing to be feasted upon, times without end, before it, too, went into the swamp.

He leaned down over Vivian, looked into her blank eyes. He touched her face with gentle, calloused fingers. He straightened slowly and from between his lips there jerked an animal sound that might have been a word.

He walked to the door of the cabin and gazed dully at Marsden, the collapsed scarecrow, lying on the grass. He moved his eyes to the place where he had seen the marsh grass bend in Womble's flight.

Better, he told himself with a bitter quirk to his mouth, that he had let them both into the shack, waved them toward the pallet where the girl's white beauty lay spread. He had killed one man and made a hidden enemy of another over a woman who, he knew now, had been dead since that last rending cry had escaped her.

Part Six

1

THE WAR moved on through the rest of 1813 and into 1814. Pitched battles, land and naval, were fought in the Great Lakes region and Andrew Jackson and Sam Houston led the soon-to-be-betrayed Cherokees against the British-officered Creeks in the Carolinas and Georgia. In New Orleans, the pirate Jean Laffite was readying himself to play his brief hero's role in history as an interlude in a cruel and bloody existence. In Georgetown, outside Washington, a young poet named Francis Scott Key wrote stormy letters to newspapers, complaining about the senselessness of this war and the need for an immediate peace with Great Britain.

In Maryland, a stalemate persisted. Baltimore was blockaded, officially, but during the winter of 1813 and 1814 the British had only a few vessels maintaining the blockade under the command of a newcomer to those waters, Captain Robert Barrie aboard the seventy-four-gun *Dragon*. Barrie was no Cockburn; the clippers still slipped in and out of Baltimore even as the captain was boasting that "not a sail has moved into or out of the port within the past two months."

Cockburn, Porter and the others spent the winter in Bermuda. Sir John Borlase Warren still fussed and doddered over his command of the fleet and predictions at the base were that he would soon be relieved with Cockburn replacing him. Cockburn thought so, himself; if he had been arrogantly contemptuous of the ancient admiral who commanded him before, he was close to openly insubordinate now.

He did not know, although Sir Peter Porter guessed from letters, that Sir George Cockburn was not in as high regard of the Admiralty as he supposed. Publicly, the British naval lords had accepted his version of the disgrace at Hampton; privately, they knew the truth. London had totted up the costs of the war in the Chesapeake and had come up with a dismal balance; Cockburn had used more than fifty ships, had employed more than eight thousand men and for two years of war on Maryland he could show—what?

He had burned Hampton, a fact which the British wanted to forget. He had occupied half a dozen small islands in the Chesapeake, none of which could be called important in themselves. He had burned Havre de Grace, a move which might by a stretch of generosity be called strategically important. And beyond that— he had levelled Frenchtown in the battle of the stage drivers, he had burned Fredericktown and Georgetown, he had destroyed Queen's Town. On the other hand, the guns of Fort McHenry and Star Fort still scowled over Baltimore harbor, the shipyards of Baltimore still rang to the tunes played by mallet and maul, regardless of Barrie's proud dispatches the clippers ranged in and out of the Bay, the fort at Annapolis was still there even if Cockburn had labelled it an impotent pile of dirt.

And Saint Michaels—the Admiralty Lords frowned over the incident of Saint Michaels. Of all the towns on the Eastern Shore, Easton Town was the acknowledged key point. Cockburn might color his journals, revise his reports, but the fact remained that the admiral had sailed an overwhelmingly-gunned fleet into the Miles River, had assaulted Saint Michaels, had suffered an early reverse that should have been merely a minor set-back, and had turned tail, never to return to the attack there again.

Granted, said the Admiralty, that Cockburn had been stunned by the death of his nephew, the loss of a man who apparently was the only person for whom he had ever warmed a human love, but that did not excuse the strangely indecisive conduct of the move that would have brought about the destruction of Easton. Advices received in London from a certain Mister Guthrie said emphatically that the Parrott's Point defense had been comprised of no more than a handful of men armed with fowling pieces and two nine-pound cannon. And this—this child's snow fort had turned back His Majesty's ships of war?

There were also reports from one of Mister Guthrie's good friends in the area, a Mister Worth, to consider. These had to deal with the fact that inspection had proved that most of the British cannon fire had overshot the town of Saint Michaels or had been far to one side or the other. There were balls lodged in treetops beyond Saint Michaels to prove this, said Mister Worth.

An admiral who could not show a better gunnery record for his command than that, the Admiralty decided, could hardly be given charge of the American War Fleet.

"Besides," one of the Lords at the long conference table added petulantly, "the feller's no gentleman. He's forever picking at his nose."

Which may have outweighed all the other considerations in the final decision to replace Sir John Borlase Warren with Vice-Admiral Sir Alexander Cochrane, by-passing George Cockburn.

Sir Peter Porter had been labelled "one of Co'burn's men" by the Admiralty and so he did not get the command he had dreamed of, captaincy of a ship of the line. He stayed aboard the *Menelaus*, the only Admiral left in command of a frigate.

He may have railed and cursed in the privacy of his cabin but outwardly he was his usual pleasant self. Perhaps he reminded himself that he was still young; there would be time enough to pace the quarterdeck of a seventy-four-gunner after this muddle had been cleared up. He had been in the Royal Navy long enough to know that subordinate officers went up and down in pace with the fortunes of their admirals; perhaps he thought that under Cochrane he could get his ship of the line command before he was thirty.

But he must tread softly, softly, and keep his fingers crossed.

2

At Easton Town and along the banks of the Miles River, life's surface showed little evidence that the war was still going on, that Spring of 1814.

Further north, at Queen's Town and Georgetown and Fredericktown, the people were rebuilding the houses and barns levelled by Sir George Cockburn but at Saint Michaels about all there was to show for the British visit were a few cannon balls, half buried high in the trunks of trees where they would remain for more than a hundred years, historical show pieces of the section.

At Larkspur Hill, Task Tillman planted more acres that Spring than he had put under cultivation since he had taken over the plantation at William's drunken death. He acquired six slaves and four mules from a landowner on the Sassafras River whose place had been wiped out by the British in the action around Georgetown; he began construction of a wing addition to the modest home Randolph Tillman had put up as a makeshift replacement for the magnificence of the original Larkspur Hill mansion.

He worked tirelessly and he seldom left his place these days. There was no need to interrupt his duties at home with the drills at Queen's Town; Joseph Nicholson's company had never been reformed after the town was burned; even the most ardent patriots knew now that all the drills and all the uniforms, all the target practice and all the planning, were mere posturing, empty boasts that collapsed in the face of actuality.

And Task Tillman's nights were empty now of all save uneasy dreams. Vivian was gone, disappeared, and although she herself had smashed Task's embryo love with a few well-chosen words before she had dropped out of sight, he sometimes awoke, even now, and found himself aching for her, wishing he could have been with her, somehow, when her fate overtook her.

Talbot County still talked of Vivian Dangerfield Worth in hushed tones, full of speculation. Talbot County sympathized with Vivian's griefstricken husband, the man who had spent a full month of days and nights riding the county, seeking some trace of his lovely wife.

"She's hidden somewhere, I tell you," he had stormed when they bade him end his wanderings. "The night the British came the poor girl was fair mad with fear—she ran off somewhere and hid and I'll find her yet!"

They did not tell Anthony the answer that was obvious to most of them, that Vivian had run off with her English countrymen during the confusion of the attack on Fairoverlea. But that was simple reasoning, wasn't it? The Redcoats had never reached the Great House—the heroic Dragon Footguards had died keeping them off—and so Vivian could not have been carried away by the British. She must have gone to them; that was as plain as the nose on your face.

And why? Well, the British had shown an unconscionable knowledge of things on the Eastern Shore. Except at Parrott's Point, the enemy had moved as though he knew which lane, which path, to use to attack from the best vantage point; he had known just where the American cannon was placed; he had acted as though every landing he had made was on familiar, well-charted ground. And that must mean that some spy had furnished the British with the information they required, and who would be a more logical spy than an Englishwoman come to the Eastern Shore only a few short years before?

Yes, the whispers agreed, Vivian Dangerfield Worth must have seen danger in the Dragons' repulse of the British at Fairoverlea. She had expected no more of Charles Rawlent's blue-blooded troop than the rest of the county had expected and she had been more rudely surprised than all the others. There was no knowing what rewards she would have enjoyed if the raid on Fairoverlea, the attack on Saint Michaels and Easton Town, had been successful but as it was she must have seen her schemes collapsed, her spy's role exposed, and she must have fled to the safety of a British warship.

And poor Anthony Worth—love made even the keenest man blind, at times. He carried on his pitiful search until even he was convinced that his young wife was not to be found anywhere on the Eastern Shore. Even then, he cried that the British had carried her off.

"She must have run straight into the hands of the murderers," he said, over and over again. "The night, the fog—ah, if she had only stayed in her room where I told her to wait for me!"

Task Tillman heard the stories of Anthony Worth's grief and bit back the exclamations that leapt to his tongue. Vivian, he knew, was dead and Anthony Worth had killed her or had ordered her killed. Titus had not lied to Gracellen; Worth had known for months that his wife had cuckold him and he had waited for his revenge as he had shown before he could wait. He had bided his time until the setting was perfect for a murder of which there never could be one speck of proof. Who could have picked that one shot, the murderer's bullet, out of the crashing confusion that shook Fairoverlea the night the British came?

Even now, eight months after the raid, there was no clear picture of what had happened that foggy, dripping night. The Dragons who had survived gave conflicting versions of the fight; some said they had been at their outposts when the British landed, others said they had been at the Great House and had met the Redcoats about halfway between Peartree Creek and the mansion. From the positions of the bodies, it appeared that the Dragons had thrown themselves at the invaders in a hollow close to the creek, then fought a hot retiring action which inflicted such heavy losses on the Lobsterbacks that the British had been glad to break off the fight without getting within a quarter of a mile from the house.

Charles Rawlent had been found close to the hollow where the main action had taken place, a bullet hole in the side of his handsome head, his sword still gripped in his hand. Beside him was a lieutenant and a serjeant named Harrison, both cruelly bayonetted as were a good many of the other slain Dragons.

They had been all but wiped out, the Dragon Footguards, but they had died as heroes. The bereavement of those dear to them was lightened by the knowledge that the Dragons, laughed at as a sort of exclusive club, had fought where other militia companies had run, had died where others had fled.

The fever to avenge the Dragons had run high in Talbot County for a time but as the weeks had passed and the British had stayed away from the Miles River, the passion for retribution had waned. Now, the Eastern Shore was content to have the war stay away from the Miles, the Chester, the Sassafras, the Choptank and her other rivers; it was enough that the Dragons' graves were carefully tended and the heroes of Fairoverlea spoken of reverently.

The live heroes, those who had manned the Parrott's Point position at Saint Michaels harbor, had received only the briefest recognition for what they had done. Scarcely had the people of Saint Michaels and Easton begun their celebration of the victory before word had come from Fairoverlea, telling of the disastrous fight there, and all attention had swung in that direction.

Which had been all right with Task Tillman; he had certainly wanted no laurel wreaths bedecking his brow. His only thought as he had slogged out of the gun emplacement the morning after the fight had been the weary realization that only inexplicable good fortune had kept the British warships from training their guns on Parrott's Point. A single shell, a bomb, a rocket, he knew, and Dodson's militiamen probably would have broken and fled as had their brothers-in-arms in every instance under British cannon fire.

Task's first thought when he had heard of the action at Fairoverlea had been for Gracellen, his second for Vivian. His relief at learning that Gracellen had found safety at her sister's in Chestertown had been spiked by the word of Vivian's disappearance. A *mysterious* disappearance, they called it, and Task could not tell them what it really was. The people might name Vivian spy and say she fled; he could not name her adulteress and say she died for her sins; all the truth would serve to do would be to lay bare Vivian's shame, and his, to no purpose.

So Task went back to Larkspur Hill and found the place undamaged—thank the amazing Dragons for that—and harvested his crops that autumn and held his counsel. To no one, not even to Squire Wills, did he refute the popular theory of what had happened to Vivian Dangerfield Worth.

His sense of guilt was not leavened by the memory that Vivian had jeered at him for thinking he was the only man with whom she had sinned. He did not spare himself a moment's bitter blame for having been one of those who had helped her down the pathway to her destruction. He tried to pray for her and found himself unworthy to whisper the simplest, most abject appeal; what Deity could be so generous as to accept the cry of a heart as black as his?

He aged that winter of 1813 and 1814 far more than could be accounted for by the hours that ticked past. He grew more and more silent, his smile vanished, his field hands muttered among themselves that he would kill himself and them, too, unless he stopped trying to do a day's work in an hour, a year's work in a week.

"You'll wear yourself out, lad," Squire Wills fretted. "No man can keep up the pace you've set, not taking a minute for rest, never stopping for an hour with a friend, a pipe and a glass."

"I've wasted far too much time at playing soldier—and at other things," Task replied brusquely. "I'm way behind in making Larkspur Hill what my father wanted it to be again."

"Your father would not ask you to make yourself a hermit," the Squire argued. "What will it benefit you to make Larkspur Hill a grand estate if the master of the place makes himself a sour sit-by-the-fire in doing it?"

398

Task shrugged. He could not tell his friend, his benefactor, that except for hard, exhausting work there was only the whiskey jug to dull his thoughts and that he was determined he would not stagger along the road his brother William had travelled.

"And what does it gain ye to bring back Larkspur Hill," Squire Wills pursued, "if there'll be no sons or daughters to make the place live?"

Task barked a harsh laugh.

"Sons and daughters?" he asked. "By God, that would be a scurvy trick, givin' innocent babes a sire like me!"

The old Squire from Easton Town surveyed Task with troubled eyes that peered out from under shaggy brows. He did not like the change in this young man who had been so brash, so fiery, a few short years before when he had thought himself the victim of a strong man's wrongdoing. War, he told himself, changed many men but this change in Task, this hardened coldness, was no product of a long campaign with all its attendant cruelties. He had first noticed the descent of this grim mood before the fight at Parrott's Point, even before Queen's Town, so it could not be pinned directly on some strange reaction from having been under fire.

"What ails ye, lad?" he asked gently. "Sometimes I think ye act like a man in torment, the way ye speak about yourself and bar all others from getting close to you."

Task's head was lowered as he made his reply in a husky voice.

"If aught torments me," he said, "'tis my own doing—and Anthony Worth's. We talked it over once, some of it, and you said I was wrong in what I knew; we'll not waste time arguing it again."

"But talk's never a waste of time, no matter what maxims say different," Squire Wills said quietly. "A man relieves himself in talk, sometimes, as completely as he rids himself of his poisons with a physic. You know me for a good friend, Task—can'st tell me what it is ye've locked up inside you?"

"Nay, Squire Wills," Task Tillman said gravely. "Good friend you are and no man had better, but if there's a thing locked up inside me, then 'tis locked with no key I can find."

Squire Wills hesitated and put a worn, wrinkled hand on Tillman's arm.

"My age," he said, "permits me the privilege of prying. Tell me, Task, does this heavy-heartedness of yours have to do with Gracellen Worth?"

"You mean the Widow Rawlent?" Task asked harshly. "I haven't seen her in a year, save for the time we luckier militiamen gave her husband and the others the military funeral. And that time, I was ashamed to look at her, remembering how I'd talked about Charley Rawlent, who proved himself a thousand times the better man than me."

"You haven't seen her," Squire Wills smiled, "but still that's not an answer to my question."

Task flung out his hands in a furious gesture and his voice hoarsened.

"Aye," he rasped. "I love her—I think you know I always have! But impossible's impossible and that's the end of it! Her father hates me as I hate him—I doubt not he'll try to kill me when the time's right, after he's waited long enough. And Gracellen must hate me, too. The last words she spoke to me were that we—I— could burn in Hell."

"A headstrong girl," Squire Wills murmured placatingly. "Red-haired, high-tempered, spoiled. She spoke in anger and meant nothing by it."

"Nay," Task said grimly. "She had good reason to wish me in Hell. She's had no cause to change her mind on that. She has a right to double her curse, remembering how I talked against Rawlent."

"We all talked against Charles Rawlent," the Squire said. "We all were wrong there. You've no reason to reproach yourself too much for what was the fault of a thousand men besides you."

"That's the least of it," Task muttered. He swung his graven face toward Squire Wills. "Don't ask me why's this and why's that, Squire," he said bluntly. "If there was aught to tell and it could do any good to anyone, I'd tell you, but, believe me, I'm better left alone with my own thoughts to chew on by myself."

3

AT FAIROVERLEA, there was a greyness that came close to matching the gloom over Larkspur Hill. The great house that had been all light and laughter, bounteous hospitality and gracious living, dwelt under a somber pall that would not be shaken off despite all Anthony Worth's efforts to lighten it.

And try he did to recapture some of the sparkle and verve, the love of life, that had belonged to the house and to Gracellen; try he did and fail, time after time, until he began to despair of ever rousing his daughter from her strange and cheerless mood.

"We cannot mourn the ones we've lost forever, my dear," he told her. "You'll find the courage to put aside your grief over Charles, I know, once you set your mind to it."

And, he asked himself, who would have guessed she'd grieve so for that useless coxcomb? If he had known Rawlent's death would have been such a blow to her, he could perhaps have made other arrangements to shut his mouth that would have still spared his life. But he had honestly thought that he was doing Gracellen a favor by removing a husband she had married on an impulse after that damned Task Tillman had been routed, a husband he had not dreamed she could love.

Still, when she had come back from Chestertown and had been told that Rawlent had died a hero's death, she had been staggered so badly that it might have been that they had told her that he, her father, had died. Anthony had been shocked as he had watched the color drain from her face and her eyes dull while she listened; he had felt the stab of jealousy bite deep as he had seen her led, half fainting, to a sofa.

He was safe, wasn't he? Fairoverlea was unharmed. That should have eased the pain of anything concerning the fool, Rawlent, her husband!

Another distressing thing was the fact that she had not joined him in his frantic search for Vivian. She had not even offered to go with him when he had ranged up and down the countryside with his cries that Vivian must be found. She had watched him silently while he had voiced his confidence that Vivian was alive somewhere, hiding in her panic.

She had fixed her grey-green eyes on him in quiet—*speculation?*

No! He was imagining things! Gracellen knew only that her stepmother suffered from brain seizures that he had kept hidden from the outside world. He had told her that and his daughter never would believe anything else. Her trust in his word was absolute; it could never be shaken. If impossibility were piled on impossibility and proof were thrown in Gracellen's lap that her father was less than he had made himself to her, she would never give the proof the dignity of consideration.

She was his daughter. She was part of him in more than other children were flesh of their fathers' flesh. Her love for him transcended any love she could have for another man. She was welded to him by a paternal natal cord that never had been severed, so she must love him as herself. And, all wise men to the contrary, there never was a love that could equal the ego's adoration of the ego.

"Listen to your old father," he begged her. "You'll do Charles's memory no good with this dragged-out mourning."

She turned her face, her set white face, away. She left the room as she invariably did when he tried to reason with her.

Damn the man, Rawlent, he cursed silently, and damn all women for finding love for a hero that had not been there when the man was a live fool. He had been wrong, he saw now, in having Rawlent killed. He could have spiked Rawlent's tongue forever in some other way, if he had put thought to it. But who had known the girl would react this way? Every time Anthony had seen the two together, and that had been seldom enough, he had thought he had seen plain boredom on his daughter's face, a constant irritation at her husband's mawkish prattle. He had thought that she would accept his removal calmly, he had even thought she would secretly welcome it, and now she acted as though she had been robbed of a treasure that never could be replaced.

Could it be that Rawlent had—*Christ, no!*

"You're looking wan and peaked," he told Gracellen. "You scarce ate any breakfast at all. Tell me, you're not—"

"No, Father," she said, looking down. "I'm not with child."

"Why then," he boomed heartily, "things are not half so bad as you'd make them seem with your long face! Look you; Charles is gone, cut off in his prime by the British, and you're still a girl. We'll find you another husband—nay, don't wince, lass—and you've a full life ahead of you. Charles would want it, my dear!"

Her hands were twisting restlessly in front of her and she regarded them as intently as though they were independent of her will. She spoke softly.

"Father—"

"Yes, my dear."

"Charles—the night the British came—I was upstairs in my room and—"

He waited a moment, the blood pulsing in his temples.

"Yes?"

"I heard his voice," she said. "He was—he was shouting something about somebody going to an outpost and—and another man yelled an insult. There was a scuffle and—"

"That!" he laughed. "My dear, is that what's bothered you?" He laid a finger to his lower lip and regarded the ceiling. "Let's see," he said ruminatively. "Charles *did* find a man of his in the parlor who'd left his post and, as I remember it, he ordered him back to duty. The man was drunk, Gracellen—one of the few who were that night—and he was insolent. There was a scuffle, yes, when the other Dragons pounced on the poor devil and, as I recall, doused him in the rain barrel outside before they sent him packing back to where he belonged."

Gracellen fingered the cloth of her dress, her eyes still downcast. He watched her, waiting for her next question, until the uneasiness bubbled from his throat.

"You believe me, don't you?" he demanded. "Why do you mistrust what I've told you?"

"I have not said—"

"But you've acted like I've fed you lies about the whole affair!" he stormed. "Even when they buried Charles, you looked at me instead of the grave he was being lowered to! Looking at me— looking at me—as though I'm to blame for what happened! Sweet Christ, I would have stopped it if I could've! I fought with 'em, I handled a carbine—ask—ask—"

She waited as he spluttered, then started to turn away. Anthony's hand shot out to grasp her arm above the elbow and swing her back to face him.

"What are you thinkin'?" he crackled. "What's behind that empty face ye've shown me lately? What else did you hear besides your husband grapplin' with that mutineer?"

Her eyes were his, he told himself, though hers were clear, unstained by all the lies that had passed under his lids.

"Nothing," she told him. Impassively, she detached her arm from his grasp and walked out of the room. She left Anthony Worth standing there, refusing to flinch under the hollow, weightless scourge of doubt.

He went to his office, splashed whiskey into a glass and gulped it. He refilled his tumbler and dropped heavily into the chair behind the desk, the liquor splashing over onto the back of the hand that held the glass. He sipped again, his eyes intent on the opposite wall.

"There's nothing," he murmured aloud, "that I did wrong. Not one thing."

Hadn't they been about to make him a hero for fighting with

the Dragons before he had hushed their praise with his keening for his lost wife, Vivian? Hadn't the men who had ridden out from Easton Town, General Benson among them, looked over the "battlefield" and found no sign of anything he had not intended them to see?

Or had they? Benson was a mask-faced old devil, impossible to read especially when he, Anthony, had had to act the distracted husband while the militia General was at Fairoverlea. Had Roan and Marsden and Womble been careless or overly careful in the placing of the bodies that were supposed to have fallen under British fire? That Harris had looked artificial lying there and the knife wounds had seemed too shallow for bayonet stabs—but Harris was deep under the dirt now with the sandstone slab at his head, proclaiming him a soldier who had died in the defense of his country, already beginning to lose the sharp edges of its carving.

Aye, he had filled the graveyards of Talbot County with heroes to bring off this success and there was not one who could find a crack in the whole thing to pry at. Vivian was known as a spy who had fled to the British when her dark plot had been upset by Charles Rawlent's fierce fight. He, Anthony, was the bereaved spouse who would not hear the whispers that his English wife had been a traitor. Fairoverlea had been a prime target for the Redcoats so Anthony Worth must certainly be their worst enemy in these parts. The Dragons' dying resistance in the hollow by Peartree Creek had smashed the British land attack on Easton Town. Was there ever a man in a better position than he?

"Anthony," he chuckled, looking down at the amber whiskey in his glass, "ye're an old woman to worry about a young girl's frown."

The knock that sounded at the passageway door brought the tail of his clubbed hair swinging around swiftly. The rap was Roan's and Anthony Worth scowled at the paper-strewn desktop. Roan—now, there was something that was not exactly right, Roan and his story of what had happened to Marsden and Womble.

He stood up slowly, watching a moth-miller that circled about

405

his desk lamp, keeping his eyes away from the bolted door. Roan —what about Roan?

"Mayhap," he told the crazily circling miller, "'tis time we dealt with Roan and so made the record clear."

He dragged his head about as the knock sounded again, impatiently. He walked over and drew the bolt, opened the door to let in his hulking overseer. Roan's small eyes swept the office and fixed themselves on Anthony. His wide mouth barely opened as he spoke.

"Ye've got to get me some help, sir," he said bluntly. "No one man can do the work that kept three busy. I'm fair wore out, tryin' t'look after Titus and the blacks besides doin' a thousand and one other things that have to be done."

His tone grated on Anthony and the Master of Fairoverlea's brows lowered thunderously. This was what was wrong with Roan; since the night the British came he had been increasingly surly, more and more outspoken in a new manner that bordered on insolence. If, Anthony Worth told himself, Will Roan thought that the little business he had taken care of with Vivian gave him some sort of special hold over his master he was due for a rude awakening. For Roan had murdered the woman, not Anthony Worth; not a man in the county would accept Roan's story over Anthony Worth's if the scar-faced bastard tried to use his knowledge to his own gain.

"I've told ye," he growled now, "t'give Titus the authority that was Marsden's. Let him handle some of the duties you three took care of."

"And I'll not be workin' with that nigger," Roan boomed. "Besides his fair chillin' my blood just to look at him, I'll not have a black eunuch ranked at my level."

Worth's lips curled in a cold smile as he turned back to his desk.

"Our Roan is a touchy gentleman," he observed mildly. "He must have men of equal excellence about him."

"Nay, sir," Roan protested, "but it'd be fair askin' fer trouble to give Titus any authority. The man hates us all, as you well know, and he's kept his place only because he's been treated like the slave he is."

"Afraid of Titus, Will?" asked Anthony, his brows rising.

"I'm afraid of no man," Roan gravelled. "I'm but lookin' to your interests, sir, in refusin' to raise Titus above his station."

"Refusing?" Anthony asked dangerously. "Since when do you refuse an order of mine?"

Roan met the other man's stare boldly, his mouth down-curved in a stubborn line.

"Our necks," he said grimly, "will act the same in a rope, even if you give the orders and I take 'em. I'm speakin' to keep the noose away from both of us, perhaps. In our position, Anthony Worth, 'twould be best to 'ware every danger, real or fancied."

"Our position, Roan?" Worth asked gently. "I fear you've mixed things up a bit. For have I any murder on *my* hands? Did I throw my dear wife into the swamp? Did I kill Womble and Marsden when they sought to interfere? Did I pistol Charles Rawlent or any of the others? Did I bash in the head of Randolph Tillman or set fire to his house or his son's tobacco barns? Think, Will Roan; how's my position the least like yours?"

Roan's scar burned dully in the light from the desk lamp and his splayed hands knotted.

"There's some," he rumbled, "would think ye were as much t'blame as if ye'd done the tricks y'rself."

"Then run to them!" Anthony Worth roared. "Go now—saddle a horse and ride to the Sheriff at Easton Town and tell him all ye know! Spill your story and see where it'll get you! By God, I think I'd welcome it, if ye're bound to be so high-and-mighty when you speak to me! I'll let the hangman rid me of a blackmailer, if that's what ye've a mind to be!"

Roan took a backward step before Anthony's fury and the knotted hands spread, rising in front of the blocky overseer in a placating gesture.

"Now sir," he said, "I meant nothin' of the kind. Why sir, ye've been my friend and my employer for too many years for me to turn against ye now! I but asked ye to get me some help in managin' the place, some men to serve as Tom and Marsden served."

"Aye," Anthony said quietly. "Tom Womble and Marsden—it was a pity that they ended as they did, eh, Roan?"

The hulking man in the striped jersey and dirty pantaloons shifted from one foot to the other, looking down at the floor.

"Aye," he muttered. "But there was no help for it."

"Tell me again," Worth said idly, leaning back in his desk chair, "just what happened that day, good Will."

"I've told ye a hundred times," Roan protested. "Ye surely know the story now."

"But I'd hear it again," Worth smiled. "It's an amusin' yarn."

Roan raised a broken-nailed hand to rub his cropped head, still looking down at his boots.

"Well—well, I was carryin' the lady to the swamp," he said hesitantly, "and I was almost to the place where she'd be—dealt with. Then Womble and Marsden come upon me. You know what Womble was like, sir, and Marsden was twice as bad, though he didn't show it. They—they were wolves, sir, where a woman was concerned and there was the lady, all—well, the way you handed her over to me—and—and those two would not be put off. They went fair mad and I had to fight them, both of them. Marsden pulled his knife and so did Womble and I—I had to defend myself, didn't I? Besides, I knew ye'd not want the two of them to have her, no matter what."

He made a half gesture with one hand.

"So—so after it was done," he said, "I got rid of them along with the lady. And that's all."

Anthony's hands were behind his head as he watched Roan recite his story. His eyes were veiled, his face impassive although within him strong currents churned and foamed. For he knew Will Roan was lying. He had killed Tom Womble and Marsden, aye, but not as he said, fighting to preserve some comic shred of honor for the harlot he'd been assigned to murder. The story was ridiculous on the face of it. No man, not even Will Roan, could battle two knife artists like Marsden and Womble while carrying a woman over his shoulder. And if he had dropped Vivian, would she have waited there obediently until he'd finished with his cronies before she offered her own neck to the blade? Yet Roan never made mention of how he'd kept Vivian from fleeing or recaptured her when she'd tried to run away.

"Tell me, Roan," he asked softly. "You did not let the bitch go, by any chance? She did not cozen you into letting her escape?"

"I swear it!" Roan burst out vehemently. "She's dead, sir, and fathoms deep in the quicksand! And Marsden, too. And Womble— I swear Womble's dead along with the others!"

"They'd better be," Anthony Worth said negligently, "for if one of 'em's alive, he or she may cost ye y'r neck, my good Will."

Roan's eyes shifted, his pitted face twitched.

"All dead," he said fiercely. "They're all as dead as dead."

He swallowed.

"Dead," he added firmly.

4

GRACELLEN RAWLENT sat in her room and looked down at the long-shadowed figure of Will Roan as he left the passageway door and stalked across the courtyard toward the quarters he shared with Womble and Marsden—*had* shared with them because Father had told her that the little fat man and the thin tomb-tenant Marsden had gone, run to Baltimore in their fear that the British would come back.

That was what Father had told her. She wondered what the truth could be. She wondered what the truth would prove about everything her father had told her, every single thing he had said to her, since she had been old enough to listen.

For her father was a liar. He must be worse than a liar; he must be a—

She cowered in her chair, her hands pressed to her face. No, she would not think it! He could not be the murderer she knew he was!

Charles—she hoped Charles had died bravely, fighting the enemy, but she could not make herself see him in the hero's role. The foggy August night the British came was still a sharp etching in her memory; she saw her husband again when he had come to their rooms, only minutes before the brawl had flared into ugly life in the parlor below. Charles Rawlent had been red-faced, reeking with brandy, uncertain in his walk, scared to a blustering bravado.

"We're fixed for 'em," he had announced with a sweep of his arm, "so let the damned Lobsterbacks try t'land in this section! We'll show 'em! The whole thing's planned and ready."

There had been a carafe of sherry on a table between the windows and he had wabbled over to it, had tilted the bottle, staining the linen cover as he missed the glass.

"I'll show Nicholson and the others where they were wrong," he had told Gracellen. "Y'can't stand up to superior forces—it's silly. What we'll do is draw 'em inshore, out of range of their warships, and then fall on 'em and cut 'em up. We'll make a stand at somewhere around Tunis Mills, if the situation's right."

"And leave Fairoverlea to the British?" she had asked.

He had teetered, the wine slopping over the rim of his glass.

"Fortunes of war," he had hiccoughed. "Can't sacrifice m'company f'r y'r father's fine house."

"But—but Father gave you money for the company when you said the Dragons would defend this place," she had protested.

"Y'r father ain't worryin'," he had grinned. "The Redcoats won't harm this place. They're much too indebted to the fine Anthony Worth to make a bonfire of Fairoverlea."

"What do you mean?"

He belched a laugh and splashed more wine on the carpet.

"He thinks I'm a blind nincompoop, does he?" he sniggered. "I know there's things goin' on here that'd open the eyes of a lot of people. And let y'r fine father complain about the way I command my company and he'll hear from me!"

He had drained the glass and set the fragile crystal down on the table with a lurch that had snapped the slender stem.

"If the British come," he told her, "ye'd be safest to stay here. No Redcoat would ever harm the daughter of Anthony Worth, their great friend."

"Charles, you're drunk to say such things!"

"Drunk? I'm never drunk enough to be called it. Stay here, I say, and ye'll be safe." He wavered to the door and turned. "And never fear," he had added with a sneer. "Your precious husband won't be touched by British lead or British steel this night, so calm y'r worries." He snickered. "As if y'had a single worry for my life," he added.

"Charles, I—"

"Y'needn't protest, Madam!" His voice had rung out surprisingly clear then. "I've never been misled to believe you married me for any other reason than to show that fine Task Tillman of yours that he meant nothin' to you! And I married you, Madam, because I was tired of pinchin' pennies on my own—and f'r no other reason!"

The door had slammed behind him and that had been Charles Rawlent's leave-taking.

And how jarringly had misfitted what had followed; her father's orders to hurry to the carriage at the first sign of the British approach; his relay of some syrupy goodbye from Charles; her being bundled into the carriage and Father's furious haste to get her away—without Vivian.

Yes, she must have known the instant that her father had told her that Vivian was not going with her that her stepmother was doomed to die that night. All the confusion, the shots, the yells, the clamor and curses of the Dragons as they fumbled their way into battle must have shown itself to her as no more than a setting for the stage where Vivian would meet her fate.

Anthony Worth had never learned that Titus had told her everything; she had discovered that the night Father had described Vivian's spells of madness. He did not know she had found out about Vivian's faithlessness with Task Tillman and all his lies had depended on her not knowing.

She had known that Vivian would be gone when she returned to Fairoverlea from Chestertown. She had prepared herself for that but she had not been ready for the news that Charles Rawlent had died, too, during that evil night. She had nerved herself to act a part when they told her Vivian was dead; she had come close to screaming collapse when she had learned that her handsome, useless, unloved husband had been killed.

And why had Charles died? Vivian had betrayed Anthony Worth and perhaps death was the meet judgment for that sin, but Charles Rawlent, the weakling, the braggart, the whining fop, had no sin to sign his death warrant beyond the iniquity of a loud and empty voice.

Which had named Anthony Worth a friend of the British!

Then she had known. Then her brain had reeled with the realization that the father she had loved with an idolization that skirted close to deep, unplumbed and fearful depths was no honest avenger but a—a murderer. Then she had known that Anthony Worth had killed Charles as certainly as he had killed Vivian. She had known that her father killed for no ennobled purpose; he struck at those, no matter how feeble, who might endanger his smiling security.

Her father's lies had robbed her of Task Tillman; that was not his least crime. His story of the insults to Johanna Worth, her mother, were false. The tobacco barn fire that Task had charged Anthony Worth with setting—no reason now to believe Task had not been right in that. And Task had shouted the accusation that her father had murdered his father, Randolph Tillman—

So she must hate him, liar, murderer, despoiler of her life that he was. All decency, all sanity, called on her to hate him.

She could not hate him, though she tried. He was branded with the mark of Cain and she, Cain's daughter, might have shuddered at his touch, the glint of his sidelong glance, his easy voice, but she kept her silence to help him hide his festering brand from the world outside Fairoverlea.

413

5

JETT WORTH paced up a brick-paved street near the Battery in Charleston with a strut to his walk that had been earned by the capture of the British sloop-of-war, *Effort*, off the Carolina coast the week before.

The *Effort's* capture had been hard-won, with no lucky shot to aid it as there had been in the capture of the brig *Unicorn*. *Lorelei* had sighted the Englishman off Gull Shoal and the sloop had tacked in a wide reach to look over the situation and size up the clipper. Jett's ship was flying no ensign nor did she show one as she bore in on the sloop until, when she came within reach with her bow-chaser, she broke out her pennant and hammered a shot, all in the same instant.

The sloop was a true specimen of her kind, low and lean, over-canvased and swift, with her lee rail closer to the water than to the sky. There lay her weakness; like most sloops she was a one-sided ship. She heeled at an angel's sigh and when she canted, the guns on her lee were useless for anything but blasting at porpoises. Knowing this, Jett swept *Lorelei* to leeward of *Effort* and broadsided the sloop from her defenseless side. *Effort* twisted away, hurt, and spun about on a shilling to answer with a hail of grape that tore through the clipper's aft starboard quarter. Greer, the first mate, and three seamen went down in that first blast, the taffrail beside Jett was shot away in splinters, but, miraculously, not a ball touched him.

Effort sliced in, intent on ramming, and the clipper went over on beam's end to avoid the crash of the sharp-prowed Britisher. The sloop dealt Jett a hammering blow at water level as she foamed past; *Lorelei's* answering fire was hurried and high. Both vessels drew off, a mile or more apart, for a second breath.

Elwood, Jett's second, reported from below that the holes in *Lorelei's* hull had been plugged with mats; the clipper was taking water but no more than the pumps could handle. Jett squinted at the sloop, at his sails, at the sky. The wind was from the southwest, brisk and gusty; *Lorelei* could crack on her studding sails and run for it and leave *Effort*, speedy as she might be, far in her wake.

"Which'd be a devilish poor way to try to win a war," Jett murmured aloud. He turned to the quartermaster at the wheel. "Put her over on port," he ordered. The clipper swung in again toward her foe.

Effort closed gladly. She was more heavily armed, she carried a bigger crew, the odds were all hers. But she reckoned without Jett's seamanship; the sloop's captain never before had met a clipper, he never before had matched his skill with a vessel that could feint and parry as nimbly as a fencing master.

The sloop's guns churned up the water a yardarm's length from *Lorelei's* hull as Jett rushed in and veered away tauntingly. The clipper's broadside bellowed as *Lorelei* leaned in again, crashed out another time before the sloop had recovered from the earlier blast. *Effort* staggered in the water, her deck a smoke-shrouded shambles, her shredded ratlines whipping in the wind, her mainsail torn to ribbons, her guns served by more dead men than live. The sloop's captain saw his vessel had been dealt a mortal blow and tried to draw *Effort* away from *Lorelei's* hungry reach.

"Grapples!" Jett roared. "We're boarding!"

There was an answering yell from the Marylanders. Over the side went the huge hooks, biting deep into *Effort*. Up and over swarmed the Eastern Shoremen, pistols cracking, cutlasses hissing, gaping mouths screaming wild and senseless cries. The British fought a hopeless battle from the start. The sloop's captain had not expected a boarding; it was wrong by every rule. He saw his decks swept by an avalanche of maddened Yankees and he did the only thing that would save his crew from annihilation; he surrendered to the slight, handsome, dark American captain who had led the rush aboard his vessel.

So *Lorelei* had come in to Charleston with the battered *Effort* in tow, a prize that, counted with the twenty dollars bounty for every British sailorman made prisoner, boosted the clipper's earnings to a dizzy figure. No wonder, then, that Jett Worth had a bit of a strut to his walk as he went along the Charleston street.

He had reason to be satisfied with himself, his ship and his crew. He had not matched Joshua Barney's record yet but he had high hopes of equalling it. He already had passed the marks set by Stafford and Dooley and Boyle. Under *Lorelei*'s guns a brig, five schooners, a dispatch cutter, three merchantmen and now this second sloop-of-war, had been sunk or captured. Another year at sea, with her good fortune supercargo on every voyage, and *Lorelei* might become the most famous clipper afloat.

Still, Jett's contentment was dimmed by the realization that he could not go back to Fairoverlea this time, while the clipper was being patched up at Charleston, the crew given shore leave to rest up. He could not go back to Talbot County on the Eastern Shore without risking a challenge to Task Tillman and, regardless of what Task had done, he had no stomach for a duel with the man who once had been his best friend. As for Vivian, he knew he could never endure being in the same house with her, knowing how falsely she had played her kind, devoted husband, Anthony Worth. He could not go back to Fairoverlea until his uncle had settled the score with Task and Vivian and even then the flavor of the place would be dulled by that pair's perfidy.

Yet he ached to see Fairoverlea again, the sunset's glow on the windows that looked down at the Miles River, the curl of smoke from the kitchen's chimneys, the white pillars stretching up from the porch, the weeping willows bowing over the lawn, the stretch of white sand beach where he had swum with Task Tillman when they both were boys.

If it had not been for Task's and Vivian's treachery he might have tried a run up the Chesapeake to Peartree Creek, blockade or no blockade. He had been told that Napoleon's final downfall had allowed the British to press their American war more closely; it would be a risky thing to try to run the Virginia Capes now but it would be worth the risk if Fairoverlea was the place it had been before he had found out about Vivian's shame and Task Tillman's crime.

His uncle had promised to deal with both the people who had wronged him; Jett wondered what shape his revenge would take.

He turned in at the door of a tavern. A dish of mullet, he told himself, would go good after the salt meat and ship's biscuit that had been his fare for weeks and a couple of tankards of ale would prove a welcome change from the everlasting blackstrap rum that was his tipple aboard the clipper. The captured sloop-of-war's grog had proved very inferior stuff, not fit for an honest Eastern Shore gullet, and Jett had promised himself his fill of foaming black and bitter ale when he reached shore.

The tavern was not Charleston's best, certainly, but the smell of frying fish from the kitchen beyond the low-ceilinged white-washed main room tickled his appetite beyond caring that the dozen or so men at the bar looked like a villainous lot. A slatternly wench in a dress that seemed to have been stitched by a seamstress who forgot the bodice should cover at least half the bosom brought him a tankard at his order and he sipped it appreciatively as he waited for his fish to be served. He wished he had a newspaper to help him catch up with what had been going on in the war while he had been at sea but one glance at this place and its customers made it obvious that no reading matter would be at hand here.

This much he had been told by the captain of a Yarmouth schooner he had met in Port au Prince when he had put in to refill his water casks: The British had invaded northern Ohio and had reached the Sandusky River before they had been defeated in

417

a battle and forced to evacuate all the territory they had grabbed; Baltimore, so far as the Yankee skipper had heard, had not been attacked although the city could hardly hope to escape the war much longer; Washington, too, was still untouched although certainly the British must have their eyes on that fledgling Capital and President Madison had gathered a great army about the town to defend its approaches. Of any action on the Eastern Shore of Maryland the schooner's captain had had no word and that, Jett told himself, must mean that the Redcoats had contented themselves with the burning of Georgetown and Queen's Town in the strange waiting game they seemed to be playing.

He looked up as the blowsy waitress slid the platter of mullet in front of him, stooping to present Jett with two reminders that more than food and ale was available at this tavern. Jett repressed a grimace; he had been long at sea and he was no saint, certainly, but there was little enticement in the grey-grimed skin offered by this unwashed coryphee.

"My room's just above," she told him, "if you've a need to rest y'rself after y'r meal."

"Another time," he smiled. "And thanks for your kind invitation."

The mullet was delicious, fresh-caught and crisply browned, with a generous dish of black-eyed peas and fried potatoes on the side. The bread was stale and the butter had turned but the excellence of the rest of the meal, the cool tang of the ale, made up for those faults.

Jett was munching on his last morsel of fish when the door opened and a round little fat man walked in out of the dazzling brilliance of the street. Jett choked on his mouthful of mullet, cleared his throat with a draught of ale.

"Tom Womble, by God!" he cried. "And what are ye doing here?"

Womble's cherub face swung toward Jett and the blue, innocent eyes widened. For a second, he appeared on the verge of turning and running out of the tavern; then his rosebud mouth assumed its familiar smile and he advanced across the room toward Jett,

418

his hand knuckling his forehead under the brown billycock hat he wore.

"Well, now, Cap'n Jett," he said happily. "A sight f'r sore eyes you are, sir!"

"And what are you doing in Charleston?" Jett demanded. "Is my uncle here? How is it you're so far from Fairoverlea? Where's Roan and Marsden? Sit down, man and explain yourself!"

Womble seated himself gingerly across the table from the skipper of the *Lorelei*, his gaze as naive as that of a child listening to the legend of Father Christmas.

"A good voyage, Cap'n?" he asked tentatively.

Jett gestured impatiently with the hand that held his fork.

"Fair enough," he said. "But tell me why you're here in Charleston, Womble. Did my uncle send you here or did you come with him?"

"Nay," Womble said, his head wagging. "*The King's* not here— or, leastwise, I hope he's not." He hunched over the table, his elbows spread. "There's been a deal of happening at Fairoverlea, Cap'n Jett, or have you heard?"

"I've heard nothing for six months and more! What happened? Is my uncle well, and my cousin?"

Womble nodded. "Well enough the last I heard," he said. He fixed his eyes on the litter on Jett's plate and ran a tongue over his lips. "I must admit," he added, "that things have not been so fine with me. Matter of fact, sir, I came in here hopin' some big-hearted gentleman would have pity on a hungry man and stand me a meal."

"God's sake, you're hungry?" Jett asked. His upraised finger brought the waitress and he gave the order. "What's this?" he asked Womble when the girl slip-slopped away from the table. "Since when hasn't *The King* seen that his men were provided for?"

"Well, sir, like I said, much has happened since you left Fairoverlea," Womble said. The gape-bloused girl slammed down two tankards of ale and the fat man reached for his thirstily. He drank and wiped the foam from his upper lip with a delicate gesture of

419

his dimpled hand. "Now Marsden, who you asked about, is dead."

"Dead?"

"Aye," Womble said. He revolved the mug between his hands. "Marsden's dead, killed by Roan. I escaped, m'self, by a chinch-bug's eyebrow, no more."

"Roan killed Marsden?"

Womble pulled at his tankard again, nodding over its rim.

"When did this happen, and why?"

"It happened the mornin' after the British came and—"

"The British attacked Fairoverlea?" Jett Worth demanded. "Give me the whole story, man, and not these dibs and dabs of information!"

Womble's eyes slid around in his chubby face.

"The whole story," he said uneasily, "is nearly past believin', Cap'n Jett, and I don't know all the facts of it. I know the British came up Peartree Creek and—and they wasn't unexpected by y'r uncle, I can say that. Now wait, sir! Don't lose y'r temper before ye heard the yarn, I beg ye!"

"I don't like the way you said the British weren't unexpected, Womble," Jett growled. "It had a curious ring."

"The whole story's got a curious ring but it's the truth I tell ye! You know me for a truthful man, Cap'n Jett—I'd not lie to you if it meant a fortune to me."

"I doubt that," Jett grunted, "but go on."

So Jett Worth learned the story of the British visit to Fairoverlea and the fight between the Redcoats and the Dragon Footguards. The fat man colored the story highly, of course, and put himself in a hero's role with many a deprecating smirk, but Anthony Worth's nephew was able to get at least an outline of the true picture and his frown deepened as the tale unfolded. All Womble's efforts to skirt outright accusation of Anthony Worth's treason failed to answer Jett's suspicion and doubt. His uncle had said one day that he was shaping his plans so that he and Fairoverlea would not be the loser, no matter which side won the war; Jett had not dreamed that Anthony would go so far as to serve his interests in the way Womble seemed to be hinting at.

420

And yet—when had Anthony Worth ever given him reason to believe other than no move could be too daringly drastic to protect Fairoverlea and his position as *The King?* Jett's mind went back to the day he had brought home the *Heron* and had expressed incautious curiosity over the shockingly bad luck Larkspur Hill had with fires. What was it his uncle had told him that day?

"There are things that don't concern you—they'll never touch you, I promise. But if you should be foolish enough to peek and pry where you shouldn't, you'll be hurt nor can I help you though you perish!"

But—but he had been a boy then, even though that had been only a few short years before. Now he was a man who had fought his ship against the British and had won; he had earned the right to know the truth. He could not be expected to knuckle his forehead unquestioningly forever; Anthony Worth was an old man with an old man's danger of mistakes made by a keen mind blunted by the years. To deal with the British—if that was what he had really done—was to invite disaster that could sweep him, Jett, to ruin along with Anthony.

"And Cap'n Rawlent," Tom Womble was saying across the table, "was killed with the others. They found him in the lane to the creek, his sword still in his hand."

"So Rawlent's dead, eh?" Jett Worth asked. "I never thought that one would have the bowels for a battle."

"Well," the fat man said with a greasy grin, "mayhap he didn't, exactly."

"Now, what's the meaning of that?"

"I had naught to do with it, Cap'n Jett—of that ye have my word. But the cutthroat Roan—and Marsden—dealt fair cruel with Cap'n Rawlent before the British ever came in sight. I saw what happened and I tried to stop it, you may be sure, but that precious pair wouldn't listen. 'Twas then, I think, that Roan made up his mind to kill me. I knew too much, y'see, and—"

"Now hold, Womble!" Jett grated. "Ye think you can make me believe Roan killed Charley Rawlent? Why, my uncle would

421

skin him alive for harming Gracellen's husband, no matter what he may have thought of him."

"I know but what I saw," the round little man said defiantly. "If ye'll not believe me, you won't, and I can't make you, but I saw Roan and Marsden knockin' Cap'n Rawlent about like a rebellious slave and it was hours before the British set foot on Fairoverlea! I swear to that, Cap'n Jett! And I saw the poor lady, *The King's* own wife, as naked as a waterfront whore, bein' mistreated by Roan. And I saw—"

"Now, for God's sake!"

Jett pushed back the bench on which he was sitting and sprang to his feet. The men in the bar turned to stare, the slatternly waitress gazed slack-jawed from the kitchen doorway. Tom Womble put up a hand to ward off the blow he thought was coming on and his voice became a whimper.

"Y'wanted the truth," he complained, "and when I try t'give it to ye, ye'd punish me for it! I say I saw Roan treatin' the poor lady wrongly and I say *The King* knew of it and did nothin' to stop it! Y'can do y'r worst, Cap'n Jett, and I'll still swear to it! That's when Roan killed Marsden, when that bag o' bones tried to get his share of the unfortunate woman. And I—I tried to rescue her but Roan came at me with his knife after he carved up Marsden— I'm not a man o' violence, sir—and I barely escaped with my life."

Jett flung himself away from the table.

"I'll not listen to your filthy lies," he growled. "You must be mad!"

"Nay, not me!" Womble shrilled after him as he stalked toward the door. " 'Tis not me that's mad but your fine uncle, *The King!* Go to him and ask him the truth, why he welcomed the British and arranged the Dragons' massacre; why he had his own daughter's husband killed; why he threw his pretty wife to Will Roan—ask him!"

Jett turned slowly and his voice was the sound of sliding shale rock.

"Aye," he said, quietly. "And you'll be with me when I ask him, Tom Womble."

6

LORELEI clawed up the coast toward the Virginia Capes, running under reefed topsails in a southeaster that lashed the Atlantic into gale-torn spume. She carried a haggard, hollow-eyed Jett Worth, a man who could not eat and would not sleep but drove his vessel relentlessly toward Peartree Creek and Fairoverlea.

Also aboard the clipper was Tom Womble, a protesting prisoner, his fat cheeks quivering with fear with every turn of the log astern that marked the knots *Lorelei* reeled off in her homebound sweep. Womble was being taken back to the Eastern Shore to face Anthony Worth and Will Roan; he knew he could not count on many days to live once Jett Worth made him repeat his charges to *The King* and the pock-marked, scar-faced killer who was *The King's* chief executioner. With every creak of the clipper's timbers he heard Marsden's last sighing groan; with every whipping crack of canvas he heard the sound of the pistol that had been held close to Charles Rawlent's head.

"You do me wrong!" he squealed to Jett. "They'll but deny everything I've told ye and cozen you into believin' them, not me! Ye're doin' naught but puttin' my neck in a noose, I tell ye!"

"And if I do," said Jett grimly, "then 'tis no more than you deserve. If what ye've told me about my father and Aunt Vivian and the others is true, I know you were in it all, up to your fat belly."

"Nay, Cap'n," Womble wept. "You wrong me, I say!"

On the decks of the clipper, *Lorelei*, Jett's crew went about their duties with troubled faces. The ship still suffered from the wounds she had taken in the battle with the sloop-of-war; the breached hull had not been fitted with new planks and in this sea the men at the pumps had to labor without respite to keep the leakage at safe levels. The clipper had not taken on any of the powder and shot she needed; her supplies were low, she was short-handed; what men she had needed rest.

And, according to all accounts, the British waited at the Capes and in the Chesapeake toward which they plunged, stronger than ever. At Charleston the word had been that the huge, eighty-gun *Tennant* had arrived on the scene, along with two new frigates, *Euryalus* and *Helrus*. Captain John Murphy, trying to run the Capes in his new clipper, *Grampus*, had been chased into the Rappahannock River and destroyed there, dying with his ship. Could Captain Jett Worth, with a holed vessel, without enough men to tend both sails and guns properly, lacking nearly everything he needed, hope to escape Murphy's fate?

Under the old Jett and with a fit ship, the men of *Lorelei* would never have hesitated to take on King George's best at any odds; with this shadow-eyed stranger in command, with a limping vessel under them, the Marylanders wondered at their chances of ever seeing home again.

Lorelei slipped through the Virginia Capes with her accustomed ease. She ran past the hulking *Tennant* and the looming *Albion* one night at such close range that it seemed impossible that some lookout did not hail her. She hugged the shore of the Bay as she had done so many times before and she scudded along unchallenged as the men's spirit's rose. Good fortune, then, was still the clipper's supercargo and why had anybody doubted that Cap'n Jett Worth could bring his ship safely into any port he chose?

It was just at dawn and the wind was giving way to the rising sun when *Lorelei* found the British frigate, *Menelaus*, bearing down on her.

7

SIR PETER PORTER was out of his bunk with a bound at the voice of the Marine corporal outside his cabin door.

"Yankee clipper, sir. We've got her dead to rights!"

He scrambled into his clothes, cursing a ruffled shirt with buttons that refused to stay in their holes, and ran topside. By the time he reached the poopdeck, *Lorelei's* guns had already opened fire.

The clipper knew she was trapped. She was too close to shore to attempt a starboard tack and a port tack would bow her neck under the frigate's broadside. Her only hope was to stand up and shoot it out with the heavier, more muscled *Menelaus*.

Or strike her colors—and Maryland clippers had a notorious reputation for refusing to do that.

She was reaching now for *Menelaus* with her waist guns. Porter watched a ball splash, bound up from a wave and skip past the frigate's stern. The clipper's bow pivot gun belched a cloud of smoke and there was a crash and rattle in the mizzen rigging over the young admiral's head. A chunk of spar, bitten off by the langrage hurled by *Lorelei*, pin-wheeled over the side, raising a geyser where it landed.

"All guns when they bear," Porter told his first lieutenant quietly. "I think we have the lady where we want her."

Within seconds, *Menelaus* erupted in a bellowing blast that slewed the frigate sideways in the water. Sir Peter Porter winced as he saw *Lorelei* take her death blow. The clipper seemed to poise there, motionless, for a long moment—and then her foremast came forward gently, her mizzen crumpled, her near rail and a whole section of her port hull planking dissolved in a burst of splinters. Again the frigate's guns spoke and again. *Lorelei* wallowed helplessly now, not answering her helm, her decks a clutter of shredded sails and tangled lines, smoke boiling from her hatches.

So died *Lorelei*, a victim of the one stroke of blind, furious doubt that had led her captain to sacrifice her. Her men died on her blood-slicked decks or in the inferno of her hold and died without a single curse to the near-madman who had brought them to this.

The clipper sought her own last resting place. She staggered toward the shore and struck on a sand bar, grated forward her own length and then struck again, listing so sharply that her lee rail went under water. As she struck, her forepeak magazine exploded with a roar. The privateer was ripped apart by ruthless, fiery claws; flames streaked through her from bowsprit to rudder and she perished there.

Sir Peter Porter used his spy glass to watch the few—the pitifully few—survivors of the clipper's last battle swim and wade to shore.

"Let 'em go," he said, when a lieutenant asked permission to swing over a longboat and take prisoners. "They've lost their ship, this war's near won, and what's served by putting those poor devils to rot in one of Co'burn's hellships?"

8

Anthony Worth was in his office at Fairoverlea that night, Will Roan across the desk from him, when the messenger, Filkey, brought word of *Lorelei's* last fight.

"Burned to the water's edge, sir," Filkey gasped, "and was fair riddled before she blew up! She ran afoul a damned British frigate and she never had a chance, they tell me who saw the thing. She—"

"My nephew?" barked Anthony Worth, grey-faced. "What about my nephew?"

Filkey shrugged and fumbled the greasy hat he held at his chest.

"They say a few came ashore," he mumbled, "but 'twasn't many and nobody's seen Cap'n Jett, sir. Knowin' him, I'd say—" He fell silent.

Anthony Worth looked down at the hand that had crumpled a sheet of foolscap into a tight ball. The inkpot, the pen, the ruler, revolved in a brief and dizzy dance. Jett gone? It could not be— *it mustn't be!* Jett, laughing, handsome, light-hearted Jett, was the sweetheart of a fortune that would never lead him under the guns of a frigate or, even if she deserted him to that extent, would reclaim him for her darling in time to arrange his escape.

It was not *Lorelei* that had been trapped by the British; it was

427

some other clipper with a captain not as clever as Jett! For why would Jett even think of so foolhardy a thing as sailing into the Chesapeake at a time when the British had more warships than ever before in that area? No, Filkey was wrong, the people who had watched some privateer with a noodle-headed skipper be trapped by a British frigate were all wrong!

"It was not Jett," he grated aloud. "It was not *Lorelei!*"

"Elwood was one o' them that saved hisself, sir," Filkey offered hesitantly. "He's bad hurt but he dragged hisself ashore and he's bein' cared for by the people that hid him. Beggin' y'r pardon, sir, but it *was* your clipper."

The feet of Anthony's chair screeched on the floor as he shoved himself back from the desk.

"Where's Elwood hid?" he demanded. "We've got to get to him and find out what happened to my nephew."

"No need, Uncle," Jett Worth said from the passageway doorway. "No need to disturb poor Elwood—I'll give you the whole shameful story."

He clung to the doorjamb as he wavered. His face and hands were mud-smeared, his wrinkled, stained, torn clothes were encrusted with sand. He was hatless, his black hair falling about his hollow, unshaven cheeks in lank strands. His eyes were dull, his lips salt-caked. He leaned there a sodden ghost, a disheveled apparition, Jett Worth, who had been the jauntiest clipper captain to ever sail the sea; Jett Worth, whose reckless quest for truth had brought him to the ruin Anthony Worth had predicted, if he peeked and pried.

Anthony was at his nephew's side before Will Roan and the man Filkey had well begun their open-mouthed stares. The tall man grasped Jett's shoulders in a joyful embrace and clasped the younger man to him.

"Jett, Jett, ye're safe!" he cried. "That's all that matters! Ye're safe and home again to Fairoverlea!"

He led his nephew toward the chair that Will Roan shoved forward. Filkey edged out of the office, closing the passageway door behind him, glad to be finished with his painful duty of telling The King that he had lost his finest vessel. Roan stood aside, his eyes fixed on Jett as he slumped in his chair. Something was wrong beyond the losing of the clipper, Will Roan told himself; he had a nose that could sniff out trouble, broken-bridged though it might be, and trouble was clouding this place thick with its skunk's stink. He started for the door after Filkey, turned at Anthony Worth's command.

"Ring for Joseph! Get brandy—this boy's close to death with weariness!"

Jett choked and spluttered over his drink. Then, as the brandy's heat flowed through him, his haggard face lost its numb expression, his eyes took on the light of returning life. Anthony pressed the second generous tumbler into his hand and he raised it to his mouth with a firming hand.

"The ship," he muttered when he had swallowed. "I lost my ship."

His uncle's clutch gripped his shoulder harder.

"You'll have another, Jett," he promised. "Finer than the *Lorelei*, you'll see! You're safe, boy—that's what counts!"

"Aye," Jett mumbled dully. "I'm safe and all those good men are dead. Wright and Lears and the Harrison brothers and—"

"War, lad!" Anthony broke in. "Ye'll not reproach yourself for that! Not a man of them but knew he took his chances."

"And Womble," Jett added carefully, thoughtfully. "Womble was killed, too. I saw him die." He looked up at Anthony's stiffened face. "You see, when the first broadside caught us I knew we had no chance so I ordered Womble freed. He came running topside and—"

"Boy, boy," Anthony said softly, "ye're ill. We'll get you to bed and—"

"—and made for the side," Jett went on. "I think he had some mad idea of swimming for it, and with the water fair foaming with every shot in that frigate's locker. He nearly made it to the rail—"

"Jett," Anthony pleaded. "It did not happen. Come to bed."

"—when the chain shot, two half-balls they were, caught him in

429

the back. He split like a pumpkin and in spite of every noise in Hell about me I heard him scream."

"He's ravin'," Will Roan creaked from where he stood. "Womble's been dead f'r nigh to a year!"

Jett's haunted eyes swung from his uncle to the scar-faced man.

"No, Roan," he corrected quietly, his head swinging. "No, you didn't kill him the day you killed Marsden, the day he said—he said my aunt"—his voice shrilled—"my aunt fell into your paws."

"He's dead, God damn you!" Roan roared. "I say Womble's dead! I killed him!"

Jett's dark eyes held themselves relentlessly on Roan's twitching face.

"You didn't bury Womble in the swamp, Will Roan," he said, "as Womble said you did so many."

The silence bellied and tautened. There was the ticking of a clock, the whinny of a horse in the stables, a lyrical laugh from the direction of the slave quarters. Then Anthony Worth let out his breath in a grating sigh.

"Womble told you that?" he asked.

Jett struggled to his feet and braced himself with a hand on the back of the chair.

"I was told everything," he said to Anthony. "About how Rawlent was killed and how you played the traitor with the British the night they came here. About Aunt Vivian and—aye, my ears were filled with a bookful of stories, right enough!"

His face twisted into a small boy's scowl and a whimper escaped him.

"And I—God help me—wouldn't believe what your look tells me is true! I was bringing him back here to have you prove him a lying dog when the duh-duh-damned British jumped us and—and—"

"Jett," Anthony Worth said quietly. He walked up to his nephew and placed a hand on his shoulder; drew it back when he saw Jett flinch. "Jett, I know you're near frantic over your ship's loss and your men killed, though you shouldn't be. It has

430

unhinged you, lad. Tom Womble's been dead a year, as Roan says. He was killed by the British, as were Marsden and Charles Rawlent. Thinking you saw him, thinking you heard him say these wild things about murder and treason, are vapours that will pass with a good night's rest. We'll talk, son, when you've had some sleep."

He ignored the shrinking of Jett's shoulder and placed his arm about his nephew as he guided him toward the door that led to the main part of the house. Jett allowed himself to be led; his head fell forward on his chest and his feet dragged leadenly; he was as helpless under the quiet hands and gentle voice of his uncle as a sleepy child being taken to bed by his mother.

Anthony had his hand on the brass knob when Will Roan's flat voice sliced out.

"No," the scar-faced man gritted. "No, ye'll not let y'r precious nephew go free to call the hangman for me!"

Anthony turned to look into the muzzle of the derringer Roan held on him.

"I've killed many a man at your bidding," the crease-faced overseer rapped out, "and now I'll have my say! This man knows everything, about your murders and our treason. 'Twould have been better if he'd ha' died aboard his ship but nobody knows he didn't, save Filkey, and he can be dealt with later. I say we save our hides now by doin' what the British should've done!"

"Put down that gun," Anthony said levelly.

"Not till it's done its work," Roan blared back. "This cockerel goes into the swamp!"

Anthony Worth dropped his arm from his nephew's shoulders and turned so that his big body covered Jett's slighter frame from the pistol's menace.

"You harm this boy," he said quietly, "and I'll see you hanged from the highest tree on Fairoverlea."

Roan's thumb knuckle crept over the hammer of the derringer and there was the click of the sear.

"Y'speak of hangin'," he grunted, "when you're the likeliest rope-stretcher ever was! Y'say rid me of this man and that man and

431

I do, but no, y'r nephew must be dandled all nice and cozy at the risk of my life! And I'll not have it, I tell ye! I'll not have him live, knowin' what he knows—about Rawlent and the rest!"

"Shut up, you fool!" Anthony shouted.

"Ah, let him hear! Let him take his information into the swamp with him! He knows most of it, in any case—that fat bastard Womble told him."

"You said you killed Womble!"

"Aye, I said that but I didn't," Roan sneered. "I was too busy with the pleasures of that fine piece you gave me. Now, stand aside!"

He twisted as Anthony flung himself at him. The toe of his thick-soled boot caught in a wrinkle of the braided rug near the desk and he missed his chance to spring clear of the raging Master of Fairoverlea. Jett Worth looked on stupidly as his uncle's huge hands gripped Will Roan's throat, as the derringer thudded its muffled hammer blow, as the two big bodies crashed to the floor.

Dazedly, Jett lurched forward. Then the hours of sleeplessness, the wrench of torturous doubt that had gripped him since Tom Womble had gabbled his story, the effort of his struggle to get to the beach after the British had torn his decks from under him, the tottering journey through marsh and pine grove, rutted field and thorn thicket, all settled their accounts as he went sprawling.

Fainted, he did not see Will Roan's knife hand rise and fall in pounding blows; he did not see Roan's face grow purple, then ashen, as Anthony Worth choked the life out of him.

He did not see the whale oil lamp on the desk toppled by the flailing of Roan's legs nor see the yellow, blue-flecked flames dance along the carpet and lick at the wall. He lay in deep exhaustion as slender, frantic hands tugged at him and dragged him from the flaming room.

9

Task Tillman was within half a mile of the fork in the road where he and Jett had talked, so many years before, when the first glare of the fire lit up the sky ahead of him.

For one heart-jolting second he thought that the torch had been put to Larkspur Hill again; then he knew that it was at Fairoverlea that this blaze flamed. As he reined Lucifer in, the sullen glow grew brighter, then waned, then bloomed again.

His first thought was the wildly glorious realization that retribution had struck at Anthony Worth. Anthony Worth had destroyed Larkspur Hill by fire; by fire his own great Fairoverlea was dying.

"Let it burn, burn, burn!" he cried aloud. "Burn to the ground with Worth's rotten carcass under it!"

The fire brightened, silhouetting the tree tops, painting the underside of the low-hanging clouds with bloody light. As he watched, grinning, Task saw sparks soaring skyward, whirling crazily as they ascended, swirling and eddying in the breeze off the river. Downwind came the acrid smell of burning paint, of cloth, of tar and wax, that indescribable blend of odors that makes up the dying breath of a flame-ravaged dwelling. Task sniffed it with the relish a woman would have given a rare perfume.

"Aye, burn," he chanted. "Burn like the hellhole you are, Fairoverlea! Burn till there's not a stick of you left or a brick that's whole! Bury him in the hottest part of you! Burn him till he's ashes and burn the ashes, too! Burn him and everything and everybody—"

His wild paean stopped as the cold hand of sanity reclaimed him.

"Gracellen!" he whispered. "Gracellen—dear God!"

He jammed his spurs into Lucifer's flanks. The black leapt forward with a snort. The stallion shot along the road until he reached the fork; there, Task had to fight the big horse to keep him from turning toward Larkspur Hill. There was a brief struggle and then the stallion laid back his ears, bunched his powerful muscles and raced along the road toward the glare that marked the blazing castle of the man some called *The King*.

As he turned into the drive he met the fleeing slaves. They ran past him, wild-eyed, shouting hysterically, screaming, singing, gone mad with the terror of the night. They flowed down the lane, barely getting out from under the hooves as horse and rider plunged ahead; the compounds had been opened or they had broken out and they were dashing for freedom from Titus's lash and Roan's cruelty.

Cursing, slashing right and left with his riding crop, Task ploughed Lucifer through the swarm and up the flame-lit drive toward the pyre that was Fairoverlea. The east wing of Fairoverlea was a roaring, crackling torch and the main section and west wing had not long to live; already ugly flickers of light glimmered fitfully in the upstairs windows of the main hall. Task's ears were filled with the sullen roar of the flames, the hiss and grumble of the fire as it reached and devoured, licked and swallowed, the majestic beauty of the mansion on the Miles.

Lucifer, snorting at the heat and smoke of the blaze, battled the bit, rearing, side-stepping, tossing his head as he walled his eyes. Fighting to keep control of his mount, Task did not see Gracellen and Jett until he was almost on top of them.

They stood in the middle of the oval made by the circling of the drive in front of Great House, so dangerously close to the flames that Jett's sodden clothes were steaming. Task slid from his saddle and let Lucifer gallop back down the drive. He ran to the girl he loved and the man who had been his friend, locked in what seemed to be a despairing embrace.

"Gracellen!" he cried. "You're safe! And Jett!"

She broke away from Jett and whirled to face him and he drew in his breath in a gasp. Her face was the tortured visage of a soul in purgatory; her eyes were stark and staring, her lips were drawn back from her teeth in a macabre grin, her hair was a tangled confusion.

"Task, Task!" she sobbed. "Thank God it's you! Make him—Father—you must make Jett let me—"

What else she said was drowned out by the thunder of something heavy falling inside the house. Gracellen stretched out both her hands to Task and he caught them. She came into his arms with a moan and her words were muffled against his chest.

"—Jett won't—Father—God's sake, help me—oh Christ, I could've saved him—Jett—"

Her voice crumpled into a succession of choked moans. Task looked over her head at Jett Worth, standing with his back to the flaming house, his hands on his hips, his feet spread wide apart.

"Where's her father?" Task yelled over the crackling of the flames.

Jett did not speak. He took one hand from his hip and jerked it laconically toward the inferno. Gracellen's hands clutched the cloth of his coat and her voice broke clear again.

"He's alive—you can save him, Task—ah, God, I could've saved him but I chose Jett instead; I don't care what he did—it's not true—all lies—all lies!"

Task half led, half carried Gracellen the few steps to in front of Jett. The slighter man looked up at him through eyes that did not seem to see.

"Your uncle's still alive in there?" Task cried. "Can we save him?"

Jett's lips barely moved but his voice, as graven as a stone statue's might be, carried over the noise of the fire.

"I don't know whether he's still alive or not," he said tonelessly. "If he lives, we will not save him."

"Task—Task," Gracellen whimpered.

Task shot a glance at the house. There, in a front window of the main hall, there was what might have been the movement of a figure, just inside the glass.

"Jett!" he cried. "I saw something—somebody! In that window by the front door. Come on—we can reach him!"

He wrenched loose from Gracellen's grip and started toward the steps to the front porch. Jett moved to block his way.

"Ye'll not try to save him," he said quietly for all the noise.

"But Jett—"

"Why should you, Task Tillman? He killed your father. He ruined you, he's ruined me, he's ruined Gracellen, he's ruined all he's touched. Let him die in this little Hell now before he goes to the one that's been waiting for him so long."

Task eyed this stranger, this Jett Worth he never had seen before. The man was not unhinged; his eyes were steady enough, though stony, his voice was not the babble of a madman.

"Jett," Task said and he kept his voice level. "I've suffered much at Anthony Worth's hand but I've wronged him, too. Maybe our sins have cancelled each other's out—in any case, I can't stand here and see a man burn to death before my eyes."

"You'll have to fight your way past me, Task," Jett said, as levelly. "You say you wronged him—I didn't. I worshipped him. So did Gracellen. And he killed Gracellen's husband, he killed all those foolish Dragons of Rawlent's—he killed my cousin's chance of happiness with you with his lies, his schemes, his thinking he was greater than anything else on earth. If he comes out of there, what's ahead of him—disgrace for all of us, shame to Gracellen, a hangman's rope? And I'll spend my life, if need be, to make sure he suffers a little, a tenth as much, at least, as he has made others suffer."

He shook his head slowly.

"You don't mean to pass, Task Tillman, but if you do, you'll have to fight your way past me."

"Task—Task—"

Task Tillman hesitated, then struck out at Jett. It was Gracellen's hands on his arm that halted the blow. He turned to shake her off and saw her staring, gape-mouthed, toward the house. He turned again, as did Jett, and saw Anthony Worth.

He sagged against the doorway; his heavy blackened head hung low between his wide shoulders, his knees sagging, his big frame wavering. He stood there while behind him the hungry flames streaked and quivered and the smoke poured out over his head, lifted by some draught from inside.

As the three watched silently, Anthony Worth staggered to the edge of the porch and stopped there.

He stood, a burned and bleeding figure, and looked at the three people on the lawn; looked full into their eyes. Gracellen gave a choked cry.

"Ye want him saved?" Jett asked leadenly. "Saved for what, Gracellen-aleen?"

The girl's head went down to her hands; she did not call to her father. Jett Worth took a step forward and stared up at his uncle, the man he had thought of as his father. The two, Anthony and Jett, communed in silence and Anthony Worth knew then what the Hell that awaited him would be.

A yell, a cry of warning, a plea for forgiveness—he did not know what it would be—wrenched at Task Tillman's tongue, struggling to make itself heard. He bit it back and drew Gracellen close to him again. Her face was pressed against him and her body shook with sobs. She did not see Anthony Worth turn slowly, inexorably, and walk, with a step grown suddenly firm, back into the furnace of Fairoverlea.

437

10

THE WAR returned to Maryland's Eastern Shore for only one brief moment. It was after Bladensburg and the burning of Washington that the British General, Sir Robert Ross, decided that the time was ripe for the taking of Baltimore. As his fleet sailed for North Point and Fort McHenry and the defeat and death that awaited him there, Ross asked Admiral Cochrane, Cockburn's successor, for a diversionary move on Rock Hall, almost directly across the Chesapeake from Baltimore.

Cochrane chose the frigate *Menelaus*, Admiral Sir Peter Porter commanding, to make the attack.

"Following which," said Admiral Cochrane's dispatch to Porter, "you will take your frigate to Bermuda where, because of your exemplary work in the conduct of this war, notably in the sinking of the American privateer *Lorelei*, a ship of the line awaits your command."

"One last frolic with the Yankees," Sir Peter exulted, "before I make m'self a crusty captain of a seventy-four-gun vessel!"

He landed two hundred and sixty men from *Menelaus*. They struck inland without encountering any opposition until they reached a place known as Caulk's Field. There, they met a handful of militia which fired a haphazard shotgun volley before they fled.

The shotguns were loaded with buckshot and buckshot makes a nasty hole in a man's side when delivered at almost point-blank range. Sir Peter Porter realized this as he stared down at himself, a second before he crumpled and pitched forward and died.

So the twenty-eight-year-old admiral finally went aboard his big ship of the line—in a cask of brandy to preserve him on his voyage home to England for burial. Aboard the 74-gunner, the *Albion*, was another cask of brandy which contained the body of General Ross who had been killed in the very first volley of the Battle of North Point.

Baltimore was saved in that battle on August 12, 1814, and the following day and night she was saved again when Fort McHenry repulsed the British fleet. But these two battles, the war's most important to Maryland, were only distant thunder to the people of Talbot County on the Eastern Shore. Their war was over with the fight at Caulk's Field; they cheered the news of North Point and McHenry, certainly, but the prime emotion was one of weary relief as the British sail stood down the Chesapeake Bay, never to return.

There was too much to be done to spend much time in celebration. Whole towns had to be rebuilt, ruined plantations brought back to production, sunken ships replaced, rotted fishing nets rewoven, life as the Eastern Shore had known it before this costly, indecisive war, recaptured.

The grass grew long, then sere, on the graves of the proud militiamen who had died through heroism and through treachery. The weeds, the brambles, and then the snow covered the great scar that had been Fairoverlea. No one, least of all Gracellen or Jett Worth, wanted to rebuild that monument to Anthony Worth's evil; the warehouses were allowed to fall to ruin, what slaves were recaptured after the mass escape on the night of the fire were sold, the fields were permitted to lie fallow and Peartree Creek's twisting channel carried no vessels bigger than a skiff up to the cove. The people of Talbot County shook their heads in wonder at the disregard of daughter and nephew of what must have been Anthony's last wishes; they spoke of disrespect to

439

a great man's memory in letting the place go to ruin but they never knew the truth.

Jett sailed away to South America, his lips still tightly sealed. Gracellen began making her new life at Larkspur Hill as Task Tillman's wife, and Anthony's name never was mentioned between the two of them.

Titus was never seen after the night of the fire. Perhaps he fled with the rest but it seemed improbable that a giant his size could hide forever. Task secretly believed that in the break from the compounds, the half-crazed pack had halted their flight long enough to deal out justice to Titus before they used the swamp as Anthony Worth had used it.

The Treaty of Ghent was signed in Flanders. Here and there could be heard the song written by Mister Francis Scott Key of Georgetown, the night he watched the Battle of Fort McHenry from a British vessel. A fair verse, folks agreed, but the tune of "Ancreon in Heaven" was too confoundedly hard to carry; it would not last long in public favor, that was one sure thing, even though its name "The Star Spangled Banner" had a pleasing ring.

Peace through what the Americans called victory and the British named stalemate, came to the Chesapeake Bay and to the Eastern Shore. Gracellen's trust in Task's love proved itself equal to the terrors of the memories that came back and back again before they finally died under the beauty of her new life, a shining thing born out of black horror, a beauty that would endure all the days of her life and Task's and survive them in their children and in Larkspur Hill.